SOMEONE IS
WATCHING

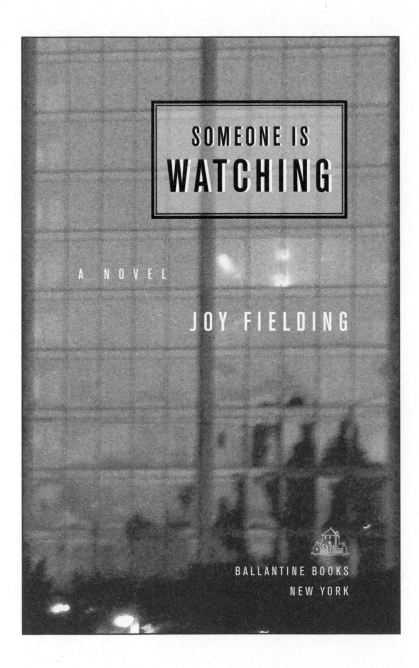

SOMEONE IS
WATCHING

A NOVEL

JOY FIELDING

BALLANTINE BOOKS
NEW YORK

Published in the United States by Ballantine Books, an imprint of Random House, a division of Random House LLC, a Penguin Random House Company, New York.

BALLANTINE and the HOUSE colophon are registered trademarks of Random House LLC.

LIBRARY OF CONGRESS CATALOGING-IN-PUBLICATION DATA

Fielding, Joy.
Someone is watching : a novel / Joy Fielding.
pages ; cm
ISBN 978-0-553-39063-6 (hardcover : acid-free paper)—
ISBN 978-0-553-39064-3 (ebook)
1. Women—Crimes against—Fiction.   2. Women—
Violence against—Fiction.   3. Voyeurism—Fiction.   I. Title.
PR9199.3.F518S66   2015
813'.54—dc23 2014037390

Printed in the United States of America on acid-free paper

www.ballantinebooks.com

987654321

First Edition

Book design and title page photo by Karin Batten

To my favorite people in the whole world:

Warren, Shannon, Annie, Renee, Courtney,

Hayden, and Skylar

SOMEONE IS
WATCHING

−ONE−

The day starts the same way it usually does. Just another monotonously gorgeous October day in Miami, the sky typically blue and cloudless, the temperature expected to reach eighty degrees by noon. There is nothing to suggest that today will vary significantly from yesterday or the day before that, nothing to suggest that today, or more specifically *tonight,* will change my life forever.

I wake up at seven. Shower and dress—a black pleated skirt and white cotton blouse, slightly more formal than my usual fare. Brush my hair, which is light brown and hangs in loose waves halfway down my back. Apply a hint of blush to my cheeks and a touch of mascara to my lashes. Make some coffee, scarf down a muffin, and call downstairs at eight thirty for one of the valets to bring up my car from the underground garage.

I could go get the vintage silver Porsche myself, but the valets get a kick out of driving it, even for the thirty seconds it takes to accelerate up the circular ramp from my parking spot on lower level three to the front entrance. This morning it's Finn, almost handsome in his uniform of khaki pants and short-sleeved, forest-green shirt, behind the wheel. "Busy day, Miss Carpenter?" he asks as we exchange positions.

"Just another day in paradise."

"Enjoy," he says, closing my door and waving me away.

I head for Biscayne Boulevard and the law offices of Holden, Cunningham, and Kravitz, where I've been employed as an investigator for almost two years. The firm, home to approximately three hundred employees, a hundred and twenty-five of whom are lawyers, occupies the top three floors of an imposing marble tower in the business heart of the city. Normally I'd enjoy another cup of coffee while exchanging pleasantries with whomever happens to be milling around the staff room, but today I'm due in court, so I park my car in the underground lot, lock my licensed Glock in the glove compartment, and hail a cab for the short ride over to 73 West Flagler Street and the Miami-Dade County Courthouse. Street parking is minimal to nonexistent in this area, and I can't afford to waste precious time looking for a spot. I've been called as a rebuttal witness in a case involving corporate espionage, and I'm anxious to take the stand. Unlike many in my profession who prefer to remain invisible, I actually enjoy testifying.

Maybe that's because, as an investigator, I spend a great deal of my time in relative isolation. My job involves gathering information that will prove useful in courtroom defense, investigating cheating spouses and suspicious employees, engaging in surveillance, taking photographs, videotaping clandestine encounters, searching out and questioning prospective witnesses, locating missing heirs, and rounding up facts, some of which turn out to be pertinent and admissible in court, others merely prurient but useful anyway. When I have gathered up all the necessary info, I sit down and write up a report. Occasionally, like today, I'm called to testify. A cursory knowledge of the law is essential, making the several years I spent at the University of Miami majoring in criminology not a total waste of time, despite my leaving before completing my degree. According to the online site where I secured my investigator's license, it is part of my job description to be clever, well-informed, dogged, methodical, resourceful, and discreet. I try to be all of those things.

There's a long lineup of people already waiting to pass through the metal detectors when I arrive at the courthouse, followed by an excruciatingly slow ride in a crowded elevator to the twenty-first floor. It seems almost laughable now to think that back when construction of this twenty-eight-story building was completed in 1928, it was not only the tallest building in Florida but the tallest building south of Ohio. Amazingly, its white limestone exterior still manages to stand out amid the largely indistinguishable glass structures that surround and dwarf it. Inside the building, it's a different and less impressive story, the lobby still awaiting funds to complete its stalled refurbishing, the majority of courtrooms feeling as stale as they occasionally smell.

"State your name and occupation," the county clerk directs as I take the stand and agree to tell the whole truth and nothing but.

"Bailey Carpenter. I'm an investigator with Holden, Cunningham, and Kravitz."

"How are you, Bailey?" Sean Holden asks as I take my seat. Sean is not only my boss but one of the firm's founding fathers and major stars, even though he's only forty-two. I watch him do up the buttons of his blue pinstriped jacket, thinking what an impressive man he is. Not good-looking in the traditional sense, his features somewhat coarse, his hazel eyes small and a little too direct, his dark hair a bit too curly, his lips a touch too full. Just a little too much of everything, which is usually just more than enough to intimidate the hell out of the other side.

The case before the court is relatively simple: Our client, the owner of a local chain of successful bakeries, is being sued for wrongful dismissal by a former employee. He is countersuing, arguing that the woman was fired for divulging trade secrets to his chief competitor. The woman has already testified that her meetings with the competitor in question were totally innocent, that she and her husband have known him since childhood, and that their meetings, all of which are detailed in my report and already entered into evidence, were for the sole purpose of planning a surprise party for her husband's fortieth birthday. She went on to volunteer that she is an honest woman who would never knowingly betray her employer's trust. That was her mistake. Witnesses should never volunteer anything.

Sean asks me a number of seemingly innocuous, job-related questions before zeroing in on the reason I'm here. "You're aware that Janice Elder has already testified under oath that she is, and I quote, 'an honest woman incapable of such betrayal.'"

"Yes, I'm aware of that."

"And you're here to refute that statement?"

"I have evidence that refutes both her assertion of honesty and that she is incapable of betrayal."

The lawyer for the other side is immediately on his feet. "Objection, Your Honor."

"Mrs. Elder opened the door to this line of questioning herself," Sean states, and the judge quickly rules in his favor.

"You said that you have evidence that refutes both her assertion of honesty and that she is incapable of betrayal?" Sean asks, repeating what I have said, word for word.

"Yes, I do."

"What is that evidence?"

I refer to my notes, although the truth is I don't need them. Sean and I have been going over my testimony for days, and I know exactly what I'm going to say. "On the night of March 12, 2013," I begin, "I followed Mrs. Elder to the Doubleday Hilton Hotel in Fort Lauderdale. . . ." Out of the corner of my eye, I see Janice Elder hastily conferring with her lawyer. I see the panic in her eyes.

"Objection," her lawyer says again.

Again, he is overruled.

"Go on, Ms. Carpenter."

"I watched her approach the reception desk and secure a room card. Room 214, registered to a Mr. Carl Segretti."

"What the hell?" a man exclaims from the bench directly behind Mrs. Elder. He is Todd Elder, Janice's husband, and he is already on his feet, a combination of shock and outrage causing his tanned skin to glow bright red, as if he has been set ablaze. "You've been sneaking around with Carl?"

"Objection, Your Honor. This has absolutely nothing to do with the case at hand."

"On the contrary, Your Honor. . . ."

"You lying little bitch!"

"Order in the court."

"You've been fucking my goddamn *cousin*?"

"Bailiff, remove that man." The judge bangs on his gavel. "Court is recessed for thirty minutes."

"Good work," Sean remarks out of the corner of his mouth as I walk past him out of the courtroom, the hostility in Mrs. Elder's eyes burning into my back like acid.

In the hallway I check my phone while waiting to see if I will be recalled to the stand. There is a message from Alissa Dunphy, a third-year associate at the firm, asking me to look into the possible reappearance of one Roland Peterson, a deadbeat dad who fled Miami some months ago rather than pay his ex-wife the several hundred thousand dollars he owes her in back alimony and child support.

"Well, that was a rather unpleasant surprise," a voice behind me says as I'm dropping the phone back into my oversized canvas bag. The voice belongs to the lawyer representing Janice Elder. His name is Owen Weaver and I estimate his age as early thirties, which makes him just a few years older than me. I note that he has a mouthful of straight white teeth that don't quite go with his engagingly crooked smile.

"Just doing my job," I tell him, only half-apologetically.

"Do you have to do it so well?" The smile spreading from his lips to his soft brown eyes tells me we're not really talking about the case at all. "Do me a favor," he says.

"If I can."

"Have dinner with me," he continues, confirming my suspicions.

"What?"

"Dinner? With me? The restaurant of your choice? Saturday night?"

"You're asking me out?"

"You're surprised?"

"Well, under the circumstances . . ."

"You mean the fact that you just blew my case out of the water?"

"There is that."

"We still have to eat."

"There's that, too." The courtroom doors burst open and Sean Holden strides purposefully toward me. "If you'll excuse me a minute . . . my boss . . ."

"Of course." Owen Weaver reaches into the inside pocket of his navy jacket and hands me his card. "Call me." He smiles, first at me, then at Sean. "Give me ten minutes with my client," he tells him before moving away.

Sean nods. "What was that all about?"

I slip Owen's card into my bag and shrug, as if to indicate our conversation was of no importance. Sean looks back toward the courtroom, my eyes following his. Mrs. Elder's husband is standing alone and stone-faced beside the door, his fists clenched at his sides, his body muscular and coiled, ready to spring into action. He catches my glance and mouths the word *bitch,* transferring his fury at his wife to me. Not the first time misplaced anger has been pointed in my direction.

By the time court resumes half an hour later, Mrs. Elder has agreed to drop her suit if our client will do the same. Our client grumbles but ultimately gives in, and nobody leaves happy, which I've heard is the sign of a good compromise. At least Sean and I are pleased. "I have to run," he tells me as we're leaving the courthouse. "I'll catch you later. And Bailey," he adds, hailing down a passing cab and climbing inside. "Congratulations. You did real good."

I watch the taxi disappear into traffic before hailing a cab of my own and returning to Biscayne Boulevard. Despite our victory in court, I'm feeling a bit let down. I guess I'd been hoping for something more than an ungrammatical pat on the back. A celebratory lunch would have been nice, I think as I locate my car in the underground garage and climb inside, unlocking the glove compartment and returning my gun to my purse, where it lands on top of Owen Weaver's business card. I'm toying with taking him up on his offer. Since breaking up with my boyfriend, I've spent far too many Saturday nights alone.

I'm still debating whether to accept his invitation some twenty minutes later as I turn the corner onto Northeast 129 Street in North Miami. Parking my car on the quiet, residential street, I head toward the lemon-yellow building at the end of a row of similarly old-fashioned, pastel-colored, low-rise condos. This is where Sara McAllister lives. Sara was Roland Peterson's girlfriend at the time he fled the city rather than support his children. My hunch is that Sara McAllister just might be the reason he came back, something I intend to find out.

Near the end of the street is an elongated circle of shrubbery, a spot both self-contained and secluded, despite its proximity to the road. I couldn't have asked for a more perfect surveillance spot. Taking a quick look around to make sure no one is watching, I retrieve my binoculars from my bag and slip into the middle of the bushes, dislodging several coral blossoms as I crouch among the flowers and raise the binoculars to my eyes. I aim them at the third-floor corner unit of the four-story building and adjust the lenses until they merge into a single image.

The drapes in Sara McAllister's living room are open, but with the lights off, it's difficult to make out much of the interior except for a white-shaded lamp positioned next to the window. The apartment appears to be empty, which isn't surprising. Sara is a saleswoman at Nordstrom and usually works till six. I decide there's little to be accomplished by hanging around now. It makes more sense to come back this evening.

I have two meetings scheduled for this afternoon as well as a backlog of paperwork to finish off. I also want to call my brother, Heath. It's been a week since we've spoken, and I can't stop worrying about him. I take one last, seemingly casual look around the old street, frozen in the sunlight as if it were frozen in time, as still as a photograph.

I'm pushing myself to my feet when I see something flash in a window across the way, a hint of someone moving just out of frame. Has someone been watching me?

I lift the binoculars back to my eyes but see no one. Professional paranoia, I decide, as I extricate myself from the bushes, brushing a fallen hibiscus blossom from the shoulder of my white blouse and swiping at the dirt clinging to my knees. I decide to change into more appropriate attire before coming back tonight, when I can use the darkness as a protective shield. I'm foolish enough to think it will keep me safe from prying eyes like mine.

— T W O —

This is what I remember: the warm night air, darkness as soft and inviting as a cashmere shawl, a gentle breeze brushing flirtatiously across the tops of the sweet-smelling shrubs in which I'm hiding, their coral flowers now folded in on themselves, closed to the dark. I'm vaguely aware of their faint aroma as I peer through my binoculars into Sara McAllister's third-floor window, my knees aching from squatting so long in the same position, my toes cramping. It's closing in on midnight, I've been here for hours, and irritability is curling around my consciousness like a hungry boa constrictor. I'm thinking that if I don't see something—*anything*—soon, I'm going to call it a night.

That's when I hear it—the snap of a twig, perhaps, although I'm not certain, that signals someone behind me. I turn to look, but it's already too late. A gloved hand quickly covers my mouth, blocking my screams. I taste leather—old, stale, earthy. And then, those hands, seemingly everywhere, on my shoulders, in my hair, snapping the binoculars from my fingers, as fists slam into my stomach and against the side of my head, causing the world around me to blur and the ground to give way beneath my feet. A pillowcase is pulled roughly over my face. I can't breathe, and I panic. Keep your wits about you, I tell myself in an effort to regain my equilibrium and hold my growing terror at bay. Keep track of everything that's happening.

Except that everything is happening too fast. Even before the pillowcase is pulled into place, the white cotton overwhelming the blackness of the night, I see nothing but a vague shape. A man, certainly, but whether he is young or old, fat or thin, black or brown or white, I have no idea. Has the man I've been waiting for been waiting for me? Did he spot me hiding in the bushes and simply bide his time?

This is good news, I assure myself. If it's Roland Peterson, he'll want only to scare me, not kill me. Killing me would invite more trouble, and he's in enough trouble as it is. He might rough me up a bit, throw the fear of God into me, but then he'll disappear. The sooner I stop struggling, the sooner he'll leave me alone.

Except he isn't leaving me alone. He's spinning me around and tearing at my clothes, his fingers ripping open the buttons of my black shirt and pushing my bra up over my breasts. "No!" I shout when I realize what is happening. Another fist crashes into my jaw, filling my mouth with blood. "Stop. Please. Don't do this." But my pleas are muffled and, if the man hears them at all, they do nothing to halt, or even slow down, the ferocity of his attack. An instant later he is tugging my jeans and panties down my hips. I kick furiously at the air, and I think my boot connects with his chest, but I'm not sure. It's possible I only wish it had.

What is happening? Where is everyone? I already know the answer. There is no one. The people who live in this neighborhood are, for the most part, on the plus side of sixty. No one goes out after ten o'clock, let alone this close to midnight. Even the most dedicated of dog walkers put little Fifi to bed hours ago.

I feel the full weight of the man's arm across my neck and shoulders, pinning me like a butterfly on a wall, as his other hand fumbles with his pants. There is the sickening sound of a zipper opening, then more fumbling, something being unwrapped. He's putting on a condom, I realize, contemplating taking advantage of this distraction when a sudden punch to my stomach leaves me barely able to breathe, let alone attempt an escape. The man quickly pries my legs apart and pushes his way inside me. I feel the sudden cold of the lubricated condom as he tears into me, his hands reaching around me to grab my buttocks. I will my body to go numb, but I can still feel every vicious thrust. After what seems an eternity, it's over. He bites down on my right breast as he climaxes, and I cry out. Seconds later, his lips approach my ear, his breath penetrating the fibers of the thin pillowcase. He smells of mouthwash, minty and crisp. "Tell me you love me," he growls. His gloved hand clutches my throat. "Tell me you love me."

I open my mouth, hear the word "bastard" tumble from my lips. That's when his hand tightens its grip. My nostrils flare against the stiff cotton of the pillowcase, and I gasp in horror, gulping at the air, swallowing blood. *I'm going to die here,* I think, not sure how long I can remain conscious. I picture my mother and father, and for the first time am glad they aren't alive to have to deal with this. The man's thumb presses down hard on my windpipe. Tiny blood vessels explode like fireworks behind my eyes. And then, finally, mercifully, the outside darkness slips beneath my eyelids and I see nothing at all.

———

When I come to, the man is gone.

The pillowcase around my head has vanished, and the night air is licking my face, like a cat. I lie still for some time, unable to move, trying to gather the thoughts that are scattered among the broken hibiscus flowers framing my face, the taste of blood fresh in my mouth, a painful throbbing between my legs, my breasts bruised and sore. I'm naked from the waist down, and even with my eyes nearly swollen shut, I can make out the rivulets of blood that crisscross my thighs. Slowly, I pull my bra back into position, gather my blouse, and reach through the broken shrubbery for my jeans. My panties are missing, as is my canvas bag, and along with it, my gun and the license to carry it, my wallet, my cell phone, my camera, my ID (both personal and professional), and the keys to both my car and my condo, although I do manage to locate my binoculars.

"Help me," I hear someone cry out, barely recognizing the voice I know is mine. "Somebody, please, help me." I struggle into my jeans, then try to stand up, but my legs have all the strength of wet noodles and they collapse underneath me, so I crawl toward the street where I remember parking my car.

Miraculously, the silver Porsche is still there. Probably too conspicuous to steal. Definitely not the most suitable car for someone in my profession, but it had belonged to my mother and I'm not about to part with it. Now I clutch at the door handle as if it is a life preserver, trying to pull myself up. The car's sophisticated alarm system instantly erupts into a cacophony of honks, bells, and whistles. I collapse onto the road, my back against the side of the door, my feet sprawled in front of me. Glancing toward the apartment I've been watching, I see a man appear at the window. Instinctively, I raise my binoculars. But the binoculars are too heavy, and I'm too weak. They fall beside me, cracking against the concrete.

The next thing I remember is waking up in the back of an ambulance. "You're going to be all right," I hear the paramedic saying.

"You're going to be all right," another voice echoes.

They're wrong.

—

That was two weeks ago. I'm home now. But I'm definitely not all right. I don't sleep, at least not without powerful medication, and I don't eat. When I try, I throw up. I've lost at least ten pounds I couldn't afford to lose, being at least ten pounds too thin to begin with. And not on purpose. I'm not one of those women who believes in dieting or even watching what she eats, and I hate exercise. At twenty-nine, I've always been naturally slender. "Skinny Minny," they used to taunt me in high school. I was the last girl in my class to wear a bra, although when my breasts finally did sprout, they grew surprisingly, even suspiciously, large and full. "Implants, obviously," I heard one woman in a group of female lawyers at Holden, Cunningham, and Kravitz whisper as I passed them in the corridor one day last month. At least I think it was last month. I'm not sure. I'm losing track of time. Another entry for my "things lost" column. Right under "confidence." Just above "sanity."

I've lost my looks, too. Before, I was pretty. Large, blue-green eyes, prominent cheekbones, a slight overbite that makes my lips seem fuller than they really are, long, thick brown hair. Now my eyes are cloudy with neverending tears and circled by bruises; my cheeks are scratched and hollow, my lips cracked and even torn from where I bite at them, a habit I used to have as a child and have now revived. My hair, once a source of great pride and joy, hangs lifeless around my face, dry from too many washings, as is my skin, which is rubbed raw from all the showers I take. But even with three and sometimes four showers a day, I don't feel clean. It's as if I've been rolling around in the muck for weeks and the dirt has seeped so deep into my pores that it has infiltrated my bloodstream. I am contaminated. Toxic. A danger to all who look at me. No wonder I barely recognize myself when I look in the mirror. I have become one of those pitiful-looking women you see on street corners, shoulders hunched, trembling hands extended and begging for spare change, the kind of woman you cross the street to avoid. The kind of woman you secretly blame for her misfortune.

This woman has become my roommate and constant companion. She follows me from room to room, like Marley's ghost, shuffling across the beige marble floors of my spacious two-bedroom condo. Together, we live on the twenty-third floor of an ultra-modern glass building in the Brickell section of Miami, an area often referred to as "Wall Street South." In addition to being the financial center of Miami, the neighborhood is full of upscale shopping malls and quality hotels, not to mention more than ten thousand condo units in luxury complexes with spectacular views of both city and ocean. The floor-to-ceiling windows in my living room look out at the beautiful Miami River, while identical windows in my bedroom overlook the backs of other glass high-rises. Unfortunately, many of the apartments sit empty, Florida real estate having been hit especially hard in the recent economic downturn. Despite this, another tall building is going up just across the street. Cranes are everywhere. The new national bird, I can hear my mother laugh. Surely we have enough tall glass buildings, I think. Still, who am I to protest? People in glass houses, after all. . . .

I moved in last year. My father bought the apartment for me, even as he insisted he would be happy if I lived at home forever. But he agreed that it was probably time for me to be on my own. It had been two years since my mother's death. I was working. I had a boyfriend. I had my whole life ahead of me.

Of course, that was then.

This is now.

Now I have nothing. My job is on hold; my boyfriend is gone; my father died of a sudden heart attack four months ago, leaving me an orphan. At least I think it's been four months since my father died. Like I said, I've lost track of time. That can happen when you stay in your apartment all day, when you jump every time the phone rings and leave your bed only to shower and go to the toilet, when your sole visitors are the police and the one sibling who isn't suing you over your father's estate.

Thank goodness for my brother, Heath, even if he's not a whole lot of help. He collapsed at the hospital when he first saw me after the attack, actually fainting dead away and almost hitting his head on the side of the gurney. It was almost funny. The doctors and nurses rushed to his side, and I was temporarily forgotten. "He's so handsome," I heard one of the nurses whisper. I can't blame her for being temporarily distracted by Heath's good looks. My brother, older than me by a scant eleven months, is by far the most beautiful of my father's children, his dark hair always falling into eyes that are an unnaturally deep shade of green, the eyelashes that frame them obscenely long and girlish. Women are always falling in love with Heath. Men, too. And Heath has always had difficulty saying no. To anyone. To anything.

At the hospital, they examined me thoroughly, then pronounced me lucky. An odd choice of words, and probably my face registered this, because they quickly qualified: By "lucky," they meant my attacker had used a condom, so he left no semen inside me. As a result, I didn't have to go on any of those awful anti-AIDS drugs or take the morning-after pill to prevent unwanted pregnancy. He spared me that. Such a considerate rapist. The downside is that he left not a hint of himself behind. There is no DNA to run through sophisticated CSI computers. Unless I can give the police something more to go on, unless I can remember something, *anything . . .*

"Think," I recall the uniformed police officer gently prompting the night of my attack. "Can you remember anything about the man, anything at all?"

I shook my head, felt my brain rattle. It hurt, but trying to talk hurt even more.

"Can we go over everything just one more time, Miss Carpenter?" another voice asked, this one female. "Sometimes the more we go over something, the more we're able to remember. Something we don't even realize might be significant. . . ."

Sure, I remember thinking. Significant. Whatever.

"Your name is Bailey Carpenter, and you live at 1228 Northeast First Avenue. Is that correct?"

"Yes, that's right."

"That's downtown. You were found in North Miami."

"Yes. As I told you, I was staking out an apartment there. I'm an investigator with Holden, Cunningham, and Kravitz."

"That's a law firm?"

"Yes. I was looking for a man named Roland Peterson who skipped town about a year ago. We represent his ex-wife, and we'd gotten wind Mr. Peterson had recently slipped back into the city, possibly to visit his old girlfriend."

"So you were watching the girlfriend's apartment?"

"Yes."

"Do you think Roland Peterson is the man who attacked you?"

"I don't know. Are you going to arrest him?"

"We'll certainly check him out."

I suspected that Roland Peterson, whether he was the man who raped me or just a deadbeat dad, was probably halfway out of Florida by now.

"Can you describe the man who attacked you?"

I shook my head again, felt my brain slide toward my left ear.

"Give yourself a few minutes," the female officer urged. I noticed that she was in plain clothes, which probably made her a detective. Detective Marx, I think the other officer called her. "I know this isn't easy, but if you could try to put yourself back in those bushes."

Is Detective Marx really so naïve? I think now. *Does she not realize I'll be in those bushes for the rest of my life?*

I remember thinking she looked too petite, too insubstantial, to be a police officer, her light gray eyes too soft, too caring. "It's just that it all happened so fast. I know that's such a cliché. I know I should have been more alert, more aware of my surroundings. . . ."

"This wasn't your fault," she interrupted.

"But I've studied judo and tae kwan do," I argued. "It's not as if I don't know how to defend myself."

"Anyone can be caught off guard. You heard nothing at all?"

"I don't know," I told her, trying to remember and not remember at the same time. "I *felt* something. A slight shift in the air. No, wait. I *did* hear something, maybe a footstep, maybe a twig breaking. I started to turn around, and then . . ." A tissue suddenly appeared in the officer's outstretched hand. I grabbed it, tearing it into pieces before it reached my eyes. "He started hitting me. He was punching me in the stomach and face. I couldn't get my bearings. He put a pillowcase over my head. I couldn't see. I couldn't breathe. I was so scared."

"Before he hit you, were you able to make out anything? A shape? A size?"

I tried to picture the man. I really did. But all I saw was the darkness of the night, followed by the suffocating whiteness of the pillowcase.

"Could you see what he was wearing?"

Yet another shake of my head. "He must have been wearing black. And jeans. He was wearing jeans." I heard the man's zipper and wanted to scream to block out the sound.

"Good. That's very good, Bailey. You *did* see things. You *can* remember."

I felt foolishly proud of myself and realized how eager I was to please this woman whose eyes were so soft and gray.

"Could you tell what color the man was, if he was black or white or Hispanic?"

"White," I said. "Maybe Hispanic. I think he had brown hair."

"What else?"

"He had big hands. He was wearing leather gloves." Once again I tasted the stale leather and swallowed the urge to gag.

"Can you estimate how tall he was?"

"I think he was average."

"Could you tell if he was overweight, skinny, muscular . . . ?"

"Average," I said again. Could I be any less informative? I've been trained to notice the smallest of details. Yet all my training evaporated with that first punch. "He was very strong."

"You struggled with him."

"Yes. But he kept hitting me, so I never got close enough to make any real contact. I never got a look at his face. It was all one big blur. And then he pulled that pillowcase over my head. . . ."

"Did you notice his shoes?"

"No. Yes!" I corrected myself, my mind flashing on the iconic Nike swoosh in the canvas of the man's sneakers. "He was wearing black Nike sneakers."

"Can you estimate what size?"

"No, damn it. I'm useless. Absolutely useless. I don't know anything."

"You *do* know," the officer said. "You remembered the sneakers."

"Half the population of Miami owns sneakers like those."

"Did he say anything?"

"No."

"You're sure?"

"He didn't say anything."

Which is when I felt the man's lips moving toward my ear, his voice penetrating the pillowcase with the same sickening force he was penetrating me. *Tell me you love me.*

My entire body started trembling. How could I forget this? How could my mind have blanked out something so obviously, terribly important?

"He told you to tell him you loved him?" Detective Marx repeated, unable to disguise her surprise or her revulsion.

"Yes. He repeated it twice."

"Did you?"

"Did I what?"

"Tell him you loved him?"

"No. I called him a bastard."

"Good for you," she said, and again I felt a surge of pride.

"Okay, Bailey. This is very important. Can you tell me what he sounded like?" She was already elaborating before I could formulate a response. "Was he American? Did he have an accent? Was his voice deep or high-pitched? Did he speak with a lisp? Did he sound young or old?"

"Young," I said. "Or at least, not old. But not a teenager," I qualified, trying to remember what teenagers sound like. "He was whispering—actually, it was more of a growl. I didn't hear an accent or a lisp."

"Good. That's very good, Bailey. You're doing great. Do you think you'd recognize him if you heard that voice again?"

Oh, God, I thought, panic making me dizzy. Please don't let me hear that voice again. "I don't know. Maybe. Like I said, he was whispering." Another surge of panic. Another onslaught of tears. Another tissue. "Please, I just want to go home."

"Just a few more questions."

"No. No more questions. I've told you everything."

What I'd told her was that the man who raped me was most likely a white male of average height and weight, between the ages of twenty and forty, with brown hair and a fondness for black Nike sneakers. In other words, I'd told her nothing.

"Okay," she agreed, although I heard the reluctance in her voice. "Is it all right if we stop by your apartment tomorrow?"

"What for?"

"In case you remember anything else. Sometimes a good night's sleep . . ."

"You think I'll sleep?"

"I think the doctors will prescribe something to help you."

"You think anything will help?"

"I know it doesn't feel that way right now," she said, placing a gentle hand on my arm. I forced myself not to recoil at her touch. "But eventually you *will* get over this. Your world *will* return to normal."

I marveled at her certainty, even as I marveled at her naïveté. When has my world ever been normal?

A brief family history. My father, Eugene Carpenter, was married three times and spawned seven children: a girl and a boy with his first wife, three boys with his second, and Heath and me with his third. A successful entrepreneur and investor who amassed his great wealth in the stock market, regularly buying low and selling high, my father was brought to the attention of state investigators on more than one occasion because of his suspiciously good fortune. But despite their best efforts, they were never able to prove anything even approaching misconduct or malfeasance, a source of deep pride to my father and equally deep frustration to his eldest son, the assistant state's attorney who initiated the original investigation. My father subsequently cut off all contact with his namesake, then cut him out of his will altogether. Hence the lawsuit over his estate, of which Heath and I are the chief beneficiaries. The rest of our half-siblings have joined the suit to claim what they insist is rightfully theirs.

I can't say I blame them. My father was, at best, a lousy husband to their mothers and an indifferent parent to all of them. What's more, he had a warped, even cruel sense of humor. He named the three sons he had with his second wife Thomas, Richard, and Harrison (Tom, Dick, and Harry), and although he always insisted this was unintentional, at least until Harry came along, one thing was indisputable: He constantly played the brothers against one another, the result being that, were it not for the lawsuit, I doubt any of them would be on speaking terms today.

Amazingly, this was not the father that either Heath or I knew. Our childhood was idyllic, our father as loving and attentive as any child could possibly wish for. I credit my mother for this. Younger than my father by eighteen years, he often proclaimed that she was the first woman he'd ever really loved, the woman who taught him how to be a man. And I guess that because he loved her, he loved us, too. The father I remember was generous and tender, soft-hearted and fiercely protective. When my mother died three years ago of ovarian cancer at the tragically young age of fifty-five, he was beside himself with grief. Still, he never deserted us, never sought escape in the man he used to be, was never the man my half-siblings all remember.

He was always there for me.

And then, suddenly, he wasn't.

The man I'd considered invincible died of a massive heart attack at the age of seventy-six.

That was four months ago.

Since he died, I've broken up with my boyfriend, Travis, and embarked on what most people would consider an ill-advised affair with a married man. Not that one thing has anything to do with the other. My relationship with Travis had been deteriorating for some time. I was reeling from my father's unexpected loss, experiencing a renewal of the daily anxiety attacks that had plagued me after my mother died, times when I couldn't move my legs, when I couldn't draw sufficient air into my lungs to breathe. I tried to hide these attacks from everyone, and I was largely successful, but there was one man who wasn't so easily fooled. "Are you going to tell me what's going on?" he'd ask. "What's *really* going on?" And so I did, reluctantly at first, then compulsively, as if once that particular tap had been turned on, it was impossible to shut off again. He quickly became my closest ally, my confidant, eventually, perhaps inevitably, my lover.

I knew right from the start that he would never leave his wife. She was the mother of his children, and he couldn't imagine being just a part-time dad, no matter how unhappy his marriage. He said that while he and his wife rarely argued, this was because they lived largely separate lives, and that although they were regularly seen together in public, they retreated to opposite ends of their house when they were alone. They hadn't made love in years.

Do I believe that? Am I really so gullible? I don't know. I only know that when I'm with him and that when we're together, I'm both where and who I want to be. It's as simple—as complicated, as complex, as awful—as that.

When I think now of the times we made love, the gentle way his fingers explored my body, the soft probing of his tongue, the expert way he brought me to orgasm, it seems impossible that an act so full of tenderness and love can, in other circumstances, be so overflowing with rage and hate, that what produces so much pleasure can inflict so much pain. I wonder if I will ever again experience the joy of a man's touch, or if every time a man enters my body, I will feel a rapist ripping into my flesh, if each time a man's lips move toward my breasts, I will convulse in horror and disgust. I wonder if I will ever be able to enjoy sex again, or if this is something else that has been forever taken from me.

When they brought me home from the hospital, after all the tests and hours of police questions, my brother was so traumatized that he chain-smoked at least four joints before he was able to calm down—"We should call Travis," he kept mumbling, and then he fell sound asleep. Even though Travis and I are no longer a couple, he is still Heath's friend. They were friends before Travis and I hooked up. In fact, it was Heath who introduced us. Heath still doesn't understand why we broke up, and I haven't told him. He's upset enough as it is.

So now I stand by my bedroom window in the apartment I never leave, staring absently at the backs of half a dozen identical glass towers, the hollow eyes of my reflection staring back at me, my fingers folded around the omnipresent binoculars that have become a virtual extension of my hands. There's a large chip in one side of them now, from when they hit the ground after my attack, and my fingers go to it automatically, as they would to a scab. I lift the binoculars to my eyes and hear my mother's voice: *Tell me what you see.* I focus on the nearby construction site, watch one worker arguing with another, his fingers poking angrily into the other man's chest, as another worker intervenes.

Slowly, I shift my focus, the two circles of the binoculars continually merging and separating as I move fleetingly from one floor to another, constantly readjusting the lens. Eventually I settle on the building directly behind mine, sliding my view from one window to the next, invading the lives of the unsuspecting and unaware, monitoring their casual routines, violating their privacy, drawing them close while keeping them at a safe distance.

The phone beside my bed rings, and I jump, although I make no move to answer it. I don't want to talk to anyone. I'm tired of reassuring people I'll be all right, that it gets a little easier every day.

It doesn't, and it won't.

I press the binoculars tighter to my face, watch the universe unfold from afar. This is as close to the outside world as I want to get.

—THREE—

People always tell you it's pointless to get upset about things you can't control. I used to agree. But that was before my mother was diagnosed with cancer, before I watched helplessly as the disease stripped her of her strength, her smile, ultimately her life. Before my father succumbed to a massive heart attack and died, just weeks after being given a clean bill of health by his doctors. Before a man found me crouching in the middle of a bunch of sweet-smelling shrubs and stripped away my clothes, my dignity, and whatever inner peace I still possessed. I know now that control is a harmless illusion at best, a harmful deceit at worst.

I've never had many close friends. I'm not sure why that is, exactly. As a rule, I'm pretty sociable. I get along well with most people. I'm good at small talk—maybe too good. Not so good at the deeper stuff. I've never felt the need to sit around discussing my feelings. I've never wanted to share the details of relationships I consider private. My friend from high school, Jocelyn, whom I haven't seen in years, used to say I was more like a boy than a girl in that regard, that I would rather talk generalities than particulars, and that while I was a great listener, I never discussed my own problems, that I never let anyone get too close. She said I had trust issues, probably because my family was so wealthy. Not to mention estranged. I'm not sure I agree. I mean, maybe I'm not great at letting other people in. Maybe I've always been more comfortable as an observer than a participant. But that's just the way I am. Maybe that's what makes me so good at my job.

At any rate, Jocelyn is long gone. She took a year off after we graduated high school to travel around Europe, then headed west to college in Berkeley. I stayed here in south Florida. We lost touch, although she did try to "friend" me on Facebook a few years ago. I meant to respond, but it was right around the time my mother was dying and I never got around to it.

Clichéd as it sounds, my mother was always my best friend. I still can't believe she's gone. I miss her every day. But as much as my body aches to feel her arms around me, to have her kiss my forehead and assure me that that kiss will make everything better, I'm supremely grateful she isn't around to see me now. Not even her kiss could fix this.

I'm friendly with Alissa Dunphy, the third-year associate I was working for the night I was attacked, and Sally Ogilby, assistant to Phil Cunningham, the firm's top family lawyer, but I rarely see them outside of work. Alissa is chained to her desk, determined to make partner before she turns thirty-five, and Sally is married, the mother of a three-year-old boy and expecting her second child, this one a girl, in a couple of months. This doesn't leave her a lot of time for other interests. Her life is very busy. Our lives are all very busy.

Correction: *Were.*

My life used to be busy. My life used to be a lot of things.

Alissa has called every day since the attack, repeatedly telling me how sorry she is, how responsible she feels, asking if there's anything she can do to help me through this difficult time. I tell her no, there's nothing, and I can almost hear her sigh with relief. "You'll tell me," she says before hanging up the phone, "if there's anything you need . . ."

I need my life back. I need things to go back to the way they were before. I need to find out who did this to me.

The police think it was a random act, a crime of opportunity, a case of wrong time, wrong place. Still, they ask: Can there be anyone I have investigated, anyone whose marriage my photographs helped scuttle, anyone whose business failed because of information I uncovered, anyone at all who hates me that much to do what he did?

I think of the testimony I gave in court the morning of my attack, the venom that shot from Todd Elder's eyes as he leaned against the wall outside the courtroom, the word *bitch* spewing silently from his lips. He fits the rapist's general description. As does Owen Weaver, I realize, recalling our short-lived flirtation and his mouthful of straight white teeth. I shudder, feeling those teeth rip into my breast. Is it possible?

"Can you remember anything about the man at all?" I ask myself daily, repeating the police officer's question.

I search my mind, scrape it clean for the tiniest of fragments, trying to be as persistent, as methodical, as resourceful in my private life as I used to be professionally. But I find nothing. I see nothing.

"It could have been worse," I recall one of the nurses saying. "He could have sodomized you. He could have forced you to use your mouth."

"I wish he had," I hear myself tell her. "I would have bitten his dick right off."

"He'd have killed you."

"It would have been worth it."

Is it possible this exchange actually took place? Or am I only imagining it? And if this conversation really occurred, what else have I suppressed? What else is out there, too terrible to see, too awful to remember?

—

A typical day, post-rape: Wake up at five in the morning after maybe an hour or two of sleep. Shake off one of several recurring nightmares—a masked man chasing me through the street, a woman watching from her balcony, doing nothing; sharks circling my feet in placid waters—climb out of bed and search through the top drawer of my nightstand, locate the large pair of scissors I have kept there ever since my attack, and begin my morning search of my apartment.

Whoever raped me stole my gun, and I have yet to replace it. But that's all right. I've decided there's something more visceral, more personal, more satisfying, about scissors. Whenever I think about striking back at the man who assaulted me—and I think about this as often as I take a breath—I never think of shooting him. I think of stabbing him, as he stabbed me. And even if I can't use my body as a weapon the same way he could, I can still tear at his flesh as he tore at mine, the scissors an extension of my arm, my fury.

Such is the person I've become. Such is the woman he made me.

Holding the scissors in front of me, I check under my bed, even though it sits too low to the ground to allow anyone to hide beneath it, then proceed down the long marble hallway, flanked on both sides by the paintings I inherited from my parents—a series of colorful hearts by Jim Dine, a Motherwell nude, an abstract pink-and-black Gottlieb, an orange-and-black Calder that looks kind of like a turkey. I do a quick search of the second bedroom that serves as my office, peeking under the Lucite-and-black-marble desk on which sits my computer and behind the purple corduroy pullout sofa where Heath sometimes sleeps. I peer into its small closet and ensuite bathroom, checking the tiny cabinet under the sink, before continuing down the hall to the main powder room. After ascertaining that no one is crouching behind the door, I move to the hall closet and look for feet hiding beneath the rack of coats. I make sure the lock on the front door is secure, then check the kitchen on my way to the living and dining area.

Two modern white sofas curve toward one another in the middle of the rectangular room, a large, square limestone coffee table between them on top of a free-form cowhide area rug. Bright purple accent pillows adorn the sofas. They match the purple velvet armchair that sits in the invisible dividing line between the living and dining areas. Ten plastic lemons fill an oblong wire bowl in the middle of the glass dining room table. A dozen pink silk roses stand tall in a lime-green vase on the serving table against the wall opposite the window, underneath a painting of two faceless women strolling hand in hand along a deserted beach. I don't remember who painted it. A local artist, I believe.

A fake palm tree beside the window stretches toward the room's high ceiling, the tree as authentic-looking as any of the ubiquitous palms that line the streets below. Artificial white orchids hang from a wall sconce next to the door to the kitchen. Everyone always assumes that the orchids are real, congratulate me on my green thumb. They look shocked when I tell them they're fake, even more shocked when I confess I prefer these imposters to the real thing. They're easy and undemanding, I explain. You don't have to take care of them. They don't die.

Of course, I have real flowers as well. In the days immediately following my rape, I received at least six different arrangements. They're mostly from my colleagues at work and are scattered throughout the apartment. Sean Holden sent two dozen pink roses. Travis sent a large pot of purple mums. He remembered that I love purple but forgot that I hate mums. Maybe he did it on purpose, or maybe I just never told him.

After I am positive that no one is hiding behind the decorative panels of the living room curtains waiting to jump out at me, I return to my bedroom, where I rifle through the clothes hanging inside my walk-in closet, making sure that no one is secreted behind my jeans and dresses. I inspect the master bathroom: the separate toilet stall, the glass-enclosed shower, even the white enamel bathtub with its brass claw feet, in case someone is coiled inside, like a snake in a basket, waiting to strike. I do the same with the white wicker hamper that sits beside the tub, removing its lid and poking through its contents with my scissors.

I perform this ritual at least three times a day, although occasionally I vary the order. Only when I am fully convinced that no

one has been able to infiltrate my glass sanctuary in the sky do I
turn on the shower. As steam fills the room, I remove my pajamas
and step inside the stall.

I take the scissors with me.

I don't so much as glance at my nude body. I can't bear the
sight of my breasts. My pubic hair repulses me. I haven't shaved
my legs or underarms since the attack. Everything hurts: my ribs,
my wrists, my back. Even my skin. I remain under the steady onslaught of hot water until I can no longer feel my flesh. I don't look
in the steam-coated mirror when I get out. I use a harsh towel to
dry myself off, then I rub myself raw. I dump my pajamas in the
overflowing hamper, exchange them for another pair, and return
to the bedroom, scissors in hand.

The room is in darkness. The sun has yet to rise. I keep my
blackout blinds closed until daylight arrives.

You never know who might be watching.

—

I sense him before I see him, smell him before I feel him moving
above me. I recognize the scent immediately: mouthwash, mentho-
lated and minty. Suddenly I feel the full weight of his body on top
of mine, his elbow lodging against my windpipe, blocking my
breath, stopping my screams before they can gain traction. "Tell
me you love me," he commands as he forces his way inside me,
setting fire to my insides, as if he is pummeling me with a lit torch.
"Tell me you love me."

"No!" I scream, my hands punching at his chest, my feet kicking at his thighs, my fingers scratching at his neck, connecting with
nothing as I flail helplessly around in my bed.

I open my eyes.

No one is there.

I sit up. It takes several minutes for my breathing to slow to
something approaching normal. The TV is still on. I grab the remote from the nightstand beside my bed and turn it off. I have no

idea what time it is, what day it is, how many hours have passed since I was last awake.

The phone rings, and I jump, then sit staring at it until it stops its awful wail. The clock beside my bed informs me that it's ten minutes after eight. I assume it's morning, although I'm not sure, and it doesn't really matter. I get up, grab the scissors from the top drawer of the nightstand, and begin my tour of the apartment. As I step into the hall, the phone starts ringing again. I ignore it.

The phone rings on and off for the ten minutes it takes me to make sure my apartment is secure. It is ringing when I return to my bedroom. Probably the police, I think, reaching for the phone just as it stops ringing. I shrug and stand there for several minutes, but the phone stubbornly refuses to ring again.

I am just stepping out of the shower when I hear voices, followed by the sound of footsteps, of people moving around my apartment. I grab my oversized white terry cloth housecoat from its hook beside the shower and wrap it around me, raising the scissors in my hand to my chest as I enter the bedroom, all the while assuring myself that I'm imagining things. It's impossible that anyone could have gotten inside my apartment. There is nobody walking down my hallway. No one is whispering outside my bedroom door.

Except there is.

A voice stabs at the air: "Bailey? Bailey, are you here?"

Followed by another voice, a man's: "Miss Carpenter? Is everything all right?"

My knees go weak. My mouth goes dry. The room spins around me.

A woman suddenly appears in the doorway, a young man's head bobbing up over her left shoulder. The woman is about five feet, four inches tall, with short blond hair and wide-set brown eyes. Her stomach is distended, heavy with the baby she is carrying.

"Sally?" I mutter, struggling to find my voice as I lower the scissors to my side.

"Is everything all right?" the young man behind her asks. Only now do his features fall into place and I recognize Finn, one of the valets who regularly works the front desk. "We tried calling and calling."

"I was in the shower," I say, trying to keep from screaming. "How did you get in here?"

"It's my fault," Sally quickly explains. "I just got so scared when you didn't answer your phone. I was afraid something might have happened to you, that maybe you'd done something. . . ." There's no need for her to finish the sentence. We both know what she was about to say.

"I'm really sorry, Miss Carpenter," Finn says, shifting his weight from one foot to the other. "We didn't mean to frighten you."

"Don't be mad," Sally says. "I forced him."

I nod. The condo rules state that the building has extra keys to all units in case of emergency. Clearly, Sally felt that this was such an emergency. "What are you doing here?"

"Don't you remember? Last night on the phone, I told you I was going to stop by this morning on my way to work."

"It slipped my mind." In truth, I have no recollection of last night's phone call at all.

"Are those scissors?" Sally asks, her wide eyes widening further.

I slip the scissors into one of the side pockets of my robe.

"Sorry again about barging into your apartment," Finn says, backing down the hall toward the door, closing it softly after him.

"That was some long shower," Sally says.

"Sorry."

"Don't apologize. I'm the one who went all crazy and broke into your apartment. Have you had breakfast yet? I brought muffins." She holds up a brown paper bag.

I make tea and we sit at my dining room table and eat our muffins and try to pretend that this is a normal day and that we are normal people having a normal conversation.

"Have you decided what you're going to name the baby?" I ask. Sally has been here for about twenty minutes, and I don't think we've talked about this yet, although I'm not sure. I've been listening with only one ear.

"Not yet. But I think we're making progress." She continues when I fail to ask any follow-up questions. "I suggested the name Avery, and Bobby didn't immediately go all ape-shit. You know how my dear husband always goes for more traditional names, like with Michael." Michael is their three-year-old. Sally wanted to name him Rafael, after the tennis player Rafael Nadal, or Stellan, after some Swedish actor she's always admired, but her husband was insistent on something more traditional. He argued in favor of Richard or Steve. They settled on Michael just as the baby's head was crowning, and Sally still isn't convinced they made the right choice. "My legs were wide open, this doctor had his hand halfway to my throat," she once told me. "I was screaming my head off. You gotta admit the man had me at a slight disadvantage."

I wince at the image.

"You don't like the name?" Sally asks.

"What?"

"I was also thinking of Nicola or Kendall."

"I like Avery," I tell her. The image fades but lingers at the periphery of my mind's eye, joining a gallery of similar images.

"You do? I'm so glad. Avery's my favorite. What's the matter— you don't like your muffin? They said it was full of cranberries, like all the way through it, not just on the top where you can see them."

The cranberries taste like sour rubber balls. "It's delicious," I lie. The berries stick to the roof of my mouth, as if they have been glued there, and even the persistent prodding of my tongue fails to dislodge them.

"I just hate when you think you're going to get this muffin that's loaded with berries, and it turns out there are only a few on the top," Sally is saying. "It's such a cheat." She smiles. "You seem much better today. Did you sleep well?"

"Much better," I say, using her words.

She reaches across the table to pat my hand. "Everybody at work keeps asking about you."

"That's nice."

"They said to say hello."

"Hello back."

Silence. She gulps down the rest of her tea, pats up the few crumbs she's left on the table with the tip of her finger, puts them in her mouth. "Well, I guess I should go."

I'm on my feet immediately. "Thanks for stopping by."

"Yeah, and scaring you half to death."

"I'm fine now."

"You look good," she says, the forced enthusiasm in her voice underlining her lie. "The bruises are pretty much gone."

Only the ones you can see, I think but don't say.

"So," she says, leaning forward to give me a tentative hug. Luckily, her growing stomach prevents her from getting too close. "I'll see you again soon."

"Sounds good."

"Any plans for the rest of the day?" she broaches as I open the door.

"Nothing definite."

"It's beautiful out," she says, as if this is unusual. Miami is full of beautiful days. "Maybe you should get out, go for a walk."

"Maybe."

She motions toward my wet hair. "Better dry it before you catch a cold." What's the point in drying it when I'm only going to shower again in a few hours?

I close the door after her, watching through the peephole as she waddles down the corridor toward the elevators. Then I run to the powder room and throw up the tea and cranberry muffin.

—FOUR—

I remember the first time a boy touched my breast. His name was Brian, and he was seventeen and a senior at a nearby high school. I was fifteen and excited that he'd even noticed me, let alone asked me out. We were going to a party, and I'd decided to wear the pretty wine-colored dress my mother had recently bought me. The dress was sleeveless, with a white lace collar and large pearl buttons up the center of the bodice. I loved it because I thought it made my still-small breasts look bigger. Was that why Brian felt he could touch them? Had the dress signaled that his touch would be welcome? Was that why he'd been so angry when I slapped his hand away? Was that why he promptly took me home, depositing me, humiliated yet defiant, on my doorstep, calling me a tease, among other choice epithets?

This memory leads to another earlier one. I am twelve, maybe thirteen. School is over for the day, and I'm about to board a bus to meet my mother downtown. I'm wearing my school uniform—a green sweater over a crisp white shirt, matching green skirt and knee socks, and black Oxfords completing the less-than-fetching ensemble—and as I lift my leg to climb onto the bus, I feel something brush across my buttocks. The touch lingers, refuses to let go, as I spin around and dig my nails into the unwanted hand. A man, short, middle-aged and balding, rubs his hand and grins, sheepishly at first, then more boldly, before backing away and disappearing into the throng still waiting to board the bus. I lurch toward the back of the bus, feeling sick to my stomach. It is years before I am able to disregard that man and his unwelcome caress, his even more unwelcome smile, a smile that said, "Don't look so shocked, little girl. You know you liked it."

Did he really believe that? I wonder now, standing by my bedroom window and staring through my binoculars at the street below. Could a grown man really think a child would welcome the unsolicited caress of a stranger? Did I do something to encourage him to grope me as I boarded the bus? Had I smiled at him provocatively? Had I lifted my leg too high, exposed too much girlish thigh? Had I sent him any sort of message to make him think he had the right to put his hands on me?

These thoughts fill my head as I train my binoculars on two young women darting between moving cars, trying to cross the street against the lights. It's about five o'clock and still light out, although not as light as it was even last week at this time. It's mid-October, and soon it will be time to change the clocks for winter. "Fall back," I hear my mother say. "Spring forward." I used to get a kick out of that. Now I think, *What difference does it make? One hour is pretty much the same as the next.*

I try to recall how I spent my day. Sally dropped by this morning, I think, then remember no, that was yesterday. Today has been relatively quiet. No visitors. No phone calls. In fact, I actually called the police this morning and not the other way around. A changing of the guard, so to speak, although the contents of the call are always the same. The police have eliminated the man I'd been watching as a suspect in my rape. It turns out it wasn't Roland Peterson after all, and Peterson's girlfriend—*ex*-girlfriend, she insisted—swore her new boyfriend, the man I saw in the window, had been with her all evening. So he has an alibi, as does Todd Elder, and we're back at square one. I ask if there are any new leads, if they are any closer to finding the man who raped me, and they ask if I've remembered anything to aid them in their search. The answer is the same in both cases: no.

The police promise to stay in touch, and I hang up the phone. I don't want to be touched.

Something is happening on the street. An altercation between two young men. I point my binoculars at them, watch as a fistfight erupts and the people around them scatter. No one interferes, which is probably smart. How many times have I read of good Samaritans being killed while trying to break up a fight?

Was someone watching the night I was attacked? I wonder, not for the first time. Did anyone see what was happening and choose not to intervene out of fear for their own safety? Was there someone who saw or heard something that could be helpful in identifying the man who raped me, someone who knows something but isn't telling?

According to the police, who claim to have questioned everyone who lives in the vicinity of where the attack took place, the answer is no. Of course, I know from professional experience that the police aren't always as thorough as they claim and that witnesses to crimes aren't necessarily as truthful or forthcoming as they should be. Not because they're bad people. Not because they don't care. They just don't want their own lives disrupted. If they can maintain a safe distance, they will choose to stay safe.

I don't judge them. Nor do I blame them. There is safety in distance, I have come to believe.

The phone rings, and I jump. Seems I spoke too soon about it being a quiet day. I move to it quickly, not wanting to risk a repeat of what happened yesterday. "Hello, Miss Carpenter. It's Finn at the concierge desk."

My heart starts pounding at the sound of the disembodied male voice speaking in my ear. I feel my rapist leaning toward me. *Tell me you love me,* he says. I calm myself by remembering that Finn always identifies himself in this manner—It's Finn, *at the concierge desk*—as if I know a plethora of Finns, and that I used to find it amusing. "Your brother is here to see you," he says.

I wonder why he is telling me this. Everyone who works here knows Heath. They know to just send him up.

"Not Heath," Finn says, as if I have voiced this thought out loud.

Another man interjects. "Let me have that. Bailey," he says in his best assistant state's attorney's voice. "It's Gene. Tell this clown to let me up."

Oh, God, I think, as my head falls toward my chest. I haven't seen Gene—more formally, Eugene, my father's first-born son and namesake—since our dad's funeral. I haven't talked to him since the launch of his lawsuit. I don't have the strength for his bluster and bullshit now.

"I'm kind of tired," I say.

"Don't make me have to call in the troops."

While I'm not sure exactly what troops he means, I know he won't leave until I've agreed to see him. "Send him up," I tell Finn. I return the phone to its charger, lay my binoculars down on the nightstand beside it and head for the door. Gene is already waiting on the other side by the time I get there.

"Why the hell didn't you tell me you were raped?" he demands even before I've fully opened the door.

I stand back to let him enter, then immediately close the door and double-lock it.

"It's not something I choose to broadcast," I hear myself say, hating the quiver in my voice.

"I'm your brother."

"You're suing me," I remind him.

"One thing has nothing to do with the other."

I find myself marveling at his ability to compartmentalize. Was this how he was able to investigate his own father for fraud? "Would you like something to drink?" I ask, not sure what else to say, not sure whether I have anything to offer him.

"I had to hear about it from the police, weeks after the fact."

"I'm sorry. I guess I should have. . . ."

"Yes, you should have. I'm an assistant state's attorney, for God's sake. And no, I don't want anything to drink. How are you doing?" His voice softens, his dark eyes narrowing with what I like to think of as concern but is more likely suspicion. He's not sure he believes my story, I understand in that moment, ushering him into the living room.

"Not great," I say.

"Maybe it would help if you got dressed."

I look down at my blue flannel pajamas, trying to remember the last time I changed them. Maybe yesterday, maybe the day before.

"You look like hell," he says.

"Thank you."

"Sorry. I'm just upset. This is very upsetting."

No kidding, I think but don't say.

"Look, I didn't come here to argue." Gene walks toward the living room window, and for the first time, I notice a slight limp. He is a big man, tall, with a linebacker's girth, which I guess isn't surprising, considering that he played football in college and was, by all accounts, headed for a pro career before being sidelined with torn ligaments in his right knee. Or maybe it was his left knee, I think, as he comes to a stop and turns around to face me. He might be more handsome if he were less severe. But he wears his thinning brown hair in an unflattering crew cut, and his lips always turn down, even when he smiles, which isn't often, at least in my presence. He unbuttons the jacket of his navy blue cotton suit to reveal a noticeable paunch pressing against the lighter blue shirt beneath. He fidgets with his too-wide, blue-striped tie. I can't remember ever seeing Gene without a tie. "Nice apartment," he says.

"Thank you."

"You have good taste."

"Thank you."

"What the hell happened?" So much for small talk.

"You know what happened. You said you spoke to the police."

"I want to hear it from you."

I can't do this. I can't keep reliving my attack for the edification of others. "Is this visit personal or professional?"

"What do you think?"

"I'm asking."

"I'm your brother."

"Who's suing me," I remind him again.

"What happened, Bailey?" His tone indicates that he will keep asking until he gets an answer.

I provide him with the bare essentials of the assault. The words stick to my teeth like toffee, and I have to pry them loose with my tongue. I watch Gene's eyes as they alternately widen and narrow. I note the creases in his forehead as his brow furrows in obvious dismay. I watch his lips turn down. "You look more like your mother than our father," I remark at the end of my story.

He looks startled. "How do you know what my mother looks like?"

"I saw a picture of her once, in one of Daddy's scrapbooks."

"I didn't realize he kept a scrapbook."

"Yes. Quite a few, actually."

"I'd like to see them sometime."

If I don't oblige, I wonder, will he sue me for them? "How's your mother doing?" I ask. I don't know Gene's mother. We've never met. But I always thought she had a kind face. Maybe that's just the way she photographs.

"She's doing well. Enjoying her retirement and her grandchildren."

Gene has two sons, ages seven and nine. I can't remember their names or the last time I saw them, probably when the youngest was a baby. "How *are* your boys?"

"They're great. But we're talking about you now," he says, as if suddenly remembering why he is here.

"There's nothing more to talk about." I used to be someone who had lots to say. I had opinions and interests. I was complicated, multifaceted. Then I was raped.

"I just don't understand," he says.

"What don't you understand?"

"How it could have happened."

I explain the situation again, how I was hiding in the bushes, how the man snuck up behind me, how he overpowered me. Was Gene not listening the first time?

"What the hell were you doing hiding in a bunch of bushes at that hour of the night?" he demands angrily. "You had to know how dangerous it would be."

"Are you implying that it was my fault?"

"No, of course I'm not implying that. I'm just saying that maybe it wasn't the smartest thing in the world for you to be doing."

"It's my job, Gene."

"Then maybe you should find another line of work."

"I like what I do." I don't tell him that I'm taking a few months off, that the mere thought of doing surveillance makes me break out in a cold sweat.

"You like hiding in bushes and chasing down lowlifes," he states more than asks.

"There's more to what I do than that."

"I thought you wanted to be a lawyer."

"I wanted to be a lot of things."

"I'm sure your mother would have liked you to go back to school and, at the very least, finish your degree."

I bite down on my lip to keep from saying something I'll regret. *How dare you?* I want to scream. You know absolutely nothing about my mother or what she might have wanted. Except I can't, because he's right. My mother *would* have liked me to go back to college and finish my education. God knows I took enough courses, left at least three different degrees unfinished, as I was never quite sure what I wanted to be: a doctor, a lawyer, a criminologist, a ballerina.

"Look," Gene says. "I'm only thinking of you here. Believe it or not, I want what's best for you."

I *don't* believe it, but I say nothing. *What do you* really *want?* I wonder as he ambles toward the sofa closest to him and sits down, carelessly tossing two of the purple throw pillows to one side. One teeters on the edge of the large cushion underneath him before tumbling to the floor. He makes no move to pick it up. "How is it, working for Sean Holden?"

"Fine."

"What's he like?"

I shrug, not sure what to say.

"I always thought he was a smart guy," Gene says, answering his own question. "A little cocky, but smart. Can't say I enjoy facing off against him in court."

"He's a good lawyer."

"A bit of a player, too, from what I understand."

"A player?"

Gene shakes his head. "You hear things, working in the State's Attorney's Office. Rumors. You know."

My heart starts pounding. Is he fishing? Is this why he is here? To glean information about Sean?

"I've been talking to the others," he says suddenly.

It takes me a minute to realize we are no longer talking about Sean Holden but about my half-sister Claire and my half-brothers Tom, Dick, and Harry. "You told them about what happened?"

"They were quite horrified."

"I'm sure they were."

"They send their best wishes for a speedy recovery." Gene looks strangely pleased with himself, although the corners of his lips continue to turn down. I wonder how his wife ever knows when he's happy. Or if she cares. "They wanted to come. . . ."

"I'm sure they did." I shudder. The thought of all my half-siblings occupying my apartment is overwhelming. Fifteen hundred square feet simply isn't enough room for all that animosity.

"Claire said she'll try to stop by after her shift." He checks his watch, a white-faced Bulova with a black leather band. "Should be any time now."

"That's really not necessary."

"She's a nurse, Bailey. She might be able to help."

"I don't see how. . . ."

The phone rings, and I jump. Gene's natural scowl deepens. "Probably that's her now," he says.

I walk into the kitchen, grab the phone, listen as Finn identifies himself, then tells me that Sean Holden is here to see me and can he send him up?

"Please," I say, mouthing a silent "Thank God" as I return to the living room, hoping this news will encourage my brother to make a hasty retreat. "Sean Holden is here."

"Well, speak of the devil."

"Thanks for stopping by, Gene." I wait for him to take the hint and leave. But he sits tight, his body language announcing that he has no intention of going anywhere.

I walk to the door and place my forehead against the cool wood, my eye peeking through the peephole into the corridor. The phone rings again, and I jump. "Do you want me to get that?" I hear Gene ask from somewhere behind me.

"No," I tell him, but he is already answering it.

"Hello?" I hear him say. Then: "Fine. Thank you. Send her up."

The elevator doors open, and Sean Holden steps into the long, beige-and-green-carpeted hall. I open my door even before he reaches it. His large arms surround me. I feel safe for the first time since his last visit, which I think was several days ago, although I'm not certain. It feels like forever. "How are you?" he whispers, his lips brushing against my perpetually damp hair. He leads me back inside my apartment, closes the door behind him.

"Okay," I tell him. "My brother's here."

Gene joins us in the foyer, extending his hand in welcome. "Well, hello there, Sean. Nice to see you again, in spite of the difficult circumstances."

I almost smile. I have become a "difficult circumstance."

"Gene," Sean acknowledges, right eyebrow arching. "I didn't expect you to be here."

"And why is that?" Gene's tone is challenging, almost belligerent, although there is no change in his expression. "Despite everything, Bailey is still family. Naturally I'm very upset about what's happened."

"Naturally," Sean agrees. "We all are."

"I would certainly think so, since it happened while she was on the job. Your firm could be held liable."

"What happened was hardly Sean's fault," I say.

"Still. That could be one hell of a lawsuit."

"You going to sue him, too?" I ask.

"Just looking out for your interests, Bailey," my brother says without a trace of irony.

"I think I may have come at a bad time," Sean says.

"No. Please, don't go," I urge.

"Yes, by all means, stick around," Gene concurs, looking toward the door. "That was Finn, from the concierge desk, on the phone just now. He said Claire walked in just after Sean did. I told him to send her up."

"Busy place," Sean remarks, and even though we are no longer touching, I can feel his body tense.

I close my eyes, feel my legs go weak. When did my right to choose who visits me and who doesn't disappear? Did the man in the bushes take that from me, too?

"Bailey," Sean says. "Are you all right?"

"I think I should sit down." But even as the words are leaving my mouth, I'm distracted by the unmistakable sound of a key turning in the lock. I watch in horror as the lock twists rapidly.

Seconds later, the door to my condo falls open. A young girl, maybe fifteen or sixteen, with blue eyes and shoulder-length blond hair framing a pretty, oval face, and a woman with almost the same face, albeit slightly fuller and several decades older, stand on the other side of the threshold. "See?" the girl exclaims, triumphantly. "I told you I could do it. These locks aren't worth shit." She returns her nail file to the oversized brown leather bag hanging from her shoulder. "Hi, everyone," she says before stepping into the foyer and dropping her bag to the beige marble floor, then brushing past me into the living room, all in one fluid motion. "Wow. Nice place."

"Jade, for God's sake," her mother says, offering an embarrassed nod in my direction. "I'm so sorry," she begins, shutting the door behind her and glancing at the two men standing beside me.

Her gaze lingers an extra second on Sean. "I'm sorry. Have we come at a bad time?"

"Claire, this is Sean Holden," Gene says, ignoring the question. "Bailey's boss."

"Oh. Very nice to meet you, Mr. Holden."

"And you." Sean smiles graciously, although I can see his eyes already plotting his escape.

"Claire is Bailey's half-sister," Gene continues unnecessarily.

"Who's suing me," I add, not quite under my breath.

"We don't have to get into all that now. Jade, get back here," Gene commands as the girl marches toward the long expanse of window to stare down at the street below. "Claire," he says. "Do something."

"Like what?" my half-sister asks. "You want me to sit on her?"

I watch their faces as they bicker. There is even less of my father in Claire than there is in Gene. Her nose is wider, her eyes a paler shade of blue. She is approximately ten years my senior, about two inches shorter than I am, and twenty pounds heavier. We both look like our mothers and absolutely nothing like each other. No one would ever take us for half-sisters. But she has a kind face, I think, although maybe what I'm seeing is fatigue. Something we have in common.

"Where the hell are you going now?" Gene shouts as my niece leaves the living room to amble down the hall toward the bedrooms.

The girl stops, spins around on her heels and swivels back toward us. She is wearing a pair of skinny jeans and a loose white T-shirt. She makes a face that says she'd rather be anywhere but here. I want to tell her I understand completely. "Sorry. Where *are* my manners?" she says with mock outrage as she comes to a stop in front of me. "You must be Bailey." Cherry red lips move furiously as she manipulates a giant wad of bubble gum from one side of her small mouth to the other. "Sorry about your rape."

"Jade, for God's sake," her mother says.

The girl's heavily shadowed blue eyes widen with disdain.

"What?" She looks toward the door. "You should get that lock replaced," she tells me. "It's a piece of shit."

"I just had it replaced," I say.

She makes another face. The face tells me to replace it again.

"How did you get it open?" I ask.

"Piece of cake." Jade returns to the door and opens it, indicating the locking device. "See this? It's really cheap stuff. All these so-called luxury condos and they all install this absolute crap. You just have to insert something long and thin, like a nail file or a bobby pin, and give it a few good twists. I thought you were a private investigator. Shouldn't you know this stuff already?"

I don't know what to say. She's right, I suppose. I should know this. And maybe I did. Before.

"Here, you want me to show you?"

I'm about to say yes, when Claire interjects. "Not now, Jade," she warns.

"What you just did is against the law," Gene says sternly. "It's called breaking and entering."

"Oh, please. You gonna arrest me?"

"Haven't you spent enough time in Juvenile Hall?"

Jade's eyes roll toward the ceiling. "Who are *you*?" she asks Sean, as if just becoming aware of his presence.

"Sean Holden." He smiles, amused by her antics.

"You Bailey's boyfriend?"

He winces, as do I. "Her boss. Who really should get going," he adds in the next breath. Jade has provided him with the perfect exit line.

I don't argue. He squeezes my hand, then leaves. I watch him through the peephole as he walks briskly down the corridor toward the bank of elevators.

"Nice of him to stop by," Claire says.

"Just protecting his ass," Gene tells her as I step away from the door, my eyes on the lock.

"Where did you learn to do that?" I ask Jade.

"*Dog the Bounty Hunter,*" she answers matter-of-factly.

"What?"

"Reality TV," her mother clarifies. "It's all she ever watches."

"You learn a lot from shows like *Dog*," Jade says. "You have a TV, don't you?"

I point down the hall. "They're in the bedrooms."

She looks relieved. "You ever watch *1000 Ways to Die*?"

"I don't think so."

"You should. It's the best." Jade's formerly sullen face is suddenly full of enthusiasm. "You wouldn't believe the stupid things people do that end up getting them killed. Like this one time, this woman had cement injected into her butt to make it bigger. . . ."

"Okay, Jade. That's enough for now." Claire turns her tired eyes toward me. "Gene told us what happened. How are you doing?"

"I'm okay. There was really no need for you to come over."

"I *told* you," Jade said.

I decide I like Jade. There's no pretense or forced concern. "You can go watch TV, if you want," I tell her.

"Great." She is already heading down the hall before her mother or uncle can object. Seconds later, we hear the TV blasting from my bedroom.

"Turn that down," Claire yells in her direction. "*Now,*" she adds when nothing happens. The television's volume lowers a barely perceptible notch.

"*More,*" Gene commands. Then: "Really, Claire. I thought you said you had a handle on things."

Claire says nothing.

"Why don't we go into the living room where we can talk like reasonable adults?" Gene suggests, as if this is his place and not mine. I bristle, my feet refusing to budge.

"I think that's up to Bailey," Claire says.

"Sure," I say. "By all means, the living room."

We arrange ourselves on the sofas, Claire sitting beside me on one, Gene sitting across from us on the other. I brace myself for the conversation of reasonable adults.

"How are you feeling?" Claire asks. "Any pain or infections?"

"No infections," I say.

"Pain?" she presses.

I shake my head. The pain I have is no longer physical.

"I see your bruises are fading. Have you been sleeping?"

"Off and on."

"Have the doctors given you anything to help you?"

I nod, although I don't like to take the pills they've prescribed. I need to stay alert. I need to be vigilant.

"You need to take them," Claire says. "You need to sleep. Have you spoken to a therapist?"

"I don't need a therapist."

"Everybody in Miami needs a therapist," she says with a wry smile. "I have the name of a good one, if you think you'd like to talk to someone."

"I'm tired of talking."

"I understand. But you may change your mind."

I shrug.

"Okay. What else can I do for you?"

"Nothing. I'm fine."

"You're not fine," Claire says, looking around. My eyes follow hers across the room. Aside from the pillows that Gene tossed to the floor earlier, everything seems to be neatly in place. Maybe there are a few dust bunnies in the corner but . . . "The windows could use a good scrubbing," she says.

"It's all the construction," I hear myself say, vaguely remembering getting a notice from the superintendent about window washers coming later in the week to clean the exteriors. "They no sooner wash them, they're dirty again." Just like me, I think, wishing everyone would leave so I can hop into the shower.

"How about the laundry? I could do a few loads while I'm here. . . ."

"It's under control," I tell her, although my hamper is overflowing. I've run out of fresh sheets. I'm all out of detergent.

"Do you need groceries?" Claire asks. "When was the last time you had something substantial to eat?"

"Heath brought over some pizza last night," I say, although it could have been the night before. Or maybe the night before that.

"You're way too thin. You need to keep your strength up."

"Why? So I can fight you guys in court?"

Claire gives Gene a wary look. "Please tell me you haven't been bothering her about that now."

"I haven't said a word."

"Okay, here's what's going to happen," Claire says. "I'm going to go through this entire apartment and see what needs doing, then Jade and I will go to Publix and get some food so I can make us supper."

"Rita's expecting me home for dinner," Gene demurs.

"Good, because you aren't invited. Now, give me some money and get out of here."

Gene is quickly on his feet, reaching into his pocket for his wallet. "How much do you need?"

"Three hundred dollars should do it."

"Three hundred dollars?"

"My guess is that Bailey's cupboard is pretty bare. Come on, little brother, let's have it."

I remember now that Claire is, in fact, older than Gene by two years and that, at almost forty, she is the oldest of my father's seven children. I am the youngest. Bookends, I think, and feel my lips relax into a smile. I'm glad she is here, whatever ulterior motives she may have. It feels nice to be taken care of again. It's been a long time.

Gene reluctantly gives his sister three hundred dollars in cash, then hands me his business card. "Call me if you feel like talking," he says, and I know he's referring to the lawsuit he and my half-siblings have launched against Heath and me over our father's estate and not my more recent trauma. Claire hurries him to the door. "And you, call me when you get home," he says as his sister is closing the door after him. Seconds later, I hear her rumbling around in my cupboards. "Jade," she calls toward the bedroom. "Turn that damn thing off and get out here. We're going to Publix."

There is no response.

"Jade, did you hear me?"

Still nothing.

"Honestly," Claire says, walking quickly down the hall. "You're going to go deaf with that damn thing on so loud."

I follow her down the hall to the master bedroom where my large-screen TV is mounted on the sliver of wall between the two large windows opposite my queen-sized bed. On the television, a man is running from the police. He leaps over a tall, chain-link fence, landing in some high grass and finding himself face to face with an angry alligator. But Jade isn't watching the TV. Instead, she is standing in front of the window, in much the same position I occupy every day, staring through my binoculars at the building directly across the way. "These are great," she says, without turning around. "You can see everything and nobody knows you're watching."

Claire quickly takes the binoculars from her hand, returning them to the nightstand beside my bed. "We're going to Publix," she tells her.

"What? You're kidding me."

"Why don't you lie down?" Claire says to me. "We'll be back in an hour." She pushes Jade toward the hall.

I hear the door to my apartment close, then do as I've been told and lie down on my bed, overwhelmed with exhaustion. My eyes stay open long enough to witness the man on TV struggling with the alligator, his legs inside the creature's mouth. The alligator becomes a shark as sleep overtakes me and my nightmares settle in, the shark's giant fin breaking through the surface of the ocean like scissors through tinsel. It glides menacingly toward where I am treading water, and I look down and see at least six more sharks circling my feet.

I swim frantically toward a distant raft, my arms and legs like propellers, chopping at the once placid water. I'm almost there.

And then I see him.

He is crouched at the edge of the raft, his body leaning forward, his face blocked by the sun. He reaches out his hand and I grab for it, about to pull myself to safety when I feel the roughness of the black leather glove he is wearing and smell my blood on its fingertips. I scream and fall back into the water as the sharks converge.

—FIVE—

I wake up bathed in sweat.

It is dark, and the TV is on. A woman on the screen is posing for photographs near the edge of a tall cliff. She is laughing and adjusting her wide-brimmed sunhat while her husband busily snaps her picture. "Back up just a bit," he motions. She complies, tripping over a small rock and losing her balance, her feet shooting out from under her as she tumbles backward over the precipice. Her screams echo throughout the giant chasm as she plunges to her death, her hat flying off her head and into the air, swooping up and down with the wind. *Falling off the Grand Canyon*, the dooms-day voice announces with barely concealed glee over the cheesy re-enactment. *Number 63 of 1000 Ways to Die.*

I grab the remote from the nightstand beside my bed and turn the TV off. I've been asleep less than an hour. At least I think it's been less than an hour since Claire and her daughter left to get groceries. If they were here at all. Maybe they came yesterday or the day before. Perhaps they were never here. Perhaps I only dreamt them.

I get out of bed, throw an old gray sweater over my shoulders and walk toward the window, grabbing my binoculars from the top of my nightstand as I go, lifting them to my eyes and adjusting their focus as I scan the exterior of the glass buildings opposite my window and direct them to the street below.

It's not quite six o'clock, and the streets are busy, people rushing off in all directions, leaving work, heading home for dinner. I see a man and woman embracing on the corner, then follow them as they continue down the street, arm in arm. From this distance, I can't make out their faces, but their posture tells me they're happy, relaxed with one another. I try to remember what that feels like. I can't.

Tell me what you see, a soft voice whispers in my ear. My mother's voice.

And just like that, I am transported from the bedroom of my glass house on the twenty-third floor of a downtown high-rise into the master bedroom of my parents' palatial estate in South Beach. My bare toes sink into the plush white broadloom as I stand by the window and gaze through the binoculars into the spectacular garden beyond, reporting on the exotic variety of birds beyond the glass. It is three years ago, a year since my mother received the devastating diagnosis that the cancer we prayed had disappeared had instead returned and that it was terminal.

In four months, she will be dead.

"I see a couple of herons and a gorgeous spoon-billed platypus," I tell her. "Come." I move quickly to her side.

But she is too weak to get out of bed, and I watch her suppress a grimace when I try to move her. She is so frail, I fear she will disintegrate in my hands, like ancient parchment. "I'll see them next time," she says, tears filling her eyes. We both know there will be no next time.

"Would you like me to read to you?" I ask, settling into the small, peach-colored chair beside her bed and opening the mystery novel I've been reading to her, a few chapters every day.

My mother always loved mysteries. When other children were listening to bedtime stories about Snow White and Cinderella, she was reading me the novels of Raymond Chandler and Agatha Christie.

Now our roles have reversed.

Occasionally we watch TV, crime shows mostly, anything to keep her mind off her pain and my mind off the fact I am losing her. "It's uncanny," she'd tell me, "the way you always know who did it."

When did that power desert me? I wonder as the ringing of the telephone yanks me from the past like a fish hooked at the end of a reel.

"It's Finn, at the concierge desk." I try to still the rapid beating of my heart as he continues. "Your sister and your niece are on their way up with what looks like a year's supply of groceries."

"Thank you." I realize I'm hungry, that I haven't eaten anything all day.

"You can tell them to put the empty carts back into the elevator when they're done with them," he says, and I say I will, although seconds later, I have no idea what he said.

I wait by the door to my apartment, listening for the sounds of the elevator down the hall. I watch through the peephole as Claire and Jade come into view, each pushing a shopping cart, both carts overflowing with bags of groceries.

"We bought out the store," Jade announces as I open the door. "Hope you're not a vegan."

"Thought I'd grill us some steaks," Claire says as she starts unloading her cart. She hands two of the bags to me.

I stand there, not sure what she expects me to do with them.

"You can start unpacking," she tells me.

I want to tell her that I don't have the strength, that I don't know where anything goes, that this whole grocery thing was her idea, not mine, but the look in her eyes tells me she will brook no such nonsense, and I don't know her well enough to argue. The truth is that I barely know her at all. We've probably spoken more today than in the past decade. So I take the two bags into the kitchen without protest and deposit them on the gold-and-brown-flecked marble counter.

"Those aren't going to unpack themselves," Claire says, following after me with two more bags that she puts down next to mine. "Come on, Bailey. You know where everything goes." She gives my arm a pat. "You can do this."

What if I don't want to? I'm about to ask, but she's already back in the hall, gathering up more supplies. What choice do I have but to comply?

It quickly becomes apparent that Claire has thought of everything. Along with at least a week's supply of fruit and vegetables, she's bought steaks, chicken, pasta and several different sauces, at least a dozen cans of soup, bread, jams, butter, milk, eggs, coffee, tea, even a bottle of wine. There is dishwashing detergent, laundry detergents for both warm and cold water washes, fabric softener and a variety of cleansers, toothpaste and a couple of fresh toothbrushes, deodorant, shampoo, body lotion, mouthwash.

I lift the large plastic bottle of emerald green liquid from the bag, my hands shaking. *Tell me you love me,* a man directs, the mintiness of his breath taking mine away, causing the bile to rise in my throat. *Tell me you love me.*

I'm not sure whether I start screaming before I drop the bottle or whether I drop the bottle and then start screaming, but one thing is certain: I am definitely screaming, as loud as I have ever screamed, my screams bringing Claire and Jade flying into the kitchen.

"What is it?" Claire is shouting, looking everywhere at once.

"Was there a spider in the bag?" Jade asks. "I saw that once on *1000 Ways to Die.* This lady . . ."

"Jade, please," her mother snaps, her eyes skipping across the kitchen floor. Then she says, "*Was* there a spider in the bag?"

I shake my head furiously from side to side, my screams having given way to sobs.

"Maybe she just doesn't like mouthwash." Jade retrieves the bottle from the floor. "Good thing it's plastic."

"Get it out of here," I manage to spit out between sobs.

"What is it?" Claire asks as Jade grabs the offensive bottle and runs from the room. I hear the door to my apartment open and close. "Bailey, what just happened?"

It takes several seconds before I'm able to explain my sudden aversion to mouthwash.

"Oh, shit," Claire exclaims as Jade returns to the kitchen. "I'm so sorry, Bailey. I had no idea."

"I threw it down the garbage chute," Jade is telling her mother as I excuse myself to double-lock the door. Not that the locks will do much good, I know, thinking of how easily Jade was able to manipulate them.

"I'll call someone in the morning about having those replaced with something sturdier," Claire says when I return.

"What was it like, being raped?" Jade asks.

"Jade," her mother says. "Honest to God . . ."

"It was awful," I answer.

"What did it feel like?" she presses.

"Oh, for God's sake . . ."

"It's all right," I tell Claire. "It felt as if someone was scraping at my insides with a razor blade."

"Ouch," Jade whispers.

"Happy now?" her mother asks.

"It's just that on TV, it always looks, you know . . ."

"No," Claire says. "We don't know."

Jade shrugs. "Kind of . . . exciting."

"You think rape is exciting?" Now Claire looks horrified.

"I just said that's how it looks. Sometimes. Women fantasize about rape all the time. I heard on Dr. Phil or, you know, one of those shows, they were having this discussion about fantasies, and they said that rape fantasies are really common among women."

"There's a big difference between fantasy and reality," her mother says sharply. "In fantasies, no one actually gets hurt." She opens the fridge and starts putting things away. "I think you should apologize to Bailey."

"What for?"

"It's all right," I say.

"You're the one who should apologize," Jade says to her mother. "You're the one who's trying to steal all her money."

Claire takes a deep breath. "Okay. I think you've said quite enough for one night."

"Can I go watch TV?"

"No," Claire says, then changes her mind: "Yes. Go. By all means, go watch TV."

Jade takes off down the hall. Seconds later, we hear the television blaring.

"I'm really sorry," Claire begins.

"It's okay."

"It's not okay. I didn't come here to upset you."

"Why *are* you here?" I ask.

She closes the refrigerator door, leans back against the counter. "Gene told me about what happened. I felt terrible. We both did. Look. I know you and I have never had much of a relationship. And I know we're suing you. But . . ." She sighs, looks me right in the eye. "But we're still family. We're still sisters. In spite of everything. And I'm a nurse. I guess I thought I might be able to help." She glances down the hall toward my bedroom, the noise from the television bouncing off the walls toward us. "Maybe this wasn't such a good idea."

"I'm glad you're here," I tell her.

"Even though I'm trying to steal all your money?" Another glance toward my bedroom.

"I know that's not what you're trying to do."

"Gene is just so adamant about the lawsuit. So are the others. They're very angry."

"And you're not?"

"Sometimes," she admits. "I mean, it hurts to be left out of your own father's will, but hell, we were pretty much left out of his life, so I guess we should be used to it by now. At least he provided for Jade and her education. Not that she's headed for Harvard."

"She may surprise you."

"You want to know what her biggest ambition is at the moment?"

I nod, realizing I am actually enjoying this conversation, that it's the first conversation I've had in weeks that isn't all about me, about being raped.

"She wants to get pregnant so she can get on one of those reality shows she's always watching, like *Teen Mom* or *16 and Pregnant*. One of those."

I laugh in spite of the serious look on Claire's face. Or maybe because of it.

"You think I'm joking? Ask her. She'll tell you."

"I think she's trying to provoke you."

"Oh, we're way past being provocative. I actually caught her with some guy last week. I came home from my shift at the hospital at about two A.M. and there they were, rolling around my living room floor, pretty much naked. I flip on the light and you know what happens? I'm the one who gets yelled at! *What are you doing home so early? You're supposed to be working till three. Are you trying to ruin my social life?* That's the kind of crap I have to put up with. Is she embarrassed? Not a bit. Is he? Not that I could tell. The idiot pulls on his jeans, then leans back against the sofa and reaches for his cigarettes. I tell him to take his filthy habit and get out of my house; Jade threatens to go with him; I tell her that her uncle Gene will have her back in Juvenile Hall so fast it'll make her head spin. And that goes double for Sir Galahad, who's already got one foot out the door. That ends that discussion. I give her the speech about the dangers of unprotected sex, which is when she informs me that she wants to get pregnant so she can be on some stupid reality show. And she's serious," Claire adds before I can say otherwise.

So I say nothing.

"Oh, and of course, she calls me a hypocrite, reminds me that I was pregnant when I married her father." Claire resumes putting the rest of the groceries in the fridge.

"What does he think of all this?" I ask. I know that Claire has been divorced a long time, but that's pretty much all I know.

Claire throws a head of lettuce into the bin, as if it is a football she's spiking after scoring a touchdown. "Eliot? How would I know? Haven't seen the prick in years. Daddy was certainly right about that one." She shakes her head, laughs her surprisingly girlish laugh. "Maybe we *should* have our own reality show."

I watch my half-sister as she begins shoving items into the pantry next to the fridge, admiring her proficiency. I used to be like that. I used to be all kinds of proficient.

"Believe it or not," Claire is saying, "Jade was a very sweet girl until her fourteenth birthday. Then she just kind of . . . turned."

"Happens to the best of us," I say.

"Really? I'm betting you didn't give your mother such a hard time."

"I'm sure I had my moments."

Claire stops what she is doing. "It must have been very hard for you when she died."

I quickly turn away so that she can't see the fresh tears that spring to my eyes. Almost three years, and I still feel the loss of my mother as acutely as if it were yesterday. "I had anxiety attacks pretty much every day for a year after she died," I confess. It's the first time I've ever told that to anyone. I'm not sure why I'm telling her.

"Did you see anyone about it?"

"You mean like a psychiatrist?"

"Or a therapist. Someone to talk to."

"I talked to Heath." Although my brother was in worse shape than I was.

She looks skeptical. Clearly, my brother's reputation has preceded him. "Was he any help?"

"We're very close," I say, although I know it doesn't answer her question. "Are you close to Gene?"

"I guess. I know he can be a little self-righteous and a bit of a prig. He thinks he's always right. And, unfortunately, he *is* right most of the time. But he's also honest and moral and all those things I'm not used to in a man, so . . . ." Her voice drifts off, the sentence lingering in the air, like smoke from a cigarette.

"What about the others?"

"You mean our esteemed half-brothers, Thomas, Richard, and

Harrison?" She endows each name with appropriate dramatic flourish.

I smile. "It's been years since I've seen them."

"Can't say I've seen very much of them either. Until recently. This lawsuit," Claire says, then breaks off abruptly. "Sorry. And sorry about the lawsuit," she adds. "If it were up to me . . ."

"I understand." Do I?

"What was your mother like?" she asks, seeking safer ground.

"She was pretty special."

"Our father was certainly besotted with her."

I smile again. *Besotted* seems such an old-fashioned word for her to use. But it's also the most accurate. "I guess he was."

"You were lucky."

The word is as strange now as when the police used it after my rape. My mother died when I was twenty-six years old. How can that be considered lucky?

It was my mother who suggested I become a private investigator. She probably wasn't serious when she said it, but I glommed onto the idea like chewing gum to the sole of a shoe. I quickly discovered I could get my license online, which allowed me the opportunity to stay home with her during those last precious months of her life. I already had years of college behind me, years spent trying to decide what I wanted to do with the rest of my life. For the previous three years, I'd been majoring in criminology. Becoming a private investigator was a natural fit, a no-brainer.

Footsteps in the hall return me to the here and now. "Haven't you started making dinner?" Jade whines from the doorway. "I'm starving. You said we were just going to eat and go home."

"Why don't you set the table?"

Jade chews angrily on her gum. A huge pink bubble blossoms between her lips, growing until it blocks out the entire bottom half of her face. She clomps toward the kitchen drawers and begins opening and closing them until she finds the one with the cutlery. "So, do the police have any suspects?" she asks, popping the bubble with her teeth, her hands dripping with forks and knives.

I picture using one of the knives to stab my attacker, my right hand balling into a tight fist as I feel the knife rip through his chest to pierce his heart.

"Earth to Bailey. Hello? Is anybody home?" Jade's voice snaps me out of my reverie.

"Sorry. What did you say?"

"I asked if the police have any suspects."

"No. None that I'm aware of."

"So, what—they think it was, like, a random attack?"

"What else would it be?"

"Maybe you were targeted," Jade says with a shrug.

"Jade, really." Claire lays a gentle hand on my arm. "We'll get those locks changed first thing in the morning."

– SIX –

"Can I speak to Detective Marx, please?" I press the phone to my ear and lean back against my pillow. The bedroom is in darkness, although it's already inching toward ten A.M. I've thought of opening the blackout blinds, of letting the relentless sun inside, but have decided against it. I'm not ready to acknowledge the start of yet another endless day, although day and night have become almost interchangeable to me. One provides no more comfort than the other.

"One minute, please," the male officer informs me. I hear an unpleasant undertone to his voice, as if I have interrupted him at something important, or at least something more important than me. *Does he recognize my voice?* I wonder as he puts me on hold, the cheery sound of Latin music instantly rushing to fill the void. I picture the officer leaning across his desk and shouting toward Detective Marx, "Hey, it's that Carpenter girl again. Third time in the last hour. You still want me to tell her you're busy?"

I understand. I really do. The sad fact is I'm yesterday's news. I have been replaced by other, newer, fresher, more interesting crimes: a woman strangled by her boyfriend after a heated argument over who deserves to be America's Next Top Model; a severed hand discovered in a swamp by the side of I-95; a shooting in a 7-Eleven that left one person dead and another clinging to life. I can't compete. I have been relegated to the proverbial back burner where I simmer on a barely perceptible flame, my essence slowly distilling into the air, like steam, until soon there will be nothing left.

"Maybe you were targeted," I hear my niece say.

Is it possible?

What if Jade is right? Although with the elimination of Roland Peterson and Todd Elder as suspects, who would target me? What motive would he have?

What am I doing? I wonder, pulling the phone away from my ear, rudely interrupting Gloria Estefan in the middle of her song. What is it I hope to accomplish by hearing the police confirm, yet again, that they have no new leads? I press the phone's *off* button, return it to its charger. There is nothing Detective Marx can tell me that I don't already know.

I push myself out of bed, stumble toward the bathroom on legs no longer used to traveling more than a few feet at a time, remove my pajamas in the dark, and get into the shower. When I am sufficiently scalded, I turn off the hot water and wrap a clean towel around my torso, saying a silent thank-you to Claire for doing at least three loads of wash before she finally left last night at just before midnight. I walk to the bedroom window, press the button on the wall that operates the blackout blinds, and watch them automatically rise toward the ceiling. A world of glass houses greets me, sunlight skating across their icy smooth surfaces.

I see them immediately, although they don't see me: the construction workers in the burgeoning building across from me, prancing around in their blue, white, and yellow hardhats. Their presence always startles me, although they are here every morning and have been for more than a year, starting their hammering at exactly eight o'clock each morning, piling one floor on top of another as easily as if they were children playing with plastic blocks. I observe them for a few minutes before reaching for my binoculars and pulling the workers closer, bringing them into sharper focus. I see one man wipe the sweat from his forehead with a white rag he pulls from the back pocket of his low-slung jeans; I see another man walk past him with a thick piece of wood slung across the tops of his broad shoulders, bare biceps carelessly on display. I see another emerging from a bright red Port-A-Potty that is situated at the far end of the open steel and concrete space. The men— I quickly count half a dozen—are between the ages of twenty and forty and of average height and weight. Two are white, three Hispanic, one the color of a latte.

Any one of them could be the man who raped me.

He could have been watching me, just as I'm watching him now. He could have spotted me one morning outside the front entrance of my building waiting for one of the valets to bring up my car from the underground garage. He could have kept track of my movements, followed my Porsche as I went about my daily routine. He could have been trailing me on the night I went in search of Roland Peterson, spying on me as I spied on Peterson's ex-girlfriend's apartment, biding his time, waiting for just the right moment to strike.

Is it possible?

The phone rings, and I jump. Probably Claire calling to see how I'm doing, I think as I lift the phone to my ear. But it isn't Claire, and I'm disappointed, which I find both curious and disconcerting.

"Bailey," Detective Marx says, her voice at once soothing and businesslike. "I'm sorry. I understand you called before. We must have been cut off." She doesn't ask how I am or if everything is all right. She already knows the answer to both these questions.

"I thought of something," I tell her, picturing the soft gray eyes I remember from the night I was raped.

"You remember something?" I picture her signaling to her partner as she reaches across her cluttered desk for her pad and pen.

"He used mouthwash."

"What?"

"The man who raped me. His breath smelled of mouthwash."

"His breath smelled of mouthwash," she repeats, her voice void of inflection.

"Mint-flavored. Spearmint," I qualify.

"Spearmint."

I'm starting to feel foolish. How useful can this be? Millions of people use mouthwash. "I just thought of it yesterday when I was unpacking some groceries." I shudder at the memory. "It's like what you said, about details suddenly coming back to me. . . ." Is that what she said?

"That's really good, Bailey. Keep trying to remember. Maybe something else will come to you."

Something that might actually help the police with their investigation.

"Is there anything else?" she asks.

"No. Just that . . ."

"Just that what?"

"Have there been any other rapes in the area where I was attacked?"

"Other rapes in the area," Detective Marx repeats, something I'm realizing she does with annoying regularity. "No, there have been no other rapes in that area."

"None at all?"

"There haven't been any assaults of any kind reported in that neighborhood in the last six months."

"What do you think that means?"

"I don't know," she admits. "What do *you* think it means?"

The words are already on the tip of my tongue, but it takes several seconds for me to gather enough strength to spit them out. "That maybe my attack wasn't random, that I might have been targeted."

"By whom?" Detective Marx asks.

"I don't know." I glance back toward the construction site outside my window, observe two workers maneuvering a long steel beam.

"Bailey," Detective Marx presses, "can you think of anyone who might want to hurt you?"

How many times have I asked myself that question? There are plenty of people who aren't happy with me, including several disgruntled members of my own family, but surely no one I know hates me enough to have done something like this. Of course they could have hired someone else to do it, I think, a gasp escaping my lungs.

"What is it?" the detective asks.

"Nothing."

A pause while we both wait for the other to speak. Finally, Detective Marx gives in, breaks the silent deadlock. "Okay, Bailey. This is what I want you to do. Are you listening?"

I nod.

"Bailey? Are you listening?"

"I'm listening."

"I want you to make a list of everyone you know, past or present, personal or professional, who might have a grudge against you. Can you do that?"

Again, I nod. I vaguely remember covering this ground before.

"We asked you about any enemies you might have made as a result of the work you do," Detective Marx continues. "Have you thought of anyone?"

"Not really," I say quickly. "You've already ruled out Todd Elder."

"No one from your past? Maybe a disgruntled ex-boyfriend?"

I haven't told her about my nasty breakup with Travis. "I'm sure I would have recognized an ex-boyfriend, even with a pillowcase over my head," I say, hearing more than a trace of agitation creep into my voice. This conversation is pointless. I'm sorry I brought the whole thing up.

"Look, Bailey," she says. "The likelihood is that you weren't assaulted by anyone you know. Or, at least, know well. It's far more likely that this was a stranger-on-stranger attack. Maybe someone saw you that night, waited for an opportune moment, then struck. Or maybe he'd been stalking you for days, even weeks. He could be someone you know casually or someone you passed on the street, maybe said hello to in passing, or *didn't* say hello to and he took it as a personal affront. There are enough weirdos in this city for anything to be possible, which is what makes finding this guy so damn difficult, why anything you can think of, any*one* you can think of, anything at all, would be helpful."

Again, I glance toward the construction site across the way. "There are all these construction workers." I tell her about the men I see every day outside my window, voice the possibility that one of them might have noticed me as well.

"Construction workers," she repeats. "Do you have any reason to suspect that one of them might be the man who attacked you?"

"Not really."

"Has any of them said anything to you or made unwanted advances . . . ?"

"No."

A sigh of defeat. "Well, we can't very well start investigating every construction worker in the area based on a sexist stereotype."

"No, of course not." She's losing patience with me. "But you *can* get a list of employees from the builder," I continue, regardless, "run their names through your computers, see if anyone has a criminal record, maybe even a prior conviction for sexual assault."

"It's a long shot," Detective Marx concedes after a long pause. "But what the hell? We're looking for that needle in the haystack."

Or a splinter of broken glass, I think, as the sun reflects off a nearby window, sending a jagged shard of light directly into my eye.

"Which doesn't mean we won't find the man who did this, Bailey."

"I know." The odds are that they will never find the man responsible unless he strikes again.

Is that what I have to hope for? That the man who raped me will consign yet another woman to this living hell? Is that the person I have become, that I look to another's misfortune for my own salvation?

"I'll get on this right away," Detective Marx says. Then, before she hangs up: "Get me that list."

I toss the phone onto the bed, find myself gravitating back toward the window. The cool breath of the air conditioner blows across my bare shoulders, and I realize I am wrapped only in a towel. *Has anyone seen me?* I wonder, knowing the angle of the sun makes this impossible, but dropping to my knees and crawling toward the closet just in case. Is it possible one of the workers from the building across the way saw me one morning as I paraded around my apartment half-dressed? Or maybe a resident in one of the other buildings? Maybe I'm not the only one in the neighborhood with a pair of binoculars.

The ringing of my phone sends me sprawling on all fours. I lie there, my face pressed into the plush beige broadloom, my heart thumping erratically. It takes several seconds for me to regain my equilibrium and reach for the phone, several more seconds to remember that it is not on its charger but somewhere on the bed where I tossed it earlier. I manage to locate it in the middle of its fourth ring, just before voice mail is programmed to answer it. "Hello?" I whisper, leaning my back against the side of the bed for support, hoping for the sound of Claire's protective voice.

"Miss Carpenter, it's Stanley from the concierge desk," the voice announces instead.

I try to picture Stanley, but I can't. There are at least half a dozen young men who work the concierge desk and double as valets, all equally presentable, all equally forgettable.

"The locksmith is here to change your locks."

"Can you give me five minutes?"

"Sure thing."

"And can you send someone up with him?"

"I'll see who's available."

"Thank you." I throw on a pair of loose-fitting khaki cotton pants and a shapeless white shirt and pull my wet hair into a ponytail at the base of my neck.

Exactly five minutes later, there is a loud knock on my door. I peer through the peephole, see two men standing on the other side, their faces distorted by their proximity and my tiny viewing space. I pull open the door, stand back to let the men inside. "Hi," I hear myself say in a voice I barely recognize as mine. "Come in."

"Hello. I am Manuel," the older of the two men says, his words buried inside a thick Cuban accent, his right hand clutching his toolbox. He is maybe forty years old, of medium height and build, with shoulder-length black hair and warm, dark eyes.

The second man is tall and slender, with a smattering of freckles across the bridge of his wide nose, and chin-length, dark blond hair. The promise of a mustache plays with his upper lip. He wears the familiar valet's uniform and his nametag identifies him as Wes. He looks all of twenty. I don't remember seeing him before.

"Are you new here?" I ask.

"Started about a month ago," he answers. "Great building."

His breath smells of mouthwash. I gasp and take a step back.

Wes stares at me, his light brown eyes gazing at me with a familiarity that is as unexpected as it is disconcerting. "Is something wrong?"

I shake my head, remind myself that millions of people use mouthwash and that this boy's mouthwash smells nothing like the one my rapist used, being more peppermint than spearmint.

Does he know what happened to me? Do any of the valets? They must suspect something, what with the obvious disruption of my normal routine and all the visits from the police. Do they whisper about it among themselves? Do they snicker behind my back? Are they titillated? Excited? Repulsed? Do they think I asked for it?

Manuel begins taking apart the existing lock. "Piece of junk," he says with a sneer, tossing it aside. "I give you something much better." He holds up another lock. "Much more substantial. You see?"

I nod. "My niece was able to open that one in about two seconds."

"She won't be able to open this one. I guarantee."

I watch Manuel's hands as they work to install my new lock. Such thick fingers, I think, feeling them press against my windpipe.

"You okay?" Wes asks suddenly.

"I'm fine. Why?"

"You shuddered. My mother used to say that when you shudder, it means someone is walking over your grave."

"We will be all finished here in just a few more minutes," Manuel says.

"Good."

"Your niece will not be able to open this lock. This is guaranteed."

Ten minutes later, Manuel drops two new shiny keys into the palm of my hand. My fingers close around them. They feel warm, melting like wax into my flesh, branding me.

"How much do I owe you?" I ask.

"Is all taken care of. Your sister . . ."

"Claire?"

"Nice lady. She take care of everything."

Manuel leaves but Wes lingers for several seconds longer. "Well, bye for now," he says, shifting his weight from one foot to the other. I realize that he is waiting for a tip, but I have no idea where my purse is, so I don't move, and he gives up after several seconds, joining Manuel at the elevator. "Enjoy your new locks," he is saying as I shut the door.

—SEVEN—

start watching the man almost by accident.

Claire sees him first. She is standing at my bedroom window, wearing dark gray pants and an unflattering white jersey that betrays a fold of flesh around her middle, her fine, chin-length blond hair in need of a good stylist. She is staring through my binoculars into the lit apartments of the building directly behind mine, her gaze swooping rhythmically through the air like a hawk, up and down, back and forth, side to side, as if carried by the wind, looking for somewhere safe to land. "My God, would you just get a load of this," she remarks, more to herself than to either Jade or me.

My niece and I are lying on top of my bed watching TV, much like I used to do with my mother. Jade is wearing a loose-fitting, pearl-pink T-shirt over a pair of black leotards, her stylish ankle boots with their needle-thin, five-inch heels on the floor beside her. She is chewing gum, playing absently with her hair, and laughing. We have just witnessed a man being sliced in half by his power mower and a woman drowning in a tar pit, numbers 547 and 212, respectively, in the random and seemingly never-ending countdown of *1000 Ways to Die.* If they ever reach the magic number, I suspect they already have a sequel waiting in the wings. *1000 More Ways to Die,* I postulate, glancing over to where Claire is looking and marveling that there are still people in the world who feel safe enough to keep their curtains open and their lights on after sunset. Don't they know someone is probably watching?

"What do you see?" I ask, hearing an echo of my mother. Jade is already off the bed and at the window, wresting the binoculars from her mother's hands.

"Holy fuck," she exclaims.

"Jade, language," Claire cautions without much conviction.

"You have to see this." Jade's hand waves, beckons me from the bed.

I shake my head. "Tell me."

"It's this guy in his apartment . . . let me see . . . three floors from the top, four windows from the left," Jade counts, then literally hoots with glee. "Oh, this is priceless. You have to see him, Bailey. He thinks he's real hot shit."

"Jade, language."

"He's parading around his bedroom half-naked. . . ."

"He's wearing jeans," Claire corrects.

"But no shirt, which makes him half-naked," Jade says impatiently. Even with the binoculars pressed tightly to her face, I can see her eyes roll toward the ceiling. "He actually has a pretty impressive six-pack."

"As if that sort of thing is important," Claire says.

"He's prancing around in front of his mirror, posing and flexing his muscles. It's hysterical. Oh, gross. He just stuck his hand down his pants and adjusted his dick."

"Jade, *language.*"

"What—you'd prefer cock?"

"Oh, for God's sake."

"Okay, okay. I get it. *Penis.* He's adjusting his *penis.* Bailey, get over here before you miss everything."

"Sorry," I mutter, fighting the urge to gag. "I think that's probably the last thing I want to see."

"Honestly, Jade." Her mother grabs the binoculars from Jade's hand and returns them to the nightstand beside my bed. "Sometimes I really wonder about you."

"I didn't mean . . . I wasn't thinking about . . ."

"That's your problem," Claire snaps. "You don't think."

"Sorry, Bailey," Jade says.

"It's okay."

"I think we should probably go," Claire says. "It's getting late."

"It's not even nine o'clock."

"You have school tomorrow."

"So?"

Almost a week has passed since their first unexpected visit. I relax into the comforting predictability of their bickering and realize how much I've come to enjoy their company. Unlike Gene, whose first visit was his last, Claire has dropped over every day since then, stopping by after her shift at the hospital to check on me before heading home. Sometimes she cooks dinner and has Jade join us. Sometimes we just sit together and watch TV. Occasionally Claire tells me about her day, the argument she had with one of the doctors, the kind look she got from a stroke victim unable to speak. She doesn't ask about my day, knowing that one is essentially the same as the next.

There is a knock on the door, followed by the ring of the doorbell.

"Who's that?" Jade asks, looking from her mother to me, as if at least one of us has the answer.

"Isn't the doorman supposed to call you before allowing anyone up?" Claire is already moving toward the hall.

"It must be Heath," I tell them. "They all know him."

"Who's Heath?" Jade asks.

"My brother."

I watch the branches of our twisted family tree arrange themselves behind her eyes. "Oh, yeah," she says. "The other chosen one."

"Jade, for God's sake. Do I have to put a gag in your mouth?"

Claire's face reflects both irritation and embarrassment. She closes her eyes, her cheeks glowing bright fuchsia. "I'm sorry, Bailey. That was before . . ."

"It's okay," I assure her. "I know."

"Where's he been all week?" Jade asks.

I shrug. Heath has always had a tendency to come and go, often disappearing for days at a time, usually into a dense, voluminous cloud of marijuana smoke. He's never been very good in a crisis, and my rape has shaken him almost as much as it has me. I know he wrestles with the same disquieting feelings of guilt and helplessness, the same impotent rage.

Truthfully, I think he was relieved when I told him about Claire and Jade during our last phone call. Their visits have taken much of the onus off of him. He no longer has to act the part of the brave older brother, a role he was never particularly suited for. Heath is a bit like all those arrangements of flowers I received just after my rape, the ones that withered and died from a lack of fresh water and attention. He requires constant nurturing, and these days I don't have the strength to provide it.

I climb out of bed to follow Claire and Jade to my front door. Jade has tried several times—and mercifully, failed—to jimmy open my new lock. "Hello, Heath," I hear Claire say, ushering my brother into the foyer, the unmistakable smell of weed coating him like a second skin. It clings to his pores and seeps right through his black leather jacket and skinny jeans. Claire's nose crinkles with recognition of the sickly sweet aroma, but she just says, "It's nice to see you again. It's been a long time."

Heath pushes his bangs away from his delicately handsome face, his dark green eyes staring blankly at his older half-sister, as if trying to place her.

"You're stoned," Jade says, giggling as she approaches.

"And you're Jade," Heath says, breaking into a wide grin. "I've heard so much about you."

"Really? I've heard nothing at all about you. At least, not from Bailey."

Heath laughs. "You're right," he says to me. "She's fabulous."

He sloughs off his leather jacket and lets it drop to the floor. Claire moves instantly to pick it up. The navy silk shirt he's wearing is buttoned incorrectly, so that the left side hangs down longer than the right, but he doesn't seem to notice. He's obviously wasted, more wasted than I've seen him since our mother's death.

"Are you all right?" I whisper under my breath.

"Perfectly peachy," he says loudly. "And you? You're out of your pajamas, I see. I guess that means the Sisters of Mercy have been taking good care of you. Good job, ladies."

"Why don't we sit down?" Claire motions toward the living room.

But Heath is already on his way to my bedroom. "I think I'd rather lie down," he says as Jade and I follow after him.

"And I think some coffee might be a good idea," Claire says, retreating to the kitchen.

"A *grand* idea." Heath enters my bedroom and stops dead in his tracks by the side of my bed, his eyes riveted to the TV. "What the hell is this?" A young woman in a low-cut blouse and tiny sliver of a skirt is climbing out of a helicopter when she steps too close to the still-whirling blades of the propeller. "Holy shit," Heath whispers as a terrifying whoosh of blood splatters across the screen.

Being beheaded by a chopper, the television announcer almost swoons. *Number 59 of 1000 Ways to Die.*

"What the hell are you watching?"

Jade explains the show's premise as Heath throws himself across my bed, bunching all the available pillows beneath his head.

"Cool," he says, closing his eyes.

I watch Jade studying his face in repose. "Your brother's really good-looking," she says.

Heath's eyes open again instantly. He props himself up on one elbow, clearly flattered, although I'm sure he's used to such unsolicited compliments by now. "Why, thank you, Jade. How kind of you to notice."

"Did you ever watch the show *Teen Mom*?" she asks.

"Can't say that I have."

Jade provides a brief synopsis of the show. "It's not on any-more, but there's talk of bringing it back, and if they do, I want to be on it," she says. "Then I could get on the cover of *US Weekly* and be famous."

"Sounds like you have to get pregnant first," Heath says.

"I know. That's where you come in."

"I come in? When did I come in?"

"You'd make the perfect baby daddy."

"Excuse me?" Heath looks toward me. "Is she joking?"

"I don't think so." I stifle the urge to laugh.

"Hear me out." Jade plops down on the side of my bed. "You know that the producers have their pick of every teenage girl in America, right? So you have to be pretty creative."

"I'm not remotely creative," Heath deadpans.

Jade ignores the comment. "You have to have a gimmick. . . ."

"You calling me a gimmick?"

Jade nods enthusiastically.

"I'm your uncle."

"Which is exactly the point, what makes this idea so irresist-ible."

"You find incest irresistible?"

"You're only my half-uncle, and besides, I barely know you."

"Which might give a normal person pause."

"I don't think either one of us is exactly normal, do you?"

Heath smiles, and I can see he's beginning to enjoy Jade as much as I do. "You may have a point there."

Claire enters the room, carrying a mug of freshly brewed cof-fee in one hand and a half-pint of cream and several packets of sugar in the other. Heath takes the mug from her hand and quickly adds cream and four sugars, then deposits the mug on the night-stand without taking a sip.

"I think we should probably get going." Claire retrieves her daughter's ankle boots from the floor and drops them in Jade's lap.

"Will you at least think about my idea?" Jade asks Heath, pulling the boots on.

"I will not."

"What idea?" Claire asks. "Never mind. I don't want to know. Nice seeing you, Heath."

"Always a pleasure," comes Heath's instant rejoinder.

"Wait!" Jade grabs my binoculars from the nightstand and hurries to the window. "Just one more look."

"What perversion is she up to now?" Heath asks.

"See for yourself." Jade offers the binoculars to Heath. "Third floor from the top, four windows from the left."

"No, thank you. It's a bit too *Rear Window*–ish for me."

"Come on," Jade teases. "You know you want to."

Her words send me skyrocketing back to the past. I'm twelve years old, wearing my school uniform, about to board the downtown bus when I feel a man's hand on my buttocks. *Don't look so shocked, little girl. You know you liked it.*

My knees buckle. I grab the nightstand for support, almost knocking over my brother's coffee. "Oh, God."

Claire is immediately at my side, holding me up. "What's wrong?"

I shake my head, fearing I will collapse to the floor if she lets go. "Nothing."

"You look like you just saw a ghost."

"I'm fine. Really." It takes all my strength and determination to remain upright.

"You're sure?"

I nod.

"Okay," she says, although I can see she's far from convinced. Eventually she loosens her grip on my arm. "We'll get out of your hair. Give you some time alone with your brother. Say goodnight, Jade."

"Goodnight, Jade," Jade says.

Heath laughs.

"Is she always like that?" he asks after they're gone.

"Pretty much."

"No wonder you're so fond of her."

I *am* fond of her. Fond of both Jade and Claire.

"Too bad they're only after your money," Heath says.

I turn off the TV and climb onto the bed beside him, pushing his legs out of the way to make room for my own. "You really think that's why they're here?"

"You don't?"

"I don't know. I guess I'd like to think . . ."

"You'd like to think . . . what? That they're here because they find you, in the words of my most formidable niece, *irresistible?*"

The private investigator in me tells me he's probably right. But I realize I don't really care why Claire and her daughter come over. "Am I so difficult to love?" I wonder, surprised to hear I've spoken the words out loud.

"What? No, of course not. Don't be silly. *I* love you, don't I? Mom and Dad loved you. And God knows Travis is still crazy about you."

"I don't want to talk about Travis."

"Really? Because you're all *he* wants to talk about. If you'd just pick up the phone and call him, I guarantee he'd be over here in two seconds flat."

"I don't want him to come over."

"Come on, Bailey. Throw the poor guy a bone. He's driving me nuts with his pining and whining."   ·

"And *you're* driving *me* nuts," I counter, grabbing my binoculars from the nightstand as I climb back off the bed and proceed to the window, more for the distraction it provides than because I am interested in anything I might see. I locate the apartment Claire and Jade were looking at, three floors from the top, four windows from the left. The light is still on, although the room appears to be empty.

"He just wants to apologize, make things right," Heath is saying.

"It's too late."

"What happened with you guys anyway? He won't tell me, you won't tell me."

I ignore the question. To say that things didn't end well with Travis would be a colossal understatement.

"So, what have you been up to all week?" I ask without turning around. "Besides smoking copious amounts of weed."

"Working on my screenplay," he says, and I sigh. Heath has been working on his screenplay for years. "And I had an audition for Whiskas cat food. It's a national spot."

"Did you get it?"

"Who knows? They had me rolling around on the floor, making a total ass of myself over some stupid cat. Is it any wonder I do drugs?"

I smile in spite of myself. "When will you find out?"

"Probably next week. It doesn't matter. I don't care one way or the other," he says, and I hear the shrug in his voice. Heath claims to be used to rejection, but I wonder if that's something any of us ever really gets used to.

That's when I see the man.

He first appears as a smudge on the lens of my binoculars, a blur that quickly morphs into a shape. He looks to be about thirty and seems reasonably handsome, his features pleasant, his posture impeccable. Dark hair, average height, a slim build. Mercifully I'm spared the sight of his "pretty impressive six-pack," as he's now wearing a shirt and toying with the idea of adding a tie, two of which he holds up to his chest in front of the full-length mirror. Probably he has a date.

I think of Owen Weaver's recent invitation to dinner, and I wonder if I would have called him. I remind myself that dating is one of the things women often forego when they get involved with married men.

Even women who haven't been raped.

After a few minutes of indecision, I watch the man reject both ties and toss them toward his bed. One misses and floats to the floor. The man disappears into his closet, returning seconds later with a sports jacket, which he puts on and adjusts carefully, studying his reflection all the while, obviously enamored with what he sees. *How can any woman compete?* I think, lowering my binoculars and turning back toward Heath. "You should see this guy," I begin. But Heath's eyes are closed and the easy regularity of his breathing tells me he is asleep.

I climb into bed beside him, toy with the idea of turning the TV back on, watching more people die in an assortment of mind-boggling ways. Instead I find myself watching my brother sleep, in much the same way I'd watch over my mother when she was sick, carefully monitoring each breath, counting the space between it and the one before, holding my own breath when hers became labored, whispering words of love into her ear as she slept, hoping that my words would penetrate her morphine-induced dreams, that they would be enough to keep death at bay for another year, another month, another day.

Of course they weren't. Words in the face of death are never enough. Neither is love. No matter what anyone tries to tell you.

I'm not sure when I first become aware that someone else is in the room. There is the sound of footsteps tiptoeing across the carpet, the floor creaking with each furtive step, and the air above my head stirring and then parting, like curtains. Someone is on top of me, his knees crushing my rib cage as a pillow is pressed against my face. I struggle, but I am helpless against his weight. An arm stretches across my windpipe, cutting off my supply of air. I scream, but the sound that emerges is more of a rattle. A death rattle. Gathering up whatever strength I have, I scratch wildly at my attacker's arm.

"What the hell!"

I open my eyes, pushing aside a nearby pillow to see my brother Heath bolt up beside me in bed, holding out his injured arm.

"What the hell are you doing?"

"Oh, my God. I'm so sorry. I was having a nightmare." I check the clock. It's after midnight.

Heath is rolling up his sleeve, although it's too dark to really see anything. "I think you drew blood."

"I'm so sorry."

He sighs. "It's okay. I'll live. A nightmare, huh? Do I have to ask what it was about?"

I shake my head as my breathing gradually returns to normal.

"Can I get you a glass of water or something?"

"No, I'm fine," I tell him, knowing this is what he needs to hear. I wipe a line of perspiration from my forehead, my body suddenly cold and clammy.

"You need your sleep, Bailey."

"I know. I'm so tired."

"Ssh. Just close your eyes. You don't have to be afraid. I'm right here beside you."

"Thank you. It means a lot."

But even as I'm saying the words I know that Heath is already drifting back to sleep. I lie there beside him for several long minutes, then carefully extricate myself from his arms and climb out of bed. I grab the scissors from the top drawer of my nightstand and do my regular check of the apartment, then proceed to the bathroom, where I take off my clothes and run the hot water. I shower in the dark, emerging fifteen minutes later into a steam-filled room, my hair wet, my body red and sore. I brush my teeth and slip into a pair of freshly washed pajamas, courtesy of Claire. I towel-dry my hair.

Walking back into the bedroom, I return the scissors to the top drawer of the nightstand, then grab my binoculars and proceed to the window. It takes only a few seconds for me to locate the right apartment—three floors down, four windows from the left. The light in the bedroom is still on, and its occupant is moving around inside. He approaches the window, his shirt unbuttoned and hanging loose, and stares down at the street below, running his hand absently through his hair. Then he turns in my direction, almost as if he knows I'm there. I watch him reach toward the turquoise lamp with its pleated white shade on the high table in front of him. I watch the room go dark.

—EIGHT—

The nightmare begins almost as soon as I close my eyes. It repeats itself over and over again, as if on an endless reel. I am being chased by a faceless man wearing black Nike sneakers. Despite the fact that I'm running as fast as I can, he is gaining on me. Across the street is a four-story, lemon-yellow building. A woman is sitting on her balcony, staring at me through a pair of binoculars. She can see everything. Surely she will call the police, and I'll be saved. Except she doesn't call the police. Instead, she inches forward in her seat, adjusting the focus of her binoculars so that she can see more clearly what is about to happen. She watches the man grab me from behind and throw me to the ground. She watches as he beats me with his fists and tears the clothes from my body. She watches as he pushes into me, pounding me repeatedly and without mercy into the cold, hard ground. Only when he is done does she lower her binoculars so that I can see her face.

My face.

I come instantly awake, gasping for air, my entire body bathed in perspiration, my sheets soaked.

I should be used to such dreams by now, but I'm not. I look

toward the clock beside my bed. It is almost ten A.M. Heath is gone. In his place is a note: *Got a callback on that Whiskas commercial. Talk to you later, H.*

I climb out of bed, walk to the bedroom window, press the button that lifts the blackout blinds. I am blinded by the bright sun shining into my face. My eyes close reflexively. I lean my head against the glass, soaking up the sun's rays, trying to gather strength from its warmth.

He's there when I open my eyes, mere inches from my face, his nose pressed against my own. I scream and stumble back toward my bed, falling to my knees and burying my face in the palms of my hands, my hands shaking. I hear laughter and force my eyes up. The man is still there, dangling just outside my window, a rope around his waist securing him to the suspended wooden platform on which he stands, a long squeegee in his hands, as he draws it back and forth against the glass. Another man is standing next to him. Both men are olive-skinned and in their early twenties. They wear baggy white uniforms with logos that identify them as "Prestige Window Cleaners."

"Sorry about that. Didn't mean to scare you," the first man shouts through the thick glass. "Didn't you get the notice we'd be working this side of the building today?"

I push myself back into a standing position, steady myself against the foot of the bed. I forgot all about this.

"You might want to close your blinds," the second man suggests.

I press the button and the blinds descend, causing the men to disappear an inch at a time, first their heads, then the logos on their uniforms, followed by their torsos, their legs, and finally their heavy work boots, as effortlessly as if I'm erasing figures from a chalkboard. Would that everything were so easy to erase.

The phone rings, and I jump.

"Hi, babe." His voice caresses my skin. "How're you doing today?"

"Okay." I'm so relieved I almost burst into tears. It's been three days since his last call.

"Just okay?"

"I'm good," I lie. I've gotten very good at telling people what they want to hear.

"I can only talk a few minutes."

"I know. You're a busy man."

"What have you been up to?"

"Not much. Claire and Jade came over last night. And Heath was here. He slept over."

"I think I'm jealous."

"He's not here now." My tone indicates that this is just a statement of fact and not an invitation to intimacy. I wonder how long it will be before I'm ready to extend that kind of invitation; I suspect he is thinking the same thing.

A moment's silence, then: "I'm in meetings all morning."

"It's been so long since we've had any time together."

"I know. Maybe later in the week . . ."

"I miss you," I tell him.

"I miss you, too."

Does he? Maybe the old Bailey, the one who didn't whine and snivel at the slightest provocation, the one who wasn't afraid of anything or anyone. Not this new Bailey, this inferior reproduction who can't stop feeling sorry for herself and who jumps at her own shadow. "I was thinking of going back to work," I say, feeling his attention waver and desperate to keep him on the line. I am paradoxically without shame and overflowing with it. The truth is that the mere thought of returning to the job I used to adore fills me with dread. Even now, I feel the start of a panic attack fluttering against my insides, like a trapped bird.

"You think you're ready?"

"Maybe in a few more weeks," I say.

Another moment's silence, this one more awkward than the first, then: "Look, sweetheart. I really have to go. I just called to see how you're doing."

"Doing okay."

"I'll stop by as soon as I can. Why don't you go out for a walk or something? It's a beautiful day."

"A walk?" I haven't left my condo since the night I was raped.

"A walk, a run. Get some fresh air, some exercise. You must be going stir-crazy in that apartment."

I latch happily onto this idea. It's because I haven't left my apartment in weeks that I'm feeling so helpless and depressed. I have cabin fever. I need to get out, take a walk, go for a run around the block.

"You don't even have to go outside. Don't you have a gym in your building?"

I picture the large room on the second floor filled with rowing machines, treadmills, free weights, elliptical machines.

"Just be careful not to overdo it. You have a tendency to do too much."

"I won't overdo it."

"You feel better already, don't you?"

"You always make me feel better."

"I really have to go."

"Call me later?"

"I'll try."

"I love you," I say.

"Take care of yourself," he says in return.

Not quite a fair exchange, and we both know it.

I shower, stealing a quick look at the teeth marks surrounding my right nipple. I wonder if this obscene imprint will ever go away. The doctors assure me that it will disappear eventually.

But I've been branded. Brands as deep as this one never go away.

The phone is ringing as I emerge from the shower. I throw on a housecoat and answer it on the third ring.

"Miss Carpenter, hi. It's Finn at the concierge desk."

"Yes?" My heart starts pounding. It seems that every time Finn calls these days, it's to tell me something I'd rather not hear. Today is no exception.

"Travis Shepherd is here to see you."

"Travis?"

"Should I send him up?"

Dear God, what does Travis want? Did Heath tell him to come over? "No. I'll come down," I blurt. I don't want to go downstairs, but I certainly don't want Travis in my apartment. Not after what happened the last time he was here. It's safer to meet him in the lobby. "I'll be down in two minutes."

I try not to panic. I remind myself that Travis is, for the most part, a good man. When we first started seeing each other, he was funny, thoughtful, and kind. He made me laugh. We'd go dancing, to the movies, and for long walks on the beach. Sometimes Heath joined us. Occasionally we'd smoke a few joints. Soon it became more than occasionally. Then it was pretty much Heath and Travis getting stoned all the time, with me watching, disapproving, from the sidelines. Arguments replaced laughter. Soon all Travis and I did was fight.

You can do this, I tell myself now. Travis is here to show support and concern, not to make a scene. I throw off my robe, climb into some exercise clothes. "You caught me just as I was going to the gym," I practice brightly in front of my mirror. My reflection looks far from convinced.

I almost don't make it to the elevators. It is only after I have fully satisfied myself that no one is lurking outside my door that I am able to step outside, lock my apartment, and proceed cautiously down the hall. I press the call button and wait for the elevator, looking from right to left, left to right, over one shoulder, then the other. Several times I decide to give up and return to my unit. Each time I take a few steps, only to stop and turn around again. I can't give up now. An elevator jerks to a stop with an audible thud. Its doors slowly open.

A man is standing inside.

I gasp and take a step back, feel my legs about to give way. "I forgot something," I mutter, tears filling my eyes as I stumble back to my apartment. I stand gripping the doorknob, my heart jumping around wildly, until I hear the elevator doors close and the elevator resume its descent. It takes several minutes before I'm able to muster enough courage to try again. I'm being silly. There was nothing to fear from the man inside that elevator. Not all men are rapists. And this one was short and stocky, not to mention at least fifty years old. He wasn't the man who attacked me.

Although, can I really be sure?

I press the call button again. The elevator doors open to reveal two young women, tall and beautiful and brimming with the kind of confidence I once possessed. They are dressed in leotards and tank tops. "Going to the gym?" one asks, her voice high-pitched and girlish.

I force my feet over the threshold. "Maybe later," I tell them, pressing the button for the lobby. The elevator descends to the second floor without further interruption.

"See you," one of the girls says as she locks arms with her friend and the two of them exit the elevator.

Luckily, no one else gets on, and I am able to steady myself with numerous deep breaths before the doors open onto the marble-and-mirrored lobby. Finn acknowledges me with a nod from the glassed-in concierge office to my right. Behind him I see a wall of surveillance TVs, their screens rotating with images of the building's common areas: the hallways, the stairwells, the elevators, the pool, even the exercise room. Cameras are everywhere. Someone is always watching.

Finn nods toward the lobby's main sitting area, where Travis has been waiting now for the better part of fifteen minutes. At first I don't see him because he is blocked by a huge arrangement of fresh flowers that all but overwhelms the glass coffee table on which it sits. He jumps to his feet as I approach, sending the mustard-colored tub chair on which he was perched into a spin. He looks good, which doesn't surprise me. Travis always looks good. Tall, slim-hipped, boyishly handsome, eyes the color of natural mink, wavy brown hair. He's wearing casual black pants and a pink golf shirt, as if he just stepped out of a brochure for the Turnberry Golf and Country Club, which is where he works, teaching golf to a bunch of mostly middle-aged men and women, the majority of whom will never break a hundred, or so he regularly complains. He dabbles a bit in modeling and acting, which is how he met my brother, at an audition.

He hurries toward me. I gird myself for an embrace that doesn't come.

"What the hell are you trying to do?" he demands. His voice is soft, as if he understands that he is in a public place, but menacing, as if he doesn't care. Two little red circles occupy the middle of his cheeks. I recognize those circles. They come out whenever he is really angry. The last time I saw those circles was the last time we were together.

"What are you talking about?"

"You sic the cops on me, for crap's sake?" Part statement, part question, part "what the hell is going on?"

"What?" I say again.

"You actually think I'm the man who raped you?"

"I don't know what you're talking about."

"Don't give me that shit. We're way past that." Travis runs an exasperated hand through his thick, wavy hair. "You weren't speaking to that cop, Detective Marcus, or whatever the hell her name is?"

I hesitate. "I spoke to Detective Marx, yes, of course. She's in charge of the investigation."

"And you told her what exactly?"

"I don't know, *exactly*," I respond, trying desperately to remember. "I asked her if she thought I might have been targeted."

"Targeted? What does that mean? That you think you knew your attacker?" he continues, answering his own question. "That you were raped by someone you know? Someone like me?"

"I never said that. In fact, I said just the opposite. That there was no way it could have been you, no way I wouldn't have recognized you, even with a pillowcase over my head."

"So you *did* mention my name."

"Detective Marx asked about disgruntled ex-boyfriends. . . ."

"That's what I am to you? A disgruntled ex-boyfriend?" Travis shakes his head, more in sadness than in anger. I can actually feel the hurt in his eyes. "How do you think I felt when Heath told me what happened to you? I wanted to kill the bastard who hurt you, for God's sake. I wanted to strangle him with my bare hands. And now I find out you think it was me?"

"But I don't think it was you."

"For God's sake, Bailey. You know I'd never hurt you."

"You hit me!" I hear myself shout, attracting Finn's attention.

Finn lowers the phone from his ear, holds it against his chest. "Everything all right, Miss Carpenter?"

"Everything's fine," Travis answers before I can find my voice.

I nod, but my eyes urge Finn to stay vigilant.

Travis lowers his voice. "You think that because I lost my cool one time during the heat of the moment . . ."

"I don't want to talk about it." Is there something about me that encourages violent behavior in men?

"I can't tell you how sorry I am about that night. I was wasted. I was upset. I was wrong. Look. I'm not trying to make excuses for what happened. And I promise you that it will never, *ever* happen again. You need me to protect you, Bailey."

"It's over, Travis," I say, as gently as I can.

"Please don't say that."

"It's over."

He shakes his head, blows a puff of invisible smoke into the air. "I didn't rape you," he says, after what feels like an eternity. The red circles have returned to his cheeks.

"I know."

"Yeah, well, try telling it to that fucking detective."

"I will."

"You know what else you can do?" he asks, the little red circles glowing brighter, as if someone has lit a match beneath his skin. "You can go straight to hell."

"Miss Carpenter?" I hear someone call, and look up to see Finn's concerned face. Travis is gone. I have no idea how long I've been there. "Are you okay?"

"Fine," I tell him, forcing myself toward the elevators. "Everything's fine."

NINE

I decide to go straight back to my apartment. My encounter with Travis has left me exhausted and confused. Am I wrong about Travis? Is it possible he could have raped me, that I wouldn't have recognized him, or that he might have hired someone to do his dirty work, someone to convince me I needed his protection? I step inside the elevator, about to press the button for the twenty-third floor when I hear a man shout, "Hang on!" Before I have time to react, he squeezes between the closing doors, pressing the button for the eighteenth floor, then notices I have yet to enter my floor. "Where you headed?" He tosses the words over his shoulder without looking back, his fingers impatiently circling the various buttons. The man is in his mid-thirties, of average height and weight. He has long fingers, large hands. I picture those hands around my throat, feel those fingers pressing down on my windpipe.

My legs buckle, and I hug the wall for support. Perspiration coats my forehead and drips into my eyes, causing everything to blur. My mouth goes dry. My heart bounces against my chest like a rubber ball against a brick wall. I grow dizzy and light-headed. I can't breathe.

I have to get off this elevator. I have to get off right now.

"Second floor," I shout, pushing past him to press the button myself, then barreling through the doors even before they have fully opened.

"Have a nice day," the man calls after me, his sarcasm pursuing me down the marbled hall.

I have no idea where I'm going. I run blindly, following the circular corridor as it twists past the spa, the pool, the massage room. Two men are walking down the hall toward me, both wearing thick white robes and flip-flops, one with a towel wrapped around his neck like a pet snake. The men are between twenty and forty and are of medium height and weight. They have deep voices with no discernible accents. One of them smiles as they draw closer. He smells of mouthwash, minty and crisp.

The carpet beneath my feet suddenly turns to quicksand, sucking me into its swirling muck. The walls around me start folding in and out, like an accordion. I struggle to stay upright. A faint cry escapes my lips, and I duck through the nearest door, find myself inside a windowless gray room—gray walls, gray carpet, gray equipment. I count five treadmills lined up side by side next to two elliptical machines, two rowing machines, and three stationary bicycles, all with tiny TVs attached, all positioned in front of a long mirrored wall that reflects the mirrored wall behind it. There are benches and free weights, various pulleys and other equipment whose purpose I don't wish to imagine. Beside me is a water cooler, a plastic hamper, and a supply of small white towels piled high on a single shelf mounted on the wall, along with a spray bottle of Lysol, a jumbo-size roll of paper towels, and a large bottle of hand sanitizer. I note the presence of a surveillance camera mounted close to the ceiling in the far right corner of the room and wonder if anyone is watching. I stand by the door until I feel my breathing return to something approaching normal and I think I can move without fainting. But I don't move. I just stand there.

"Hi," a breathy voice calls from one of the elliptical machines.

I recognize the young woman as one of the girls I saw in the elevator earlier. She is bouncing rapidly up and down, back and forth, arms and legs operating individually but in perfect coordination with one another. Her blond ponytail sways rhythmically behind her.

Her friend is on the second of the five treadmills. She is skipping and watching Judge Judy on her tiny TV. Judge Judy looks angry.

I stand by the door for several minutes, trying to decide what to do. I want to return to my condo, but that would be silly. Fate has succeeded in bringing me here to the second floor, to the gym. Fate wants me to exercise. It wants me to take back control of my life.

Get on the fucking treadmill, Fate is telling me.

I climb on the treadmill next to Judge Judy. "You're an idiot," she is shouting at some hapless young man cowering before her. "Who do you think you're talking to?"

I turn on my treadmill, feel it sputter to life beneath my feet, my body lurching forward as I try to adjust my pace. I move, slowly at first, then faster, picking up speed, eventually settling on three miles an hour. The girl on the treadmill beside me is going considerably faster and has started doing some frightening combination of skips and jumps, all without breaking a sweat. "Isn't that kind of dangerous?"

She doesn't break stride. "Nah. You get used to it."

"Looks pretty scary."

"Trust me. It's not as scary as it looks."

Do I tell her I trust no one? "Looks pretty scary," I repeat instead.

"Not nearly as scary as Judge Judy." She nods toward the television screen. "Now, *that's* one scary lady."

I watch Judge Judy shift her attention from the young man in front of her to his accuser. "And you, young lady," Judge Judy is saying, her voice as lacerating as a whip, "what were you thinking, showing up at his apartment in the middle of the night?"

"I wanted to see him," the girl whines.

"But he already told you he didn't want to see you."

"I know, but . . ."

"No buts," Judge Judy shouts.

Who are these people? I wonder, temporarily losing myself in their squabble. What are they doing on national television, airing their silly problems for everyone to witness? What happened to the desire for privacy, the very idea of it? Surely it is one thing to try to see ourselves as others see us and something else entirely to see ourselves *only* as others see us. What have we become that we achieve validation and credibility only through the eyes of others?

I turn away from the TV, shift my focus to the mirrored wall in front of me. I'm a hypocrite, I recognize. My whole career is predicated on the lack of privacy I was just condemning. What am I but a scavenger, constantly sifting through the detritus of other people's lives, digging through their garbage, spying through their windows, on the lookout for their darkest secrets?

I call it "collecting facts."

"I don't think I've seen you before," the girl on the treadmill is saying. She is turned toward me, her well-defined arms gripping the side bar of the machine as she lopes along sideways, a few delicate beads of perspiration sliding gracefully down her chest before disappearing into her cleavage. "I'm Kelly. Suite 1712."

"Nice to meet you, Kelly."

She points with her chin to the girl on the elliptical machine. "That's Sabrina. She's in 1019. You are . . . ?"

"Oh, sorry. Bailey. Bailey Carpenter."

Kelly waits a beat for me to reveal my suite number, as if my name is incomplete without it, then continues on when I don't. "Don't you just love living here? Isn't it the best? We love living here."

"I love living here," I echo.

"So, what do you do?" she asks.

The unexpected question causes my knees to buckle, and I almost trip over my feet.

"Careful," Kelly warns.

I lower my speed and manage to steady myself. "I'm kind of unemployed at the moment," I tell her, a half-truth at best, something I've become very good at.

"Been there, done that." She smiles reassuringly. "Trust me. Something will turn up."

I admire her certainty. I still don't trust her.

"I'm a bartender," she tells me. "Sabrina, too. We work at Blast-Off, over on South Miami Avenue. You know it?"

Who in Miami doesn't know Blast-Off? It's a cavernous, industrial-looking dance club that boasts music so loud you feel as if your head is literally going to explode. I went there once with Travis and my brother. They claimed they wanted to see some famous DJ who was on the schedule for that night, but it turned out that the only person they were really interested in was their dealer, and when I found this out, I headed straight for the exit. Travis and I didn't speak for two days. It was another two weeks before my ears stopped ringing. "It's kind of noisy there."

"You get used to it," Kelly says. Clearly she is a woman who gets used to things. I wonder how she would adjust to being raped. "And the money's terrific."

"Maybe I should consider it," I say, more to be polite than because the idea appeals to me. Even the thought of working in a club like Blast-Off sends fresh waves of anxiety shooting through my body.

Kelly's eyes widen in obvious surprise. I check my reflection and immediately understand why. I am skeletal beneath my shapeless clothing, my arms protruding like bones from the short sleeves of my T-shirt.

Would you buy a drink from this woman? I wonder.

"I've lost a bit of weight," I start to say. But Kelly has already turned away from me and is now facing in the opposite direction, continuing to lope, oblivious to everything but her own exertions.

I watch her from behind, noting her long, toned legs inside her tight, black, knee-length leotards, my eyes tracing the faint outline of her thong, her high round backside, her slender waist and wide shoulders. She is unaware of my gaze. Or maybe she knows I'm looking but doesn't care. She's used to being watched. Something else she's used to.

The door to the exercise room opens, and a man walks in. He

is in his mid-thirties, reasonably tall and slim, clean-shaven, with brown hair and dark eyes. He is wearing black nylon shorts and a matching T-shirt. His arms are strong but not overly muscular. All in all, not bad looking, although perhaps not quite as handsome as he thinks. I recognize him as someone who hit on me several times when I first moved into the building, although I can't remember his name. "Ladies," he says, looking from Kelly to Sabrina and then back to Kelly. He seems not to have noticed me at all, for which I'm grateful. "How's everybody doing this afternoon?"

Sabrina smiles but says nothing.

Kelly doesn't break stride. "Doing great."

The man watches her for several seconds. "I'm David Trotter. Suite 1402."

Kelly offers neither her name nor her suite number in return, a sure sign she's not interested in continuing the conversation.

David doesn't take the hint. "That's quite the routine you've got going there. You a dancer?"

"No."

"Exercise instructor?"

"Just like to work out."

"Yeah? Me, too." As if to prove his point, David moves toward the selection of free weights on the floor at the far end of the room. He picks up two thirty-pound weights and begins hoisting them up and down over his head. Immediately, his face turns beet red, and beads of sweat break out across his forehead. He stops after six repetitions, trying to catch his breath as he watches Kelly. "So, what *do* you do? Wait—don't tell me. You're a model."

Kelly all but groans. "Bartender."

"No kidding. Where?"

"Blast-Off."

"Hey. One of my favorite clubs. You gonna be there tonight?"

An almost imperceptible nod.

"Maybe I'll drop by." David resumes hoisting the barbells above his head. "You haven't told me your name."

Kelly turns off her machine and jumps off. "Sabrina, you almost done?"

Sabrina pulls the wires out of her ears. "Two more minutes."

Kelly grabs the bottle of Lysol from the shelf, spraying it into a paper towel that she uses to wipe down the treadmill.

"So, she's Sabrina," David says, refusing to give up. "And you're . . . ?"

"Kelly," she tells him, managing to keep her voice pleasant. Our eyes connect in the mirror. Help me, her eyes plead.

"You think you'd let me buy you a drink, if I were to show up tonight?"

"Sorry, but we're not allowed to drink on the job."

"How about after?"

"I work till four A.M."

Can the man really be so obtuse? Can he not see how uncomfortable he is making Kelly, how eager she is to get away from the leer in his eyes?

"You ever get a night off?" he persists.

"Not very often. Let's get a move on, Sabrina." Kelly moves toward the door.

"How about we work out together tomorrow? If I know what time you're going to be here, I could rearrange my schedule so that . . ."

"I think you should leave her alone now," I hear myself say.

"I'm sorry," David says. "What did you say?"

"I said you should leave her alone. She's clearly not interested. . . ."

"And this is *clearly* none of your business."

"Look," Kelly interrupts. "The truth of the matter is that I have a boyfriend. . . ."

I almost smile. Experience has taught me that when people say "the truth of the matter," it usually means they're about to lie.

"You have a boyfriend?" David asks. "Why didn't you say so?" He actually manages to look offended. "Of course, we wouldn't have to tell him." He runs his tongue lewdly across his upper lip.

"Why don't you just give it up?" I say, feeling the obscene wetness of his tongue against my skin.

"What the hell is your problem?" David snaps, waving one of the weights in front of him. But it is too heavy and his arm quickly collapses with the effort.

"We're out of here," Kelly says as Sabrina steps off the elliptical machine. "Nice meeting you, Bailey." She mouths a silent "thank you" as she ushers her friend from the room.

No! I think. *Don't go.* You can't leave me alone with this man.

David abandons his weights as soon as the women leave. He walks toward me.

My heartbeat quickens. My palms become cold and clammy. I have to get off this machine, but he is standing behind me, blocking my exit.

"What's with you?" he asks. "You jealous? Feeling neglected?"

My eyes look toward the surveillance camera in the upper right corner of the room, praying that someone is watching.

"Wait a minute," he says, staring at my reflection in the mirror. "I know you, don't I?"

I shake my head.

"Yeah, I do." He moves to my side, as if to get a better look at my profile.

My eyes scan the front of my treadmill for the off button. I have to get away from here. Maybe I can just jump off. I'm not going that fast. I decide to slow the machine down but press the wrong arrow and increase the speed instead. Three miles an hour quickly becomes 3.2, then 3.5.

"Didn't we go out a few years back?"

"No."

3.7 . . . 3.8 . . . 3.9 . . .

David sneers audibly but doesn't move.

I have to get away from this man. I have to get out of here.

4.0 . . . 4.1 . . . 4.2 . . .

"This building is full of women who think they're too damn good for the likes of us poor mortals."

4.5 . . . 4.6 . . . 4.8 . . . I'm running now. Maybe if I run as fast as I can . . . 5.1 . . . 5.5 . . . 5.7 . . . I hear my breath escaping in a succession of short, painful bursts. My throat is drying up. My lungs are filling with air, like balloons. Surely any more air and they will burst into thousands of pieces, splattering against the mirror, like blood.

"And I gotta admit, a lot of them *are* pretty spectacular," David continues, his attention temporarily diverted by his own reflection. "Prettiest girls in the world live in Miami. And they know it. I mean, I've been all over: New York, Las Vegas, even L.A. They got nothing on Miami. I'm talking even Brazil. Even the hookers here are better-looking."

6.0 . . . 6.2 . . . 6.5 . . .

"And they know it, man. They know they're gorgeous, and they know they have you over a barrel. You know what I mean? They know they have their pick of the litter. So, it's not enough anymore to have a Mercedes or a Jag. You gotta drive a Lamborghini or a Ferrari. You gotta wear Brioni suits, like fucking James Bond. You gotta have big muscles and a bigger . . ."

6.8 . . . 7.1 . . . 7.3 . . .

Somebody, help me. Please, help me.

"Hey, you're going awfully fast there."

7.5 . . . 7.8 . . . 7.9 . . .

"Maybe you should slow it down."

I look in the mirror, watch myself watching myself.

"I think your shoelace is coming undone."

I glance down, see that the laces of my right sneaker have indeed come loose and have started flopping noisily against the moving sidewalk of the treadmill. If I'm not careful, I'll trip over them. But I can't stop now. I have to run faster. I have to get away.

8.1 . . . 8.2 . . .

Now both shoelaces have come loose. They are snapping against my ankles, coiling over each other, like worms. I look over at David's feet, unmoving in his black sneakers with the white Nike swoosh. . . .

"No!" I cry out. "No!"

8.3 . . . 8.4 . . .

"What the hell are you doing?"

I can't escape. I'm running as fast as I can, but still, I can't get away. He doesn't even have to move to catch me. I feel my legs growing weak, giving way. I can't keep going. My eyes implore the woman watching me from the mirror. *Help me!* She stares back blankly and does nothing.

8.5 . . . 8.6 . . .

My legs shoot out from underneath me, and I scuttle backward through the air, screaming as my jaw slams against the sidebar, and I fly off the back of the treadmill into the water cooler behind me. Hand sanitizer and Lysol crash down around me from the shelf over my head. Paper towels flutter into the air, like kites without wind, as I crumple to the floor. The water cooler teeters on its side for several seconds, then miraculously rights itself before falling over.

"What the fuck . . . ?" David is shouting. "Are you all right? What the hell were you doing?" His hands reach out. He touches my arm.

"No," I scream. "Don't touch me."

"I'm only trying to . . ."

"Don't touch me!"

"What's the matter with you?"

"Get away from me."

"I'm just trying to help you, you crazy bitch."

"No! No! Get off me. Don't touch me."

I'm slapping him now, scratching and biting at his hand.

"What the . . ."

"Help me! Somebody, help me!"

And suddenly the door to the exercise room flies open and the room is full of men. Finn and Stanley and Wes and the janitor, an elderly man whose name I don't remember.

David is already on his feet. "I swear. I didn't do a damn thing to her."

"What's going on?" Finn demands, kneeling beside me, although my posture warns him to keep his hands to himself.

"She's crazy," David says softly, although still loud enough for me to hear. "She suddenly starts going like a hundred miles an hour on the damn treadmill, and I try to warn her she's going too fast. She looks like she's going to have a heart attack. But she just keeps ramping up the speed and before you know it, she's flying off the back of the stupid thing and knocking everything over, shit's flying all over the place—you almost lost that water cooler—and I go to help her, and what does she do? She starts screaming to stay away from her, like I'm attacking her or something. And I swear I never touched the crazy bitch. You can check the surveillance tapes, if you don't believe me."

I catch Stanley nod. They saw some of what went on from the lobby, I hear him confide to David. That was the reason they got here so fast.

"Are you all right, Miss Carpenter?" Finn asks.

"Is there anything we can do?" Stanley says.

"Is anything broken?" Wes adds.

I shake my head, my eyes riveted on David's black sneakers with the white Nike swoosh.

"Do you think you can stand up?" Finn asks, securing my laces with a double knot and helping me to my feet.

Is it possible that David is the man who raped me?

"Is it all right if I go now?" David says, more statement than question.

"You're sure you didn't say anything to upset her?" Stanley asks as he walks him to the door. "Anything at all?"

"Are you kidding? No. If anything, it was the other way around. She was ragging on me."

"Miss Carpenter," Finn is saying as David exits the premises. "Are you all right? Are you bleeding? You're sure nothing's broken?"

I check my forearm. It is scratched, but not bloody. I've wrenched my back, twisted my ankle. My head is throbbing. My jaw aches. But, as Kelly might say, I'm used to such things.

"You want us to call an ambulance?" Wes is asking from somewhere above my head.

"No. I'm all right." I struggle to my feet. It hurts to put weight on my ankle, but it isn't broken, and I know there's nothing a doctor can do.

"What happened here, Miss Carpenter?" Finn asks. "I'm gonna have to file a report."

Could David be the man who raped me? I wonder again, reminding myself that owning the same kind of running shoes as my attacker doesn't mean very much. I need to think things through before I start making crazy accusations. I need to shower and get into bed. I need to get away from all these men and back to my apartment as fast as possible. "I was going too fast. I tripped over my shoelaces. It was my fault," I say. "Don't worry. I'm not going to sue anyone."

"It's you we're worried about. Is there someone we can call? Your brother, maybe. . . ."

"No. Yes," I say, all in the same breath. Although I desperately want to get back to my apartment, I also know, just as desperately, that I don't want to be alone. I need someone to be with me, someone to take care of me and protect me, if only from my own crazy thoughts. "Please," I hear myself tell Finn, "call my sister. Call Claire."

—TEN—

"Okay, Bailey," Detective Marx is saying. "Let's go over what happened one more time."

The definition of insanity: doing the same thing over and over again and expecting a different result. I know this is how Detective Marx works, that she believes repetition often loosens fresh memories. But I've already told her at least three times what happened in the exercise room this afternoon.

"It's the last time. I promise." Detective Marx smiles as if she knows what I'm thinking and adjusts herself at the foot of my bed. Her partner, Detective Antony Castillo, is standing at the window, staring out at the street below. It's night, almost eight o'clock, and it's dark. Detective Castillo is in his late thirties, of medium height and weight, with black curly hair and eyes so incongruously blue I wonder if they're contacts. I also wonder if Castillo could be the man who raped me. He fits the general description.

"You want some fresh ice?" Claire asks, adjusting the pillow behind my head as I push myself up in bed, steadying the melting icepack I'm pressing against my chin.

"No. I'm okay."

"Take a deep breath," Claire instructs, and I do so, feeling the air painfully scratch at my lungs. She covers my free hand with hers, holds on through the remainder of the interview. She is still wearing her pale green nurse's scrubs, having come right from the hospital after Finn's phone call. Luckily for me, she found someone willing to take over the balance of her shift.

I clear my throat and start my story at the moment when David enters the gym, but Detective Marx stops me, makes me go back further. "What made you decide to exercise today?" she asks.

This is the first time she has asked this, and the question surprises me, even though I know that unexpected questions are another method she uses to help retrieve memories. I think about my answer for a few seconds, mutter something about it feeling like the right thing to do, a way of taking back control of my life. She doesn't bother writing this down.

"Tell me about the visit from Travis," she says, knowing from talking to Finn that he was here today. "I understand you two were arguing."

"No."

"According to the concierge . . ."

"We weren't arguing," I insist. "Travis was understandably upset about your coming to see him at work, that you consider him a suspect. . . ."

"He has no alibi for the night you were attacked," she tells me.

"Travis didn't rape me." I stop, wondering why I'm defending him, why I haven't told the police all the nasty details of our breakup, how I can be so sure it wasn't Travis, when I'm sure of so little else.

"Okay. So Travis left, and you decided to take control of your life by going to work out," Detective Castillo says from his position at the window. "Did David Trotter threaten you in any way?"

"No. He just accused me of being jealous. And then he said something about the women in Miami being the most beautiful in the world. Even the hookers."

"An odd remark." Detective Marx scribbles it down in her notebook. "You didn't mention that before."

"I didn't think it was important."

She smiles. The smile says, *Let us decide what's important.* "What else did he say?"

I shake my head, as if some other salient facts might be clinging to the inside of my skull. "Nothing I haven't already told you. Just that I was going awfully fast, that my shoelaces were coming undone."

"So he tried to warn you," Detective Castillo states.

Did he?

"Did he sound like the man who attacked you?" This, from Detective Marx.

"I don't know. Maybe."

"Did his breath smell of mouthwash?"

"Not that I noticed."

"But you *did* notice his sneakers."

"Yes. They were the same ones as the man who attacked me."

"Do you have any other reason to suspect David Trotter might be that man?"

Claire answers for me. "Well, he lives in the building, so he could easily have followed her. She rejected his advances. . . ."

"That was two years ago," Detective Marx interjects.

"Some men can harbor a grudge a very long time."

I wonder if Claire is thinking about our father or our brothers when she says this, but I decide this is not the right time to ask.

"He fits the general description," Claire adds weakly. We both know that every second man in America fits my rapist's description.

"Did he try to touch you?" Detective Castillo asks.

"Only after I fell," I admit.

"So, it's pretty much the sneakers."

I can feel Detective Castillo's disappointment. Claire squeezes my hand. She feels it, too.

"We'll pay Mr. Trotter a visit after we look at the surveillance tape."

"But you don't think it's him," I say.

"We'll definitely check him out." Detective Marx remains seated, reading over her notes, as if contemplating more questions.

"That's enough for one night." Claire lets go of my hand and slides off her side of the bed. "You'll let us know where things stand after you talk to David Trotter?"

"Of course. And if we have any more questions . . ."

"You can ask them in the morning," Claire says, now firmly in control. She leads the two detectives down the hall to the door. "Thanks for stopping by," I hear her say. It was Claire who insisted that I report my suspicions to the police, Claire who got me washed up and into a fresh pair of pajamas, Claire who dried my hair into something vaguely presentable while we waited all day for the detectives to arrive, Claire who tended to my bruises, Claire who brought me icepacks for my ankle and chin. She wanted me to go to the hospital, but I refused.

I climb carefully out of bed, mindful not to put too much weight on my sore ankle, and switch off the overhead light, pick up my binoculars, and hobble toward the window. I raise the binoculars, direct them at the building behind mine, focusing on the apartment three floors from the top, four windows from the left. The lights in the bedroom are on, although the apartment appears empty.

"Our guy up to anything interesting?" Claire asks, coming up behind me to peer over my shoulder.

I shake my head, hand her the binoculars.

"Doesn't look as if anyone's home." She waits a few seconds, then drops them back into the palm of my hand. "I should call Jade. Let her know where I am. Just in case she cares."

"She cares," I tell her.

"I'll use the phone in the kitchen," she offers. "Anything I can make you for dinner?"

"I'm not very hungry."

"I'll open a can of soup. How does that sound?"

"Sounds good." I return the binoculars to my eyes, hear Claire talking quietly on the phone in the other room. I wonder who else she's been speaking to, if she's been in touch with Gene or the others. I ask myself if Heath could be right, that Claire is only interested in my money, that that's the reason she's really here, to soften me up, to get me to loosen the purse strings.

I try to imagine how Heath will manage once the money in his bank account runs out. Gene has already succeeded in tying up our father's estate in court. It could be years before things are finally resolved. Then what would Heath do? He might actually have to get a job. Unless he lands a commercial or two. Unless he sells that screenplay he's been working on for as long as I can remember. I wonder where he is tonight, if he's somewhere with Travis, getting stoned. I picture my married lover having a late dinner with his wife and reading his daughters their favorite bedtime story. I wonder if I'll ever be part of a real family again.

And then there he is.

The man in the apartment behind mine, three floors from the top, four windows from the left.

I watch him as he enters his bedroom, his cell phone pressed against his ear. He's laughing, clearly enjoying his conversation. Something about the slouch of his shoulders and the casual thrust of his hips tells me he's talking to a woman. He is wearing a pair of tight jeans and a white shirt, open to the waist. He approaches the window and presses his forehead to the glass, talking all the while. He rubs his bare chest as he talks, and twists his head from side to side, stretching out his neck. Then he pulls his shoulders together behind him, stretching out the muscles in his back and revealing more of his bare chest. Again one hand moves lazily to caress his skin, sliding from one exposed nipple to the other. "Oh, God," I moan, feeling a wave of nausea rise in my throat. Will I ever be able to look at a man's body again and experience anything other than revulsion?

And yet, as repulsed as I am, I am powerless to look away.

"What's the matter?" Claire asks from the doorway. "Are you in pain?"

Wordlessly, I tear the binoculars from my face, extend them back toward her.

"My, my," she says, as she looks through them. "Seems like

someone's quite smitten with himself. I think we should call him Narcissus."

I recall that Narcissus was a Greek god who fell in love with his own reflection in a pool of water and drowned while trying to get a closer look. "What's he doing now?"

"He's getting undressed. Off goes the shirt. And now the pants. And now . . . my, my." She tosses the binoculars onto my bed. "Okay. Enough of that. Soup'll be ready in a few minutes."

"Did you speak to Jade?"

"I did. She said she'll try to stop by sometime tomorrow after school."

"I like Jade," I tell her as we sit at the dining room table eating our soup minutes later. Chicken with rice from a can. But it tastes good and goes down surprisingly easy. "I like her a lot."

Claire smiles. "She likes you, too."

"What kind of trouble was she in? You mentioned something about Juvenile Hall. . . ."

Claire's smile turns downward, and I am suddenly aware of her resemblance to Gene. "It was stupid. She got into a fight with some girl at school, smacked her over the head with her binder. She was expelled for two weeks, and as soon as she got back, bless her heart, she did it again. This time, she was charged with assault and got sent to Juvenile Hall. Apparently, some people have to learn the hard way."

"But she's been okay since then?"

"Okay is a relative concept where Jade is concerned, but we're hoping for the best."

"I guess that's all any of us can hope for."

"I guess." She finishes the last of her soup.

"It hasn't been easy for you," I venture. "Being a single mom and everything."

She shrugs off my concern. "I'm no different from millions of other women. It's not easy for any single parent."

"Your ex never tries to see his daughter?" I think of my lover's devotion to his children, find it hard to believe a father could be so callous, so indifferent. I know Claire would dispute me on that.

"Kind of runs in the family," Claire says, as if privy to my thoughts. "They do say we go with what's familiar."

"How long were you married?" I ask, trying to avoid a direct discussion of our father.

"Technically, four years. Accurately, thirteen months."

I can feel the look of confusion that settles on my face.

"I was pregnant when we got married, as I believe Jade already mentioned. Eliot was more than a little rough around the edges. Not exactly a parent's dream."

"I don't think I ever met him."

"You were pretty young, and the different branches of the family weren't exactly close. Dad hated him from the start, said Eliot was bad news—he was only after my inheritance. Dad threatened to cut me off entirely if I didn't stop seeing him. But hey, it's not like I saw a whole lot of the man anyway, so I didn't take his threats too seriously, which wasn't very smart. Always take a man's threats seriously." She takes a deep breath. "Then I got pregnant, which was even stupider, and Eliot and I eloped to Las Vegas. Got married by an Elvis impersonator."

"You're kidding."

"I have the pictures to prove it. Thirteen months later, Eliot took off for good."

"But you didn't get divorced for four years?"

"Eliot made things as difficult as he could for as long as he could until our father finally agreed to pay him off. End of Eliot. End of story."

"Jade's never tried to contact him?"

"Once. When she was thirteen. She did some kind of Internet search, found out where he was living, tried to reach out. He never bothered to respond." She looks away. Neither one of us says anything for several seconds. "Can I ask you something and you won't take offense?"

I brace myself for questions about our father. "Sure. Go ahead."

She takes another breath, turns her gaze toward me. "How long have you been sleeping with your boss?"

The spoon I'm holding slips through my fingers, bouncing off the glass dining room table before continuing to bounce along the marble floor. "Oh, God. What makes you think I'm sleeping with Sean Holden?"

"I saw the way you looked at him."

"I was just grateful to see him, that's all."

"Oh."

"Honestly."

"Okay."

"I swear."

"My mistake."

"Sean Holden and I are not lovers."

"I'm sorry. Forget I said anything."

"About three months," I hear myself say.

"What?"

"It's been three months."

"You've been sleeping with Sean Holden for three months?" Claire repeats.

The room is spinning. I'm dizzy. I can't breathe.

Claire is on her feet immediately, coming around to my side of the table. "It's okay, Bailey. Take deep breaths."

"I can't believe I told you that."

"It's okay."

"I shouldn't have said anything."

"I'm glad you did. There's only so much you can keep bottled up inside."

"Please. Promise me you won't tell anyone."

"Of course I won't."

"Promise me you won't tell Gene."

"I promise."

"And Jade."

A slight pause. "I think the cat's already out of the bag on that one."

"What do you mean? You told her?"

"*She* told *me*. 'So, it looks like Auntie Bailey's been banging her boss,' I believe were her exact words."

"I think I'm going to be sick."

"You aren't going to be sick. Keep taking deep breaths."

"What she must think of me."

"She thinks you're the coolest thing on earth. An affair with the boss was the cherry on the ice cream sundae. And speaking of ice cream, how about a nice big bowl?"

"No, I couldn't eat anything. Strawberry?"

"You got it."

Claire leaves my side to go to the kitchen. I push out of my chair, hop to the window, gaze out at the lights of the city. Out there are all sorts of normal people, I think. People who aren't having affairs with their married bosses, whose siblings aren't suing them, who don't fly off the backs of treadmills, who don't think every man they see is a rapist.

"Strawberry ice cream it is." Claire deposits two bowls of ice cream on the glass table. "Lots of strawberries. Lots of calories. Just what the doctor ordered. Come on, sit down. Don't let it melt."

I return to the table, plop down gracelessly in my high-backed chair. I grab my spoon and shovel a giant heap of ice cream into my mouth. "You think I'm a horrible person."

"I don't think that at all."

"You think I deserved what happened to me."

"I certainly do not. Do you? Bailey," she says, leaning forward, both elbows on the table. "Do *you* think you deserved what happened to you?"

The phone rings.

"I'll get it." Claire is already half out of her seat. "Hello," she says. "No, this is her sister. Yes, hello, Detective. . . . Yes, okay. . . . So what happens now? Okay. Yes. I'll tell her. Thank you. Good-bye." She returns to the room. "That was Detective Marx," she begins, then stops. "Bailey, what's happening?"

I realize I've been holding my breath since she stood up. The room is spinning, becoming a shifting blur, buzzing around my head like a fly. I'm about to pass out. Claire runs around the table and catches me before I fall.

"Breathe," she's telling me over and over again.

The room slowly ceases to spin. I am able to sit on my own without falling over.

"How long have these attacks been going on?" Claire asks, pulling up the chair beside me, her arms outstretched in case I start to sway.

"Three years, off and on," I tell her, thinking of my mother, my father, my rape.

"That's way too long. You need to see someone, Bailey. You need professional help. I'm going to phone that therapist I told you about and make you an appointment."

I nod, although I can't imagine it will do any good. Can a therapist undo what has already been done? Can a therapist give me back my mother, my father, my sense of self? "What did Detective Marx have to say?"

"That they haven't been able to locate David Trotter. He's not in his apartment, and he didn't go back to work after the incident in the gym. They're going to keep trying till he turns up." She stares at my barely touched bowl of ice cream. "Anyway, let's not worry about that now. Let's just get you into bed." She helps me to my feet, throwing my right arm across her shoulders, and half-walks, half-carries me to my room. She gets me settled under the covers, then goes to the bathroom, begins rifling through the drawers under the sink. "Where's the medication the doctor prescribed for you?"

"I think Heath might have taken it," I say, as a distant memory of Heath swallowing a mouthful of my pills surfaces.

"Lovely. Okay, I think I might have a few Valiums floating around the bottom of my purse. Stay here," she commands. "Don't faint. Breathe." She's back almost before I've had a chance to absorb her words, the palm of her hand open before me, two tiny white pills resting in the middle of her lifeline.

"I don't want them."

"Take the pills, Bailey. Please. For me, if not you. Jade is home alone, and I have to be at work first thing in the morning. I can't stay here all night."

I open my mouth, allow Claire to deposit the pills on the tip of my tongue. She hands me a glass of water. I drink it down.

As soon as she leaves the room, I prod the pills loose from the inside of my mouth and spit them into the palm of my hand. I hear her cleaning up and feign sleep when she checks on me half an hour later. "Good night, Bailey," she whispers from the doorway. "Sleep well."

—ELEVEN—

In my dream, I'm skinny-dipping in a secluded emerald green pond surrounded by flowering shrubs. I put my head back, feel the sun warm on my face, the fresh water cold against my neck. Gradually I become aware of a circle of sharks below me, and I start swimming for shore. A man is stretched out at the edge of the water, lost in the beauty of his own reflection. "Tell me you love me," he whispers as a shark's fin slices through his mirror image and giant teeth rip at my throat.

I scream and bolt up in bed, reaching for the light switch.

David Trotter is standing at the foot of my bed.

He is all in black and his face is in shadows, but I know instantly who he is. He moves closer. I can smell the mouthwash on his breath.

"Stay away from me!" I cry, throwing myself out of bed and landing squarely on my sore ankle. I collapse to the floor, sobbing in pain. He grabs my hair, punching at my stomach and face before I can regain my equilibrium. "No!" I shout, but his gloved hand is already curling around my throat, pressing down on my windpipe.

Somehow I get one hand free and reach up and back toward

the nightstand beside my bed. I manage to open the top drawer, my fingers searching blindly for the pair of scissors I keep there. But the drawer is empty. The scissors are gone. "Looking for these?" David asks. I look but all I see is the white of the pillow-case he is pulling over my head. This is what death looks like, I think, as he pushes my legs apart and plunges the scissors deep inside me.

I wake up screaming, my face buried in the soft creases of my pillow. The taste of cotton fills my mouth. The phone is ringing. "Goddamn it," I mutter, pushing myself into a sitting position. I stare at the phone, not completely sure if I am really awake this time or still dreaming. What does it say about me that I no longer know when I'm conscious or not? My sister is right. I need profes-sional help. I can't go on like this, night after night after night. Nightmare after nightmare after nightmare.

I pick up the phone, lift it to my ear. But I hear only a dial tone. Perhaps it didn't ring at all. It's too dark, and I'm too tired to check the caller ID.

I take a shower, shampooing the hair that Claire so painstak-ingly blow-dried earlier and exchanging my pajamas for a night-shirt. I stand beside my bed, staring at the illuminated dial of the clock and knowing I won't be able to get back to sleep. It's two thirty in the morning. I debate turning on the TV but decide against it, sensing there are more interesting things I could be watching.

I know the lights are on in the bedroom of the apartment across the way even before I lift the binoculars to my eyes. I know the man will be there—Narcissus, Claire named him—parading semi-naked in front of his window, inviting the world to watch.

Except I'm wrong. No one is there. *All Quiet on the Western Front,* I think, remembering the old movie my mother and I watched together, one of hundreds of film classics we watched dur-ing her illness. As much as I literally ache to have her arms around me, I'm relieved she isn't here to witness the sad mess I've become.

"We have to stay strong," my father said to me after her fu-neral. "We have to make her proud."

Yeah, right, I think. She'd be really proud of me now.

I'm always proud of you, I hear her say as I feel her arms surround me. *Tell me what you see,* she whispers as I lean my back against her breast, rest my cheek against hers, inhale the subtle flowers of her shampoo. She kisses the fresh bruise on my chin, and I feel the pain ebb.

I return the binoculars to my eyes.

I see an empty room. A king-sized bed, a freestanding oval mirror, a turquoise lamp with a white pleated shade sitting on a vanity table next to the window.

And a man, I realize with a start. Narcissus, home from a night on the town. He is standing in front of the oval mirror, clearly pleased with what he sees. He runs a careful hand through his hair, then removes his jacket, throws it on the bed. He pulls his cell phone from the back pocket of his jeans and walks to the window, his fingers tapping out a number before lifting the phone to his ear and staring out at the night.

My phone rings, and I jump, my head shooting toward the sound, my heart pounding, sweat erupting from my pores. I stare back through my binoculars at Narcissus, noting the phone still pressed against his ear. Could it be him? Does he know I'm watching?

I move quickly to the nightstand and just as quickly feel my ankle give out and my knees hit the floor. "Shit," I cry as the phone continues its merciless ring. This isn't happening, I tell myself. This is all still part of that stupid dream. *My Nightmare: The Sequel. Part Three. The Saga Continues. The Saga Never Ends.*

I crawl toward the phone, reach it at the start of its fourth ring. "Hello?"

A dial tone assaults my ears.

I lurch back to the window, phone in one hand, binoculars in the other, looking toward the apartment across the way. Narcissus is still at his window, his phone at his ear. He is talking and laughing.

Did my phone even ring? Or did I only imagine it?

I press *69. A recorded message curtly informs me, "We're

sorry. The number can't be reached by this method. Please hang up now."

I disconnect, trying to figure out what this means. But my brain refuses to function. Did someone actually call? Was it a wrong number? Some stupid kid playing a dumb late night prank? David Trotter? Travis? Anyone? No one?

I watch Narcissus lay the phone down on the end table beside his bed, then remove his tie and kick off his shoes. I see his head snap toward the bedroom door. I watch him leave the room. I see the light come on in the next room. I watch him walk to his door and open it. I see a young woman—slim, pretty, with long dark hair—enter. I watch him take her hand and lead her into the bedroom. I hold my breath.

From this distance, she looks a little like me. Or how I used to look anyway. He kisses her neck and she throws her head back and hugs him tight. Was she the woman he was just talking to on the phone? Did he call her and ask her to drop by? If so, she got here awfully fast. Maybe she lives in the building. Is it possible she's a hooker? Didn't David Trotter tell me that Miami has the most beautiful hookers in the world?

He's kissing her on the lips now; their kisses become increasingly passionate. His hands slide across her breasts, her buttocks, her thighs, then disappear under her short skirt. Seconds later, the skirt falls to the floor, followed in short order by her blouse and her bra. She has small breasts, breasts that are covered by his hands. Large hands, I think, my teeth tearing at my bottom lip. He pulls down her panties and kneels down, burying his head between her legs.

I gasp, feeling my stomach cramp and my knees buckle.

Soon, Narcissus is back on his feet, pushing the young woman up against the window, her naked body now on full display, his hands everywhere at once, at her breasts, between her legs. The side of her face is pressed against the glass and her eyes are closed as his fingers slide around her throat. They find her mouth and worm their way between her lips. Narcissus takes off his shirt and unzips his jeans. The palms of the woman's hands open flat against the glass of the window as he pushes into her from behind.

I cry out, feeling every thrust, but unable to turn away.

When they are done, they stagger from the window and tumble into bed. The room goes dark. I teeter into the bathroom, where I throw up the soup and ice cream I managed to get down earlier in the night. Then I return to the bedroom window and sink to the floor, where I remain, scissors in one hand, binoculars in the other, curled in a quivering, semi-fetal ball, until daylight.

—

Claire calls first thing the next morning. "How are you feeling?"

"Okay."

"Good. I've made you an appointment with a therapist. Noon today."

"Today?"

"You have other plans?"

"No, but . . ."

"No buts," she says. "Her name is Elizabeth Gordon, and she's fitting you in during her lunch hour as a special favor to me."

"I don't know."

"What don't you know?"

"Just about everything."

She laughs. "That's good, Bailey. You made a joke. That means you're getting better."

I'm not sure what she's talking about. I wasn't trying to make a joke. I was being serious.

"Bailey, are you still there?"

"I just don't think I'm up for going out today."

"And I don't think you can afford to stay cooped up in that apartment."

"I didn't get any sleep."

This seems to surprise her. "Really? Those pills should have knocked you out."

"Somebody phoned me," I say, omitting the part about my spitting the pills out. "Twice. In the middle of the night."

"What do you mean? Who?"

"I don't know. The line was dead when I picked up."

"Both times?"

"Yes. At least, I think so."

"What do you mean, you think so? You're saying someone called you twice and hung up when you answered?" I can feel her confusion even without seeing her face. "Are you sure you weren't dreaming?"

"No," I admit. I don't bother telling her about trying *69. Maybe I dreamt that part, too.

"You should call the police," she says.

"It was probably just a wrong number."

"Call them anyway," she insists. "It could be relevant."

We're both skirting the obvious, neither one us wanting to be the one who gives voice to what we are both thinking: that the calls could have come from the man who raped me. To do so would be to give the idea a reality, a validity, that it currently lacks.

"You think the calls came from the man who raped me?" Suddenly I need to hear the words out loud. Whoever attacked me stole my purse, after all. It contained all my vital information. He could have easily obtained my home phone number.

"I think we should eliminate it as a possibility."

"What can the police do?"

"You know more about that than I do, Bailey," Claire tells me. "Can't they maybe trace the call?"

"Not if it was made from one of those throwaway cells," I say, sounding like a cop on one of those *CSI* shows.

"Call the police," Claire says again. "Bailey?"

"I'll call the police."

"Good. Okay, I'm going to give you Elizabeth Gordon's address. Have you got a pen handy?"

"Yes," I lie.

She's not buying it. "No, you don't. I'll hang on while you go get one. And hurry. Don't make me late for work."

I fish through the top drawer of my nightstand for a pen and a piece of paper. "Okay. Go ahead."

"It's 2501 Southwest 18th Terrace, just west of 95. Suite 411. Did you get that?"

"Yes."

"Read it back to me."

"2501 Southwest 18th Terrace. Suite 411."

"Good. It shouldn't take you more than ten, fifteen minutes to get there by cab."

"Okay."

"Who are you seeing?"

"What?"

"The therapist. What's her name?"

"Elizabeth."

"Elizabeth Gordon. What's her address?"

"2501 Southwest 18th Street."

"Terrace," Claire corrects. "Are you sure you wrote that down?"

"Terrace," I repeat. "Suite 411," I add, before she can ask.

"Good. Now I have to go to work, but I'll call you later. Have you had breakfast yet?"

"No."

"Okay, I want you to go into the kitchen and make yourself some toast and coffee. And an egg. Have an egg. It's protein."

"I don't think I can eat anything."

"Have an egg, Bailey."

"Okay."

"Good girl. I'll call you later."

I hang up the phone, leaving the slip of paper with Elizabeth Gordon's address on top of the nightstand, and hobble into the kitchen, make myself some toast and coffee. And an egg, which is actually quite delicious. I'd forgotten how much I like eggs. I've forgotten how much I used to enjoy a lot of things.

The phone rings, and I jump, my stomach lurching, the egg I've just enjoyed threatening to come back up. I move to the phone as quickly as I can, although I don't pick it up. *Unknown caller,* reads my caller ID. I hesitate, debating whether to let voice mail take it. Ultimately, my curiosity gets the better of me, and I lift the phone to my ear.

"Hey, Bailey," Heath says. "What took you so long?"

"Why do you block your calls?" I say instead of hello.

"What?"

"Why do you block your calls so I can't see it's you phoning?"

"I block all my calls. It's automatic. I pay extra," he starts to explain.

"Did you call me last night?"

"Huh?"

"At around two in the morning. Did you phone?"

Silence. Then: "I don't know," he admits. "I was with Travis. We got pretty wasted. We might have made a few calls."

"You were with Travis?"

"What's going on, Bailey? He says you think he's the guy who raped you, that you sicced the police on him."

"I didn't sic the police on him. And I don't think he raped me." Do I?

"The guy loves you, Bailey."

"And I love *you*, Heath. But, I swear, if I hear you defend that man one more time . . ."

"Whoa. Okay. Wait. I'm on your side, remember?"

"Then start acting like it."

Silence. I know I've hurt his feelings, something I've always taken great pains not to do, but I'm tired and crabby and everything hurts and Claire has made this appointment for me with a therapist who's giving up her lunch hour to fit me in, so how can I even be thinking of not showing up, which is exactly what I'm thinking?

"I'm sorry, Bailey. I'm an ass. . . ."

"Can you give me a lift somewhere?" I don't want to end up consoling Heath, which is where I know this discussion is headed. "I have to be over on Southwest 18th by noon."

"What's on Southwest 18th?"

I tell him about the appointment Claire has set up for me.

"Beware of scheming step-siblings who are only after your money."

"Can you take me?" I ask again, ignoring his remark.

"Sure. Oh, wait. Noon, you said? No, I can't. I have another callback for that Whiskas commercial at 11:45. It's my second callback. Apparently it's between me and this one other guy. What about Saint Claire? Can't she take you?"

"She works, Heath."

"How convenient."

I'm losing patience with the conversation. "Was there some other reason you called?"

"Just to find out how you're doing. And since you're being a bit of a bitch, I guess that means you're getting better."

It's interesting how different people interpret getting better. To Claire, it comes down to a sense of humor; to Heath, it means being a bitch. "I'll talk to you later."

"Love you," he coos as I disconnect.

I call the police. They tell me they still haven't been able to locate David Trotter, that they'll keep me posted. I decide not to tell them about last night's phone calls. I don't want to get my brother in trouble. Or Travis, who is probably the one who made the calls, with Heath just covering for him, hiding behind drug-induced amnesia. If the calls continue, I'll report them. In the meantime, I should get ready for my appointment. It's still hours away, but I might as well get a head start. God knows I don't have anything else to do.

I head for my bathroom, purposefully avoiding the binoculars still lying on the floor beside the bedroom window. I'm through with being a voyeur, I tell myself as I step into the shower, laying my scissors down on the gray-and-white marble shelf built into the shower's marble wall. I stand beneath the torrent of blistering hot water, feeling my hair flatten against my scalp like seaweed. When I have finished scrubbing myself so raw I can actually see patches of bloody skin around my elbows and knees, I thoroughly wash and condition my hair, although the conditioner has ceased to have any effect, undone by too much shampoo. Permanent knots have replaced the waves in my long hair. Its once-shiny brown has lost its luster.

I do a cursory job of drying it, then pull it into a large scrunchie at the nape of my neck. I apply concealer to my eyes, then smear some tinted moisturizer on my face. This is followed by some cream blush and a few strokes of mascara.

I look like a clown, I decide, staring slack-jawed at my reflection for several seconds before wiping everything off and starting over again. The second time is even worse. I rub the mascara off with a tissue, find myself face to face with a wild-eyed raccoon.

Ultimately, I step back into the shower, start the whole process over again. This time I decide not to bother with makeup. Elizabeth Gordon will just have to take me as I am, dry scaly skin and corpselike complexion.

The phone rings, and I jump. "Hello?" I say, picking it up before the end of its first ring.

"What's the address?" Claire asks, and I laugh.

"2501 Southwest 18th Terrace."

"Suite number?"

"411."

"Good girl. You almost ready?"

"Almost."

"Do you want me to arrange a cab for you?"

"No, that's all right. I was thinking I might drive." This statement catches both of us by surprise. When was I thinking any such thing?

"I thought whoever attacked you stole your car keys."

"The valets keep a second set."

"What about your license?"

"I have a photocopy," I lie.

"I'm not sure it's such a good idea."

"I am," I say, growing increasingly adamant.

"Well, okay then. I guess."

"Okay, then," I repeat.

"Call me when you get home."

I promise I will, then hang up the phone. I walk gingerly into the closet, careful not to put much weight on my sore ankle and wondering if, in fact, it's a good idea for me to drive. But I've always loved driving. And sitting behind the wheel of the car that once belonged to my mother has always soothed me.

I select a pair of loose-fitting black pants and a white shirt to wear on this, my first outing in three weeks. I'm almost giddy. Driving will do more for me than any therapist.

At eleven fifteen, I call down to the concierge and ask Finn to have someone bring up my car.

"Sure thing, Miss Carpenter."

"And could you send someone up to escort me down in the elevator?" I ask, feeling a lump in my throat, a constriction in my chest. "Normally, I wouldn't ask. But after yesterday . . ."

"I'll be right up and escort you down myself," Finn says without hesitation.

Two minutes later, he's at my door.

"I'm probably being silly," I tell him, growing dizzy and fighting to stay upright as he walks beside me down the hall.

"Never hurts to be cautious."

The elevator arrives and we step inside. I close my eyes as Finn presses the button for the lobby, and we ride all the way down without interruption. "Here comes your car now." Finn points toward the silver Porsche pulling around the corner into view.

Wes jumps out of the still-running sports car as Finn holds open the lobby door.

I walk slowly toward the car I inherited from my mother, its exterior shiny and clean, its silver metal reflecting the blinding midday Florida sun. The last time I saw my car it was night on a quiet residential street in North Miami. The last time I touched the door handle was the night I was raped. "I can do this," I mutter as I crawl in behind the wheel.

Wes closes the door after me and leans in through the open window. "Drive carefully," he says, the strong, medicinal scent of his mouthwash bringing tears to my eyes.

—TWELVE—

My father bought my mother the silver sports car as a present on her fiftieth birthday. It was love at first sight, and she swore she'd drive it forever. Forever turned out to be less than three years. After she got too sick to drive, it sat in the garage. "My baby feels neglected," she'd say periodically from her bed, her head swiveling on her pillow in the direction of the four-car garage. "When are you going to get your father to teach you to drive shift?"

"It's *your* baby," I'd reply with a stubborn shake of my head. "It wants its Mommy." *I* want my Mommy, I'd add silently. *Please, Mommy. Don't die. Don't die.*

So much for silent prayers.

The car is now eight years old and in the years since my father patiently taught me how to drive a stick shift, I've more than tripled the mileage. Still, it feels brand new. Every time I climb behind the wheel, I feel my mother's comforting arms surround me. I inhale the quiet citrus of her perfume.

Until today.

Today the car feels foreign and unfamiliar. The buttery smooth black leather feels harsh and prickly against my skin. The seat sits too low to the ground and no longer cups my back like the palm of a hand. My legs have to stretch to reach the pedals; my hands slide from the steering wheel as if it's been greased. My mother is nowhere to be found.

Wes has made a mistake, I decide. He's new to the building and has mixed things up and brought me the wrong car. "This isn't my car," I shout out the window, but Wes is back at the front entrance talking to Finn and doesn't hear me. I'm not sure what to do, so I do nothing, just sit there. Of course this is my car, I assure myself. It just doesn't feel like mine because Wes has adjusted the seat to fit his own frame. It's a simple matter to return everything to its rightful position.

I press a button to adjust the seat, which lifts the seat up instead of forward, and when I press the button again, it moves the seat back further than it was before, making everything worse. I press a button on the side of the door, causing the window beside my head to rise, cutting off my supply of outside air. The car's air conditioner is off, and I've forgotten which switch will turn it on. The car is hot and growing hotter and more humid by the second. I can't breathe. "Okay, stay calm," I whisper, taking a bunch of deep breaths, trying not to give in to my growing panic as I start pushing one button after another.

The seat suddenly vaults forward, then back again, then forward, before locking into place with a jolt so intense it jostles my right hand, throwing the car into first gear. My left foot automatically lifts off the clutch as my right presses down on the accelerator. "The car practically drives itself," I hear my mother proclaim proudly as the silver Porsche literally bounces out of the driveway.

In my rearview mirror, I see Wes turn around, his mouth opening in alarm as he watches my car lurching toward the street. I've forgotten where I'm going. I fish in my handbag for the address I scribbled on a piece of paper, but I can't find it. What's more, the sun is blinding, and I realize I've forgotten my sunglasses.

Reflexively, I lift one hand from the wheel to shield my eyes from the sun's glare and feel the car veer sharply to the left. Such a powerful engine. "Too powerful for a girl," Travis once scoffed, although I think he was just peeved because I wouldn't let him drive. But maybe he was right after all.

Can a girl ever have too much power? I wonder, trying to keep another more worrisome thought at bay. The thought asserts itself anyway: when did I stop being a woman and regress into a girl? I shake my head, already knowing the answer. Another wave of disgust washes over me. I am drowning in disgust. I press down harder on the accelerator and shift the car into second gear. A mistake. It's too early to shift gears. I'm not going fast enough. I'm barely out of the driveway, for God's sake.

A half-finished building suddenly looms large in front of me. I tighten my grip on the wheel, spin it to the left to avoid a collision with a car approaching from the right, not seeing until it is too late that several construction workers are crossing the road directly in my path. I see their faces contort with fear, hear the frenzied cries of onlookers, hear my own scream rise above theirs as I struggle to control the wheel. Tires squeal as the car mounts the sidewalk, continuing its sickening path toward the orange wire fence surrounding the construction site.

"What the hell?" someone shouts as the front of the Porsche crashes into the chain-link fence, causing the wire to crumple and collapse. It falls across the hood of my car like netting from a hat.

"Are you crazy?" another voice cries as instinct takes over and I manage to wrest the key from the ignition, stopping the car once and for all.

I push open the door and stagger out.

"Miss Carpenter," Wes is shouting from somewhere behind me. "Are you all right?"

"What happened?" Finn demands, both men racing across the street toward me.

And then, a succession of overlapping voices: "Are you hurt?" "For God's sake, you almost killed us." "What's the matter with you?" "Are you sick?" "What were you thinking?"

"I have to go," I tell the blur of bodies moving around me.

"I think you should sit down."

"I have to go."

"Do you want me to call your sister?" Finn asks.

How many times has he asked me that lately? I find it ironic that a week ago, Claire barely existed. My half-sister in theory perhaps, but in reality little more than a name scribbled on the back of an old photograph. She was half of nothing. Now she is the half that makes me whole. I couldn't have survived this past week without her. So why didn't I listen to her when she warned me not to drive? Why didn't I call a cab?

My eyes shoot from side to side. I notice steam rising from the engine of my car and a large scratch etched across its hood like a deep scar. I see a woman ushering a small child away from the scene, as if staring too long in my direction might permanently damage her son's vision, like gazing at a solar eclipse. I watch a few people starting to wander off even as several others jockey to improve their positions.

I see David Trotter.

He is standing by himself on the other side of the street, perusing the scene with cold, dispassionate eyes. He shifts from one foot to the other as his mouth curls into an insolent smile.

"No!" I gasp, turning away.

"What is it?" Finn asks.

I dismiss his concern with a shake of my head. When I work up enough courage to look back in David Trotter's direction, he is gone.

Was he ever really there?

A construction worker touches my arm. He is about thirty and of medium height and weight. "Are you okay?" he asks. His breath carries traces of the spearmint gum he is chewing.

I cry out, as if I've been burned by the lit end of a stray cigarette and take a step back as a gloved hand reaches for my shoulder. I break from the crowd and take off down the street.

"Hey, you can't just leave the scene of an accident."

"Miss Carpenter . . ."

As if by prior arrangement, a cab suddenly pulls to a stop in front of me. I open the door and hop in, not fully convinced the taxi isn't a mirage. It is only when the stale aroma of perspiration

emanating from the cracked green vinyl of the cab's interior assaults my nostrils and I hear the driver's heavy Cuban accent that
I begin to accept this is actually happening. "Where you go?" the
man asks.

I struggle to remember the address. Then I hear Claire's calm
voice in my ear, reminding me. "2501 Southwest 18th Terrace," I
tell the driver. "Can you get there as fast as you can?"

The driver smiles at me in his rearview mirror. I note with relief
that he is about sixty, with salt-and-pepper hair and a paunch so
pronounced that it actually crowds the steering wheel. He is not
the man who raped me. For the time being, I can relax. "Hang
on," he says.

—

Suite 411 is on the fourth floor of a six-story, bubblegum-pink
building, directly across the hall from the elevator. I am both
sweating from the outside heat and shivering from the inside air-
conditioning, an unsettling combination. I knock on the heavy
wood door and wait, but there is no answer. I check my watch and
see that I am twelve minutes late. Elizabeth Gordon has probably
given up on me, I think with a mixture of disappointment and relief, about to turn away when the door opens and a pretty woman
with frizzy brown hair and a mouthful of tuna sandwich stands
before me. She is about forty years old, almost six feet tall, and
dressed casually in gray slacks and a powder blue cotton shirt. A
thin gold pendant dangles from her swanlike neck, matching the
small gold loops in her ears and wide gold band on the third finger
of her left hand. She wears minimal makeup, and she is smiling as
she discreetly pries several stray flakes of tuna from her teeth with
her tongue and wipes her right hand on the side of her pants before
extending it toward me. I shake it, deciding she must be Dr. Gordon's receptionist. "You must be Bailey," she says, ushering me
inside the small waiting room lined with high-backed plastic
chairs. "I almost didn't hear you. Sorry about the tuna. I was trying to wolf it down before you got here."

"No, I'm sorry. I'm the one who's late. Did Dr. Gordon leave?"

"I'm Elizabeth Gordon, and I'm not a doctor."

Only then do I notice the framed diplomas on the pale blue wall. One boasts an undergraduate degree from Vassar, the other a Master of Social Work from Yale. No medical degree, but impressive nonetheless.

"Why don't we go into my office?" Elizabeth Gordon opens another door to reveal a modestly larger room than the one we've just been in, which is painted the same soothing shade of blue. On one side of the room sits a desk, piled high with files and loose pieces of paper covered in illegible scribbling. On the other side are grouped a tan-colored sofa and two mismatched chairs, one green, the other navy, an attempt, I decide, to appear casual and get clients to relax and open up. I wonder if the tuna sandwich was another such ploy.

"Sorry I'm late," I apologize again, as she motions for me to have a seat on the sofa.

I sit down at the far end while she folds herself into the navy chair across from me, crossing one long leg over the other and resting her hands in her lap. "You seem to be upset about that."

"I don't like being late."

"Why?"

"I think it's rude. It shows a disrespect for other people's time." I recall that my father was a stickler for promptness. But I don't tell her that.

"Being late makes you anxious?"

"Doesn't everything?"

"I don't know. Does it?" She smiles. What exactly does she expect me to say? "I understand from your sister that you've been going through a difficult time."

I almost laugh, roll my eyes instead, the way Jade often does when talking to her mother. "I guess you could say that."

Elizabeth Gordon jots something down on the pad of foolscap she is holding. I don't remember seeing this pad in her hands before and wonder where it came from. "Do you want to talk about it?"

"Not really."

"Okay. What *would* you like to talk about?"

"I don't know."

She waits. "Why did you come to see me, Bailey?"

"My sister thought it would be a good idea."

"Yes. She told me you've been having crippling anxiety attacks for some time now."

"It hasn't been that long."

"I understand they've been going on ever since your mother died."

"I guess."

"Approximately three years."

"I guess," I say again, although I know exactly—almost to the minute—how long it's been.

"Claire tells me that your father died recently as well."

"That's right."

"And that a few weeks ago you were beaten and raped."

"My sister has been quite the blabbermouth."

"I think she was just trying to be helpful."

"Did she also tell you I'm having an affair with my married boss?" I watch Elizabeth Gordon's face for any sign of disapproval, but her face remains impassive and judgment-free.

"She left that part out. Is *that* what you'd like to talk about?"

I feel a burning sensation in my chest that causes my face to flush. "No."

She chooses her next words with obvious care. "Look. I know from your sister that the rape has been an awful setback for you, and I can see you have a lot of feelings related to all the things you're dealing with. I hope you'll feel comfortable enough to start putting those feelings into words, that we can work together to integrate those feelings with your cognition of what happened, with the eventual hope of getting better. . . ."

"I have absolutely no idea what you're talking about."

"I realize certain events are harder to talk about than others. . . ."

"What is it you want from me?"

"I think the question is, what do *you* want from *me*?"

"I want . . . ," I begin, then stop. "I don't know. I don't know what I want." I shake my head, lower my eyes to the beige shag carpet at my feet. When I finally look up again, my voice is a whisper. "I just want to stop feeling so damn scared all the time."

"What are you scared of?"

"What do you think?" The sneer in my voice matches the sneer on my lips. "I was raped, for God's sake. The man almost killed me."

"You're afraid it might happen again?"

"He's still out there, isn't he?"

"That's a pretty frightening thought."

"Is this what therapists do—state the obvious?" I'm being deliberately provocative, although I'm not sure why.

"No. Therapists try to understand and assist the people who come to them for help," she says, refusing to rise to the bait. "You seem frightened and hostile, Bailey. Both edgy and on the edge. I'd like to know what is most upsetting to you now."

"Are you fishing for details of my rape, Dr. Gordon?"

"Elizabeth," she corrects gently, "I'm not a doctor, remember? And no, I'm not looking for specifics. I'm just trying to get you to put into words what is most troubling you. That's the only way I'll be able to help. People usually feel better when they leave their problems here. But I know it's a difficult process, and there's a lot going on with you. It will take time. The good thing is that we have as much time as we need."

"We have less than an hour."

She checks her watch. "Today, yes. But I'm hoping you'll trust me enough to want to come back."

"I'm not sure what good it will do."

"Well, you don't have to make any decisions right this minute. Why don't we see how the rest of the session goes first? Sound fair to you?" she asks when I fail to respond.

"I guess."

"Why don't we start with your telling me a bit about yourself. How old are you?"

"Twenty-nine." I wait for her to tell me I look much younger, which would be a lie, but she doesn't, which I appreciate. I tell her about my job, supply vague facts about my life, steering well clear of any more intimate revelations.

"Tell me about your mother," she says.

My eyes fill with tears. "What can I say? She was wonderful. The best mother . . . my best friend."

"It must have been terrible to lose her so young."

"She was only fifty-five."

"I was talking about you," she corrects gently. "And your father? I understand from Claire . . ."

"Then you understand nothing," I say sharply, my muscles tensing.

". . . that he was quite a bit older than your mother," she continues, finishing her thought, "that she was his secretary."

Again I feel my muscles constricting. "I'm sure Claire told you all about their affair."

"Actually, no. You're saying your father was married when he started seeing your mother?"

"I know what you're getting at," I say, impatiently.

"What am I getting at?" She looks genuinely confused. Which only makes me more impatient.

"You think that because my mother had an affair with her boss when he was married to another woman that I think it's okay to sleep with mine?"

"Is that what *you* think?"

"I don't think my mother has anything to do with my affair, that's what I think."

"Okay. Fair enough."

"Do *you* think my mother has something to do with it?" I ask after a pause in which my heart is pumping so fast and hard it threatens to burst from my chest.

"I think there are all sorts of reasons why women get involved with married men. Sometimes they're lonely. Sometimes they have nothing better to do. Sometimes the man isn't fully honest about his circumstances." She pauses briefly. "In some cases, getting in-

volved with a married man keeps them from dealing with the demands of a more normal relationship. . . ."

"You think that's the case with me?"

"In your case," Elizabeth Gordon says, and I can see her
weighing her answer carefully before she continues, "I don't know.
We'll see. It might speak to some yearning you have to understand
your mother better."

I fall back in my chair, expelling all the air in my lungs with a
deep whoosh, as if I've been kicked in the chest. Once again, my
eyes fill with tears.

"What is it, Bailey?"

"I can't do this." I jump to my feet. "I have to go." I'm at the
door, my hand on the brass knob. "This is not why I came here."

"Tell me what you're feeling right now, Bailey."

I look toward the ceiling, then down at the floor. I will my
hand to open the door, but it remains immobile. I command my
feet to move, but they refuse to budge. "I just feel so stuck," I cry,
pushing the words from my mouth.

"How about vulnerable?" Elizabeth Gordon asks, rising to her
feet.

"Of course I feel vulnerable. How could I not?"

"Is it the stuck or the vulnerable that's making you so frightened and angry?"

"It *all* makes me angry."

"Then let's look at the *all*. The rape, the loss of your mother,
the death of your father, the sleeping with your boss."

I try to speak, but no words come. Instead I just stand there
and cry, my shoulders convulsing with each sob.

"I see we struck a chord," she says gently. "Tell me what you're
feeling, Bailey. Try to put it into words."

I'm silent for several more seconds, then surprisingly, I hear the
words tumble from my mouth. "I just feel so sad."

"Then I think you're ready to start therapy," Elizabeth Gordon says simply, putting her arm around me and leading me back
to my chair.

THIRTEEN

"Well, you've certainly had an eventful day," Jade says as we enter my apartment together.

I am almost giddy with delight at the sight of my familiar walls. I feel as if I have just made a successful emergency landing after a dangerously turbulent flight. I want to kiss the marble floor of my foyer with the same reverence that soldiers kiss the ground after returning from a tour of duty in a hostile foreign land.

Jade is unaware of the emotions raging inside me. She walks directly into the kitchen and opens the fridge door, almost as if she is the one who lives here and not me. "Feel like something to drink? I'm dying of thirst."

I realize I am equally parched. "Is there any Coke?"

She retrieves a can and opens it as I lean against the counter, grateful for its support and enviously watching the ease with which she moves. There is nothing tentative about her. She pours half the contents into a glass and hands it to me, then sips the rest directly from the can. "I like the fizz," she explains.

I fight the urge to walk over and take her in my arms. Has she any idea how happy I am to see her? I'd been dreading the scene I imagined I'd be returning to—the fallout from my leaving the scene of an accident I was responsible for, even though no one had been hurt. But when I stepped out of the taxi in front of my condominium, I discovered that my car had already been towed to a service station and that my sixteen-year-old niece, who'd skipped her afternoon classes to check up on me and was waiting at the concierge desk wearing cut-off jeans and a lime green halter top, had managed to mollify both the construction workers and the police. "How'd you manage that?" I asked in the elevator on the way up to my apartment.

"I promised them all blow jobs." She laughed when she saw the horrified expression on my face. "Just kidding. Only the cute ones. *Kidding*," she added again quickly, twirling several strands of long blond hair between her fingers before letting them fall back across her bare shoulders. "I just explained the situation, told them that you've been under a lot of stress and stuff and were on your way to see your therapist when the accident happened, and that the police should check with Detective Marx—that's her name, right?—if they needed further clarification. I think the 'further clarification' part might have sealed the deal."

Again I smile. "Something else you got from *Dog the Bounty Hunter*?"

"CourtTV. Anyway, the cops said they might have some questions for you later."

"I'm sure they will." I try not to think about what those questions might be.

She finishes her drink, then tosses the empty can into the recycling bin under the sink. "So, what was it like? Therapy, I mean."

"Pretty good."

"What'd you talk about?"

I shake my head. "Everything."

"In one hour? You must talk pretty fast."

"I booked some more appointments. Every Wednesday at one o'clock for the foreseeable future."

"Mother will be very pleased. I know Elizabeth Gordon was a big help to her when I was in juvie."

"What was *that* like?" I ask, relieved the focus of the conversation has shifted.

"About what you'd imagine."

"I can't imagine," I say honestly. "Tell me."

"Can we go watch TV?" she asks instead, already moving toward the hall. "*Millionaire Matchmaker* should be on."

"What's that?"

"Oh, my God. You've never watched *Millionaire Matchmaker*? Patti Stanger's the best."

"Who's Patti . . ." But Jade has already disappeared into my bedroom; I have little choice but to follow. I enter my bedroom to see a pretty, dark-haired woman with remarkable cleavage filling my TV screen. She is lecturing a group of nubile young women in the art of seducing a millionaire.

"No sex without monogamy," Patty proclaims as I collapse on top of my bed, exhaustion covering me like a heavy blanket.

"Oh, crap. I've seen this one." Jade leans back on the pillow beside me. "This couple ends up having sex on their first date, which is like this big no-no for Patty. She says you have to be in a committed relationship before you sleep with the guy, or you don't feel safe, and it won't work out. Do you agree with that?"

"Makes sense." I wonder if I'll ever feel safe again where men are concerned. I wonder if I ever have.

"Do you think you'll ever have sex again?" Jade asks.

I swallow the impulse to gag. "What?"

"Sorry. I guess that qualifies as none of my business. My mother says that I ask too many questions, and that sometimes I'm just plain rude. . . ."

"I don't think you're rude, just . . ."

"Inappropriate?"

"Let's say inquisitive. Tell you what," I continue, surprising both of us. "You answer my question, and I'll answer yours."

"What question was that?"

"What was it like in Juvenile Hall?"

"To be perfectly honest, it wasn't all that awful. Everybody was pretty nice. They wanted to help. Kind of like your therapist,

I guess." She shrugs. "But you're still locked up. You can't watch your programs or go out when you feel like it. And I hated having to make my bed a certain way and share a room with a bunch of psychos. But it's not like anybody raped me with a broomstick or anything."

I feel the color instantly drain from my face.

"Oh, shit. Sorry. I didn't mean . . ."

"I know."

"I wasn't thinking."

"It's okay."

"It's not okay. My mother's right. I need to think before I speak. I'm really sorry, Bailey."

I take a long, deep breath. "How long were you there?"

"Less than a month. Uncle Gene pulled some strings, got me out early. He denies it, of course. He pretends to be such a hard-ass. . . ." She begins flipping through the stations. A succession of images assaults my eyes as one channel disappears into another. "So, your turn. Think you'll ever have sex again?"

Truthfully, the thought of having sex again terrifies me. The idea of a man, *any* man, even Sean, touching me in an intimate manner sends spasms of revulsion through my body. "I hope I'll enjoy sex again one day," I say, but my words sound hollow and unconvincing, even to my own ears.

"Can I ask you another question?"

"Can you make it an easy one?" This is worse than therapy, I think.

"Did you like sex before you were raped?" Jade leans forward, staring at me intently, the television temporarily forgotten.

"Yes."

"Did you have orgasms?"

I want to tell her this is *really* none of her business, but I don't. Instead I answer the question. "Sometimes."

She sighs. "I've never had an orgasm."

"You're sixteen," I remind her.

"I read that some women *never* have orgasms. Maybe I'll be one of them."

"Somehow I doubt that."

She giggles. "So whose fault would it be if I don't, the guy's or mine?"

"I don't know that it's a question of fault," I begin, choosing each word with care. "It's more a matter of finding out what works for you and what doesn't, and being able to express—"

"Did you have a lot of lovers?" she interrupts, my answer clearly much too long and earnest to sustain her interest.

I do a quick count. "Does six qualify as a lot?"

"Are you kidding? For a single woman your age that's, like, nothing."

"What about you?"

She is silent for several long seconds. "Promise you won't tell my mother?"

I nod, regretting now that I've asked the question.

"Just one," she tells me so quietly I almost don't hear.

"Just one?"

"I know. My mother thinks there've been, like, what—twenty?" She sits up ramrod straight. "You promised you wouldn't tell her."

"I won't. But frankly, I think she'd be relieved."

"Who says I want her to be relieved?"

I laugh.

Jade looks offended. "You think this is a joke?"

"No, not at all. I just meant . . . She worries about you. That's all."

"She worries about everything."

"She does?"

"You seem surprised."

"I guess I am," I admit. Claire always seems in such control.

"She worries about money, mostly," Jade says.

I feel a stab of guilt. It's because of me that Claire worries about money. It's not right I have so much and she so little. "So, tell me about this guy," I say in an effort not to think about such things. "Is he the one your mom caught you with?"

"Nah. He was this boy in my English class last year, but his family moved to Arizona in July, and that was the end of that. No big loss. I mean, the whole thing was pretty forgettable, although they say you never forget your first love."

"They say a lot of things. Most of them aren't true." I pause, thinking of Sean. "I think it's your last love that counts."

She seems to weigh this thought seriously, her forehead creasing in concentration. "Are you in love now?" she asks.

Am I? I used to think so. "I don't know."

The phone rings, and I jump.

"Want me to get it?" Jade's hand stretches toward the end table. I nod as she checks the caller ID. "Somebody's ears were obviously burning," she says, picking up the phone and handing me the receiver. "It's your boss," she mouths.

I think Bailey's banging her boss, I hear Claire say.

I take the phone, press it tight against my cheek, as if trying to prevent any words from escaping. "Hi," I whisper, my heart already pounding. I'm seized with the notion that Sean was somehow able to hear everything Jade and I have been talking about. I signal for Jade to leave the room, but she stubbornly refuses to take the hint. Instead, she leans forward, elbows resting on crossed knees, her eyes fastened on mine.

"How are you?" Sean asks.

"Good."

"I thought I'd stop by later, if you're going to be alone."

"I'd like that."

"Around five?"

"Sounds good."

"I'll see you then." He hangs up without saying goodbye. Sean was never one for beating around the bush, in the courtroom or anywhere else. His philosophy has always been, Keep it simple. Make your point. Then get the hell out.

"What sounds good?" Jade asks as I drop the phone to the bed.

I shake my head. It's one thing to talk about Sean with my sister or my therapist. But I draw the line at discussing him with a sixteen-year-old girl.

"He's coming over, isn't he?"

"Jade . . ."

"Now? Is he coming over now? Do you want me to leave?"

"He's not coming over now."

"But he *is* coming over."

"Around five," I admit, recognizing it's a lost cause to do otherwise.

"You want me to stick around? *Kidding*," she says immediately. "I'll be long gone by then. Promise. And just so you know," she adds, "anything you tell me is just between us. Like with your therapist."

I smile. "You'd make a very good therapist."

"You think so?"

"Absolutely."

"How about a private investigator, like you?"

"I think you'll be great at whatever you decide to do."

"Thanks."

"And just so *you* know, whatever you say to me is strictly confidential as well."

She uncrosses her legs and leans back against the pillows, returning her attention to the TV, the channel back to *The Millionaire Matchmaker*. One episode is just ending and another beginning. "I like you," Jade says without looking at me.

"I like you, too."

—

It's almost six o'clock when Sean knocks on my door. Jade left almost two hours ago. I've showered and changed into a pair of white cotton jeans and a loose-fitting gray jersey. I've even made a stab at blow-drying my hair and applying a bit of makeup. The result, while not a total success, is not an unmitigated disaster. At least I don't look as if I'm about to keel over dead.

"Sorry I'm late," he says as I open the door to let him in.

In the next minute, I'm in his arms. He is holding me very gently, as if he is afraid too much pressure on my back might cause it to break. His lips brush against my hair, although they don't linger. I feel his breath against the skin of my neck. I lift my face to his, and he kisses me tenderly, although briefly and without passion, as if he is aware another man is hovering, waiting to pounce.

"How are you?" he asks.

"Better, now that you're here." I take his hand, guide him toward the living room.

"I can't stay long."

"I figured as much." I know he likes to be home in time to tuck his daughters into bed.

"I was hoping to get away earlier, but you know how it is. Something always comes up just when you've got one foot out the door."

We sit side by side on one of the sofas, our fingers touching, although just barely. "Are you very busy at work?" I ask, although I already know the answer. He is always busy at work.

"The usual. Nothing I can't handle."

"Hopefully I'll be back in the office soon to help out." I do my best to sound more convincing than I feel.

"Take your time. There's no rush." He lifts his hand to caress my cheek. Instantly I feel my jaw clench and my ribs constrict. "Sorry," he says, returning his hand to his lap.

"It's not you," I offer.

"I know."

"It'll just take time."

"I know," he says again.

I take his hand in mine, guide it back to my face, press it against my cheek, then kiss his open palm. Is it possible that Elizabeth Gordon is right about him? Could this affair be my attempt to understand my mother better?

"What were you thinking just now?" he asks.

"Nothing."

"Yes, you were. I could see all this stuff going on behind your eyes."

I laugh to hide my embarrassment at being so easily read. "I don't know. I guess I'm just so glad to see you."

"How are you feeling . . . *really*?" he presses.

The easy answer would be to tell him I'm feeling better. But the truth is I feel the same as I did yesterday and the day before that. The relief I felt when talking to Elizabeth Gordon was only temporary. "Better," I lie.

"Well, you certainly look better."

"Makeup."

"No, it's more than that. I'm seeing a bit of the old spark coming back."

We see what we want to see, I think. "I went to a therapist this afternoon. Elizabeth Gordon."

He shakes his head at the name. "Don't know her. Any good?"

"I hope so."

"I think it's a good idea, that you're seeing her," he says after a pause. "I think it'll help."

"I hope so," I say again. I wait for him to ask what we talked about, to grill me as Jade did earlier, but he doesn't. Does he wonder if we talked about him? He doesn't ask that either.

"Any interesting new cases?" I ask after a silence of several seconds.

"Not really. Same old, same old," he adds for emphasis, as if to convince me I'm not missing much.

"No juicy office gossip?"

He hesitates. "None that I can think of."

"What?" I ask.

"What?" he repeats.

"You thought of something," I tell him, a repeat of our earlier exchange, although our roles have reversed. "There was all this stuff going on behind your eyes."

"Just trying to see if I could come up with anything sufficiently juicy. Guess you'll have to talk to Sally about that sort of thing." He looks toward the window, stares absently at the horizon.

I'm holding my breath. We've never had a problem talking to each other before. Words always flowed so effortlessly between us. Although truthfully, we never had much need for very many words.

"I ran into your brother this morning," he says finally.

"Heath?" I haven't heard from him today. I wonder how his callback went, if he got the Whiskas commercial. I hope he did. Heath needs for something good to happen.

"Gene," Sean corrects.

I grimace. I'd forgotten about Gene. I'm used to thinking I have only one brother.

"He asked how you were coming along, if I'd spoken to you since that memorable afternoon here."

"What'd you tell him?"

"That your recovery might proceed faster if he'd drop his lawsuit."

I can't help but laugh. "And what did he say to that?"

"That he was open to discussing the matter whenever you felt up to it."

"Lovely. I feel better already." I'm reminded of Claire, her worries about money. "Do you think I should settle?"

"I think that's entirely up to you and Heath."

"My father would have a fit. You know he would. You were his lawyer."

Sean shakes his head. "Your father was a stubborn man, Bailey. And much as I respected him, he wasn't always right."

"So you think I should settle?" I repeat.

"I don't think you should decide anything until you're feeling stronger. Just remember that there's lots of money to go around, and it's your health that's important here. At some point, it might be best to cut your losses, make peace with your family, and move on with your life." He reaches over and pats my knee. "I should go."

"Now? You just got here."

He checks his watch as he rises to his feet. "It's getting late. The girls . . ."

". . . like their father to be home to kiss them goodnight."

He's walking toward the foyer. I reach out and grab his hand, feel his fingers sliding from mine as he moves to open the door. "Listen. There's something I have to tell you. I'm going away for a week."

"What? When?"

"We leave Saturday. It's this family cruise Kathy booked months ago. The Caribbean. Believe me, this was not my idea."

I bite down hard on my lower lip to keep from saying something I'll regret.

"I'll miss you," I tell him. What else can I say?

"I'll miss you, too."

He leans over and kisses me. The kiss is soft and tender, longer than the one he gave me when he arrived. I can't help wonder if there's something more, something he isn't telling me. I long to grab him close, to keep him from leaving. My arms stretch toward his neck. But he is already pulling away from me, and my hands brush ineffectually across his shoulders as he steps across the threshold.

"Take good care of yourself until I get back," he says. And then he is gone.

I run down the hall to my room, grab my binoculars and stare down at the street, watching for his car. But it is dark, and one car looks pretty much the same as the next. I watch them as, one after another, they disappear into the night, taking their secrets with them.

FOURTEEN

It's just after midnight, and a light rain is starting to fall when the lights go on in the apartment across the way. Immediately I raise my binoculars to my eyes, watching as Narcissus enters his bedroom. He's not alone. A woman is with him, but I'm pretty sure she's not the same woman he was with last night. This woman appears both taller and thinner, although she has the same long, dark hair as the previous one. She seems to be laughing, but I can't tell for sure.

I adjust the lens to get a better look. The circles refuse to align properly. Everything remains hazy. Maybe it's the rain. Maybe it's because I'm so tired. Earlier I pulled the desk chair from my office into the bedroom, and I've been dozing in it on and off for the last few hours, alternating between the worlds of dreams and reality, unable to decipher which is which, equally uncomfortable in both.

The fog surrounding me suddenly lifts. The rain disappears. Everything becomes crystal clear, so clear that I find myself standing right behind the young woman with the slim build and long, dark hair as Narcissus offers her a drink. I can even make out the painted olives decorating the side of her glass as we reach for the drink together. I feel it cold against my fingers.

Narcissus and the woman raise the glasses to their lips, and I feel the liquor burn my throat as they drink it down. He mutters something in her ear; she smiles and mutters something back. Despite our close proximity, I am unable to hear their voices. We listen, but we don't hear, I think. No matter how close we stand to one another, we somehow fail to connect.

The woman is laughing again, and I wonder what Narcissus said that was so funny. He strikes me as too self-absorbed to have much of a sense of humor, but perhaps I'm wrong about that. The young woman seems mesmerized by what he is saying. She is younger than his conquest of the night before, although not quite as pretty. She clicks her glass against his in an impromptu toast. To what? To life, to health and wealth, to people who live in glass houses?

I watch as Narcissus takes the now-empty glass from her hands and deposits it on the table by the window, then wraps her in his arms. I watch him kiss her, his arms moving up her back in a virtual replay of last night's activities. A man who likes routine. I find myself as powerless to look away as I was the night before. I see him unzipping the back of her short red dress. I see it fall to the floor. Shockingly, she is naked beneath it, and I gasp as his hands reach around to clasp her buttocks.

His head snaps up, as if he heard me, and he smiles, as if he knows I'm watching. Does he? Is it possible?

I'm being ridiculous. There's no way he knows I'm here, no way he can see me sitting here in the darkness of my bedroom. But the smirk pulling on his lips taunts me. *I know you're there,* his eyes shout at mine. *I know you're watching.* I drop the binoculars to my lap. There's no way he can see me.

Enough of this nonsense. Enough hiding in the dark, spying on neighbors, no matter how recklessly they choose to display themselves. I'm too exhausted to think clearly, too hungry to function properly. It's time to grab something to eat and get into bed.

But of course I do no such thing.

I see that Narcissus is naked now as well, and I watch a rerun of the same show I saw last night: the woman's bare breasts and stomach pressed against the wide windowpane as the rain picks up its pace, the man's groping hands, their hungry mouths. I watch her eyes close even as his remain open, staring toward me provocatively as he pounds into her from behind. And just like last night, I am as transfixed as I am revolted.

Soon, he is leading her toward the bed. *Has he even changed the sheets?* I wonder as he throws her down and climbs on top of her, lifting her legs toward the ceiling as he thrusts into her again, each thrust a dagger in my groin.

It is almost two o'clock when the lights in his bedroom finally go out. I push myself slowly out of my chair, bathed in sweat. I take another shower, do a final search of my apartment, and climb into bed, beyond tired, desperate for a sleep that never comes.

—

The same scene is repeated again the next night at eight o'clock. And the night after that. I watch Narcissus get ready to go out. He performs virtually the same pre-game ritual each time, choosing between two ties, holding one and then the other up against his shirt, then tossing the unwanted one toward the bed. Some nights his toss is good, and the tie reaches its destination. Other nights, the silk column unfurls in midair and falls to the floor, where it remains, to be trampled on later.

I observe him as he combs his hair and prances half-naked around the room, stopping only to periodically admire his reflection in the mirror before administering whatever final touches are required prior to turning out the lights and leaving his apartment. I watch him return at midnight with a different woman, although they all share similar characteristics. All are reasonably tall and slim, with dark hair that cascades down their backs like a waterfall.

All look vaguely like me.

Or maybe I'm just imagining a resemblance. In fact, maybe I'm imagining the whole thing. It's possible. It's been raining for days. Lots of thunder and lightning. I haven't slept. Or maybe the reverse is true. Maybe sleep is all I've been doing. Maybe none of this is real. Maybe it's all a dream.

The phone rings, and I jump, glancing at the clock. It is seven o'clock on a Saturday night. Who would be calling me? Claire is working the late shift at the hospital; Jade is spending the weekend at a classmate's beach house on Fisher Island; Sean is off cruising the Caribbean; Heath has dropped off the face of the earth; the police haven't called in days.

Caller ID identifies the person on the other end as my friend Sally. She's called several times, and I haven't picked up or returned her calls. I know she means well, but I simply haven't had the energy for her benign chatter. Work is what brought us together, and I don't know that our friendship will survive my prolonged absence. Still, maybe she's phoning to inform me that she had her baby early or that, God forbid, something went wrong. Maybe she's calling to tell me there's been a tragedy at sea, that the cruise ship Sean is on was struck by lightning and has capsized and sunk. Maybe someone else at the office has been beaten and raped. . . .

"Hi," I say, picking up the phone before I'm overwhelmed by maybes.

"Finally," she says, with obvious relief. "You're a hard girl to get a hold of. When are you going to get a new cell phone? Then we can at least text."

"Soon," I say. "Things have been a little hectic."

"Yeah?" she asks hopefully. "Is there anything new . . . ?"

"No," I say. "Nothing."

"Oh." The disappointment in her voice is palpable. "But you're feeling better," she states more than asks. "You sound better."

"I feel better," I say, and if she knows I'm lying, she doesn't let on. "How are *you*?" I ask. If I can't be honest, at least I can be polite. "The baby . . . ?"

"Still cooking. And kicking."

"Good."

"I'm sorry I didn't have a chance to drop by this week. It's been a madhouse at work." Without any prompting, she launches into a story about the high-profile divorce case that the firm just landed.

My attention is diverted by the lights snapping on in the bedroom across the way. I watch as Narcissus strolls into the room, chest bare, pants unbuttoned at the waist. I grab my binoculars and creep toward the window as Sally's voice continues in my ear.

"Anyway, this is all very hush-hush, of course," she is saying, "but guess who hubby's been sleeping with? Bailey? Bailey, come on. Take a guess."

What is she talking about? "What?"

"Didn't you hear me?"

"The firm got this big divorce case. . . ."

"Not just big. Huge. Aurora and Poppy Gomez! We're repping Aurora, thank God. Turns out Poppy's been screwing around on her for years. Can you imagine? The sexiest woman on the planet, not to mention she's sold . . . what? Three *billion* records? And he's this ugly little gnome and he still plays around. I don't get it. What's wrong with these guys? So, are you going to take a guess?"

"At what?"

"At who he's been sleeping with in his South Beach mansion while she's busy touring the universe in order to keep him living in the style to which he's become accustomed?"

"I haven't got a clue."

"Oh, this is just too good. Are you ready?"

"I'm ready," I say, obligingly.

"Little Miss Pop Tart, 'I'm-Saving-It-For-Marriage'—Diana Bishop, herself."

"You're kidding." I utter this as if I'm truly shocked, but the fact is I have no idea who Diana Bishop is and what exactly she's saving for marriage. The name is vaguely familiar, someone I probably knew from my previous life, I think as I watch Narcissus walk toward his window and stare out at the storm, his hand disappearing down the front of his pants.

"Can you imagine? The shit is going to majorly hit the fan in the next couple of days. We've been trying to keep it quiet, but we're already fielding calls from *Entertainment Tonight* and *Inside Edition*. Plus *National Enquirer* is all but camped out in our reception area. *Sources say this; sources say that.* You know how it goes. You can't believe anybody. And we have to dig up as much dirt on Poppy as we can as fast as we can. Dirt we can actually use in court, that is. Which is, of course, where you come in. Turns out Aurora's pre-nup—which our firm didn't draw up; when will they ever learn?—isn't quite as iron-clad as she thought it was. So, any idea when you're coming back to work?"

"What?"

"We could really use your help on this one."

"I can't."

"This request is coming straight from Phil Cunningham himself."

"I'm not ready, Sally."

"You don't think it might be good for you? Getting back in the saddle and all that."

"I can't," I say again. "Not yet. I'm sorry."

"Well, do us both a favor and think about it some more. Okay? It might help get your mind off, you know, stuff."

Stuff. Such a strange word to describe what I've been through.

"Anyway, that's not the only reason I'm calling."

I hold my breath, afraid of what fresh horrors await me. I note that Narcissus is now openly masturbating, his hand working furiously inside his pants, his head lolling from side to side, his jaw slack, his mouth open.

"You're coming to the shower, aren't you?"

"What?"

"I knew it. You forgot all about it, didn't you?"

What is Sally talking about now?

"The baby shower Alissa's throwing for me. Tomorrow night at seven. Her place. You RSVP'd weeks ago. Before . . . ," she says, then breaks off. There's no need to continue. We both know what comes after "before."

"I can't."

"There you go again. Of course you can. It'll be good for you to get out."

It seems Sally has become quite the expert on what is good for me. I bite my tongue to keep from voicing this thought out loud.

"I mean, you just can't stay cooped up in your apartment all day and night. It's not healthy. And this is a joyous occasion, a reason to celebrate. I'm having a baby and you said you'd be there. . . ."

"Before," I remind her, watching Narcissus's frantic exertions come to a satisfied halt.

"Everyone from the office is coming, and Alissa's doing this whole pink theme, on account of the baby being a girl. We've decided to call her Avery. Did I tell you that? Anyway, Alissa's serving pink sandwiches and a pink cake, and you probably don't remember but she even requested all pink presents. Not that you have to buy me anything. Your presence will be present enough." She laughs nervously.

I nod, my head spinning. I watch as Narcissus extricates a tissue from his pocket and wipes his hands.

"So you'll try to make it?"

"I can't. I'm sorry, Sally. I just can't."

Silence. For a minute, I wonder if Sally has hung up, and I'm about to do the same when she speaks. "Okay." Another second's silence. "I understand. Really. I do."

"Thank you."

"We'll miss you."

"I'll miss you, too," I say, the words reminding me of Sean's last visit.

"And while we're on the subject of babies, what do you think about Sean Holden?" she asks brightly, as if my thoughts have somehow prompted hers.

I brace myself as Narcissus turns his head in my direction, a bolt of lightning flashing in the distance. "What are you talking about?"

"Nobody told you? Sean's wife is pregnant!" Sally exclaims as my entire body goes numb. "Nobody's supposed to know yet, of course. But apparently, she blurted the news to Sean's assistant. I can never remember that girl's name. . . ."

"Jillian," I say in a voice not my own.

"That's right. Jillian. Don't know why I can never remember that name. Anyway, she swore Jillian to silence, but word kind of got out once they left on their Caribbean cruise. The first vacation he's taken in years. Can you imagine? Nice to know they're still doing it at their age. Bailey? Bailey, are you there?"

"I have to go." I disconnect before she can utter one more awful word. I stand in front of the window, my eyes closed against the small, hard circles of my binoculars. So this is what Sean came over to tell me. This was the secret behind his eyes.

Another flash of lightning turns the sky from black to white. I see Narcissus standing at his window, a pair of binoculars at his eyes, trained directly at my apartment. I cry out, my body folding in on itself, collapsing forward from the waist in slow motion, as if I've been kicked in the gut. My whole body is on fire.

But when I look back moments later, Narcissus is gone and his apartment is in darkness. I'm left wondering if he was ever there at all.

—

"Of course he was there," Claire is saying. "You saw him, didn't you?"

It's Sunday, around six P.M. Claire has today and tomorrow off from work. She came over so that we can have Sunday night dinner together. Jade won't be back from Fisher Island until later.

"I don't know," I tell her honestly. "It was raining and I was tired and upset. Maybe I imagined it."

"You didn't imagine anything," Claire says. Then: "What were you upset about?"

I begin pacing back and forth in front of my bedroom window.

The rain has finally stopped. The lights in my room are on, the blinds closed. I'm not sure I'll ever open them again. "I'd just heard something. . . ."

"From the police?"

I tell her about Sally's phone call, about Sean's wife being pregnant. I wait for her rebuke: *That's what you get for wasting your time with a married man.* But instead she says, "I'm sorry, Bailey. That must have been so hard for you."

"I feel like such an idiot."

"He's the idiot. You should have called me."

"I'm not going to bother you every time I get upset, especially when you're working. I probably just imagined the whole thing."

"Just because you were upset doesn't mean you were hallucinating," Claire says. "You said you were watching Narcissus, that he was masturbating in front of the window."

I shudder at the memory. "I closed my eyes, and when I opened them again, he was staring right at me."

"Through binoculars."

"Yes."

"Well, if you didn't have your lights on, he couldn't see a damn thing," she assures me, the same thing I've been telling myself repeatedly since last night. It was pitch black in my bedroom. Even with the lightning, there was no way he could have seen me.

"I was so scared."

"Well, no wonder. It's creepy as hell. It would have freaked me out." She looks toward the closed blinds of my window. "No shortage of crazy people in this world, that's for sure."

"Careful. I'm one of them."

"You're not crazy, Bailey. You've been through a highly traumatic ordeal. You're not sleeping. You're having nightmares, experiencing flashbacks. It's only natural that you'd . . ."

". . . be seeing things that aren't there?"

She shrugs and for an instant, I see traces of Jade. "I don't believe that for a second. I think we should call the police."

"What? Why?"

"Tell them what happened."

"Tell them what exactly? That I'm some sort of weird Peeping Tom who may or may not have seen her neighbor masturbating in the privacy of his very own bedroom. . . ."

"It's not exactly private when you do it in front of your window with all the lights on," Claire argues.

"I'm the one spying on him through binoculars! Why do you want me to call the police? What aren't you saying?"

Claire hesitates.

"What?"

"It's probably nothing."

"What?" I say again.

"I don't want to alarm you. . . ."

"For God's sake, just spit it out."

She takes a deep breath and pushes the reluctant words from her mouth. "It can't have escaped your notice that the man you've been watching fits the general description of the man who raped you." She takes another deep breath and holds it, waiting for my reaction.

Of course this hasn't escaped my notice. But I wrote it off as too coincidental, another by-product of my growing paranoia. "You really think it could be him?"

"All I'm saying is that he fits the general description. And he's an exhibitionist and a pervert who lives right across the way. He might have noticed you, liked what he saw, and started following you." She pauses, watching my face for signs her words are sinking in. "I don't know about you, but the more I think about it, the less crazy it sounds and the more worried I get. I'm calling the police."

—

Detective Castillo arrives at my door, along with another uniformed officer he introduces as Officer Dube—"spelled Dube, pronounced Dubie," he explains—some forty minutes later. Detective Marx got married on Friday and is off on her honeymoon. I feel a slight sense of betrayal, not so much that she has deserted me but that she didn't tell me her good news. I wonder if she felt I couldn't handle her happiness.

I note that Officer Dube is tall and slender with reddish blond hair and a tiny scar that wiggles across the bridge of his nose. He looks barely out of his teens. I usher the two men into my living room. Claire and I sit together on one sofa, our hands entwined; the police officers perch on either end of the other, facing us. Claire explains the situation as Detective Castillo, casual as always in a short-sleeved, green-and-white-checkered Brooks Brothers shirt and brown pants, takes notes. "Okay, so just so I have this right: You think this neighbor you saw masturbating last night might be the guy who attacked you."

"That's correct," Claire tells him.

"You were looking through your binoculars," Castillo says to me, then stops abruptly. "Do you mind my asking why?"

"It's just something I do," I explain weakly.

"Often?"

"Force of habit. It was part of my job." Part of who I am.

"But you're not working now."

"No."

"You're missing the point here, Detective," Claire says.

"The point being . . . ?"

"That not only has this man been deliberately parading around naked in front of his window and entertaining an assortment of young women, also naked and on full display," Claire says, "but he was also spying on Bailey. She saw him staring at her last night."

"Through *his* binoculars," Detective Castillo states. "A bit of a coincidence, don't you think?"

"I don't think so at all. Who knows how long he's been spying on her? He knows Bailey is an investigator—he attacked her while she was on surveillance—and he thinks it's fun watching her now, catching up on his handiwork. The only *coincidence,* if you insist on calling it that, is that Bailey inadvertently started watching him as well."

The two officers exchange glances. "You have to admit it's a bit far-fetched."

"I told you we shouldn't have called."

"Are you going to arrest him or not?" Claire asks.

"On what grounds? For looking at his neighbors through binoculars? I'd have to arrest you, too," he tells me.

"Are you at least going to bring him in for questioning?" Claire persists.

"You can't just bring people in for questioning without proper cause. You work for a law firm," he says to me. "You know that." Castillo runs his hand through his hair, clearly exasperated. "All right. Let's have a look."

Claire is immediately on her feet, marching toward my bedroom. The detective and officer follow after her, and I trail after them. "He's home," Claire says, triumphantly. "His lights are on." She grabs the binoculars off my bed and passes them to the police detective. "Three floors from the top, four windows from the left."

"Were the lights in your bedroom on when you were watching him last night?" Officer Dube asks.

"No," Claire and I say together.

"It was dark," I add unnecessarily.

"Then there's no way he could have seen you," Castillo remarks. "I doubt he could even differentiate one apartment from the other, especially with the rain." He sighs and hands the binoculars back to Claire. "Okay. We'll go talk to him."

"Can you do that without letting him know we've been watching him?"

I hear the fear in Claire's voice, and I can't help feel responsible.

"Suppose you leave the police work to us." It's more an order than a request.

The phone rings, and I jump at the sound.

"Aren't you going to get that?" Officer Dube asks after the second ring.

I walk to the phone, lift the receiver to my ear. "Hello, Miss Carpenter?" the voice says, and I feel a familiar dread. "It's Finn, at the concierge desk."

What bad news is he about to deliver? "Yes?"

"Can I speak to that police detective?"

For an instant I wonder how Finn knows the police are here. Then I remember he was the one who called to announce their arrival. I hold the phone out to Detective Castillo.

"Castillo," he says instead of "Hello." Several seconds elapse, then: "When was that? Okay, yes, thank you. What's the suite number again? Okay, yes. Thanks." He hands me back the phone. "It seems that our boy, David Trotter, has resurfaced. I'm afraid the man across the way is going to have to wait."

— FIFTEEN —

This is what happens after the police leave my apartment: Nothing.

Claire and I wait for over an hour, but they don't come back. They don't call. "What do you suppose it means?" I ask Claire.

"It means we should get dinner started," she tells me.

We go to the kitchen where I watch her season the salmon fillets she bought earlier, then peel and slice a bunch of potatoes before smothering them in olive oil and basil and putting them in the oven. I admire her skill, remembering when I, too, used to possess such easy competence. I impulsively decide to make my favorite salad, consisting of watermelon, cucumbers, and feta cheese, a recipe I got from my mother. "That looks delicious," Claire tells me, and I feel a surge of pride.

I set the table in the dining room, deciding to use my good china and favorite linen napkins. What am I saving them for, after all? "How about some wine?" I ask. I haven't touched alcohol of any kind since my attack, although I don't know why. Nobody said I couldn't. Probably Elizabeth Gordon would say that such abstinence has something to do with control and my fear of losing it, of my need to be ever vigilant. Something to talk about in our next session.

"I think a glass of wine is a *great* idea," Claire says. "There just happens to be a very nice California chardonnay in the fridge that I picked up on my way over. . . ."

"You shouldn't have done that."

"You don't like chardonnay?"

"Of course, I like it. That's not the point."

"Then I'm confused," she says. "What *is* the point?"

"The point is that you shouldn't be spending your money on me." I remember Jade telling me that Claire worries a lot about money. "You keep bringing over food and groceries. You buy me magazines and now wine. . . ."

"The wine's not just for you."

"I know that, but . . ."

"But what?"

"You shouldn't."

"Why shouldn't I?"

"Because it's not right."

"Why isn't it right?"

"Claire," I say, sighing in frustration. We're going around in circles.

"Bailey," she says in return, tired eyes sparkling.

"You work too hard for your money," I tell her. "I don't want you spending it on me."

"You're my sister," she reminds me. "And you're going through a difficult time right now. Relax, Bailey. It's not going to last forever. Pretty soon you'll start feeling stronger. You'll go back to work. You'll get your life in order. You won't need me to come around so often."

"What if I want you to come around?"

"Then I will," Claire says with a smile. "And I'll bring the wine. Now get the bottle out of the fridge, find me some wineglasses, and let's get this show on the road." I bring her the bottle, and she twists open the top while I locate a couple of wine-glasses in the cupboard over the sink. "Amazing," she marvels, pouring us each a glass. "You don't even need a corkscrew any-more. The miracle of modern technology." I raise the glass to my lips, about to take a sip when she stops me. "Wait. We have to make a toast."

Instantly I picture Narcissus and his various conquests toasting each other with martinis. I wonder what the police are doing, if they've questioned him yet or whether they've decided not to bother. I know that if they do question him, it is strictly to mollify me, to satisfy what they undoubtedly perceive as my growing paranoia. I'm aware of the veiled glances and raised eyebrows that passed between Detective Castillo and Officer Dube. I know that they view me as a pathetic hysteric, a woman unhinged by what happened to her. *Am* I paranoid? Are they right?

"To brighter days ahead," Claire says, clinking her glass against mine.

"To brighter days," I mimic, taking a tentative sip of the smooth yellow-gold liquid and watching her do the same.

"Mmm. Good stuff," she says.

Stuff, I repeat silently, inhaling the intoxicating combination of apple-cinnamon and tropical fruit, a mixture of butter and oak lingering on my tongue. At least Claire doesn't think I'm paranoid. "To sisters," I say.

"To sisters." Her eyes fill with unexpected tears, and she turns away, swiping at her cheeks with the back of her free hand. "I al-most forgot. I have something to show you." She picks up her floppy brown leather purse from the floor next to the counter and rifles through it, her hand emerging seconds later with a white envelope. "For your amusement," she says, handing it to me.

"What's this?" I take another sip of my wine before lowering my glass to the counter. Then I open the unsealed envelope and pull out three photographs. At first I think I'm looking at pictures of Jade. Then I realize it's not Jade, but her mother, taken some sixteen years ago. Her hair is longer than it is now and is secured behind one ear by a spray of plastic lilacs. She is wearing a short white satin dress that is neither stylish nor flattering, but the resemblance to Jade is startling. Even more startling is the man standing beside her. The man is Elvis Presley. "Oh, my God. Is this . . . ?"

"My wedding pictures, as promised. That's the Elvis impersonator who married us, and this," she says, indicating the sullenfaced youth wearing a leather jacket and jeans who is standing beside her in the remaining two photographs, "this is Eliot. Notice the beady little eyes and the nasty, self-satisfied expression."

Claire isn't being cruel. Nor is she exaggerating. It's hard to miss either the groom's eyes or his expression. The cat who not only swallowed the canary but chewed it up. "A weasel," I hear my father shout from beyond the grave. "What's the matter with that girl? She married a goddamn weasel. Can't she see he only married her to get at her inheritance?" As usual, he was right. Eliot does look like a weasel, and he did marry her for her projected inheritance, an inheritance that my father, in keeping with his earlier threats, then revoked. It's hard now to understand what Claire saw in the rodent-faced young man, so profoundly different is he from our handsome, charismatic father. Unless that's exactly what she found so attractive.

But Eliot is long gone, and I have the power to return to Claire at least a portion of her birthright. I wonder if Heath would be agreeable, if he'd even entertain the possibility of sharing part of our estate. Would he consent to a meeting with our half-siblings in an effort to settle the lawsuit hanging over all our heads, a lawsuit that keeps us stuck in a past full of old grievances, that prevents us from moving forward, from getting on with our lives, as Sean has suggested? Of course, Sean has already moved on with *his* life. And my brother has vanished into thin air, as is his frequent wont. Where the hell is he? Why hasn't he called?

"You notice how neither the bride nor the groom is smiling," Claire remarks.

"At least Elvis looks happy," I remark.

"I'll drink to that," she says.

And we do.

—

It is almost two hours later. We have finished our dinner and are halfway through our second bottle of wine when the phone rings. I jump at the sound and drop my knife. It hits the marble floor and disappears underneath the dining room table.

"My mother used to say that, according to ancient superstition, when you drop a knife it means a man is coming over," Claire says, and I shudder, struggling to retrieve the knife and almost falling off my chair in the process. Maybe if I pick it up fast enough, the man, whoever he may be, will be persuaded to stay away.

"I'll answer it." Claire pushes back her chair and heads into the kitchen. I notice a slight wobble to her gait. "Hello?" she says. "Okay. Good. Yes, you can send them up. Thank you. That was Stanley, from the concierge desk," she announces as she returns to the room. "Seems the police are on their way back up."

I stagger to my feet. I've had way too much to drink and the room is spinning. I grab the table to keep from falling over. *This is not good*, I think as both Claire and I move unsteadily toward the door.

"Gentlemen," I say as I usher the two officers into the apartment moments later. I can smell wine on my breath, and I can see by the sudden twitch of Detective Castillo's nose that he has detected it, too. Not just a paranoid hysteric, he is thinking. But a drunk, as well.

"Sorry to be getting back to you this late," he says politely, his words belying the thinly veiled disapproval in his eyes.

How late is it? I glance at my wrist, although I'm not wearing a watch. In fact, I haven't worn one since the night I was attacked. What difference does it make what time it is? Time has all but stopped.

"We wanted to give you an update." A look of fear fills the

detective's face. He takes a step back, points toward my right hand. "Is that a knife?"

I look down, see the knife I'm holding, and laugh. "Your mother was right," I say to Claire. "She said that when you drop a knife," I explain to the officers, "it means a man is coming over."

"I'm not sure I understand," Officer Dube says.

"Suppose you give me that," says Detective Castillo.

"It's not very sharp." I'm giggling as I hand it over. "Smells of salmon."

"I see you've had a few," Castillo remarks.

"California's finest," I say as Claire lifts a finger to her pursed lips, warning me to keep quiet. "Would you like some?" I ask anyway, disregarding her signal. It's not like Claire to be such a stick-in-the-mud.

"No, thank you. We're still on duty."

"Did you talk to David Trotter?" Claire asks.

I struggle to remember who David Trotter is, why his name seems so familiar.

"We did. It seems his mother suffered a stroke the night of the incident in the gym," Castillo begins.

What has any of this to do with me? What incident in what gym, and what has David Trotter's mother got to do with anything?

"She lives up in Palm Beach, and he took off as soon as he heard the news, didn't get back till tonight. That's why we've been unable to locate him."

"Did you question him about Bailey?" Claire asks.

"We did. He claims he was attending some big dinner with at least half a dozen potential investors on the night Bailey was attacked."

"Do you believe him?"

"We'll check out his alibi. As well as the story about his mother."

"How is she?" I ask.

The detective looks surprised by my question. "I believe he said she's recovering nicely."

"Glad to hear it." I feel my body begin to sway. Nice to hear that someone is recovering nicely.

"Maybe we should sit down," Claire says.

"What about Narcissus?" I ask.

"Who?" both policemen ask together.

"The man who's been staring at me through his binoculars," I explain, impatiently.

"The man we talked to is named Paul Giller," Officer Dube says, checking his notes. "What did you just call him?"

"Narcis . . . ," I begin.

"It's the name we gave him because he spends so much time looking in the mirror," Claire explains.

"You know, the old Greek myth," I add as Officer Dube rolls his eyes and Detective Castillo shakes his head.

"What did this Paul Giller have to say for himself?" Claire asks.

"Well, you understand we had to be careful. You can't just come out and tell a man you suspect him of rape without pretty substantial evidence to back you up, which we obviously don't have. Also, if he is our man, we don't want to go tipping our hand before we acquire that evidence."

"What did he say, Detective?" Claire asks again, as I lean back against the nearest wall. My head is starting to clear. A dull headache is waiting behind my eyes. "Does he have an alibi for the night my sister was attacked?"

"We didn't get into that."

"What do you mean? Wasn't that the whole point of going over there? What exactly did you say to the man?"

"We told him that we'd had a few complaints from neighbors who claimed to have seen him staring through binoculars. . . ."

"And?"

"He denied it. Said they must be mistaken, that he doesn't even own a pair of binoculars."

"Well, of course he'd say that."

"He offered to let us search the apartment," Officer Dube says, as if this ends the discussion once and for all.

"And did you?" Claire asks.

"No," Castillo says. "We'd made our point."

"What exactly *was* your point, pray tell?"

"That spying on your neighbors with binoculars could land you in court as a Peeping Tom," he says. "A point you ladies would do well to remember."

"And that's it? That's the end of your investigation?"

"No. We'll run a background check on this Paul Giller, find out what he does for a living, if he has a record, that sort of thing. But other than that, there's really not much else we can do. Unless you're ready to make a positive identification . . . ," he adds, looking at me.

I shake my head, watch the room tilt dangerously on its side.

"You're sure you had the right apartment?" Claire asks.

"Suite 2706. Third floor from the top, four windows from the left," Officer Dube says, once again referring to his notes. "That's the information you gave us. Is it incorrect?"

"Third floor from the top, four windows from the left. That's right."

"Then I'm sorry," Castillo says. "But unless you can come up with something more substantial, our hands are pretty much tied."

"I understand," I say, and I do. That's why there are private investigators, I think, people like me, who are under no such restrictions. Except that I am no longer a person like me. "Thanks for bringing us up to date."

"We'll keep you posted if there are any new developments."

I open the door. The men step into the corridor. Detective Castillo stops, hands me back my knife.

"Put this away," he says.

I take the knife and shut the door.

"I need a drink," Claire says.

—

"Oh my God. Would you just look at this!" Claire is laughing. We're sitting on the floor of my walk-in closet, our legs extended out in front of us, a box full of old photographs emptied around us, surrounding our bodies like an old-fashioned crinoline. "Look at my hair!"

"I think you look sweet."

"You're drunk."

"Yes, I am." I grab another handful of pictures, personal items left to me and Heath after our father died, although Heath showed little interest in any of the photographs he wasn't in. There are several old scrapbooks as well, filled with snapshots from our father's previous two marriages, photos of Claire squeezed between her parents, her mother's stomach swollen with baby Gene, of both children gazing adoringly at their father as their father gazes at something off in the distance.

I open another album and see my half-brothers Thomas, Richard, and Harrison spring to life, and I follow their development from infancy through adolescence. There's even a picture of Gene as a teenager in full football regalia. I notice the resemblance between wives number one and two, how different they were from my mother.

"They look so sad, don't they?" Claire states, the same sadness radiating through her own eyes.

I want to hug her, but I don't. Instead, I push myself to my feet and begin searching through the drawers of my built-in cabinets.

"What are you doing?" she asks.

I finally locate what I'm looking for in the bottom drawer: a stack of unused checkbooks. I grab one, then begin searching for a pen.

"What are you doing?" Claire asks again.

I find one at the back of the drawer and quickly write out a check. "For you," I say, handing it to her as I plop back down on the floor, harder than I should, although all the alcohol in my system cushions the fall.

"What's this?"

"I want you to have it."

"It's ten thousand dollars! I can't take this." Claire tries to push the check back into my hand.

"It's the least I can do after all you've done for me."

"You've had too much to drink, Bailey," she cautions. "You don't know what you're doing."

"I know exactly what I'm doing," I tell her. "Consider it an advance."

"What does that mean?"

What *does* it mean? That I'm seriously considering settling my half-siblings' lawsuit, dividing up the family fortune? Shouldn't I be discussing this with Heath first?

"I think you'd better talk this over with Heath," Claire says, echoing my thoughts. She drops the check into my lap.

"It's not fair that you worry about money," I protest.

"Who says I worry . . . ? Oh. Jade's been telling tales out of school, I gather."

"She just said sometimes you worry."

"We're doing fine, Bailey. I have a steady job. Gene helps out whenever he can. He's paying for that fancy private school she goes to, the one with the classmates whose parents can afford beach homes on Fisher Island."

"But our father made provisions for Jade's education. . . ."

"*College* education," Claire reminds me. "Who knows if that's ever going to happen."

"It'll happen," I state with absolute certainty. About the only thing I'm sure of these days is that Jade will one day make us proud. Once again, I hold out the check. "Please . . . take it."

Claire hesitates, then sighs and tucks the check into the side pocket of her pants. "But I'm not going to cash it, in case you change your mind when you sober up."

"I won't change my mind."

Tears fill her eyes for the second time tonight. This time she makes no effort to turn away. "I don't know what to say."

"You don't have to say anything."

Claire reaches over and takes me in her arms, hugs me close. I feel safe, as if I've come home at last. Then her cell phone rings, and I jump and pull away. It's Jade, calling to report that she's back from Fisher Island. "I should go," Claire says.

"Wait. Take these with you." I gather up the photo albums and stray snapshots of my half-siblings and follow her out of the closet into the bedroom. The lights are on, the blinds down. "You can divide these with Gene and the others."

She takes them from me. "Thank you. For everything."

"Thank *you*. For more."

Claire is almost at the bedroom door when she stops and turns around, her eyebrows arching playfully. "What do you say? One last peek, for old time's sake?" I hang back as she drops the photos to the bed, then presses the button that turns off the lights, followed by the one that opens the blinds. She grabs my binoculars and approaches the window. "Doesn't look like he's home," she says after a pause of several seconds. "Oh, well. It's probably for the best." She gathers up the photographs again and walks into the hall, hugging me when we reach the door. I melt into her arms. "I'll call you tomorrow."

I feel words forming in my mouth, approaching the tip of my tongue. But Claire opens the door before I can give them a voice. The door closes behind her, and I watch through the peephole as she walks down the corridor. "I love you," I whisper, my words trailing after her. She stops suddenly and turns around, as if she heard me. She gives a little wave, walks into the waiting elevator, and is gone.

—

The light in Paul Giller's apartment is on when I return to my bedroom. Holding my breath, I grab my binoculars and march to the window. Through small circles of glass, I see a man and a woman moving awkwardly around the room. I glance back at the clock beside my bed, the numbers illuminated in red. Not even eleven o'clock, too early for the man I think of as Narcissus to be home. Although perhaps now that he is just ordinary Paul Giller, he's moved everything up an hour.

Except something else is different as well.

It's the woman. I adjust and then readjust my lens in an effort to bring her into sharper focus. This woman is noticeably plainer than the women I've seen him with all week, and her hair is both shorter and lighter. And far from hanging all over her, Paul Giller is standing on the other side of the room, fully dressed and flipping through the pages of a magazine.

What's going on?

It's then that I notice a suitcase open on the bed. Is he going somewhere? Has tonight's visit by the police prompted him to take off for a few days, in much the same way David Trotter took off earlier in the week? I wonder if Paul Giller also has a mother who's conveniently been rushed to the hospital.

Paul looks up from his magazine as the woman walks to the bed and starts removing items from the suitcase: a denim jacket, then a blouse, then another blouse, followed by a pair of jeans and a peasant skirt, then a pair of flat shoes. Casual attire, for the most part. Nothing particularly exciting. No frilly nightgowns or racy underwear. I watch the woman disappear into the closet and come back with a handful of hangers. She hangs up the skirt, jeans, and jacket, then returns them to the closet. She drops the blouses into a laundry basket located on the far side of the bed. She deposits the shoes in a shoe bag that hangs on the inside of the closet door. She is obviously comfortable in this space. She belongs here.

His wife? I zero in on her hands, trying to make out the presence of a gold band on the appropriate finger. But I'm too far away. I can't be sure.

Experience tells me she's probably his wife and she's been away all week, leaving Paul alone to morph into Narcissus and indulge his most wanton fantasies. Does she have any clue who he is when she's not around? Would she care if she did?

She goes into their en suite bathroom and closes the door. Paul promptly strips down to his briefs and climbs into bed. This time there is no preening in front of the mirror, no parading nude in front of the window, no spying on my apartment through binoculars. Maybe the police warning scared him. Maybe, as he told them, he doesn't even own binoculars. Maybe I imagined the whole thing, as Detective Castillo and Officer Dube have no doubt decided.

Paul flips lazily through the pages of his magazine as his wife, if that's who she is, returns to the bedroom, wearing a delicate pink lace negligee. She's brushed her hair and made an effort to look pretty. But Paul doesn't seem to notice until she moves to turn off the light. He raises his hand to stop her, indicating with a visible degree of annoyance the magazine he is reading.

I watch Paul's wife pull back the covers and crawl into bed beside him. She leans back against the headboard, glancing anxiously toward her husband, as if willing him to stop what he is doing and take her in his arms. After several minutes, she decides to take the initiative, her hand moving tentatively to stroke his thigh. He lowers his magazine and shakes his head. "It's late, I'm tired," I can almost hear him say. She nods and removes her hand, sitting in silence for several minutes before scooting down in the bed and pulling the blanket up over her head to block out the light. Or maybe to hide her tears. Even through the covers, her shame is palpable.

Less than five minutes later, Paul, alias Narcissus, tosses his magazine to the floor and stretches to turn off the light. I am left in the dark, nursing the image of Paul's wife with the blanket covering her head. I feel a pillowcase being dragged over my face, my own shame spreading throughout my bloodstream and racing toward my heart.

—SIXTEEN—

The phone rings at just before seven o'clock the next morning.

The sound jolts me awake, although I can't even remember climbing into bed last night, let alone falling asleep. Obviously I did both at some point. I have vague memories of sharks swimming menacingly beneath my feet, of faceless men extending gloved hands toward me, of passive women watching me from distant balconies. My head is pounding and the leftover taste of wine lies flat across my tongue, an unpleasant reminder of all the alcohol I consumed last night. "Hello?" I whisper, pressing the phone to my ear, and then again, despite the busy signal that greets me: "Hello?" I say it a third time. "Is somebody there?"

I drop the phone and flop back onto my pillow, dozing off again for approximately another hour until a shrill ring once again shakes me into consciousness, like a hand on my shoulder. This time I think to check the caller ID. *Unknown caller.* "Heath?" I say, instead of hello, the dull throb of my hangover pushing against the insides of my eyes. "Heath, is that you?" There is no answer, and I'm about to disconnect, to dismiss this latest call the way I did the first, as nothing more than an early morning extension of my nightmares, when I hear the sound of breathing.

The voice, when it comes, is low and filled with dust, like tires on a gravel-filled road. "Tell me you love me," it growls in my ear.

I scream and drop the phone, watching as it bounces across the floor toward the bathroom, coming to a stop on the marble tile of the bathroom floor. "No," I cry, falling to my knees beside my bed. "No, no, no, no."

The phone rings again almost immediately. Once . . . twice . . . three times . . . four, each ring a dagger thrusting into my chest. If the phone doesn't stop ringing, I will die.

It stops, and only then am I able to breathe, although just barely. Hands shaking, I crawl to where the phone is lying on its back on the bathroom floor, like an upturned insect. I glance at the caller ID, expecting to see the familiar words: *Unknown caller.* Instead I see *Carlito's on Third,* followed by a number. Who or what is "Carlito"? What does this mean? I quickly press in the number for *Carlito's on Third.* It's picked up immediately. "Hello," I say before anyone can speak.

Tell me you love me, a gravelly voice whispers lewdly.

"No!" Immediately I drop the phone and burst into tears.

Seconds later, the phone rings again. *Carlito's on Third,* caller ID boldly proclaims, and again I don't answer, listening as it rings four times before being transferred to voice mail. "You have two new messages," voice mail informs me seconds later. "To listen to your messages, press 1." I do as instructed. "First new message."

"Hi. This is Johnny K. from Carlito's Auto Repair," a voice informs me. "I'm just calling to tell you that the work has been completed on your Porsche, and you can come by to pick it up any time." He leaves a number where he can be reached.

"Oh, God." I'm overwhelmed by a fresh onslaught of tears. What does this mean?

Tell me you love me.

"Second new message," voice mail continues as I try to separate fantasy from reality.

"Hi. This is Jasmine from Carlito's Auto Repair," a woman is saying. "Did you just call here? I think we got cut off." She leaves the same contact number.

I call back. Again, the line is picked up before the first ring is complete. This time I give the person on the other end time to speak. "Carlito's on Third. Jasmine speaking. How can I direct your call?"

"Can I speak to Johnny?" I ask.

"Johnny K. or Johnny R.?"

"What?"

"Johnny R. or Johnny K.?" she says, reversing the order.

"I'm not sure. Wait." I replay the earlier message in my head: *This is Johnny K. from Carlito's Auto Repair.* "Johnny K.," I say, louder than I intended. I picture the poor woman pushing the phone away from her ear to escape the sound of my voice.

"Did you call here a few minutes ago?" she asks.

"I think we got cut off," I lie.

"Sounded like somebody yelled 'No!' or something. It was weird."

"Really? That *is* weird."

"Hold on and I'll connect you to Johnny."

A brief interlude of salsa music follows. "This is Johnny Kroft."

The same voice as on my voice mail. Nothing like that other voice.

"This is Bailey Carpenter. I believe you phoned about my car."

"Right. The silver Porsche."

"That's the one."

"Yeah, sorry for calling so early. I wanted to catch you before you left for work."

"At seven o'clock this morning?"

"Seven? No. It was only about ten minutes ago."

Ten minutes ago, I repeat silently. "You said my car is ready?"

"Yep. There was a pretty deep scratch across the hood and one of the headlights was damaged, plus there were a few minor dents along the driver's side that we took care of. Bill comes to four thousand seven hundred dollars and twenty-six cents."

Tell me you love me.

"What?"

"Sorry. I know it's a lot," Johnny Kroft apologizes.

What's happening?

"But what can you do?" he asks. "It's a Porsche, right? Expensive car, expensive repair bill."

"What did you just say to me?"

Tell me you love me.

"What did I just say to you?" he repeats. " 'Expensive car, expensive repair bill'?" he asks, as if he's not sure. "I'm sorry. I don't mean to be flip. Of course it's a lot of money. . . ."

"You didn't just tell me to . . . ?" I stop. Obviously he said nothing of the sort. We're operating in two different realities. My reality is that I'm stark raving mad. "So my car is ready to be picked up?"

"Anytime you're ready to stop by." He gives me the address, at the corner of Third Street and Northwest 1st Avenue, within walking distance of my condo. I tell him I'll drop by sometime this morning. He says he'll look forward to showing me exactly what was done, adding that he thinks I'll be pleased.

Tell me you love me.

I hang up. But the words tunnel into my brain: *Tell me you love me. Tell me you love me. Tell me you love me.* They follow me into the shower. *Tell me you love me. Tell me you love me.* "You are officially off your rocker," I acknowledge, pulling my wet hair into a ponytail as I emerge from the shower and get dressed— baggy white jeans and a loose black jersey top—before opening the blinds and staring toward Paul Giller's apartment. Even without my binoculars I can see Paul and his wife moving about their bedroom. They are dressed—he in a casual shirt and jeans, she in some kind of uniform, like the kind my dental hygienist wears. They pass each other in front of their bed without touching.

The phone rings, and I jump. "Hello?"

"It's Claire. Did I wake you?"

"No. I'm up." I don't tell her that I've been up since seven, when the first phone call of the morning jolted me rudely awake, because I'm no longer sure of any such thing. I remind myself that Claire and I drank almost two bottles of wine last night and that the alcohol is still in my system, no doubt causing me to hear things that aren't there. There were no phone calls from the man who raped me, no voices commanding me to say anything. The only calls I got were from Carlito's Auto Repair. Everything else is a product of my paranoid, alcohol-soaked brain. "My car's ready," I tell Claire. "I was just going to walk over and pick it up."

"Please tell me you aren't planning to drive it home." She doesn't wait for me to answer. "I'll be right over."

"No, Claire. It's your day off. You're supposed to be relaxing and taking it easy. . . ."

"Don't argue," she says. "I've always wanted to drive a Porsche."

She hangs up and I return to the window. *It can't have escaped your notice that the man you've been watching fits the description of the man who raped you,* Claire said. Is it possible?

Just who is Paul Giller anyway?

Seconds later, I'm in the next room, leaning over my desk and accessing my computer. I haven't so much as glanced at my Mac in weeks. My hands hover over the keyboard, shaking. This is who you are, I remind myself. This is what you do. And if you don't start doing something soon, something concrete, you will never regain your sanity.

I google the name "Paul Giller."

My computer screen immediately fills with more than a dozen listings. I dismiss several of these immediately. Two are for a photographer named Paul Giller who lives in Texas, another for a Paul Giller who, at a hundred and six, is Ohio's oldest living resident. But the next five are for a Paul Giller who lives right here in Miami, a Paul Giller whose row of handsome headshots closely resembles the man who lives across the way. An actor, according to his Internet Movie Database profile. *More at IMDbPro,* the listing informs me. *Contact info; View agent; Add or change photos.* I wonder if Heath knows him.

In minutes, I learn his middle name (Timothy), his date of birth (March 12, 1983), his birthplace (Buffalo, New York), that he was the son of a highly respected, now-deceased symphony conductor (Andrew Giller), and that he has his very own website (www.paulgiller.com). I check it immediately.

It contains a short biography, a list of contact numbers for agents, all of which I jot down, and his résumé (bit parts in several locally shot movies and a minor, although recurring, role in a now-canceled TV series that was shot in L.A. several years ago.)

His brief bio informs me he is six feet one, and 190 pounds. Experience has taught me to automatically subtract two inches and add ten pounds, but in Paul Giller's case, the description seems accurate. According to his bio, he also spent some time in Nashville, where he recorded an album, now available on iTunes. (I can sample a selection, if I so choose, which I don't.) Also listed are a few commercials, mostly local.

Again, the disconcerting thought enters my mind that he might know Heath. Could there be a connection between them? "Don't be ridiculous," I say out loud, suddenly angry, although I'm not sure why. I quit Paul Giller's site and log onto Facebook.

Since I'm not an official "friend" of Paul's, I have limited access to his page. What I *am* permitted to view is more photographs of the man, some serious, some smiling, some in profile, a few without a shirt. There are no pictures of him with anyone else, male or female, no photographs of the woman I saw him with last night and this morning or any of the women I saw him with last week. There is no mention anywhere of a wife.

According to the half dozen "get well soon" messages I see posted on the part of his wall to which I'm granted access, I gather that Paul Giller recently spent a few days in the hospital with a virulent strain of pneumonia. If he was in the hospital the night I was attacked, that would obviously eliminate him as a suspect.

I click out of Facebook and phone the number for Paul's agent.

"You have reached the offices of Reed, Johnson, and Associates, representing the finest talent Miami has to offer," the recorded female voice announces. "The office is now closed. If you want to leave a message for Selma Reed, press 1. If you want to leave a message for Mark Johnson, press 2. If you want to . . ."

"I don't want to," I say, hanging up the phone and returning to my bedroom. What was I thinking? Of course the office is closed. It's barely eight thirty in the morning.

I move to the window, grabbing my binoculars. Paul and the woman are still in their bedroom, still largely ignoring one another, careful to avoid contact as they move about the small room. The woman reaches into her purse for her lipstick and applies it without looking in the mirror, then she marches purposefully from the room, Paul following right behind.

Where are they going?

The woman's clothes indicate that she's dressed for work, as does the hour. Paul's clothes tell me nothing. Where is he off to, so early in the morning?

Before I can think twice about what I'm doing, before I even *know* what I'm doing, I'm racing down the hall of my apartment, grabbing my purse, and heading out the door. If I stop to think, even for one minute, I will stop this craziness and return to the safety of my bed.

Except I'm going crazy there as well.

The elevator arrives within seconds of my pressing the call button, and I am about to step inside when I see a man standing off to the right. He is tall and heavyset, with graying hair and a nose that is too narrow for his wide-set eyes. My knees almost buckle with relief. He is not the man who raped me.

Although, can I really be sure?

"Going my way?" he asks with a smile.

I hesitate only briefly before my investigator's instinct pushes me inside. This is what you do. This is who you are. And the only way to regain control of your life is by taking it. If the police lack the authority to investigate Paul Giller, I lack no such power. If there are rules against them tailing him without sufficient so-called cause, I am under no such restrictions.

I can follow him at will. No one can stop me.

The elevator stops on the twentieth floor and a middle-aged man and woman step inside. They smile. There's nothing to be afraid of. You're getting better, taking control. These are my thoughts as the elevator makes another stop, this time on the fourteenth floor.

The doors open and David Trotter steps inside.

I cry out, everyone turning toward me as I back into the corner. I will myself to disappear, but it is too late. David Trotter has already seen me. He is staring right at me.

"What the hell is your problem?" he demands as the elevator doors close behind him. "What have I ever done to you?"

"Please leave me alone."

"Leave *you* alone? My mother had a stroke, for God's sake! She's in the hospital up in Palm Beach, I have to drive all the way up there, I don't sleep for days, and I come home to find the police on my doorstep. . . ."

"I'm sorry. It was all a misunderstanding. . . ."

"You bet it was."

"Please . . ."

"Take it easy," the gray-haired man advises.

"I was trying to help you!"

"It was a mistake."

"Relax, mister," the woman says. "You're scaring her."

"Scaring her? The bitch accused me of rape!"

"Oh, God." I feel myself sinking to the floor as the elevator comes to a stop on the ground floor, its doors opening into the sun-filled lobby.

"Just stay the hell away from me," David Trotter warns, the index finger of his right hand pointing at me like a gun. Then he turns and exits the elevator.

"Can I help you, Miss?" the gray-haired man is asking, his hand extended toward me.

I shake my head as I scramble to my feet. Then I push past him out the elevator. "What was that all about?" I hear somebody ask as I hurtle past the concierge desk.

"Miss Carpenter," another voice calls out, but I don't stop.

Minutes later, I find myself standing outside Paul Giller's building. I'm not sure exactly what I intend to do, but I most definitely intend to do something.

—

The building in which Paul Giller lives—and in front of whose ornate wrought-iron-and-glass-paneled doors I am currently standing—is several stories taller than the one in which I live and more austerely modern in appearance. Or maybe it's just more austere. The lobby is white on white—white marble walls and floors, a single white sofa, fake white flowers reaching toward the high ceiling from a tall white porcelain vase that stands in a corner. Not nearly enough furniture for the space, which is perhaps indicative of the building itself, which has remained more than half-empty since it was completed. Originally intended as a luxury condominium complex, much like mine, construction was already well under way when the economy suddenly tanked. Owners fled in droves. Prices dropped precipitously. Buyers dried up, then disappeared altogether.

The builders regrouped, deciding to rent out the remaining units, although judging by the large signs that hang along the exterior walls—LUXURY UNITS FOR RENT BY THE MONTH. NO LONG-TERM LEASE REQUIRED—they've had only limited success. I note that there is no concierge and that a resident directory is posted just inside the lobby doors. I open them—they are lighter, less substantial than they appear—and approach the directory, locating Paul Giller's name and the number of his apartment. I also note there is a building manager, but when I press his number—drawing up a list of questions in my head to ask him—there is no answer.

Which is when I see them.

They are walking side by side across the lobby, and while they aren't touching, they seem friendly enough. Friendlier, certainly, than they were moments ago in their apartment. He's leaning toward her, and she's smiling at something clever he's said. Perhaps he apologized for last night's boorish behavior on the elevator ride down, spoke the words she needed to hear. Who knows? We see what we want to see. We hear what we want to hear.

Not always, I remind myself.

Tell me you love me.

I spin around. A man brushes past me, his shoulder slamming into mine as he hurries outside, as if I'm invisible.

I no longer have any sense of myself, I realize, panicking as my reflection in a nearby square of glass disappears in a sudden streak of sunlight. I no longer know what is real and what is imaginary. I no longer know who I am.

Except I *do* know. I'm a private investigator. And I'm doing what I do best: I'm watching.

I lower my head as Paul Giller and his wife, if that's who she is, stride past me, almost close enough to touch, then exit the building. I watch as they approach the curb and wait to cross the street with the lights.

The same impulse that brought me here compels me to follow them.

They still haven't noticed me, and I'm careful to stay a safe distance behind them. They stop at the next corner, then kiss briefly before going their separate ways. I hesitate, not sure whom to follow. But the choice is made easy when Paul hails a passing cab and climbs inside, disappearing into the morning rush hour traffic. Mrs. Paul, as I have chosen to think of her, continues on by foot.

I scramble to catch up to her.

The neighborhood is a curious mix of old and new, of tall glass high-rises and single-story specialty shops, of sophisticated restaurants and rickety fruit juice stands, of the ethnic and the home-grown, all existing side by side, interwoven and inseparable, although not always compatible. And while English is considered the official language of the financial district, it's mostly Spanish one sees and hears.

But this morning I see and hear nothing. I am aware only of a woman in a pale blue uniform walking briskly down the street, her arms swinging at her sides.

I am only a few steps behind her when she stops suddenly and

swings around. I brace myself for a confrontation. "Are you following me?"

Except she does no such thing. Instead, she approaches a shop
window to take in a display of neon-colored shoes. I wait, holding
my breath. After a few moments of staring wistfully at a pair of
outrageously high-heeled, raspberry-and-purple pumps, she steps
away from the window. I squat down on one knee, pretend to be
tying my shoelace, although if Mrs. Paul were to take a good look,
she'd notice the flip-flops I'm wearing have no laces. I push myself
unsteadily to my feet as Mrs. Paul continues on her way.

A young man brushes past me with such speed that he almost
knocks me over. *"Scuse,"* he mumbles over his shoulder, continuing on his way without stopping, even as I spin around, hands
shooting out in front of me, my body tipping toward the concrete
of the sidewalk. Luckily, other hands reach out to prevent my fall.
One hand brushes against the side of my breast.

I slap it away, recoiling as if I've been shot.

"Take it easy," a middle-aged man says, lifting his hands into
the air as if someone is pointing a gun at his back. He shakes his
head and walks away, mumbling.

"Are you all right?" a woman asks warily.

"Yes," I say, and then, as she is walking away, "Thank you."

But if she hears me, she gives no sign. I lose her in the crowd.

I have lost Mrs. Paul as well. I spin around, looking in all directions, but she is nowhere to be found.

I am as much relieved as disappointed. What did I hope to
achieve by following her?

It's better this way, I tell myself, deciding to talk to Paul Giller's
building manager instead, glean any information I might need
from him.

And then, of course, there she is.

As I am turning around, I catch my reflection in the front window of a hairdressing salon, just opening for business. And there
she is behind the reception counter, alongside another young
woman, this one with long curly dark hair and huge hoop earrings. They are laughing. I push open the door, a cold blast of air-

conditioning raining down on my head from the overhead vents. The women continue their conversation, ignoring me as I approach.

"So who's my first appointment?" Mrs. Paul is asking the woman with the giant hoop earrings.

The other woman checks her computer screen. "Loreta De Sousa, in half an hour."

Mrs. Paul's shoulders slump visibly. "Shit. What a way to start the week. She's never happy with the color she chooses. Never has the patience to sit still and let her nails dry properly. Then she smudges them, and insists I do them all again. Shit."

So, not a dental assistant after all. A beautician.

"Excuse me," I venture.

Two sets of startled eyes turn toward me.

"Can I help you?" the woman with the giant hoop earrings asks.

I look directly at Mrs. Paul. "I'd like a manicure."

— SEVENTEEN —

The salon is clean and modern, with white walls, black sinks, and burgundy leather swivel chairs, mirrors everywhere. And even though it is first thing on a Monday morning, when many hairdressing salons remain closed, this place is bustling. There are already a handful of clients present, one woman chattering away while getting her hair washed, her head thrown back to expose her jugular, another whose eyes are closed and whose head is completely covered with strips of aluminum foil, and another talking into her cell phone and thumbing through a celebrity tabloid while her stylist, a slim-hipped young man with pink-highlighted, platinum hair and tight, leopard-print pants, flits around her head with a pair of scissors, like a giant gnat.

"Sorry we don't have enough time for a pedicure, too. I have this client coming in half an hour," Mrs. Paul says.

"Loreta De Sousa."

"What?" She stops, spins around, brown eyes widening with alarm. "You know her?"

"I heard you mention her name when I walked in."

Mrs. Paul sighs with relief, then shakes her head in obvious dismay. "Sorry about that. Never good business for one client to hear the staff bad-mouthing another. Tabatha would be horrified."

"Tabatha? Is she the owner?"

"Oh, God, no. You've never watched *Tabatha Takes Over?*"

I shake my head.

"It's this show on Bravo. It's great," she says, directing me to a chair in front of a small manicure table. "Tabatha's this really cool blonde who takes over small businesses, like hair salons, that are struggling, and plants hidden cameras so she can spy on everyone, and then she tells them what they're doing wrong and what they should be doing to make it right. She changes people's lives. She really does."

"Amazing," I say. What I find truly amazing is that my niece is far from alone in her obsession with reality TV. Tabatha and her various clones are indeed changing people's lives because reality TV is changing the face of reality itself. This thought makes me almost dizzy, and I look around the room, trying to ground myself.

On the wall beside me are several rows of Plexiglas shelves filled with small bottles of colorful nail polishes, from the palest white to the darkest black. Behind me are shelves filled with a variety of beauty products—facial cleansers, body lotions, anti-aging creams—and two big burgundy leather chairs used for pedicures. "They're massage chairs," Mrs. Paul tells me, following the direction of my gaze. "Absolutely fabulous. Too bad we don't have time for a pedicure. Maybe next time. Do you know what color you want for your nails?"

I shrug. "What do you suggest?"

She gives me a quick once-over. "Well, you don't strike me as much of a pastel person. Am I right?"

I nod.

"How about red? This is a great new shade." She holds up a tiny round bottle of thick red liquid. It looks pretty much the same as all the other bottles of red liquid on the shelf, but then, she's the expert.

"Great."

She deposits the bottle of polish on the table and then busies herself at the sink. I estimate her age as early thirties and note that she is about five feet, six inches tall and approximately one hundred and forty pounds. Her hair is chin-length and light brown. She is pretty in an ordinary, everyday sort of way. Her eyes are brown, her nose narrow, her lips—probably her best feature— pleasantly bow-shaped. If there is nothing unappealing about her, neither is there anything spectacular. Other than liberally applied mascara, she wears very little makeup. It's hard to picture her as the wife of Paul Giller, alias Narcissus, a man whose tastes veer toward the noticeably younger and more wantonly seductive.

Mrs. Paul turns toward me. "I'm sorry. I just realized I don't know your name."

"It's Avery," I say, the first name that pops into my head. "And yours?"

"Elena." She extends her right hand toward me, and I notice her fingers are free of rings. That doesn't necessarily mean anything. The woman is a manicurist after all.

She deposits a plastic container full of soapy warm liquid on the table and directs my right hand into it while examining my left. "You ever had a manicure before?"

"Yes, of course."

"Not in some time, I'll bet. Your hands are a mess. How long have you been picking at your cuticles?"

I feel instantly self-conscious. I used to pick at my cuticles whenever I got nervous, although I had that nasty habit pretty much under control at the time I was raped. Truthfully, I have no recollection of starting it again, but there is no denying the evidence. I try to pull my hand away but she holds tight.

"You see these ridges?" She points to the thin lines cutting into the surface of my nails. "I'll try to buff these out a bit, but if you don't stop picking, you'll make them permanent. And it would be a shame because, otherwise, you have very pretty hands." She picks up an emery board and brushes it across the nails of my left hand as I ponder the best way to proceed. "So, you're here bright and early on a Monday morning," she says before I can decide. "What is it you do, Avery?"

"What do I do?" I repeat.

"Hard question?" She looks up from what she is doing, her brow furrowing.

"I'm between jobs," I say. Not quite a lie.

"You get laid off?"

I nod. Talk about getting laid, I think, wondering where I have suddenly acquired this macabre sense of humor.

"From what?"

Another pause. Another half-truth. "Legal assistant."

"What's that mean?"

"Damned if I know." I'm grateful when she laughs.

"Probably why you got laid off," she says.

My turn to laugh. I like Elena, I decide. She deserves better than Paul Giller.

"Seriously," she says. "Just what does a legal assistant actually do? And please don't say 'assists lawyers.'"

"Glorified secretary," I offer instead.

This seems to satisfy her. "Must be hard. All those egos."

I picture the lawyers of Holden, Cunningham, and Kravitz, as if assembled for a group photograph. Sean Holden pushes himself front and center, relegating everyone else to background, supporting roles. Even in my imagination, even knowing what I know now, the sight of him induces a palpable pull, and I feel my body sway toward him.

Without warning, a pregnant woman emerges from behind his back. At her side are two young girls, their faces blurred although their eyes are clear. They stare at me, accusingly. "Leave our father alone," they warn silently. I will them to disappear.

"So what happened?" Elena is asking. "Was your firm downsizing?"

"Actually, I got sick," I say, retrieving my footing and remembering why I'm here. "Pneumonia." I lift my eyes to hers, hoping she'll take the bait, tell me about Paul Giller's recent hospital stay.

"No kidding. And they fired you for that?"

"I missed a lot of work."

"I don't think they're allowed to fire you for getting sick. I realize you know a lot of lawyers, but I have a cousin who's an attorney and he's really good. Maybe you should speak to him."

I flinch, pull my hand away.

"Sorry," she says. "Did I nick you?"

"No. It's okay."

"His name is Peter Sullivan. My cousin, that is. He's with Ron Baker and Associates. You know them?"

Luckily, I've never heard of Ron Baker and Associates. Miami has hundreds of law firms, maybe even thousands.

"So, what firm were you with?"

I hesitate, coughing into the side of my arm in order to buy time. "Bennett, Robinson," I offer, combining the first names of two well-known firms.

"Don't know them. I think you should call my cousin," she says, more emphatically than she did the first time, guiding my left hand to the soapy water and starting work on my right. "Sounds like you have a good case for wrongful dismissal. Avery . . ."

I look around to see who else has entered the room.

"Avery?" she says again, which is when I realize she is talking to me.

"Oh, sorry."

"Forget your name?"

"You were saying?"

"That pneumonia is one nasty piece of work," she says. "My mother had it a few years back. And then this guy I know was in the hospital with it a little while ago."

This guy I know?

A little while ago?

"He was really sick with it. They had him on IVs, the whole works."

"That's awful. Did he lose *his* job?"

"Nah. He's an actor. He doesn't work half the time anyway. He's with this temp agency. They get him part-time work. Odd jobs. Nothing to do with acting. Hey, maybe that's what you should do, sign up for something like that."

"Maybe." So we *are* talking about Paul Giller.

She begins chopping at my nails with an oversized clipper. "Your nails are really strong."

I'm not sure if her remark is an observation or a compliment. I want to ask her more about *this guy she knows* but have to move slowly. "So, have you been working here long?" I venture, deciding to go off in another direction, then circle back.

"A couple of years."

I take another cursory glance around. "Seems like a pretty nice place."

"I like it."

"You live around here?"

"Pretty close."

"There's so much construction," I remark.

"Yeah," she agrees, offering nothing further.

"Are you married?" What the hell, I think.

"No. You?"

"No."

She finishes clipping my nails, begins filing them with the emery board. "Square or round?"

"What?"

"Your nails. Do you prefer them square-cut or round? Like diamonds," she adds with a laugh.

"I don't know."

"I think round's better, personally. They're a little easier to take care of that way, and you obviously don't spend a lot of time on your nails."

I feel her rebuke like a slap on the wrist, and again, pull my hand away.

"Sorry. Did that hurt?"

"No. I just . . . Let's go with round."

"Round it is." She resumes her filing.

"So, no special someone?" I prod, half-expecting her to tell me to mind my own business.

Elena stops filing, relaxing her grip on my fingers. She gets the kind of wistful look in her eyes I probably get when I think of Sean. "Sort of. There's this one guy. But it's more an on-and-off kind of thing."

I feel my heartbeat quicken. "The guy who had pneumonia?"

"How'd you know?"

"Lucky guess. You said he was in the hospital."

"Yeah."

"Was he there long?"

"Couple of days." She shakes her head at the memory. "But he was flat on his back for weeks after that. Literally couldn't get out of bed. I moved in. Took care of him. Nursed him back to health. You know what men are like when they get sick. It was pathetic."

"How long ago was that?"

"I think it was August. Maybe late July. One month kind of blends into the next around here. You know how it is."

I know exactly how it is. I also know it means Paul Giller was out of the hospital when I was attacked and doesn't eliminate him as a suspect. I watch as she begins work on my cuticles.

"These really are an awful mess," she says.

"I guess you can blame my ex for that."

"How's that?"

"Caught him cheating on me."

"What happened?"

"I had to go out of town for a few days. Came back earlier than I expected. Earlier than *he* expected," I clarify, watching Elena's face. "Found him in bed with my best friend."

"Shit. Why is it always the best friend? What'd you do?"

"Kicked him out."

"And your friend?"

"What friend?"

She nods. The nod says, *I've been there,* although she says nothing more. If she suspects Paul Giller of cheating on her, she's not about to confide in me. I've likely learned everything of significance from Elena that I'm going to.

I try a few more questions, asking if she likes to travel, and she says, "No, not especially." I tell her I'm thinking of using my enforced free time to take a trip and ask if she can recommend any-where. She says San Francisco is always nice. I ask if she's been there recently and she says no. I'm wondering about the trip she just returned from, but I can't think of a way to ask about it with-out tipping her to the fact that I've been spying on her boyfriend's apartment and that I saw her unpacking her suitcase. Besides, what difference does it make where she's been? The only thing that matters is that Paul Giller was not in the hospital at the time I was attacked, that I can't eliminate him as a suspect.

"Can you relax your hand a little?" Elena asks as she starts applying color to my nails. "Actually, a lot," she qualifies. "You're stiff as a board."

"Sorry." I do my best to comply. "Better?"

"It'll have to do."

We sit in silence for the remainder of my manicure. When we are done, I glance down at my hands. It looks as if someone has chopped off the tips of my fingers and all that remains are ten bloody stumps.

"What do you think?" she asks.

"Very nice."

"They need to dry." She puts a small heating device on the table and directs my hands inside it. "I hope you don't have to rush off anywhere."

I suddenly remember that Claire is waiting for me at Carlito's Auto Repair. What's the matter with me? How could I have for-gotten this? I look down at my wrist, but I'm not wearing a watch. "What time is it?" I ask, much louder than I intended, so that Elena recoils, clearly alarmed.

"Almost ten o'clock."

"Shit!" I pull my hands from the small heater, jumping to my feet with such speed that the chair in which I've been sitting top-ples over on its side.

"Careful with your nails," Elena warns.

"I have to go." I grab my purse.

"You can pay at the front desk," she calls after me.

I have no idea how much I owe, nor the time to ask, so I reach into my purse and pull two twenty-dollar bills out of my wallet, throwing them toward the reception counter as I race out the door. "Why do I always get the crazy ones?" I hear Elena saying to the woman with the gold-hoop earrings as the door slams shut behind me.

—

"Where the hell have you been?" Claire demands as I burst through the front doors of Carlito's On Third.

"I'm sorry. I got a little side-tracked."

"Oh, my God," she says, the color draining from her face as she stares down at my hands. "What have you done?"

My eyes follow hers to my fingers, where I see what is left of my manicure, polish streaking across the backs of both my hands like rivulets of dried blood. "I'm fine. It's just nail polish."

"Polish?" Claire grabs my fingers and checks for herself.

"It's a long story."

"It better be a good one."

"Miss Carpenter?" a man asks, approaching.

My sister falls silent, and for the first time I take note of my surroundings. We are standing in what appears to be a giant glass bubble. The walls on all sides are curved and transparent, so that it feels as if we are not inside at all, but standing right in the middle of the busy outside corner. The floor is limestone and has the look and feel of a sidewalk, albeit one with strategically placed, color-fully woven area rugs. A variety of fake trees provide accents of luscious green. The buttery yellow leather furniture in the reception area is ultramodern, all sloping lines and gentle curves. A gorgeous, dark-skinned young woman sits at a Lucite reception desk, the computer in front of her seeming to float in mid-air. She is wearing a deep purple T-shirt with a plunging neckline, the not-so-subtle projection of her implants on display, as if she is saying, "I paid for them. I'm going to show them off." I wonder at such confidence. I worry about it. About how it might be misinter-preted.

I was completely covered up the night I was attacked, I remind myself. There was nothing at all provocative about what I was wearing. I should be ashamed of such thoughts. I know better. I know that rape is not about sex, that it is about power, fury, and hate.

"Miss Carpenter?"

I find myself staring at a nice-looking man in his late thirties, with straight brown hair falling into hazel eyes that crowd the bridge of his aquiline nose. Although it is only mid-morning, his cheeks already look as if he could use a shave. Despite his easy smile, this premature five o'clock shadow casts a somewhat sinister aura. He is wearing jeans and a blue-and-white checked shirt, a nameplate—*Hi, I'm Johnny K.*—pinned to its breast pocket. Could Johnny K. be the man who raped me? I take a step back, inadvertently stomping all over Claire's toes.

"Nice to see you finally got here. Your sister was getting worried."

"Sorry."

He laughs, as if I've just said something terribly clever. "Come on. Let me show you what we did to your car."

Claire and I follow him out the back of the glass dome into a large concrete garage filled with luxury cars in various stages of repair. I note a chocolate-brown Mercedes hoisted high in the air, two men working on its undercarriage; I see a pale blue Jaguar being painstakingly repainted; I see a brand new, bright red Ferrari with a big dent in its side.

"Are you all right?" Claire asks. "You're kind of pale. Do you want to sit down?"

I shake my head, counting at least six mechanics at work. With one exception, all are dark-haired, between twenty and forty, and of average height and weight. The lone exception is a man probably closer to fifty and balding, although he, too, is of average height and weight. Any one of these men could be the man who raped me.

"What are you thinking?" Claire asks, eyes narrowing.

"Nothing."

"Liar." She gently squeezes my arm.

"As you can see," Johnny Kroft explains, "we ironed out the dents and filled in the scratches, gave it a coat of fresh paint and a good washing, and voilà, as good as new. Great car. You ever want to sell it, you call me first."

"I'll never sell this car," I tell him.

"No? Well, can't say I blame you. Anyway, here's your invoice." He hands me the itemized list of charges. "You can pay the receptionist. I'll have your car brought around front."

Claire and I thank him and return to the main part of the building.

"I'm sorry," the receptionist says, "but we don't accept personal checks. We take Visa, MasterCard, American Express . . ."

"I don't have . . . they were stolen," I say, as Claire pulls out her wallet and hands the young woman her credit card. "What are you doing?"

"It's all right. I just came into some money."

"No! That money was for you."

She shrugs. "Easy come, easy go."

"I'll make it up to you," I insist, knowing I have no other choice.

"We'll talk about it later," she says. "First, let's get you home."

—EIGHTEEN—

We don't go home.

Instead we find ourselves driving down Brickell Bay Drive, the ocean roaring along beside us, in the direction of South Beach. I suggested going for a ride as we pulled out of Carlito's lot, and Claire quickly agreed. It would be good to get away from my apartment for a while, I reasoned, good to experience a change of scenery, good to put a smile back on my sister's face.

"Is there a more beautiful strip of land anywhere in the world?" Claire asks, shifting gears with obvious enjoyment as I lean back in the passenger seat and inhale the sheer majesty: the cloudless skies, the towering palms, the sandy strip of beach, the thrilling expanse of deep blue sea.

It is the first time I have allowed anyone else to drive my car. Not even Heath has been permitted to get behind the wheel. I love my brother dearly, but even he admits he's easily distracted and more than occasionally reckless. Where is he? I wonder again. It's not like him to disappear for this long without so much as a phone call. Why haven't I heard from him? Why hasn't he returned any of the half-dozen messages I've left on his voice mail?

"I've always wanted to go to Paris," Claire is saying.

"We should go," I tell her. "Maybe this summer when Jade is out of school. The three of us could . . ."

She shakes her head. "Nice idea, but there's no way I can afford—"

"There's a way," I insist. "You'll see. I'll call Dad's travel agent and have her start looking into things."

Claire shakes her head.

"What?" I ask.

"You make it sound so easy."

"It *is* easy."

"Not in my experience."

Our lives have been so different, I think, not for the first time. I grew up in a loving home with two parents who adored me. I was pampered and indulged, my every need anticipated, my every wish granted. Trips abroad, expensive gifts, a high-rise condo. All I had to do was ask. Usually even that was unnecessary. Claire had none of these things. She's had to struggle all her life, to work hard for every dollar she earns, every vacation she takes. She has every reason to resent me. And yet here she is. "I can't thank you enough," I tell her.

"For what?"

"For everything you've done . . . everything you're doing."

"Please," she says dismissively. "You'd do it for me."

"I wouldn't have," I say honestly. If the reverse were true, if it had been Claire who'd been raped and not me, I might have felt bad, maybe even called to ask if there was anything I could do, the way people do when they don't really expect to be taken up on their offer, but that would likely have been the extent of my efforts. We may share my father's DNA, but we've shared very little else over the years. Until a few weeks ago, we were virtual strangers. Now, I think with a surge of pride, we're sisters.

"You hungry?" Claire asks as we cross over into Miami Beach, proceeding at a snail's pace down perennially congested Collins Avenue.

I realize I've forgotten to have breakfast. "I am, yes."

We both laugh at the unexpected vehemence of my response. "Then I vote we stop somewhere soon for lunch."

South Beach is famous for its restaurants. I'm about to suggest one of my favorites, an "in" spot called Afterglow, located on Washington Avenue, a place frequented by the young and the beautiful that boasts an ultra-healthy and mostly raw menu, but then I remember it also boasts some of the highest prices in town. There are a bunch of similarly overpriced restaurants in the area, but since I don't have any credit cards, I decide it would probably be best to stick to something I can cover with cash. I make a mental note to start calling the appropriate people and get the ball rolling on replacing my stolen cards. I can't keep relying on Claire to bail me out.

"Remind me to call the banks later and get you some new credit cards," Claire says, as if reading my mind.

I reach over and fold my hand across hers. "You're amazing."

"Oh, please. Don't you dare start getting all gooey, sentimental on me," she warns. "I don't do sentimental very well."

I wipe at my budding tears with the back of my polish-streaked hand.

"You think I'm kidding? Ask Jade. Or better yet, ask my ex-husband, if you can find the bastard. They'll tell you I don't have a sentimental bone in my body. Or a romantic one either, for that matter. Too damn practical, I guess."

"Can't you be romantic *and* practical?"

"Not in my experience," she says again.

We fall comfortably silent, not speaking again until we reach South Beach, where we park in a lot off Lincoln Road and set out on foot. The streets are crowded, as they always are: spoiled club kids in designer duds and rollerblades whipping past gray-haired pensioners pushing walkers; black-suited, serious-faced Hasidim doing their best to ignore the elaborately costumed drag queens standing in front of the magical, pastel-colored art deco buildings; straw-hatted tourists trying to tame unruly street maps while firmly holding their ground against would-be encroachers.

We walk along the ocean boulevard. The wind has picked up

and plays havoc with our hair. It feels great. For the first time in longer than I care to remember, I feel like a real human being. I am no longer a victim. I am a girl walking with her sister along a crowded beach, the wind blowing hope through her hair.

Until I see him standing on the corner.

"What is it?" Claire asks. "What's wrong?"

The man is in his late twenties or early thirties, of medium height and weight, with dark hair and a gaze so intense it burns into my skin like a branding iron.

"Bailey, what is it?"

I lower my head, point with my chin, while keeping my eyes on the ground. My heart is pounding wildly, reaching up into my throat, strangling my words before they have a chance to form. When my voice finally manages to push its way out, it is unrecognizable. "That man over there."

"Which one?"

I raise my head, see at least a dozen people gathered on the corner, waiting for the light to change. A third of them are women, and of the men, easily half are in their late twenties or early thirties, of average height and weight, with dark hair. None seems even vaguely aware of my existence. No one is looking at me.

The man with the piercing gaze is gone.

Was he ever really there?

"False alarm," I tell Claire, forcing a stiff smile onto my face.

"You're sure you're okay?"

"Fine." I take a furtive glance around, see no one who warrants further suspicion.

Except, of course, every man I see.

I have to stop doing this. I'll make myself crazy.

Too late! a little voice shouts from somewhere inside my head, and I bite my tongue in an effort to quiet it, grabbing Claire's hand as we cross the street, allowing her to guide me.

Eventually we move away from the ocean, looking for a restaurant that doesn't sport a line stretching halfway down the block. We finally find a small café on Michigan Avenue with only a minimal wait time to be seated. A hostess with long, brown hair, a sly wiggle, and heels that boast more inches than the tiny black skirt that barely covers her backside finally leads us through the cool, dimly-lit interior to a small table in the far corner of the rear outdoor patio. The patio is enclosed by bushes of brilliant purple bougainvillea and dotted with coral-and-white striped umbrellas to protect diners against the sun. We settle into the rounded chairs of our wrought iron, glass-topped table for two. Seconds later, a waiter approaches with our menus. He is maybe twenty-five, of average height and weight, with brown hair and eyes. His hands are large. I stare through the glass top of the table at the cobblestone tile floor below and try not to picture those hands around my throat. "Tell me you love me," the waiter says as he leans over my shoulder to hand me my menu.

My eyes shoot toward his. "What?"

"Can I get you ladies something to drink?" he repeats with an easy smile.

"I'll have a glass of the house white," Claire says, eyeing me suspiciously. "Bailey?"

"Just water."

"You're sure?"

I nod, regretting that we have come here, that I ever suggested going for a ride, that I left my apartment in the first place.

"Bottled or tap?" the waiter asks.

"Bailey . . . ?" Claire prompts again.

I have no idea how much time has elapsed since the question was asked. I'm no longer even sure what the question was. "Bottled."

"Plain or carbonated?"

I break into a sweat. "Carbonated."

"Perrier or San Pellegrino?"

"I'll just have wine," I say, waving the waiter away with an impatient hand.

"Two house whites coming right up," he says cheerfully.

"Since when did it get more complicated to order water than wine?" I ask Claire.

"You're sure you're okay?"

"Just hungry."

"Well, that's a good sign . . . your appetite coming back."

I manage another smile. I remember reading somewhere that if you pretend something long enough, you might actually start to feel it. I hope this is true, although I doubt I can sustain the pretense long enough for reality to take its place.

"So," Claire says, examining her menu, "the poached salmon looks pretty good."

"It does," I agree, although I have no idea where on the menu she is looking. All I see is a jumble of letters.

"Bailey," Claire says, and I realize by the concerned look on her face that this isn't the first time she's said my name, "Bailey, what's going on?"

"Too many choices," I say as the waiter returns with our wine.

"Would you like to hear the specials?" He proceeds to list them, then offers us a few minutes to decide.

"They all sound so fabulous," Claire says.

I have already forgotten the choices.

"I'll have the lobster-and-grapefruit salad special," Claire tells the young man upon his return, and I nod my head in agreement. It's easier that way. Besides, I've lost my appetite. The thought of food makes me want to retch. "To better days ahead," Claire says, raising her wineglass in a toast and clinking it against mine.

"Better days ahead," I agree, taking a sip.

"So," Claire says, looking suddenly very serious, "I think I've been very patient. Are you ever going to tell me what happened?"

"What happened?" I have no idea what she's talking about.

"This morning," she explains. "The sudden urge for a manicure."

I take a deep breath, running through the events of this morning in my head, trying to arrange them in an order that will make sense to both Claire and me. Strangely enough, thinking about all this, recalling the details, helps calm me down. I am able to tell her, clearly and unemotionally, about the Internet search I did on Paul Giller, about following him and his wife, a woman whose name is actually Elena and who is, in fact, *not* his wife. I watch Claire's face move from interest to concern to outright alarm.

"Wait a minute," she interrupts before I'm done. "You're telling me you did an Internet search of Paul Giller? What did you find out?"

"Not much. Just that he's an actor, and that he recently had pneumonia so bad he had to be hospitalized."

"Shit," Claire mutters. "And you actually went to his apartment?"

"To his building," I correct.

"Do you have any idea how dangerous that was? I mean, what if he *is* the man who raped you? Think about it for a minute, Bailey. What if he saw you?"

"He didn't."

"Are you sure?"

"I'm positive." Am I? When was the last time I was positive about anything?

"And then you followed him?"

"Until he got into a cab. Then I followed her."

Claire is trying both to absorb and discount this latest tidbit. She leans across the table. "Bailey, I need you to promise me something."

"What?"

"I need you to promise me that you aren't going to go anywhere near Paul Giller's apartment again, that you're going to leave the detective work to the real detectives."

"I am a real detective," I remind her.

"You're also the victim."

I open my mouth to protest, but she is already continuing.

"I know you want to do something. I know you want results. But it's one thing to spy on a man from the safety of your apartment and another thing to actually seek him out, to follow him and question his girlfriend. That's just . . ."

". . . crazy?"

". . . asking for trouble. Promise me you aren't going to do anything like that ever again."

"Claire . . ."

"Bailey . . . ," she says, my name serving as a resounding exclamation point, ending the discussion once and for all. "Promise me," she says again, as the waiter approaches with our lobster-and-grapefruit salads.

"Enjoy," he says.

"Promise me," Claire repeats as soon as he is gone.

"I promise," I agree reluctantly.

"Okay." She takes a long, deep breath. "We won't mention this again. Eat up."

I spear a piece of lobster, along with a wedge of grapefruit, pop the whole thing in my mouth and swallow it.

"I think you're supposed to chew it," Claire says.

I spear another piece, deliberately exaggerating each chew.

"Smart-ass," Claire says. Then, after a slight pause, "So, what's the verdict?"

"Delicious," I say, although I don't taste a thing.

Claire's face radiates worry, a series of small lines bracketing her mouth, the indentations at the bridge of her nose burrowing in noticeably deeper than even a week ago, threatening to become permanent. I am sorry to be the source of that worry, to be adding to the concerns she already has. I resolve not to do anything to upset her further. I will keep my promise to stay away from Paul Giller. I will let the police handle things. I will get my life back in order.

"This is on me," I say when the waiter reappears at the conclusion of our meal to hand us the bill. I pretend to check the addition, although the jumble of numbers I see is meaningless. I reach into my purse, pull out a handful of twenty-dollar bills, hope they add up to the correct amount.

"Cash? Haven't seen that in a long time." The waiter laughs, revealing two large canine teeth.

I feel those teeth biting into my breast, and I gasp.

"Is there a problem?" he asks.

"No problem at all," I say.

"Be back in a minute with your change."

"Unnecessary." I just want him to go away.

"Well, then, thank you very much, ladies. It's been my pleasure serving you. Have a lovely afternoon."

—

"Feel like doing some window-shopping?" I ask Claire. All I really want to do is go home and climb into bed, but I'm afraid to tell her that. I don't want her to lose patience, lose interest, lose confidence in my recovery and her role in it.

We spend the next hour looking in the windows of seemingly every shop in South Beach. "God, I wish I could still fit into something like that," Claire remarks upon seeing a blue-and-white string bikini in one of the many bathing suit stores that line the ocean strip. Then: "Who am I kidding? I could never fit into something like that. Even in my so-called heyday. Inherited my mother's hips," she says with a laugh.

While I inherited our father's money, I add silently. "I think you're beautiful," I say out loud.

Her eyes grow misty, and she turns away. We cross the road to walk along the beach, and I take off my shoes, feel the sand scratch against the insides of my toes. How long has it been since I've walked this stretch of beach? I used to come here every day when my mother was dying. I loved the sound of the ocean, its waves crashing against the shore. I found comfort in its continual ebb and flow, its constant renewal, its permanence.

"You used to live around here, didn't you?" Claire remarks.

"Up the way a little bit. A few blocks west." It strikes me as both strange and sad that Claire has never seen the house I grew up in, that my father was so able to compartmentalize the various aspects of his life, to keep them separate. "You want to have a look?"

"If you'd like to show me."

"I would." I take her hand and guide her back across the street. "I'd like that very much."

—NINETEEN—

The mansion I grew up in is a sprawling, single-story, twelve-thousand-square-foot Spanish-style hacienda with a coral tile roof, ceilings that are twenty-five feet high, and Italian marble floors. An ornately carved, black wrought iron gate separates the street from the semi-circular, orange-and-gray brick driveway, a driveway that can comfortably hold up to half a dozen cars. To the left of the main entrance is a four-car garage that once housed a black Rolls, a copper-toned Bentley, and a fire engine red Maserati as well as the silver Porsche I inherited from my mother. My father eventually got rid of both the Rolls and the Bentley, and Heath was supposed to inherit the Maserati but has been temporarily prevented from claiming ownership by the lawsuit launched by our half-siblings. Likewise, this lawsuit has prevented us from selling the house until all such issues have been resolved. It sits empty, its furnishings in place and intact, the estate committed to maintaining its upkeep, both inside and out.

I have always loved that house. The rooms, while undeniably large, are warmly decorated in an assortment of earth tones and filled with oversized, overstuffed sofas and chairs, antique wooden tables, and finely textured area rugs. Brightly colored abstract paintings by artists both well known and obscure cover the walls. Even as a small child, I felt comfortable moving about the labyrinth of rooms, exploring each twist and turn of the classic Spanish architecture. I especially loved the large and open inner courtyard filled with flowers and tall blossoming trees. Heath and I used to consider this courtyard our personal playground. We'd hide among the shrubs and jump out at each other from behind the blue and pink hydrangeas.

"We won't be able to go inside," I tell Claire as we turn the corner onto my old street. "I don't have a key." Normally, I have two keys to the house. One lies in my desk drawer at home. The other was on the same keychain as the key to my condo and was stolen the night I was attacked.

"It's the one on the end, isn't it?" Claire asks.

I nod, and we walk toward it.

I know something is wrong from almost half a block away. The gate, normally closed, is wide open. As we draw closer, I see several cars crowding the driveway, one with its tail end up over the curb and resting on the grass, its heavy tires flattening a row of delicate white and purple impatiens. "Looks like you have visitors," Claire says, pulling her cell phone out of her purse.

"What are you doing?"

"Calling the police."

"No," I tell her, recognizing the dark green Volvo. "I know that car."

"You do?"

"It belongs to Travis."

"Your old boyfriend?" More statement than question, although Claire looks to me for confirmation. "What would he be doing here? How would he get in?"

"I have no idea." We walk through the open gate, approach the massive wood-and-glass front doors, and try to peer around the intricately carved design of floating palm leaves in the etched surface. I see the marble foyer with a large oak table containing a spectacular arrangement of eerily real-looking artificial flowers.

Beyond that is the central courtyard where Heath and I used to play. It appears empty.

I try the front door. It opens.

"I'm calling the police," Claire says again.

"Wait," I urge, as the unmistakable odor of marijuana wafts toward my nose. If Travis is here, that means Heath must also be here. Heath has a key, and Travis doesn't. Unless he stole it from my purse the night I was raped. Which means he's the one who raped me. Which is impossible. I know that. Don't I? "Please, just wait."

Claire lowers her phone.

"Heath," I call out. "Heath, are you here?"

We glance down the corridors leading to the left and right wings of the house. "You really think your brother is stupid enough to violate a court order?"

Heath is not stupid. But neither is he famous for his good judgment.

We turn a corner into the first of the home's three living rooms. I hear a moan and sense movement to my left. I freeze as a slender arm drapes across the top of a sand-colored sofa, a mop of un-combed, curly red hair popping into view. Half-closed eyes squint, although the sunlight is behind her. "Who are you?" a sleepy, dope-induced voice inquires.

"I'm Bailey. This is my house."

"No shit. Nice to meet you, Bailey. I'm Samantha." The girl, who can't be more than eighteen, tries to stand up, which is when I see that she is naked. Luckily, she tumbles back to the sofa before she is fully upright and doesn't bother trying to get up again.

"I don't believe this," Claire says.

"Is Heath here?" I ask Samantha, the words scratching against my throat.

"Who's Heath?" comes the slurred reply.

"What about Travis?"

"Oh, yeah, Travis," Samantha says, as if this is all the answer I need.

I struggle to find my footing as we turn to leave, a now-familiar panic building with each step.

"Nice meeting you," Samantha calls out as we exit the room and continue on down the hall.

"This is like something out of the movies," Claire says as we walk through the dining room, with its skinny, medieval-looking oak table that seats twelve, into the large modern kitchen and equally large breakfast room. Other than Samantha, we encounter no one. We turn and retrace our steps, heading back down the corridor in the opposite direction.

We walk through the second living room and my father's impressive book-lined office as well as the media room, with its huge, high-definition television screen mounted on the wall opposite eight large burgundy leather chairs arranged in two rows of four. The blinds are closed, and the television is on, although there is no sound, and no one is watching. "Heath," I call, locating the remote control button on the seat of one of the chairs and clicking off the TV. The motion makes me dizzy. I fight the almost overwhelming urge to flee.

We enter the third and smallest of the living rooms, its four sofas arranged in a neat square in the center of the room, then peek into the four guest bedrooms, each of them empty, although the cloyingly sweet smell of marijuana grows stronger with each step. We finally reach the end of the wide, winding corridor to find the door to the master bedroom closed. Claire and I exchange glances as my hand grips the doorknob. She lifts the phone in her hand, as if raising a weapon, her fingers ready to press 9-1-1. My heart is pounding so hard, it feels as if it's about to explode.

The bedroom is in darkness, so at first I don't see them. "Ouch," someone says as the door connects with a mound of flesh lying only inches from my feet. I fumble for the light switch and flip on the overhead pot lights. The room is flooded with light.

"Holy crap," a man's voice exclaims from the bed in the middle of the room.

Heath?

"Turn that damn thing off, will you?"

"What the hell . . . ?" another male voice demands from the floor at the foot of the bed, an unfamiliar head appearing, an unlit joint dangling from thin, half-parted lips. Almost immediately, the man slinks from sight again.

Despite the light, it's hard to make out how many people are actually in the room. In addition to my brother and the man at the foot of the bed, I make out two women in differing stages of undress sprawled across the bed's down comforter. There is also the matter of the semi-conscious body, whose sex I have yet to determine, on the floor in front of the bedroom door.

"Good God," Claire says as the door to the en suite bathroom opens and Travis appears, a look of embarrassment sweeping across his handsome face when he sees me. He's wearing jeans and an oversized Tommy Bahama shirt I've never seen before. His feet are bare.

"Bailey," he acknowledges. "What are you doing here?"

My heart rate steadies. Outrage overtakes panic. "What am *I* doing here?"

"I know this must look pretty bad. . . ."

"Trust me—you have no idea how bad this looks," Claire says.

"Who are *you?*" Travis asks.

"What the hell is going on here?" I demand.

"I think you should probably talk to your brother about that." Travis motions toward the bed as Heath's hand reaches out from underneath the covers to heap a pillow over his head.

"Get out," I say quietly.

"Bailey . . ."

"And take your friends with you."

Travis acknowledges my directive with a silent nod. He walks to the foot of the bed, bends down, and slaps at the head of the man lying there. The unlit joint tumbles from the man's lips, although even this fails to rouse him. Travis lowers himself to the bed between the two semi-comatose, semi-dressed women. "Okay, ladies. Party's over. Time to get up."

"I want all of you out of my house," I tell them.

"Last I heard, this was my house, too," Heath volunteers from underneath his pillow.

"Last I heard," Claire says, "that was up to the courts to decide."

"Who *are* you?" Travis asks again.

"Wait," Heath says, his face still hidden. "Let me guess. Is it a bird? Is it a plane?" He sits up abruptly, the pillow sliding from his face, dragging his unwashed hair across his forehead into his eyes. "No! It's Super-Claire!"

"Heath, for God's sake . . ."

"You probably didn't recognize her, Travis, because she's in her everyday disguise as mild-mannered nurse and savior of troubled, long-lost sisters, but don't be fooled. Super-Claire has a secret identity. Beneath that unflattering blue blouse and too-tight khaki pants lurks the blue-and-red spandex of a true schemer, false friend, and looter of lost inheritances. I don't need X-ray vision to see through you," he says to Claire, pointing a wobbly finger in her direction before collapsing back on the bed in a fit of boyish giggles.

"Are you done?" I ask him.

"Are *you* done?" he repeats.

"Please don't make me call the police," I say.

The word *police* seems to wake everyone up at once. The two women wrapped in the comforter push themselves into a sitting position, bare arms overlapping, bare legs casually entwined, so that it is impossible to tell where one ends and the other begins. "Where are my panties?" one girl mutters, hands searching blindly through the pile of crumpled bed sheets.

"Don't think you wore any, sweet cheeks," Heath says, giving her naked bottom a playful slap as she dangles over the side of the bed, searching.

The two men on the floor rise up, their eyes glazed, their movements stiff, although strangely graceful. Everything feels as if it is happening in slow motion. The young man at the foot of the bed—he is about twenty-five with dark hair and a skinny, hairless torso stretching out of the top of his unzipped, skinny black jeans—glances toward the door. "Did someone mention the police?"

"I could use a glass of water," says the other man, now leaning against the bedroom door. He says this to me, as if I am here to service him, his eyes growing noticeably impatient when I fail to respond. He is wearing a pair of boxer shorts festooned with images of Mickey Mouse, although he must be at least thirty, and his wild, shoulder-length hair is an unnatural, almost neon shade of yellow that puts me in mind of a large dandelion. Dark roots peek out from the surface of his scalp. I estimate by the size of his roots that he probably dyed his hair himself sometime in the last month. Possibly around the time I was attacked. Possibly soon after. I close my eyes and try to will such thoughts from my brain. What is my brother doing with these people?

"I think you should get your clothes on and get out of here," Claire says.

"I think you should go take care of sick people," Heath retorts, laughing.

"Heath," I warn. "Please. This isn't funny."

"You're certainly right about that." He pushes away the sheets gathered in his lap. "It's pathetic."

Claire throws a pair of jeans directly at his head. I don't know where she found them. I don't know if they even belong to Heath. "For God's sake, cover yourself up. Don't you know this is the last thing your sister needs?"

"The last thing my sister needs," Heath repeats, refusing to be cowed, "is people pretending to give a damn about her when they're only thinking about themselves."

"And who could that be?" Claire asks, staring him down.

"What's going on?" asks one of the girls as Heath pushes his legs into his jeans and, as discreetly as he can, pulls them up over his slender hips.

"I thought the police were here," says her friend.

"Are you cops?" the man with the hairless torso asks.

Is this the man who raped me? Could someone who looks so insubstantial have been able to overtake me so easily?

The man looks from Claire to me, then over at Travis, "Are they cops or what?"

"I could really use a glass of water," the dandelion says.

"I'm giving everyone two minutes, and then I'm calling the police," Claire tells them.

"Oh, come on, man," whines the dandelion. "You gotta give us longer than that. I don't even know where my pants are."

"Where's Samantha?" one of the girls asks, her hand rifling through the bedcovers, as if her friend might be lost somewhere inside the folds.

"I believe she's in the living room," Claire says.

"What's she doing there?"

"Suppose you ask her on your way out."

"I'm really sorry about this," Travis says. "Honestly, Bailey, I . . ."

"Just go."

Travis turns toward Heath. "Come on, man. Let's get out of here."

"I don't think so."

"You're in violation of a court order," Claire reminds him.

"So sue me," Heath says. "Oh, I forgot. You're already suing me. Sue me again," he says, even more provocatively. "What are you doing here anyway? Don't you know you're in violation of a court order?"

I'm about to explain that I merely intended to show Claire the exterior of the house where I grew up, when Claire stops me. "Don't waste your breath." She checks her watch. "One minute," she warns.

Everyone scurries into whatever clothes they manage to locate, then flees the room.

Everyone except Travis and Heath.

"Bailey, please . . . ," Travis says again.

"Just leave."

Travis offers no further protest as he walks from the room. Heath pushes himself off the bed, about to follow.

"Not you," I tell him.

"You just said . . ."

"Not you," I repeat.

"I'll make you a deal," Heath says. "I'll stay . . . if Florence Nightingale goes."

"Heath . . ."

"Take it or leave it." He turns to Claire. "You can spare her for a few minutes, can't you, sainted sister? You can go keep Travis company. Get to know him better. I think you'll find you have a lot in common. He's a bit of leech as well."

"Bailey?" Claire asks.

"It's okay."

"It's okay," Heath repeats.

Claire reluctantly exits the room. Heath kicks the door shut after her with his bare foot.

"What's going on, Heath?"

"Nothing's going on. You're overreacting. I had a few friends over. So what?"

"Those are your friends?"

"What's wrong with them?"

"Do you even know their names?"

"What difference does it make what their names are? They're upstanding citizens, fellow actors and future stars, every one."

"They're lowlifes."

"That's a little harsh."

"Wait a minute. You said they're actors?" My mind is racing. What am I thinking? "Do you know Paul Giller?"

"Who?" Heath looks toward the door, then at the floor, anywhere but at me.

"Paul Giller. He's an actor. Do you know him?"

"Should I?"

"Why aren't you looking at me?"

"Why are you yelling?"

"Do you know Paul Giller?" I ask again.

"I already told you—no. What's your problem?"

"*You're* my problem," I cry, frustration getting the better of me. "You bring these strangers into our parents' home, you get wasted out of your mind in the middle of the afternoon, you break in . . ."

"I didn't break in. I have a key, remember? I don't get why you're so upset. What's the big deal? This is my house. *Our* house. Our father left it to *us,* along with his considerable fortune, and our greedy half-siblings, including the sainted Claire, have absolutely no right to any of it. I will fight them to my dying day before I let them have a single dime."

"With what?" I ask plainly.

"What do you mean, with what?"

"You need more than willpower to fight them. Gene is threatening to tie us up in court for years, and he has the power and the know-how to do just that. Sooner or later, whatever money we've managed to save up is going to run out. I have no idea when I'll feel strong enough to return to work, and you don't have a job."

"What? You think I'm not trying?"

"I didn't say that."

"I came this close, *this* close," he says, bringing his thumb and index finger almost together for emphasis, "to getting that damn Whiskas commercial. I rolled around on that stupid floor for hours, *hours,* with that fucking cat licking my face, giving the director exactly what he said he wanted. The commercial's in the bag, my agent tells me, a national spot, residuals up the wazoo. And then at the last minute they decide they want to go in a different direction. Nothing personal, my agent tells me. The director loved what I was doing. It's just that I'm a little too good-looking for what the client has in mind. After reviewing the audition tapes, the client's worried I might upstage the fucking cat. So they've decided to go with more of an everyday Joe, someone the average-looking cat-lover can relate to."

"I'm sorry, Heath," I tell him. "I know how frustrating it must be."

"You have no idea how frustrating it is," he snaps. "You have no idea what it's like to keep getting the door slammed in your face. Time after time after time. Everything's always come so easy for you."

Can he be serious? His self-absorption takes my breath away. Heath has always been self-absorbed—interestingly, that's part of his appeal—but can he really be so oblivious as to what I've been going through these past weeks?

As if my thoughts have suddenly appeared in bright lights across my forehead, he softens. "I'm sorry," he says, hand over his heart. "That was insensitive. Even for me." He offers his best "forgive me" little half-smile. "I don't mean to dump on you. I know things have been kind of messed up for you lately. . . ."

Heath has never been good at dealing with any kind of unpleasantness. I understand that he has to keep what happened to me at arm's length, minimize its trauma, or he will fall apart.

"It's just that I've been dealing with this sort of crap all my life," he continues, returning to his comfortable oblivion as my legs grow weak and I sink down on the edge of the bed to keep from crumpling to the floor. "I'm either too handsome or not handsome enough," he is saying. "Either too tall or too short, too thin or too muscular. Whatever it is, I'm never just right. I'm never good enough."

I know he's referring to more than his erstwhile career, that he is no doubt referencing the look of disappointment he claimed he always saw on our father's face, but I don't have the strength to go into that now. "It's the nature of the business," I offer instead, my heart aching for my brother despite his profound self-involvement. "You knew that going in."

"It's not that I'm sitting around on my ass. I'm going on auditions; I'm putting myself out there."

"What about your writing?"

"What about it?"

"That screenplay you've been working on—"

"Still working on it," he says, cutting me off. "What are you getting at, Bailey? Are you saying that I should give up my dreams and settle for some stupid nine-to-five job? Is that where this is leading?"

"No, of course not." I say this despite what I am really thinking, that regardless of what you hear on TV shows like *American Idol,* where the tearful winner urges all those watching from their living rooms to hang on to their dreams, no matter what—

forgetting about the thousands of other contestants, the millions of other desperate wannabes whose dreams of stardom will *never* come true—that sometimes it's just better to choose another dream, that living an actual life is better than just dreaming about a life that will never be. "It's just that there's no money coming in, and all our assets have been frozen. . . ."

"All I need is a couple of national spots and I won't have to rely on Dad's money, no matter what the courts eventually decide. I'll even have enough money to take care of you for a change, the way you've always taken care of me. Please don't be mad at me, Bailey. I can't stand it when you're mad at me. I love you more than anything in the world. You're all I've got."

"I love you, too." I fight the impulse to take him in my arms. "I was just thinking it might be smarter in the long run to settle this thing. . . ."

"Are you kidding me? Is she kidding me?" he asks the surrounding walls.

"Heath, listen to me. It's not like there isn't plenty of money to go around. We're talking about millions of dollars. Tens of millions . . ."

"I'm not giving those vultures ten cents."

I lower my head. This is not what I wanted to talk to Heath about, although I no longer have any idea *what* I wanted to talk to him about. I almost smile. Heath has that power.

"It's just that if Dad wanted to divide his estate evenly," my brother continues, "he would have done just that."

"I know." In truth, I know no such thing. The fact is that there was nothing our father relished more than a good fight. Claire would probably say that this lawsuit is what he'd been hoping for all along.

"And we have to respect Dad's wishes," Heath is saying. "We can't just take the easy way out. In spite of everything we've been going through lately."

Everything *we've* been going through, I repeat silently. What I say out loud is, "You're sure you don't know Paul Giller?"

"Never heard of him."

I have no choice but to believe him. "Promise me you won't do anything like this again? That you'll respect the court order and stay away from here?"

"I'll be a good boy from now on. I swear."

"You don't have to swear. Just promise."

He gives me one of his most genuine smiles, one he once confided he spent hours, if not days, perfecting in front of his mirror. If I were a producer looking to cast the part of the hapless heroine's sensitive, deeply misunderstood older brother, he'd be perfect for the role. The smile deepens. "I promise," he says.

—TWENTY—

"I'm really upset with my brother right now."

I am perched on the tan sofa in Elizabeth Gordon's inner office, and she is sitting in the navy chair across from me, in virtually the same positions we occupied a week ago.

"What is it that's upsetting you?"

I tell her about the incident at my parents' house.

"What upsets you more—the fact that your brother disobeyed a court order or that he was there at all?" she probes.

"That he disobeyed a court order," I answer quickly. Too quickly, I think, understanding she is probably thinking the same thing. "It's more than that," I continue, although I have no idea what I'm about to add.

"I can see you're conflicted," Elizabeth says. "Try to put whatever you're feeling into words."

How many times have I overheard young parents encouraging frustrated three-year-olds to "use their words"? Has my rape rendered me so infantile? "It's not just that he was in the house. It's that there was something so sordid about the whole thing." I tell her about the state of the various rooms and the hangers-on my brother surrounds himself with. I don't tell her my gut says that Heath is hiding something from me.

"Were you frightened?"

"No. Why would I be frightened?"

"A bedroom full of stoned, naked men," she remarks. "I can certainly understand why that might be intimidating to you." She tilts her head, her frizzy brown hair falling across her right shoulder, revealing a delicate diamond stud in her left ear.

"You're wearing different earrings," I say.

Her left hand reaches absently for her earlobe. "What earrings did I have on last time?"

"Small gold hoops."

"You're very observant." She leans forward. "Why don't you tell me what you're experiencing."

"That's just the problem."

"What is?"

"I'm not sure *what* I'm experiencing anymore."

"How so?"

"I just feel so strange all the time."

"How so?" she asks again. "Are we talking panic attacks?"

"Sometimes. But it's more than that."

"How is this different? You can trust me, Bailey," she says after a pause. "I understand you've had it very rough lately—"

I interrupt. "Rough doesn't begin to sum it up."

"What does?"

"It feels as if I can't breathe. It feels as if I'm losing my mind."

"This is good, Bailey."

"*How* is this good? What possible good is this doing?"

"Listen to me." She leans forward in her chair. "It's hard for people to understand how this process works. But by explaining things to me, you're also explaining them to yourself." She lays her pen across the notepad in her lap. "Picture yourself on a skating rink. You're worried about falling through because the ice is so thin. Therapy allows the ice to get thicker so you can skate better. With confidence. Right now you're not skating on very thick ice."

She pauses to let the image set. "I understand that these things are very upsetting for you to think about, let alone talk about, but it will be helpful to you if you can just put it out there. . . ."

I glance down at the beige shag carpet at my feet. "I don't know if I can. I don't know."

"It's better to share whatever's going on inside you right now—to put those feelings into words—than to try to keep those feelings all bottled up, waiting to explode. Now I know you don't have a lot of trust in people right now. But the important thing is, can you trust *me*? Can you trust me—and yourself—enough to put these feelings into words? If you can, I promise it will help relieve your intense anxiety."

"How can you promise that?"

"Because I can help you, Bailey, if you'll let me."

"I just don't know if I'm ready to do this."

"I'm here, Bailey. *Whenever* you're ready."

"You can't imagine what's been going on with me."

"Well, then, *tell* me precisely what's been going on."

"I don't sleep. I have such awful dreams. But then I wake up, and I'm even more anxious."

"Tell me about your dreams. Describe them in as much detail as you can."

I recount my recurring nightmares: of sharks swimming beneath my feet in placid waters; of faceless men waiting for me on the shore; of a woman watching me through a pair of binoculars from the balcony of her apartment, the woman's face my own.

"These are anxiety dreams," Elizabeth tells me. "You feel helpless and confused and frightened, maybe even a little guilty."

"Guilty?"

"I sense you feel some responsibility for what happened to you."

"I know I shouldn't. . . ."

"Forget about 'should' and 'shouldn't.' The fact is, you *do*. Just what do you think you could have done differently, Bailey?"

"I could have been more observant, more aware."

"I could have been shorter," she says with a shrug.

"It's not a valid comparison. You have no control over how tall you are."

"And it's important to feel in control?"

"Isn't it?"

She scribbles the word *control* across the middle of the piece of paper on her lap before she catches me looking and gently shifts the pad out of my line of vision. "I think everyone likes to feel in control."

"Except there is no such thing, is there? Is that what you're trying to tell me? That I had no more control over the situation than you had over your height?"

"I'm not trying to tell you anything. You tell *me* something," she continues. "Would having been more observant that night, more aware, have changed anything?"

"I might have heard him earlier. I might have seen him. I might have stopped him."

"Really?" she says. "Realistically. You think you could have stopped him?"

I see myself crouching in the dark inside a clump of flowering shrubs, staring through my binoculars at the building across the way. I hear the sound of twigs snapping behind me and experience the slight shift in the air. Once again, I taste the gloved hand that covers my mouth and blocks my screams and feel the flurry of fists at my stomach and face, overpowering my resistance and bringing me to the brink of unconsciousness. Could I have done anything differently? "I don't know."

"I do," she says. "Nothing you could have done would have stopped him."

"I could have screamed."

"You think anyone would have heard you?"

"I don't know." It was late. Most people would have been in bed or glued to their TVs. Their windows would have been closed to the outside heat, their air conditioners on full-blast to keep out the humidity. Even if anyone had heard me, chances are my screams would have been discounted or ignored. Even had people glanced out their windows, the odds are they wouldn't have seen anything. I had been well hidden.

I suddenly remembered the feeling I'd had of being watched by someone in one of the overlooking apartments when I'd gone to scout things out that morning. I'd dismissed the feeling as professional paranoia, but maybe it hadn't been. Maybe someone had been watching me. Maybe even the man who raped me.

"Ultimately what you might have seen or done doesn't really matter," Elizabeth is saying, unaware of my inner musings, "because the only thing that *does* matter is what you *did* see and what *did* happen. And that's more than enough to deal with without trying to deal with what *might* have been. It's the *might haves* that are keeping you stuck, Bailey, keeping you from dealing with your real issues."

"Which are?"

"You tell me."

"What if I don't know?"

"Then, that's what we'll have to figure out," Elizabeth tells me. "That's what we'll have to work on together."

I nod, half-expecting her to tell me that our hour is up, that this will be a good starting-off point for our next session. Instead, a glance at my watch tells me the session has barely begun.

"Perhaps you have more to tell me," she says.

"Like what?"

"I don't know. Aside from the incident with your brother, what else has been happening?"

Can I do this? Can I really tell her *everything*? Can I trust her with *crazy*? I take a deep breath, then release it slowly, the air escaping my body like air from a balloon. I push the words from my mouth. "I think I might be losing my mind."

"In what way?"

"I see him everywhere."

"The man who raped you?"

"Yes." I shake my head. "I mean, weird, huh? I didn't see him, and yet I see him everywhere. Every man between the ages of twenty and forty, white or black or anything in between, as long as he's of medium height and build, I look at him, and I think, it could be him."

"Doesn't sound crazy to me at all," Elizabeth says. "You're right. It *could* be him."

"The other day I thought I saw him on a street corner in South Beach," I continue, refusing to be comforted so easily.

"Go on."

"I think I hear his voice whispering in my ear, telling me to tell him I love him. Sometimes I wake up in the middle of the night, convinced the phone is ringing, but when I answer it, there's just a dial tone. When I check the phone's history, I see that yes, some-body *did* call, and I think it must be the man who raped me. Ex-cept maybe it isn't. Maybe it's just my brother. . . ."

"Why would your brother call you in the middle of the night and then hang up?"

"I don't know."

"Surely the police have ways of checking. . . ."

"The police already think I'm crazy."

"Why is that?"

I recount the earlier episode with David Trotter. "And then there's this guy . . . ," I begin.

"What guy?"

What the hell? I think again. I've gone this far; I might as well go the rest of the way. "His name is Paul Giller. He lives in one of the apartment buildings behind mine."

"Is he a friend?"

"No," I say loudly. Too loudly. Elizabeth jots something on her piece of foolscap. "I don't know him at all."

"But you know his name."

"Yes. The police told me."

"Is he a suspect?"

"They don't think so."

"But *you* do."

I tell her about Paul Giller, alias Narcissus, how I started watching him, why I continue to do so, how I can't seem to stop. "I should probably be ashamed to be telling you this."

"There's no reason to be ashamed. You're just telling me what's on your mind."

"But I've been watching him having sex. . . ."

"In front of his window, with all the lights on, and his curtains open," she reminds me.

"I don't think he has any curtains," I correct. "I think they might have just moved in."

"They?"

I tell her about Elena, and about following her to her place of work, of the information I gathered from her during the course of my impromptu manicure. "Crazy, right?"

"It doesn't sound crazy to me at all," Elizabeth counters. "Risky, maybe. But not crazy. You were taking control of the situation in the best way you know how. You were doing what you've been trained to do."

I bury my hands between my knees to keep from clapping. *She doesn't think I'm crazy*, a voice inside me is shouting. *She thinks I'm taking control.*

"And one night you actually caught this man staring back at you through binoculars?"

"I *thought* I did. But when the police went to check him out, he claimed he doesn't even own a pair of binoculars. He offered to let them search his apartment."

"And did they?"

"No."

Elizabeth gives her shoulders an exaggerated shrug, as if to say, it figures. "So he could have been lying. Does Paul Giller have an alibi for the night of your attack?"

"The police claim they can't ask him that without sufficient cause. You really don't think I'm crazy?"

"Well, let's recap what we know so far, shall we? You discover a man who fits the general description of the man who raped you living in the apartment building directly behind yours; your sister and your niece also see him. Correct?"

"Correct."

"So we know he isn't a figment of your imagination. We know

he's real. And that he likes to parade around naked in front of his window, for all the world to see."

"Well, he *is* twenty-four floors up. . . ."

"Okay. So, for *half* the world to see," she amends, with a smile. "And your sister and your niece have witnessed this behavior as well."

"Yes."

"So we know *that's* real. And that he likes to have sex in front of the window."

"Well, I'm the only one who's actually seen him having sex," I tell her, my voice growing suddenly weak.

"Are you saying it might not have happened?"

"I don't know."

"Do you *think* you only imagined it?"

"No."

"What?"

"No," I repeat, my voice stronger with the repetition.

"Good. Neither do I."

"And you don't think I'm paranoid? Or psychotic?"

"You're hardly psychotic. And I'd say you have good reason to be a little paranoid. You were beaten and raped. Your world has been turned upside down. You have every right to feel the way you do."

I have a right, I think. *I'm not crazy.*

"You've been through hell, Bailey. And this creep you've been watching—whether he knows you've been watching or not, whether he's the man who raped you or not—certainly isn't helping things. You're obviously tense and on guard. The dreams you've been having signify your feelings of being out of control, as does your overall anxiety. You made a very interesting distinction today: that you don't know what's real and what isn't. This doesn't mean you're psychotic."

I'm not crazy.

"You're familiar with the term *post-traumatic stress disorder*?"

"Of course. Aren't hallucinations a symptom?"

"They can be. It still doesn't mean you're crazy."

I'm suffering from post-traumatic stress. I'm not crazy.

"So what can I do about it?"

"Exactly what you're doing. Coming here. Talking about it. You're smiling. What are you thinking?"

I feel the smile I hadn't realized was on my lips grow wider, stretching across my cheeks. "Just that it's funny."

"What is?"

"I feel better."

"How so?"

"You just said I'm not crazy, even though I feel crazy. So maybe I'm not crazy after all. Crazy, huh?" I laugh.

"You're not losing your grip on reality. You're just stressed out and traumatized."

"Thank you." I want to stand up, to leave, to get out of her office before this feeling of euphoria dissipates. "Thank you so much."

"We still have a lot of work to do, Bailey."

"I know. But just knowing that you don't think I'm crazy makes me feel more in control."

"You *aren't* crazy."

"I'm not crazy."

"Can you remember the last time you felt you had control, Bailey?" Elizabeth asks.

I search my memory, feeling my newfound confidence starting to wane. "I don't know. Probably before my mother died," I admit. "Everything has seemed so helter-skelter since then."

"You certainly had no control over what happened to your mother. But you did find a way to cope. You found a way to take control of your life."

"You mean by becoming a detective?"

"I don't think your choice was happenstance. Or helter-skelter, as you called it. You wanted answers. You chose a profession that allows you to actively search them out. It was the same thing after your father died. Your work helped you deal with his passing, helped you move on with your life. And even now, when the police refused to investigate Paul Giller, you took matters into your own hands, investigated him yourself. It may not have been the most prudent thing in the world for you to do, but it certainly made you feel less victimized. It made you feel more in control."

She's right, I think. I'm never more in control than when I'm working.

"Except I was raped when I was working," I say out loud before she can ask me to put my thoughts into words.

"Which has made this all the more traumatic for you. You were attacked in the very place you felt most in control."

This time I do stand up. "You've given me a great deal to think about."

"I hope it's been helpful."

"I think maybe you cured me." I laugh as if to underline my meager attempt at humor. Although what I'm really hoping she'll say is that it's not a joke, that I *am* cured, that there's no need for me to come back, that my anxieties have been banished for all time because *I'm not crazy, I'm not crazy, I'm not crazy.*

"We're just scratching the surface, Bailey," she says instead. "We still have a great deal to talk about."

"Such as?"

"Well, for starters, we've never really talked about your father."

"I think he's Claire's issue, not mine."

"You have nothing to say about him?"

"Just that I miss him."

"I'm sure you do. So, are you saying that some men are good?"

I smile. "I guess I am."

"I think that's a nice note to end on for today. Don't you?"

—

I all but fly out of Elizabeth Gordon's office, walking to the corner and hailing down the first cab I see.

I'm not crazy.

Not all men are irresponsible liars. They don't beat up on their girlfriends or lie about not sleeping with their wives; they don't have drug-induced orgies in their dead father's bedroom. They aren't all rapists.

I'm not crazy.

"Where to?" the cab driver asks.

He is about forty, with broad shoulders, a strong back, a mustache, and wavy dark hair. Normally this would trigger a panic attack, but this is not the man who raped me. Not all men are rapists. Some men are good.

I'm not crazy.

I am about to give the driver my address when I change my mind. *I'm never more in control than when I'm working.*

It's time to get to work. The police claim they've questioned everyone who lives in the immediate vicinity of where I was raped. But so far, their investigations have turned up nothing. And if the police can't help me, I'll have to help myself.

Which means returning to the proverbial scene of the crime.

To borrow a page from Elizabeth Gordon's notepad, it might not be the most prudent course of action, but it might make me feel less victimized, more in control. I take a deep breath. "Northeast 152 Street in North Miami."

—TWENTY-ONE—

The street looks so benign in the daytime, I think, glancing down the row of pastel-colored buildings, none higher than six stories, all neat and tidy and speaking to a decidedly different era, a time before towering glass houses became the norm. Palm trees cast long, lazy shadows across the center of the wide road. The cab driver pulls to a stop in one such shady patch, about half a block down from where I'd parked my car the night I was attacked. "This okay?" he asks.

"Fine," I say, although it isn't. I started trembling approximately ten minutes into the ride, the tremors getting worse the closer we got, and now my hands are shaking so badly I all but throw the money for my fare at the driver's head, then push open the rear passenger door with such force, it actually feels as if it might snap off. I jump from the cab before I can tell the driver I've changed my mind, that I was mistaken, that this isn't where I wanted to go, that it is, in fact, the last place on earth I want to be.

The taxi pulls away from the curb, leaving me standing in an unexpected circle of sun, as if a spotlight has just found me. *Ladies and gentlemen,* an invisible voice declares, *look who we have here!*

Why, it's none other than Bailey Carpenter, returning to the place where it all began—or should we say, the place where it all fell apart? What are you doing here, Bailey? Tell your adoring public what you think you can accomplish.

Tell me you love me.

I take a couple of tentative steps before my knees give way and I'm forced to stop before I fall to the sidewalk. I breathe deeply half a dozen times, releasing each breath slowly, trying to quell my growing panic. I'm taking control.

I'm not crazy.

"Excuse me. Can I help you?" The woman's voice is small and friendly, as is the woman herself. She is maybe five feet tall and at least eighty years old, her face a tanned canvas of lines and creases. Another throwback, I find myself thinking. To the days before plastic surgery turned women's faces into ghostly, expressionless masks. She is wearing a floral print blouse and a pair of pink-and-white-checkered capris that shouldn't go together but do, and I watch her as she approaches, pulling her small dog on a neon green leash behind her. The dog, a pudgy little Yorkshire terrier, has a matching green bow in its thick, silky hair, and when the woman stops, perhaps a foot in front of me, the dog curls up at her sandaled feet, its breath emerging in a series of short, uneven pants, its little tongue hanging over the side of its tiny mouth as he stares up at me, questioningly, as if he knows I don't belong here. "You look lost," the woman says.

I decide this is as good a word to describe me as any. "No," I say anyway. "I'm okay, thank you."

"It's sure a hot one," the woman says. "Ninety-two, according to the morning paper." She pushes some damp, thinning gray hairs away from her face. "Same as me. Ninety-two last week."

How is it that some women get to be ninety-two while others die at fifty-five? "Congratulations," I offer, trying not to begrudge this woman her longevity. "You look amazing."

She acknowledges my compliment with a girlish giggle and a shy wave of her noticeably arthritic fingers. "I try to get out for a little walk several times a day, although this humidity is just murder on my hair. But Poopsie here needs his bathroom breaks. Don't you, Poopsie?"

Poopsie looks up at his mistress with large, baleful brown eyes, as if trying to assess how long they are going to linger and whether or not he should bother getting up.

"Do you live around here?"

"The pink building right behind you." She points with her chin at a square, five-story building with white shutters. "My daughter's been trying to convince me to move into one of those assisted living communities, says it'll make my life easier. I think what she really means is that it'll make *her* life easier. And I kind of like my life the way it is. Of course, I've had to give up golf," she adds wistfully.

I think of Travis. He taught me to play, and I was actually getting pretty good at it, which didn't surprise him, that I'd cottoned on to the game so quickly. "Is there anything you can't do?" he'd asked, a slight edge to his admiration. I picture him standing in the doorway of my father's en suite bathroom, his feet bare, a guilty look on his handsome face.

Was he feeling guilty because he was embarrassed, possibly even ashamed? Or was it something else? Something more.

"Can I ask you something?" I ask the old woman.

"Of course."

"I understand a young woman was raped recently on this street. . . ."

"Really?" Watery hazel eyes grow wide with alarm. "Where did you hear that?"

I shrug, as if I can't quite remember. "It happened about a month ago. . . ."

"I had no idea." She clutches the collar of her floral print blouse with her free hand, bringing the two sides together at the base of her wrinkled neck.

"You haven't heard anything about it?"

"No. You're sure it was this street?"

"Positive. The police never talked to you?"

"No. Not a word. Oh, dear. This is normally such a safe area. You're sure it was *North*east 152, and not *South*east?"

I point to the clump of bushes at the end of the road, feeling my hand shake and immediately lowering it to my side. "I think it happened over there."

"My goodness. I can hardly believe it. That's just so awful. Poor thing. Is she all right?"

"I don't know," I tell her truthfully.

"Did you hear that, Poopsie?" the woman mutters as she turns away. "A woman was raped on our street. It might be time for us to move after all." She looks back at me. "Would you mind waiting," she asks, "until I'm safely inside?"

"Of course." I watch as she walks up the path to the front entrance of her building and pushes open the lobby door, then stops and waves me away. I head off down the street, my breathing becoming more labored, less steady, with each step. I try to convince myself that this is a result of the oppressive humidity, but I know that's not true.

I am nearing the spot where I parked my car that night. A white Honda Civic is parked there now, and I stop in front of it, trying not to see myself splayed out carelessly at the foot of its passenger door, my arm raised up behind my head to grip the door handle, my body all but vibrating with pain. I try not to hear the car's alarm bells lulling me into unconsciousness.

According to the police, an elderly resident from a nearby condo heard the alarm and looked out to see me lying there, then phoned 9-1-1. No, he hadn't seen what happened, he told the officers who questioned him. Nor had he witnessed either the attack or anyone suspicious fleeing the scene. He'd simply heard a car alarm going off and looked out his window to see a woman lying on the side of the road.

I wonder which resident it was as I continue down the sidewalk, stopping beside the elongated circle of shrubbery near the far corner, directly across the road from the four-story, lemon-yellow building I'd been watching the night of my attack. It had been so easy to slip into the middle of the bushes, to crouch among their flowers and disappear into the night.

Except I didn't disappear.

Someone had seen me. Someone was watching.

Someone is always watching.

I crouch down. Or do my legs collapse? Supporting myself on unsteady ankles, I swivel toward the building across the street, raising imaginary binoculars toward the third-floor corner apartment, the exact position I was in when I heard the sound of twigs breaking and felt the air part behind me, like curtains.

Instinctively I spin around, my body bracing for a fresh barrage of fists, my arms lifting to protect my head. I bite my tongue to keep from crying out, although several sobs escape when I realize no one is there. My eyes search the top floors of the buildings behind me. It's entirely possible that someone could have seen me, that someone might have witnessed the entire attack. Or worse: The man who raped me could actually live in one of these units. Have the police really questioned everyone?

I determine that the two apartments on the top floor of the cream-colored building directly to my right would have the clearest, most unimpeded view of the area. I jump to my feet, deciding to start with the people who occupy those units.

"Hey, there!" a young man exclaims from the sidewalk, less than two feet away from the shrubs in which I'm standing, as startled by my sudden appearance as I am by his.

I gasp, the gasp as loud as any scream.

"Sorry," he says quickly. "I didn't mean to scare you. I just wasn't expecting to see anyone."

"Me neither," I say.

The man is about thirty, tall and slender, with light brown hair and dimples, exactly the sort of man I would have found attractive just a month ago. A half-empty bottle of water dangles from the fingers of his right hand. He is wearing the traditional jogger's uniform of T-shirt, knee-length nylon shorts, and sneakers. I search their sides for the familiar Nike swoosh. Mercifully, there isn't one.

Of course, this means nothing. Whoever raped me likely owns more than one pair of sneakers. I cast a wary glance around the empty street, reaching into my purse for my gun before I remember that I no longer have one. Nor do I have any pepper spray or mace. Not even any perfume I can spray in the man's eyes, should he get too close. Nor have I gotten around to replacing my cell phone. There's no one I can call, nothing I can do.

"Lose something?" the man asks, his voice relaxed and friendly, sounding nothing at all like the man who raped me.

"An earring," I say, the first thing that comes to mind. Hopefully he won't notice I'm not wearing any.

"You need some help looking?"

"No. That's fine. I found it." I indicate my handbag, as if the wayward earring is now safely inside it.

"That was lucky. How'd it get all the way in those bushes?"

Why are we having this conversation? Where did he come from? How long has he been here? Is it possible he's been spying on me ever since I stepped out of the taxi? Was he watching me the night of my attack? Is he the man who raped me?

He has a nice face. He doesn't look or sound like a rapist. He jogs, for God's sake. But whoever said joggers can't be rapists and rapists can't be soft-spoken and nice-looking? "My dog ran in here the other night," I lie. "The earring probably fell off when I was trying to drag him out."

"Talk about your needle in the haystack."

"Yeah." Why is he still here?

"What kind of dog do you have?"

"What?"

"Wait. Let me guess. Something exotic, I bet. Portuguese Water Dog?"

"Doberman," I say, as if the word itself will be enough to inspire fear.

"Really? I never would have pegged you as a Doberman lover."

Again I wonder why we're having this conversation, why I find myself willingly prolonging it. I am standing in the exact spot where I was attacked, talking to man I don't know, a stranger who

fits the general description of the man who beat and raped me.
Why? "You don't know anything about me."

"I'd like to."

"What?"

"You have time for a cup of coffee?"

What?

"There's a Starbucks not too far from here. . . ."

Is he hitting on me? Or is he one of those sick bastards who get
a perverted kick out of first stalking the women they rape and then
befriending them in the aftermath of the attack, ingratiating themselves into their victims' lives, becoming their confidants, their
boyfriends, sometimes even their husbands, relishing their hold
over these unsuspecting women, victimizing them over and over
again?

"Are you hitting on me?"

"Well . . . yes. It would seem that's exactly what I'm doing.
Normally, that's not my thing, picking up strange women standing
around in bushes, but I don't know . . . the way you just popped
up like that . . . it seems kind of like serendipity. You know, like in
the movies. What they call 'meeting cute.' The name's Colin, by
the way. Colin Lesser. And you are?"

"Bailey. Bailey Carpenter." What's the matter with me? What
on earth possessed me to give him my name? "I don't want coffee," I add quickly.

"Well, you don't have to have coffee. You could have a
smoothie or a muffin. . . ."

"I don't want anything."

"Okay. I get it. No worries. Sorry to have bothered you."

As he turns to leave, I notice a woman wheeling a baby carriage up the street toward us and feel emboldened. "Wait."

Not all men are rapists. Some men are good.

He turns back.

"Do you live around here?" I ask.

He checks his watch. "About a forty-minute run that way." He
points south, then looks back at me, as if waiting for me to make
the next move.

"You've been running for forty minutes in this heat?"

"You grow up in Miami, you kind of get used to it." He takes a long swig of his water. "You're very observant."

"So they tell me."

"Who's they?"

"You run every day?" I ask, ignoring his question.

"Pretty much. Can I ask *you* something now?"

I nod, hear a baby's cries as the woman with the carriage draws closer.

"Are you ever going to come out of those bushes?"

I try not to smile. "What do you do?" I ask, again ignoring his question and staying resolutely in place, "that allows you to go jogging on hot Wednesday afternoons?"

"Chiropractor," he answers, too easily for it to be a lie. "I take Wednesday afternoons off. What about you? Gardener? Landscape architect?" The twinkle is back in his blue eyes.

"Temporarily unemployed."

"From doing what?"

"I worked for a bunch of lawyers."

"Tough crowd. Tougher times. You get laid off?"

"You could say that."

"What would *you* say?"

"I prefer to think of it as a temporary sabbatical."

He smiles. A nice smile. "Good way of looking at things," he says. "A glass-half-full kind of approach to life. I like that." I watch the dimples in his cheeks deepen.

"Glad you approve."

"So, you come here often, Bailey Carpenter?" he asks, and I try not to cringe at the effortless familiarity of my name on his lips.

Not all men are rapists. Some men are good.

"No. This really isn't my neighborhood." Does he already know where I live?

"You just come here to walk your dog," he states.

"Sometimes. Yes."

"Your Doberman."

"That's right."

"What's your dog's name?"

I hesitate, trying to come up with an appropriately sinister name for a Doberman. All I can think about is the old woman and her Yorkshire terrier I saw earlier. "Poopsie," I say.

"Poopsie? You're sure about that?"

"It was meant to be ironic."

"You don't have a dog, do you?"

I shake my head. "No, I don't."

"And you didn't lose an earring."

"No, I didn't."

"You just like standing around in bushes in the middle of strange neighborhoods?"

Again I hesitate. The woman pushing the baby carriage draws closer, her baby's cries louder. "Do you know anything about a rape that happened on this street about a month ago?" I ask suddenly, watching for any change in Colin Lesser's expression. Why not just come right out and ask? Even if he *is* the man who raped me, surely he's not crazy enough to try anything now, not with a witness less than ten feet away.

"No. I don't know anything about a rape." He points to where I'm standing. "Is this where it happened?"

"Yes."

"Are you a cop?"

"No."

"Then why are you standing there?"

The woman with the baby carriage approaches, smiling at Colin and looking warily at me as she continues on her way.

I am now alone with Colin Lesser. Hopefully, he's exactly what he seems. A naturally friendly guy, out for an afternoon jog. I watch his lips as they take another sip from his bottle of water, imagine those same lips biting down on my breast.

"Are you all right?" he asks.

"Yes. Why?"

"You winced. Like you had a sudden pain."

"No." More constant than sudden, I think.

"I'm a chiropractor, remember. I'm very good with aches and

pains." He reaches into the pocket of his shorts, pulls out a business card, holds it out for me to take, then laughs self-consciously. "I always carry a few of these with me."

I have to stretch in order to reach it, somehow managing to take it from his hand without allowing our fingers to touch. DR. COLIN LESSER, CHIROPRACTOR, I read, along with the address and phone number of his office, which I can't help notice is on Biscayne Boulevard, only a few short blocks from Holden, Cunningham, and Kravitz.

Did he notice me when I was working there? Did he secretly stalk me? Is he the man who raped me?

Not all men are rapists. Some men are good.

"You're looking a little pale. Are you sure you wouldn't like to go somewhere and sit down?" he is asking. "It doesn't have to be Starbucks."

"I can't."

"We could talk about what happened here, if you'd like."

"What?"

"Only if you want to," he adds.

"You said you didn't know anything."

"Well, that's not exactly true. I know a few things."

I hold my breath.

"Just not about a rape." His voice softens. Brackets of concern replace the dimples at the sides of his mouth. "It was you, wasn't it?"

"What?"

"The woman who was raped. . . ."

"Why would you say that?"

"The way you look, the way you're acting . . ."

"You're wrong."

"Okay. Sorry."

"And I don't want coffee. I don't want to go anywhere with you."

"Sorry. I didn't mean to upset you."

"You didn't upset me."

"Good."

"Good," I repeat. If I say anything else, I'm likely to burst into tears.

"Well, it was very nice—if a little strange—meeting you," he says, about to turn away when he stops. "If you ever change your mind about that coffee, well . . . you have my card."

"Enjoy the rest of your run."

I wait until he is safely out of sight before exiting the bushes, impatiently brushing away the assortment of leaves that cling to my white cotton pants. A large orange blossom protrudes from my side pocket. Once, not too long ago, I might have tucked it playfully behind one ear. Now I toss it to the ground, along with Colin Lesser's business card.

Immediately I scoop up the card again, thrusting it deep inside the side pocket of my pants. Is it possible he is who he says he is?

I recall another nice-looking man, another invitation, another business card. That morning in court the day I was attacked. Does Owen Weaver wonder why I never called him? Has he thought about me at all? Has he heard about what happened to me? Could he be the man responsible?

Not all men are rapists. Some men are good.

I look up at the two apartments that are the most likely places for someone to have had a good view of everything that happened that night. One is the apartment where I thought I saw the curtains stir earlier in the day. Can I really do this? Am I crazy?

I'm taking control, I remind myself as I edge closer to the cream-colored building.

I'm not crazy.

—TWENTY-TWO—

The inside of the building has definitely seen better days. Unlike the exterior, which has recently been given a fresh coat of paint, the interior is musty in both appearance and odor. The air conditioning system, if indeed there is one, is more loud than effective, its fan circulating air that is more stale than cool. The lobby is right out of the fifties: old-fashioned green-bamboo-stalk-patterned wallpaper on a white background, once-stylish wicker furniture, a wool carpet that is all green and pink swirls. Despite the happy colors—or maybe because of them—the lobby feels sad, as if it knows its best days are behind it, an over-dressed, forty-year-old chaperone at a high-school dance.

I approach the directory beside the locked set of glass doors leading to the interior elevators and scan the names of the residents, debating whether or not to press all the buzzers in the hope that someone will be foolish enough to buzz me inside without asking questions. Amazingly, despite everything we know, or should know, or *think* we know about crime and how best to prevent it, this old trick still works at least fifty percent of the time. I am jiggling the door handle, wondering how long it would take

my niece to dispatch the lock, when I see a pair of elderly gentlemen exiting one of the two inside elevators and walking toward
me. I make an elaborate show of pretending to talk to someone on
the intercom as they draw closer. "Allow me," the first man says,
holding the door open for me, and bowing to reveal a prominent
bald spot interrupted with wisps of fine, white hair.

I slip inside. "Thank you."

"Have a nice day."

"Who was that?" his companion mutters as the door closes
behind me.

I walk to the elevators before anyone can challenge my right to
be here. The doors close, and the elevator begins its squeak-filled
ascent. Seconds later, it stops on the second floor. I lower my head
as the doors slide open, then watch two pairs of swollen ankles
shuffle inside, accompanied by a cane and a walker. I move to the
rear of the elevator. The doors close on the now full cab. The elevator resumes its jerky climb.

"We're going up? Why are we going up?" a woman says, accusingly. "Sidney, did you press *up*?"

"You're standing right beside me, Miriam. When did I press
anything?"

"Then why are we going up?"

"I pressed it," I admit, feeling strangely guilty, and lifting my
eyes to see two puzzled, old faces staring back at me.

"My wife and I wanted to go down," Sidney says.

"I'm sorry," I mutter. "I'll be getting off in a few seconds. . . ."

"You never look," Miriam scolds her husband. "Now we have
to go all the way up. We're going to be late."

"We're just going for a walk," Sidney counters. "How can we
be late?"

Their bickering has the curious effect of relaxing me, distract-
ing me from the task at hand. Although not for long. By the time
we reach the sixth floor, my nerves have returned.

"Have a nice day," I say as I step off the elevator into the sixth-
floor corridor.

Miriam sighs. "For God's sake, Sidney," she says, "press the damn button, or we'll be here forever."

I follow the corridor around the side of the building that overlooks the street until I reach the far end. The narrow hall smells of cooking, a riot of pungent oils and spices that clings to its off-white walls and radiates off the worn green carpet. The hall has the same amount of minimal air-conditioning as the lobby, and by the time I reach the last two units, dots of sweat are staining the front of my T-shirt.

I stand in front of apartment 612, silently rehearsing what I'm about to say as I ring the bell. A middle-aged man with a comb-over of wiry salt-and-pepper hair and a matching full beard opens the door. He is wearing a short-sleeved navy-and-white shirt over a pair of baggy gray pants, and when he narrows his gray-blue eyes, the bushy unibrow above them rearranges itself into a wiggly line, like a worm on a hook. "What are you selling, young lady?"

"Who is it, Eddy?" a woman calls from inside the apartment.

"That's what I'm about to find out," he calls back. "You aren't one of those Jehovah's Witnesses, are you?"

"No. My name is Bailey Carpenter." I have decided at the last minute to use my real name. There seems no reason not to.

A woman materializes at Eddy's shoulder. She has pale skin and shoulder-length, Alice in Wonderland–styled blond hair. Her lips have been plumped to twice their normal size, and her already narrow face has been pulled tighter than a drum. She looks more amphibian than human, like an animated fish in a Disney cartoon. "Who is it?" she asks her husband, her face betraying no emotion whatsoever. "We always vote Republican," she adds before I can say anything.

"Good to know," I say. "But actually, I'm looking into the attack that happened in front of your building about a month ago."

"You mean the rape?" The woman reaches for her husband's arm.

"Yes."

"You're with the police?"

"I'm an investigator."

"Because we already told the police everything we know," Eddy says.

"I was wondering if we could go over a few of the details again."

"What details?" the woman asks suspiciously, although again, her face remains resolutely placid, revealing nothing. "Like we told the police, we didn't see anything."

"Nothing at all?"

"Nothing. I take it the police haven't caught the guy yet."

"Not yet, no. Your balcony overlooks the bushes where the attack occurred," I venture.

Eddy glances over his shoulder toward the interior of the apartment. "Yeah, but we weren't on the balcony when it happened."

"We were watching TV," his wife says. "*Criminal Minds* was on."

"And you didn't hear anything?"

"Heard a car alarm going off." Eddy shrugs. "Apparently that was after it was all over."

"What about your neighbors?"

"As far as we know," Eddy's wife says, "nobody saw or heard anything."

"Have you noticed any of your neighbors behaving in a suspicious manner?"

Eddy chuckles. "Well, they're all pretty peculiar."

"Eddy," his wife scolds.

"I was wondering if you think there's a chance that . . ."

"What? That one of the residents in this building could have raped that woman?" She shakes her head. "Have you seen the people who live here, Miss Carpenter? They're all a hundred years old! We're the youngest people in the building by at least three decades."

I take a step back. I'm not going to learn anything here. "I'm sorry I bothered you. Thank you for your time."

"You should talk to Mrs. Harkness next door," Eddy mumbles as he's closing the door.

"Eddy, for God's sake," his wife says. "Stop making trouble for that poor woman. She has enough on her plate."

"Who's Mrs. Harkness?"

"Woman in the next apartment. She's got the same view as we do." He sticks his head out the door. "Plus she's got this weird grandson who practically lives here," he whispers.

"Eddy!"

"There's something off about that kid and you know it," he shouts.

Eddy's wife appears in the doorway's narrow crack. I can see the anger in her eyes. "We can't help you," she says, reaching past her husband to close the door in my face.

I stand there for several long seconds, trying to digest what I've just been told. It seems this Mrs. Harkness not only has a view that overlooks the area where I was attacked, she also has a grandson whom her closest neighbor considers "off." Do the police know about him?

Seconds later, determined to ignore the pounding in my chest and the warning bells going off inside my brain, I am ringing the bell for apartment 611. I can hear several people arguing inside and am straining to make out what is being said when the door opens.

A robust-looking woman of about seventy-five stands before me. She is approximately my height, with a slim build and large, inquisitive brown eyes. Her hair is short, blond, and curly, with a halo of gray roots sprouting up around her temples. She wears a velour hot-pink tracksuit with the words JUICY GIRL prominently displayed across her equally prominent bosom.

"Mrs. Harkness?"

"Yes? What can I do for you?"

"I'm sorry to be disturbing you. . . ."

"Just watching my soaps." She waves toward the TV in the living room behind her. "They can wait. Nothing ever happens anyway. What can I do for you?" she asks again. Behind her, I can feel cold air blasting.

"I was wondering if I could ask you a few questions."

"About?"

"About the rape that happened in front of your building about a month ago."

Her smile disappears; her shoulders visibly tense. "I've already spoken to the police."

"Yes, I know. There are just a few things I'd like to go over with you."

Mrs. Harkness looks toward her feet. She is wearing a pair of white sneakers, and I try not to notice the subtle white Nike swoosh sewn into the canvas. My breathing becomes more constricted, as if someone is standing behind me, squeezing my chest. The pressure makes my ribs feel as if they're about to crack open. "I have nothing to add to what I've already told you."

She assumes I'm with the police, and I don't bother to correct her. "Sometimes the more times we go over something . . . ," I say, borrowing one of Detective Marx's favorite phrases.

"I'm quite positive I don't know anything," Mrs. Harkness insists.

I'm equally positive she is lying. She has a pretty obvious tell, tucking some invisible hairs behind her right ear and pursing her lips with each fresh falsehood.

"I was asleep when it happened. Didn't see anything. Didn't hear anything."

"Would you mind if I had a look from your balcony?" I ask, already half-inside her apartment before she can stop me.

"I don't understand what good that will do."

"It'll only take a minute."

"Well, all right." She deliberately looks the other way as we walk past the closed door at the end of her hallway. Why? Is someone there?

Her apartment is freezing. Most older people prefer being too warm to being too cold. I wonder if it is her "weird grandson" who likes things so frigid. I also wonder where he is now, if he is the one behind the closed door at the end of the hall, if he knows anything about my attack, if he is, in fact, the one who attacked me. I decide I should probably get the hell out of here, but of course I do no such thing. I've come this far. It would be crazy to leave now. And *I'm not crazy.*

A beige leather sectional and matching armchair are grouped in front of the high-definition TV mounted on the far wall beside the door leading to the balcony. To the left of it are a small dining area and tiny galley kitchen. I note a can of Coke and a half-empty bottle of beer in the middle of a glass coffee table as I cut across the living room. A thin, blue blanket is folded up on one pillow of the sofa and a stack of magazines beside it rests on the floor, the top one bearing the title *Motorcycle Mania.* "You like motorcycles?" I ask.

Mrs. Harkness purses her lips and tucks several nonexistent hairs behind her ear. "I do, yes. My late husband used to own one."

I have to admire her skill. Were it not for her tell, Mrs. Harkness would be a first-class liar. "Oh my goodness," I say suddenly, as if just noticing the bottle of beer. "You have company!" I feign looking around. "I'm so sorry. . . ."

Mrs. Harkness tucks more invisible hairs behind her right ear. "I don't have company," she says quickly. "Just couldn't decide what I felt like drinking." Another purse of her lips, another unnecessary tuck of hair behind her ear. "I know they say that things go better with Coke," she says with a laugh. "But sometimes there's nothing like an ice-cold beer."

That's another thing about liars. They always feel the need to embellish.

"This is really a lovely apartment," I say. "One bedroom or two?"

"Just one. Don't need more space than that. Since my husband died."

"How long ago was that?" I ask, keeping my voice determinedly casual as I unlatch the door to the balcony and slide it open.

"Three years. Do you think we could speed this up? I'm missing my soap. . . ."

"I shouldn't be much longer." I step out onto the balcony, the onslaught of warm air covering my head like a pillowcase. I gasp, throwing my head back, my body slamming into the railing overlooking the street below.

I tell myself to calm down. This is a simple episode of posttraumatic stress. That's all it is. *I'm not crazy.*

Looking down, I see an unimpeded view of the bushes where I was raped. In the daytime, everything is visible: the flowers, the shrubs, the space in the middle of those shrubs where I was crouching when I was overpowered, the exact spot where I was violated. There is a street light at the corner, so even in the black of night, it's entirely possible for someone standing on this balcony to have seen at least some of what went down. Was that what happened? Had someone been standing on this balcony and witnessed the attack, or had that someone seen me crouching in those bushes earlier that day and decided to launch an attack of his own? And did that someone like beer, motorcycle magazines, and the air conditioning turned to high? Could that someone be described as weird or a little "off"? And could that someone be hiding in the bedroom of his grandmother's apartment at this very minute, someone who is creeping steadily toward me. . . .

I spin around, my hands shooting out to thwart my attacker, a strangled cry escaping my lips, becoming louder, as whatever semblance of control I had goes flying off the side of the balcony.

Mrs. Harkness underlines my scream with her own. She backs into the living room, her eyes spinning around wildly, as if afraid to settle. "What's wrong? What's happening?"

I take a minute to catch my breath and pull myself together. Tears are cascading down my cheeks. No one is there. Only Mrs. Harkness.

"What's wrong?" she asks, clearly unnerved by my behavior.

I stumble back into the frigid interior of the apartment, wiping away my tears with the back of my hand. "Could I trouble you for a glass of water?"

Mrs. Harkness moves swiftly to the tiny galley kitchen and returns with a plastic glass of cold water, holding it out for me. I gulp it down, my hands shaking so badly that I lose at least half the water down the front of my T-shirt. "Who are you? What's going on?" she asks, her eyes glued to my every twitch. "You're not with the police, are you?"

I shake my head.

"You're that woman, aren't you?" she says after a lengthy pause. "The one who was raped."

I shudder at being so easily unmasked. First Colin Lesser, now Mrs. Harkness. I might as well wear a sign.

"Do the police know you're here?"

"I was hoping I might be able to discover something they missed," I explain when I'm reasonably sure I can speak without my voice breaking.

"And have you?"

"Possibly," I tell her, too exhausted to lie. "I understand you have a grandson."

"Who told you that?"

"Is he here now?"

"I bet it was Mr. Saunders, from next door. He's always trying to make trouble for me. That bastard's had his eye on this apartment ever since he moved in, wants it for himself. He's been trying to get me to move out ever since my husband died."

"Is your grandson here now, Mrs. Harkness?"

Mrs. Harkness purses her lips and pushes her hair behind her right ear. "I never said I have a grandson."

"Well, I guess that's something the police can find out easily enough."

Her face crumples in on itself in defeat. She suddenly looks every one of her seventy-plus years. "That bastard's always complaining about Jason, that he makes too much noise or plays his music too loud. But he doesn't. And nobody else has ever complained. Only Mr. Saunders. And only because he has way too much time on his hands. He was let go from his job about six months ago and can't find anybody else who wants to hire him. Surprise, surprise."

"Is Jason here now, in this apartment?" I ask.

"I'd like you to leave," she responds.

"Are you sure that's really what you want? Because it will only throw more suspicion your grandson's way. The police can get a search warrant."

"They won't find anything. My grandson is a fine young man."

"I just want to talk to him."

"He had nothing whatsoever to do with what happened to you."

"Then he has nothing to be afraid of."

"I saw you that day, you know," she says accusingly.

"You saw me?"

"Saw you hiding in the bushes. Staring at the apartment across the way through your binoculars. I almost called the police to report we had a Peeping Tom."

"Why didn't you?"

"I decided it was probably best not to get involved."

"Because of Jason?"

"Of course not." Another pursing of her lips, another tug of her hair.

"Jason was here that night, wasn't he?"

"That's irrelevant. Jason has been staying with me off and on since the summer. He doesn't get along with his stepfather. I said he was always welcome to come here, that I was grateful for the company. . . ."

"Did you tell the police that Jason has been staying with you?"

"I didn't see any reason to. Neither of us saw the actual attack. We were both asleep when it happened."

"You said you have only one bedroom. . . ."

"Yes. So what?"

"I'm assuming that Jason sleeps out here, on the sofa." I glance toward the blanket resting in the corner of the leather sectional.

"What exactly are you getting at?"

"That you don't really know where Jason was at the time I was attacked, do you? That he could have easily slipped out after you went to bed, and that that's the reason you failed to mention him to the police. . . ."

"That's utter nonsense. What were you doing hiding out there in the bushes anyway, spying on people? If you ask me, you were just asking for trouble."

Her words hit me like a slap on the face, producing a fresh barrage of tears. I turn away.

Which is when I see him.

A young man of medium height and weight, in his late teens or early twenties, with chin-length brown hair and impenetrable brown eyes. He is standing no more than ten feet from me, and although his arms hang still at his sides, I can feel them reaching for my throat. "What's going on, Nana?" he asks.

Tell me you love me.

"Oh, God." I feel my legs wobbling beneath me. The glass of water slips through my fingers and falls to the floor.

Instantly Jason is at my elbow, pulling me toward the armchair, pushing me into the seat.

"Take your hands off me!" I cry, swatting him away.

"Hey," he says, his voice suddenly angry. "What the hell . . . ?"

"Jason, sweetheart," his grandmother says, her voice soothing and low, "go back into the bedroom, darling. This lady was just about to leave."

"What'd she hit me for? You don't hit," he warns.

"Please, darling. Go back to the bedroom."

He releases his grip on my elbow, although he continues to stare at me through dark, angry eyes. "I want her to leave," he says.

"She's going, sweetheart. In just a few minutes."

"What's she doing here anyway?"

"She just came to ask a few questions."

"What kind of questions? About me? Something about me you want to know?" he demands.

I shake my head, tears springing to my eyes.

"Just give us another minute and she'll be gone."

Jason shoots me a look that is equal parts impatience and fury. Then he turns and skulks back toward the bedroom, leaving me trembling in the seat where he has placed me.

"I'm sure you can understand now why I didn't tell the police about Jason. He's obviously different. . . ."

"He's obviously angry."

"Jason has had a very difficult life. His mother, my former daughter-in-law, was addicted to drugs and alcohol. Jason was born with fetal-alcohol syndrome. My son isn't the most responsible of fathers, and unfortunately Jason's stepfather is even worse. Jason has struggled all his life. But, I promise you, he's a good boy. He didn't rape you."

"You're aware he fits the general description of the man who did."

"Jason is not the man responsible."

"How can you be so sure?"

"Because I know my grandson. Now," she says, walking to the door and opening it, "I'm afraid I have to insist that you leave. Or this time I *will* call the police."

I remain in my seat. "Please do," I say.

—TWENTY-THREE—

"Are you crazy? What in God's name were you thinking?"

Detective Castillo has been taking me to task for much of the past hour, ever since we left Mrs. Harkness's apartment and returned to my own. I understand his exasperation. I've been asking myself the same question, although I would never say as much to him.

"You *do* realize you could have blown this whole investigation?"

"What investigation?" I demand. "You didn't even know Mrs. Harkness *had* a grandson."

"We would have found out."

"Really? When?"

"That's not the point."

"What *is* the point?"

"The point is that you had no business going to see Mrs. Harkness in the first place." He runs a hand through his thick, black hair and turns to stare out my living room window.

"I had every right."

"You know I could arrest you for impersonating a police officer," Castillo tells me.

He has implied this several times already. "I never told Mrs. Harkness I was a police officer."

"You led her to believe . . ."

"I did no such thing. I have no control over what she may or may not have assumed."

"Be that as it may—"

"Look, Detective Castillo," I interrupt, losing patience with the conversation. "I did nothing wrong or illegal. I am perfectly within my rights to question potential witnesses. I am a licensed investigator. . . ."

"You are the *victim*."

The victim, I repeat silently, bristling at the immediate and total reduction in my status, of having been relegated to that unfortunate sub-species of human being known simply as *victim*. "Thank you for that little reminder, Detective. I'd almost forgotten. But *be that as it may*," I continue, throwing his words back at him, "I think you know that I can be of significant help to you."

"How? By interfering in our investigation, by intimidating potential witnesses, by prejudicing our case. . . ."

"What case? You have no case. If it weren't for me, you wouldn't even have a suspect."

"Are you saying you're ready to identify Jason Harkness as the man who raped you?" Officer Dube asks. Until now, he has remained largely silent, seemingly content to stand in the background and watch me spar with Detective Castillo.

I glare at Officer Dube. He knows I can't say for sure that Jason Harkness is the man who raped me, that I have only the vaguest sense of the man responsible. There's no way I can make a positive identification.

"What about his voice?" Castillo asks, his own voice softening.

"What about it?"

"Jason Harkness spoke to you. Did he sound like the man who raped you?"

I close my eyes, hear my rapist whispering in my ear. *Tell me you love me.*

I sink to the closest sofa at hand, a wave of dizziness sweeping over my head as I try to reconcile the two disparate voices, to fit one on top of the other, mingle the two of them together, to force a fit. "I don't know."

"You don't know?"

"I can't be sure. It's possible. . . ."

"Possible," Officer Dube repeats with a none-too-subtle shake of his head. "We should have no trouble at all securing a warrant with that resounding endorsement."

"Here's what I *do* know," I tell the two men. "Jason Harkness fits the general description of the man who raped me. He was in the area the night it happened. His grandmother's apartment over-looks the exact spot where I was attacked, so he had both access and opportunity. Furthermore, he's a damaged, angry young man whom I'm guessing was probably abused or, at the very least, ne-glected during his formative years, making him a pretty good can-didate to commit future acts of violence. Have you even checked to see if he has a record?"

"First thing I did when we got here," Castillo answers, indicat-ing the cell phone in his hand.

"And?"

"Just waiting for someone to get back to me."

There is a moment of silence for which I sense we are all pro-foundly grateful. It gives us a chance to remember that we are not adversaries, that we are, in fact, on the same side, and that we all want the same thing: to find the man who did this to me and put him behind bars.

Actually, I want more than that. I want to scratch out his eyes and rip out his throat, then castrate him and beat him to a bloody pulp before flinging his battered, mutilated corpse to the sharks that swim through my nightmares. That's what I want. But I'll settle for finding him and putting him behind bars.

"I'm sorry," I offer. "I really didn't mean to step on anyone's toes. . . ."

"It's not a question of stepping on toes," Castillo says. "It's a matter of using your head. You're way too close to this, Bailey. I understand your wanting to help, but you can't. What you're liable to do is get yourself killed."

"I think you're being a touch dramatic."

"Think about it, Bailey. What if Jason Harkness *is* the man who raped you? And what if you'd gone to his grandmother's apartment and she hadn't been home? But he *was* home. Have you thought about what could have happened then?"

I have to admit that I hadn't even considered this possibility. Considering it now sends shivers up and down my spine.

"You're shooting from the hip, Bailey. Firing off blindly in all directions at once. A few days ago you were convinced it was Paul Giller who raped you. . . ."

"I never said I was convinced," I argue, although my heart is no longer in it.

"Okay," the detective says. "I don't think there's anything to be gained by rehashing everything again."

I nod my head in agreement. "So what now?"

"You let us do our job. You get on with your life," he adds, almost as an afterthought.

What do you think I'm trying to do? I want to ask him, but I decide it would be more prudent to remain silent. There's nothing to be gained by challenging him. "There's someone else you should probably check on," I say instead, pulling Colin Lesser's business card out of my pocket and handing it to the detective.

He glances at the card, then back at me. "Who's this?"

"Someone I met this afternoon."

"I take it your meeting had nothing to do with the fact that he's a chiropractor."

I do my best to downplay the absurdity of our meeting.

"He was jogging; you were standing in the bushes where you were raped," Castillo reiterates, refusing to let me off the hook so easily. He massages the bridge of his nose, as if trying to ward off a budding migraine.

"I just thought it might be worth your taking a look. . . ."

"Of course. We'll do a background check on the man." He pockets Colin's card. "We should probably get going," he says to his partner.

The phone rings, and I jump.

"Why don't you get that," Castillo says. "We can show ourselves out."

They are approaching the door as I reach the kitchen and pick up the phone. It's Finn from the concierge desk. "I know the cops are there," he begins, "and I thought I should give you a heads up. Your brother, Heath, is on his way up. He's pretty wasted. . . ."

A wave of panic sweeps over me as I realize that Heath is already on one side of my door, the cops on the other. "Bailey?" I hear him call out, proceeding to knock loudly and repeatedly. "Bailey? I know you're still pissed, and I'm here to apologize and beg forgiveness."

The fact that my brother is either drunk or stoned or, very likely, both is not missed by either of the two officers. "For what?" Castillo asks me as I approach. "Anything we should be aware of?"

I shake my head. I haven't said anything to the police about the incident at my parents' house. What would be the point?

I pull open the door. Heath all but falls inside, his breath reeking of alcohol, his head buried inside the cloud of smoke emanating from the joint in his hand.

"You gotta be kidding me," Detective Castillo states, taking several steps back as Heath tumbles toward him.

"Uh-oh." Heath dissolves in a fit of giggles at the sight of the two police officers.

"Heath, for God's sake . . ."

"Suppose you hand that over." Castillo lifts the lit joint from between Heath's fingers and pinches it out.

"Hey . . ."

"Bailey, I think your brother could use a glass of water," he suggests.

"Or even better, a nice tall gin and tonic," Heath calls after me as I hurry back into the kitchen.

"Suppose we go into the living room," I hear Officer Dube say.

"And who exactly is doing this supposing?" Heath asks. "I don't believe we've been properly introduced."

"This is Officer Dube," Castillo is saying as I return with Heath's water.

"You're kidding me, right?" comes Heath's instant reply, followed by another round of giggles. "Officer Doobie? Is he kidding me, Bailey?"

"Shut up, Heath," I tell him, following the men into the living room and pushing the glass into my brother's hands. We stand in a loose square in front of the sofas. Nobody sits down.

Detective Castillo is glaring at Heath. "Just what do you think you're doing?"

"What am I doing?" Heath repeats. "I'm here to support my baby sister during her time of need."

"You think this sort of behavior is helping her?"

"More than you are, I bet." He takes a long sip from his glass. "Love your shirt, by the way. There's just something about those bold Hawaiian prints that screams competence."

"Please, Heath. Be quiet."

"Tell me you didn't drive here," Officer Dube says.

"Okay," Heath replies with a smirk. "Have it your way. I didn't drive here."

"Don't be a smart-ass."

"Or what? You'll haul my smart ass off to jail?"

Detective Castillo drops Heath's joint into the same pocket as he put Colin Lesser's business card. "You have any more of these on you?"

"You looking to score?"

"Heath . . ."

"Regrettably, no, I have no more doobies, Officer Doobie," Heath says. "Oh, no, wait. That's Officer Doobie over there, isn't it?" He turns away, singing, "Doobie, doobie, do . . ."

"Heath . . ."

"You're welcome to search me, if you'd like." He plops down on the sofa, stretching his long legs out in front of him and cradling the back of his head in the palms of his hands, as if relaxing in a hammock on the beach.

"Please don't arrest him," I say, wanting to kick Heath's feet out from under him.

Detective Castillo nods. "Just don't let him leave here until he sobers up."

"I won't. Thank you."

Detective Castillo's cell phone rings, and he answers it before it can ring a second time. "Castillo," he says. I watch his face as he listens. "Really? Okay, thanks. That's very interesting." He's looking at me as he disconnects. "Apparently Jason Harkness does indeed have a record."

"What for?"

"Don't know. The record's sealed."

"What do you mean it's sealed?"

"Just that. Apparently whatever offense he committed happened when he was a juvenile, and his record was sealed."

"Can you get it unsealed?"

"Come on, Bailey," Heath says. "Even I know better than that. Once a record's sealed, it's sealed."

"Your brother's right," Castillo says. "Unless, of course, someone at the District Attorney's Office happens to hear about this and pulls a few strings."

Can I ask Gene to do this? Would he even consider it? And in the unlikely possibility my half-brother were to agree to peek into Jason Harkness's juvenile files, what would he ask for in return? "I'm sorry. I can't ask him. . . ."

"I'm not asking you to. Don't worry. I'm sure someone will bring it to his attention. Not that we'd be able to use any evidence obtained in those records in court. It would be inadmissible," he reminds me.

"It would still be helpful," I counter. "If there's a conviction for any kind of assault in those files, it would give us leverage. We might be able to use it to extract a confession. . . ."

"*We* won't be doing anything," Castillo says, emphasizing the pronoun. "I thought I had made that clear."

"Of course. It was just a figure of speech."

"Who's Jason Harkness?" Heath asks. "Is he a suspect?"

"I'll let your sister explain," Castillo says, as he and Officer Dube step into the hall. "Get your act together," he advises Heath.

"Get your act together," Heath mimics after they're gone and the door is safely closed. "Who the hell does he think he is?"

"He's a police detective, you idiot."

"Well, he's not a very good one." Heath kicks off his shoes, and half a dozen hand-rolled cigarettes immediately scatter across the marble floor. He is instantly on his hands and knees, scooping them up.

"What is the matter with you?" I ask. "Are you *trying* to get arrested?"

He dismisses my concern with a shake of his hand. "They never look in your shoes."

"You deliberately tried to provoke them. . . ."

"In my defense, I didn't know they'd be here."

"How is that any kind of defense?"

"I was caught off guard. You know I always go on the offensive when I'm surprised."

"Well, you were offensive all right."

"Whoa! Welcome back, little sister. Nice to see you're finally starting to get your mojo back. I've missed you."

His comment momentarily takes my breath away. I sink to the sofa across from him. Is he right?

"Look. I just came by to tell you I'm really sorry about the other day. You were right. I shouldn't have disobeyed a court order. I shouldn't have brought those people into our father's house. My behavior was unacceptable, not to mention reckless and maybe even stupid. I did a bad thing and I apologize. How's that for sounding like a grown-up?"

"Not half-bad."

"Good. I think this calls for a celebration." Heath holds up one of his newly recaptured joints. "A smoke of the old peace pipe?"

"Put those damn things away."

"Not until you have a puff. Come on, Bailey. It won't kill you to relax a little." He pulls a tattered book of matches from the side pocket of his tight leather pants and lights a joint, inhaling deeply. He tucks the others in his pocket, along with the matchbook. Then he holds the cigarette out for me to take.

I haven't smoked weed since I broke things off with Travis, and even before that, I was an infrequent user who never particularly enjoyed getting high. I take the joint from his hand, intending to do as Detective Castillo did earlier and extinguish it between my fingers. But instead of butting it out, I find myself lifting it to my lips and taking a drag. I feel the smoke fill my throat and settle deep into my lungs.

"Atta girl, Bailey," Heath says proudly, reaching across the coffee table to take a toke of his own.

We spend the next fifteen minutes passing the joint back and forth, smoking it down until it literally disintegrates in my hands. I am very pleasantly stoned, and wondering when exactly that happened. I didn't feel anything for most of those fifteen minutes, convinced my long layoff had left me immune to the drug's supposed charms, and yet here I am, feeling quite mellow and even a bit serene.

The phone rings, and for the first time since my attack, I don't jump. Instead my head turns lazily toward the sound.

"Who is it?" Heath asks. "Don't answer it," he advises in his next breath.

But I'm already on my feet, the ringing pulling me like a magnet. "Hello?"

"Bailey?"

"Claire?"

"Were you sleeping? Did I wake you up?"

"No. What time is it?"

"Just after six. You sound funny. Are you feeling okay?"

I try to pull myself together. Claire would definitely not approve of my getting stoned. "I'm fine."

"Are you having a panic attack?"

"No. I'm just a little tired."

"So how'd it go this afternoon?" she asks.

Have the police already contacted her? I wonder.

"With Elizabeth Gordon," she qualifies, as if sensing my confusion. "You went, didn't you?"

I breathe a sigh of relief, although the relief is tinged with guilt. I don't like lying to Claire. I don't like keeping things from her. "Yes. Yes, of course I went."

"And? How'd it go?"

"It went well."

"You think she's helping?"

"I do. I really do."

"Doobie, doobie, do," I hear Heath sing out from the other room, and I can't help myself—I laugh.

"Bailey, Bailey, what's going on? Is someone there?"

"No, of course not. Nobody's here. Nothing's going on." I force a cough from my lungs. "I think I might be coming down with something."

"Shit. I knew you sounded a bit off."

A bit off, I repeat silently, trying to remember where I've heard something like that before.

"You want me to bring over some chicken soup when I'm finished work?"

"No, that's all right. I was actually thinking of getting into bed early."

"That's probably a good idea. You sure you don't want me to drop by?"

"What I want is for you to go home to Jade and stop worrying about me."

"Okay. But feel free to call me if you start to feel worse. Don't worry about the time. I'll probably be up."

"I'll call you tomorrow," I tell her.

"Feel better," she says.

I hang up the phone, feeling the pleasant buzz I'd been experiencing already starting to dissipate. I return to the living room and stand in the doorway, watching as Heath lights up another joint and extends it lazily toward me. I shake my head and continue down the hall toward the bedroom. I crawl into my unmade bed and pull the covers up over my head to block out the evening sun.

—

The phone rings, and I open my eyes to darkness. I check the clock as I reach for the receiver, see that it is almost midnight. I raise the phone to my ear, about to say hello when I realize there is no one on the other end. Just a dial tone. I return the phone to its charger.

My head feels as if it is weighted down with sandbags, and my throat is so dry I can barely muster up enough saliva to swallow. I get out of bed and shuffle to the bathroom, pour myself a glass of water. *I think your brother could use a glass of water,* I hear Detective Castillo say. When was that? How long ago?

I have a sudden image of Heath sprawled out across my living room sofa, his head lolling back against its pillows, his beautiful face hidden inside a cloud of marijuana smoke. Everything falls into place. "Damn it." What the hell was I thinking?

I return to the bedroom and grab the scissors from my nightstand, carrying them in front of me as I proceed down the corridor. "Heath?" I call out, flipping on the light when I reach the living room and looking toward the sofa where I last saw him.

He's not there.

Nor is he on the other sofa or on the floor or in the kitchen, the powder room, or sprawled across the sofa bed in my office. "Heath," I call again, even though I know he's no longer anywhere in my apartment, that he must have slipped out sometime after I fell asleep.

Which means that he left the door to my condo unlocked.

Immediately I secure the lock, then do another search of my apartment, my heart racing, my legs shaking, my panic building, as I peek into every nook and cranny, all traces of my drug-induced calm now gone, although the suffocating scent of marijuana trails after me.

I return to my bedroom, understanding full well that I won't be able to sleep. Instead, I grab my binoculars off the nightstand and push the button that raises the blinds, knowing that the lights in Paul Giller's apartment will be on. I'm aware I'm disobeying another police directive, that they have warned me against spying on my neighbors, but what the hell? I'm already in their bad books, and this beats staying up all night, wandering the halls and berating myself for my stupidity.

I see them.

They are standing in front of the bed and they are arguing. Even with no sound, I can hear Paul's voice rising in anger as his hands wave theatrically in front of him, the index finger of his right hand jabbing repeatedly at the air. Elena is shaking her head and crying—pleading, interrupting, trying to get a word in.

I move closer to the window, adjusting the lens of my binoculars in an effort to bring these two strangers closer. If the expression on Paul's face is indicative of the tone of his voice, he is only seconds away from losing control. I watch, helpless and spellbound, as he advances menacingly toward Elena, backing her against the window.

They remain in their respective positions for several minutes: Paul shouting, Elena cowering: Paul accusing, Elena denying. And then Elena has had all she can take. She tries to break away, getting as far as the bed before Paul physically restrains her, grabbing her elbow with his hand and spinning her around. Elena attempts to pull out of his reach, which only enrages Paul further. He slaps her hard across the face, so hard that she falls back across the bed, and when she tries to get up, he slaps her again.

And he doesn't stop.

"No!" I cry out, my cheeks on fire from the force of his slaps, my ears ringing as he climbs on top of her, straddling her while continuing to pummel her with his fists. "No!" I shout as he pulls up her nightgown and unzips his jeans. "No!" I scream as he pushes his way roughly inside her.

I am sobbing as I stumble across the room and reach for the phone.

Feel free to call me, Claire said. *As late as you want.* "Bailey?" she says when she picks up the phone. "What is it? Are you okay?"

I tell her what I've just witnessed.

"Call the police," she says. "I'll be right over."

—TWENTY-FOUR—

Twenty minutes later, Claire is at my door. She is wearing gray sweatpants, a rumpled gray T-shirt, and lime-green Crocs. Her face is devoid of makeup, and her hair is pulled into a loose ponytail at the base of her neck.

"What's happening?" she asks, heading straight for the bedroom and grabbing my binoculars off the floor where I dropped them earlier. "Have the police shown up yet?"

"No."

"I can't see anything," she says, sweeping the binoculars across the side of Paul's building. "All the lights are out."

"What? No—they were on a minute ago."

Claire hands me the binoculars for me to check for myself.

I shake my head. Paul must have turned the lights off when I left the room to answer the door.

"You *did* call the police, didn't you?" Claire says.

"I told them that a woman was being attacked in her apartment. I gave them the address and apartment number."

"What did they say?"

"I didn't give them a chance to say anything. I just told them a woman was being attacked and hung up."

"You didn't tell them your name?"

I shake my head again, trying to shake away lingering feelings of guilt. I know the police aren't always quick about following through on anonymous tips. I should have given them my name.

Claire takes a moment to think this through. "Okay. Okay. Let's wait and see what happens. How are you doing? Are you feeling any better?"

"I don't know."

She reaches out and takes me in her arms. "I'm so sorry, Bailey. I should have been here."

"No. I told you not to come."

"I shouldn't have listened. I could tell something wasn't right." She puts her hand on my forehead. "You're feeling a little flushed. Do you have a thermometer?"

"I don't have a fever."

"I don't know. You're a little warm."

"It's nothing." I look toward the floor as another wave of guilt sweeps over me. "It happens sometimes when I get stoned."

"What?"

"I was stoned," I whisper.

"*What?*" she says again.

"Heath was here," I add, as if this explains everything.

"You got high?"

I shrug. What is there to say? "I'm sorry."

"You don't owe me any apologies, Bailey. You're a big girl. It's just that . . ."

"What?"

"Are you sure about what you saw?" she asks, as direct as ever.

"You think I made it up?"

"No. Of course I don't think that. But if you were stoned . . ."

"You think I might have been hallucinating?"

"It's a possibility, isn't it? We get all sorts of people turning up in the ER who got a little more than they bargained for when they lit up a supposedly innocent joint. What Heath gave you could have been laced with some pretty potent stuff. . . ."

"But that was hours ago."

"If it was laced with LSD, it could stay in your system for days. You know that. Is there any chance you might have been dreaming?"

Is there? The only thing I know for certain is that for the first time, I see doubt in Claire's eyes. And I hate it. "I don't know. I was asleep. The phone rang. . . ."

"The phone rang?" she repeats. "Who called?"

"I don't know. There was just a dial tone. Maybe it didn't even ring. Maybe I *was* dreaming. . . ."

"Where is Heath now?" Claire looks toward the hallway, as if he might be lurking in the shadows.

"He was gone when I woke up."

"So he wasn't here when you saw . . ." Her voice trails off. The question remains unfinished.

"No. He wasn't here. He didn't see anything." Did *I*? I can't help wonder, knowing Claire is thinking the same thing. "He can't back me up."

Claire's cheeks redden, as if I've physically struck her. "It's not that I don't believe you. It's just that . . ."

"You have doubts," I say, finishing the sentence for her.

She opens her mouth to speak, but only a sigh escapes.

The phone rings, and we both jump at the unexpected sound. "Okay. This is definitely no dream," Claire says, plucking the phone from its stand. "Hello?" Her shoulders stiffen, then relax. "Okay. Thank you. Yes. You can send them up." She hangs up the phone. I realize I'm holding my breath. "That was Stanley, from the concierge desk. The police are here."

"They're *here*? What does that mean?"

"I guess we're about to find out."

The two uniformed policemen notice the smell of marijuana as soon as I open the door, their noses sniffing at the air like dogs after a scent. One officer nods knowingly toward the other as the two men enter my foyer. Immediately I recognize the younger of the two from various cases I've worked on, although I can't for the life of me remember his name.

"Bailey," he says in greeting.

"Sam," I hear myself say, his name appearing out of the blue and landing on my lips just in the nick of time.

"I heard about what happened," he says. "I'm very sorry."

It takes me a few moments to realize that he is referring to my rape.

"This is my partner," Sam says. "Patrick Llewellyn."

"Officer," my sister and I say at the same time.

Patrick Llewellyn is several inches taller and at least a decade older than his partner whose last name, I remember now, is Turnbull. He is as white as Sam is black, his hair as fine and red as Sam's is dark and curly. Both are handsome in that rough, offhand way that cops often possess, their uniforms enhancing their appeal. "You are . . . ?" Sam asks Claire.

Claire introduces herself as my sister, no halfs or hyphens attached, for which I am beyond grateful. "What can we do for you, officers?"

"I think you know why we're here," Patrick Llewellyn says.

Sam clears his throat. "Maybe we should sit down. . . ."

"Of course." Claire leads them into the living room, motioning them toward the sofas.

I follow, the distinct scent of marijuana becoming stronger with each step. I wince as Officer Llewellyn lowers himself into almost the exact spot where Heath lay puffing languorously away a few short hours ago. Sam lowers himself to the seat beside his partner while Claire and I perch on the opposite sofa.

"Can I get either of you something to drink?" Claire offers, as if it is perfectly normal to have two policemen sitting in your living room at this hour of the night, the lingering smell of weed circling everyone's heads like a noxious cloud, strong enough to induce light-headedness, even now. "Some water or juice?"

"Nothing, thank you," Llewellyn says as his partner nods. "Do you want to tell us what exactly happened tonight? You called the precinct to report a woman being attacked," he clarifies when I hesitate.

"Yes."

"You didn't leave your name."

"No."

"Mind my asking why?"

"I didn't think it was relevant."

"You know better than that," Sam says, and I feel the sting of his rebuke. "What exactly happened?" he asks again, notepad in hand, pen poised and waiting for my response.

I describe what I saw take place in Paul Giller's apartment, careful to keep my eyes on the floor so that I don't have to see the looks on the officers' faces.

"This isn't the first time you've reported Paul Giller's behavior to the police, I understand," Llewellyn says, flipping through his notepad, as if making sure of his facts.

"Did Paul Giller tell you that?"

"Is it true?"

"Yes," I admit.

"What has that got to do with anything?" Claire asks impatiently. "Surely what's important here are the events Bailey witnessed tonight."

"Which are what, exactly?" Sam asks again.

"That a woman was beaten and—"

"Were you here?" Sam interrupts Claire to ask.

"No. I—"

"So you didn't actually see anything?"

"No, but—"

"Then, you wouldn't mind letting your sister answer the question." Again, more an order than a request.

Claire sits back in her seat, covering her nose with the back of her hand when the motion results in a fresh current of marijuana-laced air.

"I saw Paul Giller beat and rape his girlfriend," I tell the officers.

"You're positive about that?"

I look toward Claire. Am I?

"How do you know the woman you saw is his girlfriend?" Sam asks.

I decide it is best not to tell them about my earlier exploits, understanding that I am likely to be viewed as a stalker. "I just assumed . . ."

Sam's attention is suddenly diverted by something on the floor. He bends over and reaches underneath the coffee table. When he straightens up again, he is holding one of Heath's errant, suspiciously hand-rolled cigarettes between his fingers.

Claire rolls her eyes and I close mine, picturing the joints flying from Heath's shoe and watching his mad scramble to retrieve them. Clearly, he missed one.

"Look, I know you've been through a pretty hard time lately, and I understand your needing a little escape, I really do," Sam says, "but if you were stoned at the time you made that call . . ."

"I wasn't stoned."

"You're saying you hadn't smoked a little weed—"

"More than a little, by the smell of things," Patrick Llewellyn interrupts.

"Okay, I might have been a little high earlier. But I wasn't when I saw Paul Giller. You don't believe me," I state, unable to ignore the looks on their faces any longer.

"What we believe isn't important," Sam says. "What's important is what happened."

"Which was, apparently, nothing," Llewellyn says.

"We went over to Paul Giller's apartment and questioned both him and his girlfriend," Sam continues. "The bedroom shows absolutely no signs of any disturbance, and they both vehemently deny an assault of any kind took place."

"Well, of course *she'd* deny it," Claire says, rushing to my defense. "If he was standing right beside her. . . ."

"There wasn't a bruise on her."

I go completely numb, recalling the bruises that covered most of my body in the immediate aftermath of my attack, bruises that have only recently begun to disappear.

"Look," Llewellyn says. "There's not much we can do when both parties insist no assault took place. You want my advice? Stop spying on your neighbors."

"I'm not spying."

"Really? What would you call it? Using binoculars to check out your neighbors might not technically be a crime, but making false accusations most definitely is."

"Please tell me you're not blaming the victim," Claire says.

"Your sister is not the victim here," he reminds her. "At least not tonight."

"You have to look at this from our perspective," Sam says, interrupting. "A month ago, you suffered a grievous assault. Since then, I understand you've made a number of unsubstantiated accusations against not only this Paul Giller but several other men as well, including David Trotter and Jason Harkness."

I gasp. So they already know about Jason Harkness.

"It's in your file," Sam says before I have the chance to inquire.

"Who's Jason Harkness?" Claire asks.

"You were also involved in a minor car accident a week ago," Sam continues, again checking his notes. "And tonight you placed an anonymous call to the police to report an assault that both the alleged assailant and his purported victim swear up and down never happened. Not only that, but we find evidence of marijuana in your apartment. . . ."

"Which I don't have to remind you is still illegal in the state of Florida," Llewellyn adds.

My head is spinning. What are they saying? "Are you going to arrest me?"

"No. We're going to pass on that. . . ."

"And Paul Giller? He gets a pass, too?" Claire asks.

"Luckily for your sister, Mr. Giller has declined to press charges," Llewellyn tells her.

"Charges? For what?" I ask.

"Harassment, for starters."

"Harassment? That's ridiculous."

"Is it? I'd say Paul Giller has good reason to be feeling more than a little pissed. He thinks you have some sort of vendetta against him."

Claire jumps to her feet. Clearly she's heard more than enough. "Sorry we wasted your time, gentlemen."

"Maybe you should think about getting some help," Sam whispers to me on their way out.

"Thank you," Claire tells them, closing the door before they can offer any more parting advice. "Who the hell is Jason Harkness?" she asks, spinning toward me as soon as they are gone.

I start walking to the bedroom. "I'm really tired, Claire. Can we do this another time?"

She is right behind me. "No, we can't do this another time. Who the hell is Jason Harkness?" she asks again. "What haven't you been telling me?"

I sink down on my bed, reluctantly confiding in her everything that happened after I left Elizabeth Gordon's office this afternoon and watching her expression shift from curiosity to mild alarm to total disbelief, as I knew it would.

"I don't understand. . . ."

"I just wanted to be doing something . . . taking control of my life . . . instead of sitting around, being so damn passive and afraid all the time."

"That's not what I'm talking about," she corrects. "Doing something, taking control, *that* I understand. What I can't wrap my head around is why you didn't tell me. What is it, Bailey? Don't you trust me?"

"Of course I trust you."

"Then why didn't you tell me what you were planning?"

"Because there *was* no plan. Things just . . . kind of happened."

Several seconds pass before she speaks. "Did anything else just *kind of happen* that I should know about?"

I shake my head, deciding not to mention my encounter with Colin Lesser. There's only so much that one rational human being can be expected to understand, only so much sympathy to go around.

Claire walks to the window and stares toward Paul Giller's

apartment. "So you think that maybe this Jason Harkness could be the man who raped you?"

I shrug. I don't know what I think anymore.

"And Paul Giller?" she asks. "What about him?"

"I don't know." I fall back so that I'm stretched horizontally across my bed, my right arm raised and draped across my eyes. "You think I'm crazy, don't you?"

"No, I don't think you're crazy. Well," Claire demurs, "maybe just a little." Her voice is soft, even kind. I hear the gentle whir of my bedroom blinds being lowered, and I remove my arm from across my eyes and turn my head toward her. She is getting undressed.

"What are you doing?"

"Getting ready for bed." She pulls a toothbrush out of the side pocket of her sweatpants. "See? I came prepared."

"What? No. You can't stay here."

"You really think you have the strength to kick me out?"

"What about Jade?"

"Sleeping like a baby when I left. I wrote her a note and I'll leave a message on her voice mail."

"No. I can't ask you to do this."

"You're not asking. I'm telling. Now shut up and get ready for bed. I don't have to be at work until noon." She walks toward the bathroom.

"Claire . . ."

"You're welcome," she says before I can formulate the words to thank her. "Now get some sleep."

—

I'm in the middle of a nightmare in which I'm being chased along the ocean road by a jogger wielding a large butcher knife. Across the street, in front of a small church, I see Heath sharing a joint with Paul Giller. My assailant catches up to me, grabbing my hair and pulling my head back, his knife slicing effortlessly across my throat. I collapse to the sidewalk, my life bleeding onto the hard concrete, as all around me, the sky fills with the sound of laughter and church bells explode in song.

I know it's the phone even before I'm fully awake, that its ringing has infiltrated my dream. I sit up and look over at Claire, who is sleeping beside me, undisturbed by either bad dreams or the untimely ringing of the telephone. Is it possible she doesn't hear it? Is it ringing at all? Am I still dreaming? "Claire," I say, my hand brushing against her shoulder. "Claire . . ."

She stirs, flips over onto her back. "Hmm?"

"The phone . . ."

She twists her head in my direction and opens her eyes. "What?" She pushes herself into a sitting position. "What's happening?"

"Do you hear the phone?"

Her head shoots toward the nightstand. "Somebody phoned?"

I realize the phone has stopped ringing.

"Were you having a nightmare?"

"I guess," I say, deciding it's easier this way.

She takes me in her arms. "Go back to sleep, sweetie," she says, drawing me back down and laying her head next to mine on the pillow, one arm draped protectively across my hip. "You're exhausted," she says, already drifting back toward unconsciousness. "You need your sleep."

I feel her breath warm on the nape of my neck as she succumbs to the sleep I know will elude me for the balance of the night. Instead I lie there beside her, afraid to close my eyes, waiting for the phone to ring again.

—

It rings at just after eight o'clock the next morning.

It isn't really ringing, I tell myself.

"Aren't you going to answer that?" Claire asks, rubbing her eyes and sitting up in bed.

"You can hear that?"

"Of course I can hear it."

I reach for the phone. "Hello?"

"It's Jade," the voice informs me without unnecessary preamble. "Is my mother still there?"

"Right beside me." I hand the phone to my sister, then proceed into the bathroom, deciding to forego my usual early morning search of the premises. I don't want to alarm Claire any more than is absolutely necessary.

When I return to the bedroom some twenty minutes later, scrubbed clean and wrapped in my voluminous terry cloth robe, Claire is already dressed and waiting for me with a hot cup of freshly brewed coffee. "Everything all right with Jade?" I ask.

"She's fine. Just wanted to know how late I'd be getting home tonight. Which means she probably has something devious in mind. Teenagers—what can I tell you?"

I feel guilty that I have taken Claire away from her daughter.

"Don't give me that look," Claire says. "This has nothing to do with you. How's your coffee? Strong enough?"

Claire has become so adept at reading my thoughts. "It's perfect," I tell her, even before I've taken a sip.

"So, what are the plans for today?" she asks as the phone rings again. "Want me to get that?" She glances at the caller ID. "Unknown caller," she remarks, picking up the phone before it can ring again. "Hello?" A slight pause. "No, this is her sister. Who can I say is calling?" Claire holds the phone out for me to take. "It's a Dr. Lesser," she whispers, eyebrows raised.

I feel the color drain from my face. It takes all my willpower to force a smile onto my lips, all my strength to exchange the coffee in my hand for the phone in hers. Why is he calling? What does he want? How did he get my number? "Hello?"

"Hi, there. Remember me?"

"Of course."

"Sorry to be calling so early, but I wanted to catch you before you went out."

Why is he calling? How did he get my number?

"Look. I'll get right to the point," he continues. "I find you . . . interesting, to say the least, and I'm calling because I was hoping I could persuade you to have dinner with me. I googled you, in case you're wondering how. . . ."

Someone else who can read my mind, I think, aware that Claire is watching me with curious eyes. "I can't."

"Can't or just don't find me as interesting as I find you?"

"Thank you very much for calling," I tell him. "I'll make another appointment as soon as I know my schedule." I disconnect the line before he can say another word. "My dentist," I lie. "Apparently I missed my last appointment."

"And he called you himself?"

"Must be a slow morning," I offer as the phone in my hand rings again.

"Not around here," Claire says.

I lift the phone to my ear, a series of disconcerting thoughts swirling through my brain: *Why did I lie to Claire? What was Colin's real motive for calling me? Is it possible he's exactly as he presents—a man who finds me "interesting" and wants to take me to dinner?* "Hello?" I all but shout into the receiver in an effort to send such thoughts scattering.

I listen to the familiar voice on the other end of the line, my heart moving to my mouth, my breath freezing in my lungs.

Tell me you love me.

"Oh, God." I click off the phone and let it fall to the floor.

"What is it?" Claire asks. "Who was that, Bailey?"

"It was Detective Castillo," I answer when I'm able to find my voice.

"What did he say? *Tell me.*"

"Apparently another woman was raped last night about ten blocks from where I was attacked. They have a man in custody, and they want me to come to the station to see if I can identify him."

"When?"

"As soon as possible."

Claire lowers my cup of coffee to the nightstand. "Let's go."

—TWENTY-FIVE—

Approximately forty minutes later Claire pulls my car into the parking lot of the police station at 400 Northwest 2nd Avenue in the part of downtown Miami known as Little Havana. The sky is threatening rain, and the winds, already blowing at twenty-five miles an hour, are picking up speed. According to the weather report on the all-news radio station we've been listening to, a tropical storm is gathering strength somewhere east of Cuba, although there's still hope it will miss Florida, dying an inauspicious death somewhere in the middle of the Atlantic.

"Ready?" Claire asks, turning off the engine and unbuckling her seat belt.

Ready to meet the man who raped you?

"You can do this." She reaches over to pat my hand.

I look toward the modern mainly white structure that is something of an architectural hodgepodge, with its angular, McDonald's-esque exoskeleton frame jutting from its sides to wrap around the upper floors. The building is three, maybe four stories high, it's hard to tell from this angle. Bold blue letters across the top of its exterior spell out MIAMI POLICE DEPARTMENT. Tall, leafy trees—

the kind whose names I should know but never seem to remember—line the sidewalk and walkway leading to the front door.

You can do this, I repeat silently. *You can do this.*

I don't move.

"We can just sit here a while," Claire says, although I know she doesn't have all day, that she has to be at work by noon. "This is such an interesting area," she comments, looking down the decidedly blue-collar street that contains little of note. "Did you know that originally this area was chock-a-block with Jewish delis? Then came the Cuban bodegas and espresso shops. And now the Latinos have pretty much taken over."

"Interesting," I say, although I've only heard snatches of what she's been saying. "How do you know all this?" We both know I'm not really interested in Claire's answer, that I'm simply trying to prolong the conversation, a conversation it's clear Claire only initiated to distract me from my swelling panic.

"Jade's been studying local history in school. Or more accurately, *I've* been studying, and she's been goofing off. Oh, well. Maybe she'll learn by osmosis."

"You're a good mom."

"The jury's still out on that one," she demurs.

"And a great sister."

She laughs, a surprisingly hollow sound. "Heath doesn't think so."

Heath doesn't think, I correct silently, although I would never voice this thought out loud. To do so would be disloyal to the only real sibling I've ever known. Until now. "That's just because he doesn't know you."

"Nor does he want to."

"He'll change his mind."

"Maybe." Claire checks her watch. "You ready to do this?"

"How can I identify a man I never saw?"

"You'll take a good look. You'll take your time. You'll do your best. That's all anyone can ask."

I nod and push open the passenger door, feeling the wind pushing back, as if warning me to stay put. Claire comes around to my side of the car and grabs my hand, guiding me across the parking lot. The wind is whipping my hair into a frenzy. It shoots out in all directions, as if I've just stepped on a live wire, each strand a tiny whip lashing at my cheeks and eyes. "It's funny the way things work out, isn't it?" I ask, coming to a sudden halt behind an ancient black Buick, amazed at what I'm about to say.

"How so?"

"If everything hadn't happened," I begin, "if I hadn't been raped . . . then you and I might never have connected."

"That's true."

"So maybe I should thank him."

"How about you just kick him in the balls?"

I actually smile. "Definitely a better idea."

—

Detective Castillo is waiting for us in the lobby.

The first floor of the station is airy and bright, despite the gloom-filled skies outside the wrap-around windows and the seriousness of what goes on inside the maze of interior offices. I've been here many times in the course of various investigations, and I've always found the building to be relatively pleasant, despite the mug shots and photos of America's Ten Most Wanted that line the corridors. This is the first time I've ever felt it to be intimidating.

"Bailey. . . . Claire," Castillo says by way of greeting. "Thanks for getting here so quickly. Looks like we might be in for quite the storm."

"Hopefully, we'll miss the worst of it," Claire comments.

"You look nervous," the detective tells me as I smooth my hair away from my face. "How are you feeling?"

"Terrified." I wonder if he's been briefed about the events of last night.

"Don't be. Just remember, you can see them but they can't see you."

Knowing this doesn't help at all.

He leads us down a hallway whose walls are covered with re-cruitment posters, notices, and announcements for upcoming events as well as framed and formally posed photographs of high-ranking members of the force. "I understand some officers dropped by to see you last night," he says, his voice casual, as if what he is saying is of little importance. "We'll talk about it later," he adds ominously as he opens the door to one of the inner offices.

"Shit," I mutter underneath my breath.

"You can do this," Claire says again, misinterpreting the ex-pletive.

We are joined by Officer Dube, who follows us into the room and closes the door behind him. He says hello, asks how I'm doing, tells me there's no need to be nervous because although I'll be able to see the suspects, they won't be able to see me. It still doesn't help.

The room in which we find ourselves is small and windowless. Recessed lighting, a nondescript tile floor. Except for a couple of orange plastic chairs pushed against the eggshell-colored wall to my left, the room is devoid of furniture. There are no photographs on display, no decorative watercolors, nothing at all to distract from the purpose of the place, which is to view the suspects who will soon be lining up on the other side of the glass partition that takes up most of the far wall. I tuck my navy-striped jersey inside my white cotton pants—the same pants I was wearing yesterday, I realize, noting the streaks of dirt across my hips—and clear my throat. I used to be so fastidious about what I wore.

"Would you like something to drink?" Castillo asks.

"I'd love some water."

Officer Dube leaves the room.

"Nothing for me," Claire says, although she hasn't been asked. "So, you think you have the man who raped my sister?"

"We have a suspect in custody with regard to another rape that occurred last night in the same general vicinity as where Bailey was attacked."

The same area I returned to yesterday afternoon, I think, suppressing an involuntary shudder. I find myself wondering if my visit had something to do with this latest assault. Could I be responsible in any way?

"The same M.O.?" I hear Claire ask, the initials sounding so foreign on her tongue that I almost laugh out loud.

"There are some differences."

"What do you mean, differences?"

"Why don't we wait until after your sister has had a chance to view the suspects," Castillo says as the door to the room opens again and Officer Dube reenters with my glass of water. He places a paper cup filled with water into my noticeably trembling hands. I take a sip before the water can spill out onto the floor.

"There's no reason to be nervous," Officer Dube tells me again. "You can see them, but they can't see you."

The door opens. A young woman enters. She is tall and gangly, with long arms and wide hips. Chin-length jet-black hair frames a somewhat horsey face. Apparently she's with the Public Defender's Office.

"Hello," she says in a Marilyn Monroe–like whisper that is as incongruous as it is disconcerting.

"I'm sure you're familiar with the procedure," Castillo states, before going on to describe it. "We'll bring in five men. They'll each step forward so that you can get a good look at them, then turn so that you can view them in profile. We'll also be asking them to speak, to say the words the rapist said to you. . . ."

Tell me you love me.

My knees buckle. My hands begin to shake uncontrollably. The paper cup filled with water slips through my fingers and falls to the tile floor. I cry out.

"Just leave it," Castillo directs, although Officer Dube is already bending down to scoop up the now-empty cup and reaching for a paper towel to wipe the water from the floor. "I know how difficult this is for you, Bailey, but it's also really important. You may not have gotten a good look at him, but you heard his voice. You can do this," he says, as Claire said earlier.

She reaches over to grip my hand.

"I'm afraid I'm going to have to ask Bailey's sister to leave the room," the woman from the Public Defender's Office states.

"Please," I beg Detective Castillo. "Can't she stay?"

"We can't have anyone potentially influencing the witness," comes the breathy whisper that is starting to irritate me.

Officer Dube opens the door. "You can have a seat out here," he tells Claire, directing her to the row of orange plastic chairs that lines the hallway.

Claire hugs me. "Take a deep breath," she reminds me. "Take a good look. Take your time. Do your best. I'll be right outside this door." She gives my hand one last squeeze, then leaves the room.

"Ready?" Castillo asks as soon as she is gone. His finger is already on the intercom, and as soon as I nod, he gives the order to send the men in.

Take a deep breath.

I inhale, releasing it slowly as I watch five men enter the well-lit space on the other side of the glass. Each man carries a small sign numbered one through five and holds it against his chest. On cue, they all turn to face me, five pairs of eyes blank and staring straight ahead. According to the chart behind them, the men hover between five feet nine and five feet eleven inches. Each is of average weight and build, although numbers one and five are noticeably more muscular than the other three. All have brown hair. Numbers two and four appear to be in their twenties, numbers one and five slightly older, number three the oldest by at least a decade. Numbers three and four are likely Spanish, the other three white. All are dressed in dark T-shirts and blue jeans.

All seem vaguely familiar.

Number five in particular. I've definitely seen him before.

Take a good look.

"Number one, please step forward."

Number one steps forward.

I take him in from head to toe.

"Turn to your left. Now your right."

In profile, the man is slightly better looking than he is head-on, although he stops well short of handsome. The overhead light exaggerates the cut of his biceps, making the muscles in his arms seem even more pronounced than they were before.

Can this be the man who raped me?

"Say *Tell me you love me,*" Castillo directs, and I shudder at the sound of those words on his lips.

"Tell me you love me," number one barks without inflection.

I shake my head. I don't think this is the man who raped me.

"Step back."

Number one returns to his original position.

"Number two, please step forward."

Number two takes a lazy step forward, his shoulders slouched, a bored look on his acne-scarred face. He is instructed to turn left and then right, and to say *Tell me you love me.*

Even though he sounds nothing like the man who raped me, I have to fight the urge to throw up. There is something so menacing about his tone, something so effortlessly angry in the insolent slouch of his shoulders. I shake my head, stealing a glance toward number five, my panic escalating. Is this the man the police apprehended last night, the man who raped another woman not far from the spot where I was attacked? Could number five be the man who raped me?

"Step back. Number three, step forward please."

Number three looks to be about forty. In addition to being the oldest, he's the most jittery. He bounces into position, swaying from one foot to the other and all but vibrating as he turns first to his left, then his right. He spits out *Tell me you love me* as directed, tiny traces of an accent in the words.

He is not the man who raped me.

"Number four."

Number four is both the youngest and the tallest of the five men. He is also the skinniest. He turns left, then right, and mangles the words he is directed to say, so that he is instructed to say them again, not once but twice. The repetition only serves to make it clear that he is not the man who attacked me.

Number five steps forward as number four is stepping back.

He is the best looking of the five men, and he looks the strongest. He is also deeply tanned, even a little sunburned. He doesn't wait for instructions, turning left and then right before being directed to do so.

"Somebody's hot to trot," Officer Dube states.

"Say *Tell me you love me,*" Castillo instructs.

"Tell me you love me," he responds. Loudly. Clearly. Definitively.

I feel my knees buckle. The room tilts on its side. The floor rushes toward my head.

Detective Castillo catches me before I can fall. "Take deep breaths," he urges as I gulp at the air.

"Is it him?" Officer Dube asks. "Did you recognize his voice?"

I shake my head. Tears I didn't know had formed drop toward my chin. "It's not him."

"You're sure?"

"He looks so familiar . . . I thought maybe . . . but his voice . . ."

"I think we're done here," the public defender says in her breathy, little-girl whisper. "Thank you, gentlemen. Miss Carpenter," she says instead of goodbye.

She leaves the room, and my sister immediately rushes in.

"What happened?" Claire asks, instantly at my side as, on the other side of the glass partition, the five men are led away. "Are you all right? Were you able to identify him?" She leads me to the orange chairs against the wall, sitting down beside me.

"Your sister was unable to positively identify any of the men," Castillo says, careful to keep his obvious disappointment out of his voice.

"Are you sure?" Claire asks me.

I shake my head. "Number five looked so familiar," I marvel out loud.

"That might be because he's working construction on the building going up behind you. You've probably seen him in the area."

"Or through your binoculars," Officer Dube adds, his words a clear, if unnecessary, reprimand.

"He's on probation for assault," Castillo adds. "Which is why we were able to bring him in."

"Sexual?"

"No. Bar fight. Five years ago. Still, it was worth a shot."

"Is he your suspect in the other rape?" I ask.

"No. That was number two."

I picture the young man's slouched shoulders and acne-scarred face. *Tell me you love me,* I hear him snarl. Just not the snarl of the man who raped me.

"What about number one? It might have been him. . . ."

"That would be Officer Walter Johnston. One of Miami's finest."

My head drops toward my chest. "Shit. I'm sorry."

"Don't be. He's not the nicest guy in the world. But he does have an airtight alibi for the night you were attacked. He was on the job, surrounded by dozens of fellow officers."

"I'm sorry," I say again, because I can't think of anything else to say.

"Hey, we tried, you tried. If our guy wasn't up there, we'll just have to keep searching."

"You did your best," Claire tells me.

"We need to talk," Castillo says, "about last night."

"Oh, God. I really don't think I'm up for a lecture right now."

"You know what you did is stupid, right?" Officer Dube asks, not bothering to elaborate. There are so many stupid things I've done lately, I would be hard pressed to choose just one.

"I guess it can wait," Castillo says. "Just do me a favor, will you, and don't make any more anonymous calls to the station. It doesn't help your credibility." He pulls a card out of his back pocket and hands it to me. "Call me directly," he says. "My home number's on the back."

"Thank you." I tuck his card inside my pocket. Another card to add to my growing collection.

"Are you all right? Can I get you anything? Some more water . . . ?"

"I just need a few minutes."

"Take your time." He leaves the room, followed by Officer Dube.

"Have you any idea how proud of you I am right now?" Claire asks as soon as they are gone.

"You're proud of me? For what?"

"It took enormous courage to do what you just did."

"I didn't do anything."

"Don't minimize what just happened because it didn't yield the results you hoped for. You faced your worst fears, Bailey. You stared five potential rapists right in the face. You didn't run. You didn't hide. You didn't fall apart. That's got to count for something. And that something is a whole lot in my book."

I fall into her arms, my head resting against her chest. "I love you," I tell her, realizing this is true.

"I love you, too," she says, choking back tears. She quickly pulls herself together. "Come on. Let's get you home."

—

There are two messages waiting at home for me when I check my voice mail. The first one is from Sally, apologizing for not calling in a few days, it's just been so busy at work and her son has this terrible cold, and why haven't I gotten around to replacing my cell phone so we can at least text? She adds that it's a madhouse at work now that Sean Holden is back from his cruise. . . .

"Shit," I mutter. Sean's back, and he hasn't called me. What does it mean? More important, why do I care? Sean might be a brilliant lawyer, but he is also a liar and a cheat. "You're such a fool," I tell myself. Upset because a married man, your boss no less, cheated on you . . . with his wife! "Idiot," I say, waiting for the second message, hoping it is from Sean, regardless.

"Bailey, it's Gene," my half-brother suddenly bellows in my ear. "I need to speak to you as soon as possible."

"Shit," I say again, deleting both messages. Seconds later, the phone rings.

"Hi, Miss Carpenter," the voice says as soon as I pick up. "It's Finn, from the concierge desk. Your brother is here. The big one," he adds, his voice a whisper.

Panic wells up inside me. Damn it. I'm really not up for this. "Okay. I guess you better send him up."

"You didn't return my call," Gene says, striding into my apartment as if prepared to tackle anyone in his way.

It is at times like this that Bailey regrets keeping a landline. Most of the people she knows have done away with theirs long ago. Maybe once she replaces her stolen cell phone . . . "I just got home. I was at the police station, a lineup. . . ."

"They got the guy?"

"No. I wasn't able to. . . ."

"That's too bad." He scratches the side of his thin nose. My father's nose, I realize, in the middle of his mother's face. Gene proceeds, uninvited, into my living room and sits down, adjusting his dark blue tie. I notice drops of rain on the shoulders of his blue-and-white seersucker suit. "What's this about wanting me to peek into a sealed record?"

"What? No. I. . . ."

"You know I can't do that."

"I never suggested. . . . I would never have asked. . . ."

"You *do* know such information is inadmissible in court."

"I know that. I'm really sorry."

"Sit down, Bailey," he directs, as if we are in his office and not my apartment. "And listen carefully because I'm not going to repeat what I'm about to say. Ever. Is that clear?"

I nod, holding my breath.

"Jason Harkness broke into a 7-Eleven when he was fifteen years old, hitting the store clerk over the head with a bottle and making off with forty-three dollars and nineteen cents," he tells me, his voice flat and matter-of-fact. "He did sixteen months in juvie and then petitioned to have his record sealed. He's been clean ever since. There's nothing in his files to suggest rapist tendencies, yet he's clearly capable of violence. So, whether this helps or not, I can't say. That's it. That's all she wrote." He folds his hands inside his lap.

"Thank you." I try to comprehend the implications of what

I've just learned. I'm also waiting for the other shoe to drop. I don't know Gene well, but I know him well enough to know he doesn't give without expecting something in return.

I don't have to wait long.

"Look," he says, clearing his throat. "This is obviously a very stressful time for you. And we—your brothers and sister and I—don't want to be the source of any more stress for you."

Has Claire been talking to them? Has she persuaded her brothers to drop their lawsuit?

"We were thinking—hoping—you'd want to settle," he says before I can ask.

"Settle?"

"The last thing that any of us wants, and surely the last thing you need, is a bitter and very public court battle, especially now, when you're trying to recover from this hideous attack. It would be a tragedy were this lawsuit to interfere with the progress you've been making. . . ."

"You're only thinking of my best interests." Sarcasm clings to my voice like honey to a spoon.

Gene pretends not to notice. "Yes, exactly. I'm positive that if we were all just to sit down and talk this through like reasonable adults. . . ."

"You think that suing me for virtually my father's entire estate is reasonable?"

"He was my father, too, Bailey. He had seven children, not just two. And we're only asking for our fair share." Gene is growing red in the face. His right foot taps impatiently on my cowhide rug. He doesn't like being challenged, which must be difficult in his line of work. "Look, Bailey. It's obvious that our father wasn't in his right mind when he changed his will," he says, trying a different approach. "He was depressed over your mother's death and angry at what he perceived as his older children's indifference to what you were all going through."

"Are you saying he shouldn't have been depressed, that he had no right to be angry?"

"He had no right to disinherit us."

"It was *his* money."

"It was *family* money," Gene insists. "You're forgetting that my mother worked very hard to support him when they were first married. . . ."

"And you're forgetting that our father provided for her very well after their divorce. If I'm not mistaken, he gave both of his ex-wives several million dollars in their divorce settlements and also provided very generous child support."

"All of which pales in comparison to the windfall you and Heath will receive. And speaking of Heath," he continues in the same breath, trying yet another tack, "I doubt our father would want your brother pissing away his fortune on drugs and dissolute hangers-on."

"Dissolute hangers-on," I repeat, managing to sound outraged despite having had the same thoughts myself. "That's quite the mouthful."

"Facts are facts," Gene states, as if delivering his summation to a jury. "Heath likes to party, his friends are dicey at best, he's never held a job in his life. . . ."

"He's an actor and a screenwriter. . . ."

"Really? What movies has he acted in? What scripts has he written?"

"You know it's not easy these days. It takes time. He's try-ing. . . ."

"Bailey . . ."

"Eugene," I say pointedly, using the name I know he hates.

He'll take our father's money but won't use his name. Before this visit, I was actually leaning toward reaching some sort of set-tlement with him and the rest of my half-siblings.

"I just think it would be a mistake to put that kind of money into the hands of someone who will more than likely turn around and blow it out his nose," Gene says, sealing his fate once and for all.

"And I think it's time for you to leave."

"Be reasonable, Bailey. . . ."

I stand up and walk toward the front door. Gene sighs and follows. I open the door and he steps reluctantly into the hallway.

"I want to thank you for the photographs you gave Claire," he says, in what is clearly an afterthought. "That was very kind of you."

"Consider us even," I say. Then I shut the door in his face.

— TWENTY-SIX —

An hour later I am standing at the bank of elevators in the lobby of the gleaming white marble tower that houses the law offices of Holden, Cunningham, and Kravitz. I have only an indistinct sense of how I got here—a bumpy cab ride through the rain-lashed streets of Miami—and an even less distinct sense of why I'm here at all. Did I come to see Sally? To confront Sean? To escape Gene, whose stubborn presence continues to haunt my apartment, a place that has started to feel more like a prison than the safe haven it's always been?

But here I stand. A sudden, overwhelming anxiety has seized control of my legs and rooted them to the floor as deeply as the decorative marble columns nearby. I watch the half-dozen elevators arrive and depart at steady, if irregular, intervals, brass art deco doors opening and closing, busy well-dressed people making entrances and exits, the process repeated so many times it becomes meaningless, the same way a word loses its meaning through too much repetition. I feel an unpleasant numbness spread from the bottoms of my feet and curl around my toes, then move up my legs toward my thighs and creep between my legs.

I am experiencing an episode of post-traumatic shock, I tell myself. *I am not crazy.*

"Bailey?"

A loud guttural protest escapes my lips, causing those in my immediate vicinity to take a cautionary step back.

"Sorry," a young woman says, although the way she's looking at me suggests I should be the one apologizing to her. "I thought it was you. It's Vicki, from accounting?" she asks, as if she isn't sure. "My God, you're soaking wet."

"Am I?" A quick glance tells me that Vicki from accounting is right. Water is dripping from my shoulders and forming puddles on the floor around me.

She laughs. "Well . . . yes, you are!" She stares at me as if she's half-expecting me to burst into flames. "Are you all right?"

"Fine."

Vicki from accounting is a pretty girl with straight brown hair that falls almost to her waist. She is wearing a gray dress and black heels that are so high I wonder how she manages to stand in them, let alone walk. I used to wear shoes like that, I think, looking down at my flat sandals. I used to have no trouble at all walking.

"Are you headed upstairs?" She pushes the call button, although it is already lit. I nod, and she smiles. "How's everything going?"

Exactly how much does she know, how much information, both true and false, has the office gossip mill generated? "Getting a little better every day."

"Thinking about coming back soon?"

"Maybe."

"I hope you do. We miss you."

I find this odd, since this exchange is probably the longest we've ever shared. "I miss you, too," I tell her, partly because it is expected and partly because it is, surprisingly, true.

An elevator arrives, and the doors slide open. "Coming?" Vicki from accounting asks, stepping inside and waiting for me to do the same. The door knocks against her shoulder and the buzzer starts to sound when my feet refuse to budge, and I delay too long. "Bailey? Are you coming?"

A man pushes past me, the sudden motion serving to propel me inside.

Vicki from accounting presses the button for the twenty-fifth floor, then glances over at me, her fingers hovering in front of the panel. "Mr. Holden's on twenty-seven, right?"

Why does she assume I'm here to see Sean? Does she know of our affair? Is this another piece of juicy office gossip I'm responsible for?

"Twenty-six," I say. "I thought I'd say hello to Sally first."

"Oh, yeah. Talk about crazy busy. She's working on the Aurora and Poppy Gomez divorce. Can you believe what's going on there? They say he slept with over a thousand women in the last two years alone. That's like one a *night.*"

I try to convince myself that Vicki from accounting is merely exaggerating to make a point and that this is not an indication of her actual accounting skills.

"Excuse me," a woman says from somewhere in the back of the cab as the elevator doors open onto the seventeenth floor. I feel several bodies rearrange themselves behind me as she pushes her way to the door, exiting as a man gets on. The man is about thirty-five and of average height and weight. He smells of expensive soap and mouthwash, crisp and clean.

Tell me you love me.

I reach for the nearest wall, telling myself to stay calm. This is not the man who raped me. The lineup this morning has upset my balance, throwing my imagination into overdrive. *I am not crazy.*

Seconds later, we arrive at the twenty-fifth floor, and Vicki steps out into the impressive, green marble-paneled reception area of Holden, Cunningham, and Kravitz. She turns around to say goodbye and finds me just inches from her face. "Oh," she says, startled at finding me so close. "I thought you were going to twenty-six."

"I should probably call Sally first," I say, pretending to be searching through my purse for my stolen cell phone. "You said she was crazy busy. . . ."

Vicki from accounting smiles awkwardly. "Well, it was nice seeing you again. Good luck with everything."

"Thank you." I watch her greet the receptionist, then walk through the glass doors toward the offices on the east side of the building. Beyond those doors is the steady hum of people going about their business.

I used to be part of that hum. I used to have business to go about.

"Excuse me. Can I help you?" the receptionist asks. I've never seen her before. She must be new. And she's gorgeous—there's no other word for it.

"I'm Bailey Carpenter," I tell her, approaching the massive green granite counter she sits behind. "I work here. I'm on a short leave of absence," I continue, unprompted.

I am temporarily blinded by her movie star smile. "Are you here to see anyone in particular?" she asks.

I hesitate, deciding in that instant that I never should have come, that I have to get out of here right now. I turn back toward the elevators just as one opens and Sean Holden steps into the foyer.

Unless he doesn't.

Unless I'm only imagining him and the "Oh shit" look in his eyes.

"Bailey," he says, walking toward me, arms extended. "I wasn't expecting to see you. What are you doing here?"

My throat goes dry. I feel dizzy, light-headed, faint. "I work here. Remember?"

And suddenly I'm in his arms. Although only for a second. Only for as long as it takes him to whisper, "I've been meaning to call. . . ." And then backing away, saying, "I see somebody got caught in the rain." He swats at the dampness my hug has deposited on his beige linen jacket.

"Forgot my umbrella," I manage to stutter.

"How are you doing?"

"When did you get back?" The questions overlap.

"On Sunday. Uh . . . give me a minute, okay?" He walks toward the receptionist's desk.

"Mr. Holden?" she says brightly, and I can't help notice the way she looks at him, navy blue eyes all but twinkling. Is he looking at her with the same twinkle? I wonder.

I hear he's quite the player, Gene once said to me. Was I always this blind? Was I always this stupid?

Stupid enough not to take an umbrella, despite warnings of a major storm front. Stupid enough to have an affair with a married man, despite knowing it would end badly. Stupid enough to still go all weak in the knees at the very sight of him.

"Would you tell Barry York that I'll be a few minutes late?"

"Certainly, Mr. Holden."

"Is anyone using Conference Room B?"

The receptionist checks the large appointment book in front of her. "Not a soul."

Sean returns to my side. "Come on." He takes my arm and guides me toward the glass doors opposite the ones that Vicki from accounting walked through earlier.

Conference Room B is a small rectangle of a room whose floor-to-ceiling windows face west into the city, although at the moment all that is visible are black skies and a steady downpour. "It's turning into a pretty nasty day," Sean remarks, and I briefly wonder if he is referring to the weather or my unexpected visit. He closes the solid oak door behind him, giving me another quick hug and then breaking away before I can reciprocate. He motions for me to sit down in one of the twelve upholstered red chairs grouped around the long oak table, and I all but fall into the seat as he pulls up the chair beside me. He swivels it around, sitting down and facing me so that our knees are touching, then reaches over and takes my hands, his eyes searching mine. "How are you, Bailey? You look so tired."

I shrug, afraid to say anything for fear I'll burst into tears. Why has he picked now, of all times, to be honest with me?

"I'm so sorry," he says, and I know he's referring to more than his remark about my appearance.

I lower my head as my tears start to fall. I'm not ready to have this discussion. Not yet. "How was your trip?"

"Good. It was good. The girls seemed to enjoy it."

"And you?"

"Well, cruises aren't exactly my thing, as you know."

How would I know? "You should have told me," I say, unable to keep the words at bay any longer. "About the baby."

He sighs. "I know. I wanted to. I came over that afternoon to tell you, but I . . . I just couldn't. Not after everything you've been going through."

Lucky for you my rape was so convenient, I think, but resist the urge to say.

"What can I tell you, Bailey? That I'm a coward, that I'm a bastard? . . . Feel free to stop me any time," he adds with a forced chuckle and a squeeze of my hand. "It was just one time, Bailey. One night when we had a few too many drinks at dinner and . . ."

"Oh, please," I interrupt, my voice louder than either of us expected, causing Sean to glance over his shoulder toward the door. "Don't insult my intelligence."

"It's complicated."

"You've been sleeping with your wife, Sean. Sounds simple enough to me."

"It has nothing to do with us."

"It has *everything* to do with us."

"It doesn't mean I don't care about you, Bailey."

"Just that you care about yourself more."

"That's not fair."

"A lawyer who expects fairness? How unusual."

"I care deeply about you, Bailey. You know that."

"You have a funny way of showing it."

Silence.

"You're angry," he says finally. "And understandably upset."

"I'm so glad you understand."

"This couldn't have come at a worse time for you. . . ."

"Yes. First I get raped, then my lover gets his wife pregnant. The timing pretty much sucks."

Again, Sean glances self-consciously toward the door. "Maybe we should bring this down a notch. . . ."

"When's the baby due, Sean?"

"February."

"So, you've known about this for quite a while."

"A few months," he admits.

"Girl or boy?"

"A boy," he says with a smile. "How about that?" He looks at me for approval, as if we are just two old friends celebrating his good fortune.

"Congratulations." I push myself to my feet. "I guess I should get going. I'll email you my resignation this afternoon."

"Bailey, no. That's completely unnecessary. I'm not asking for your resignation."

"And I'm not asking for your permission."

Another sigh. "Okay. As you wish," he says formally, having the good grace not to look overly relieved. "Are you going to be all right?"

My lungs fill with false bravado, and I all but puff out my chest. "Count on it."

—

Somehow I manage to keep it together after I leave the conference room, forcing one foot in front of the other, my tears in check, my head held high as I wait for the elevator. I close my eyes to block out the other passengers as I step inside, only opening them again when we reach the ground floor, remaining upright by sheer force of will as I cut across the lobby and step into the blustery afternoon. The rain has temporarily let up, although the sky remains dark and the winds are blowing as fiercely as ever.

I see him as soon as I exit the building.

He is standing on the sidewalk, struggling to fix his umbrella, which the wind has blown inside out. Even though he has exchanged his jogger's uniform for a pair of black pants and a sports jacket, I recognize Colin Lesser immediately. I know he works in the area and that it's lunchtime, so it's not out of the question that we would run into each other. Still, it seems more than mere coincidence that he would be in this spot at precisely the same time I am. Has he been following me?

"What are you doing here?" I demand.

He looks up, startled. "What?"

"I'm so sorry," I say, realizing only then that the man I have just accosted is not Colin Lesser at all. "I thought you were someone else."

The man mumbles something unintelligible before hurrying away.

What's the matter with me? Probably I have Colin Lesser on the brain because of his phone call this morning. I close my eyes, picturing the address printed at the bottom of his business card; his office is approximately three blocks from here, not even a two-minute sprint away. What am I thinking?

Clearly I'm not thinking at all, I decide, as I begin hurrying toward it.

—

Colin Lesser's office is on the second floor of an eighteen-story, baby pink building less than three blocks from Holden, Cunningham, and Kravitz. I take the stairs, relieved at not having to get into another elevator, and locate his office, which is halfway down the long hall. I'm here to apologize for my puzzling and probably rude behavior this morning on the phone and to explain that, while he is an attractive and no doubt fascinating man, it would not be a good idea for us to have dinner anytime soon. This is what I tell myself. Perhaps I even believe it.

The office appears to be empty, which isn't surprising, given that it's lunchtime. There is no one sitting at the receptionist's tidy desk, no patients waiting in the cozy waiting area, with its long, green leather sectional across from a large TV, which is currently tuned to CNN. An espresso machine is built into the pale green wall alongside several impressive abstract oils, and on the limestone top of a wide coffee table are several of the latest in celebrity gossip magazines.

"Can I help you?" The voice is familiar and I turn toward it, expecting to see Colin. Instead I come face to face with a balding man with kind eyes and a gentle smile, some three decades Colin's senior.

"I'm looking for Dr. Lesser."

"You found him."

"You're Dr. Lesser?" What does this mean? That Colin isn't who he claimed to be? That everything he told me was a lie? That our meeting was far from chance and even farther from "cute," that he has, in fact, been stalking me, that he is the man who raped me. . . .

"Do you have an appointment?"

"What? No. I . . . I've made a mistake. . . ." I head to the door.

"Wait. Perhaps you're here to see my . . ."

"Bailey?" I hear.

I turn around, watching the Colin Lesser I know emerge from one of the inner rooms to walk toward me. He is wearing a white lab coat over a checkered shirt and a pair of khaki pants. Even from this distance, his dimples are clearly visible.

"What are you doing here?"

"I . . . I . . ."

"I see you've met my father."

"If you'll excuse me," the older man says, retreating down the inner corridor.

"What are you doing here?" Colin asks again.

"I'm hungry," I tell him, surprised to realize that this is true. "I was hoping you might be free for lunch."

—

"So you quit?" he is asking, putting his elbows on the Formica-topped table and leaning toward me.

"I didn't really feel I had any other choice. I mean, it was stupid, right?" I say. "Having an affair with a married man who also happens to be my boss. . . ." I glance at Colin Lesser's plate, his enormous corned beef sandwich sitting, half-eaten, in front of him. He is staring at me, his dark blue eyes fastened on my lips, which haven't stopped moving since we sat down.

After asking a few perfunctory questions—How long have you been in practice? What's it like working with your father? Have you ever been married?—and receiving some mercifully ordinary answers—Four years; it's great; my girlfriend and I broke up about a year ago—I completely steamrolled the conversation. I was talking even as I wolfed down the diner's hot turkey special, and now I can't seem to stop. I'm pouring my heart out to a man I barely know, a man I suspected less than an hour ago could be the man who raped me. "I don't know why I'm telling you all this."

"Sounds like you have a pretty good case for sexual harassment," he offers.

"I was hardly harassed. He didn't force himself on me."

"But somebody did," Colin says after a pause.

"Yes," I hear myself admit. Why am I confiding in this man? Because he has the same kind eyes as his father? *Because he's here?* The truth is, he *wasn't* here. The truth is that I went out of my way to bring him here. Why? Because I'm angry at Sean? Because I want to prove to myself that a man—a seemingly sane, reasonable man whom I might normally find attractive—might find me attractive as well? Because I desperately want to believe that despite what has happened, *some men are good*? Or do I harbor deeper, darker, suspicions? "Was it you?" I hear myself ask.

"What do you mean?"

"Are you the man who raped me?"

"What!?"

The waitress approaches our table. She is about sixty years old and speaks with a thick Hungarian accent. Her pendulous breasts strain against the front of her mustard-colored uniform, its round black buttons threatening to pop right off. "What's the matter?"

she asks Colin, whose face has gone ghostly white. "You don't like your sandwich?"

"What did you say?" he asks me, ignoring her question. "What on earth would make you think that?"

"Dessert? Coffee?" the waitress asks.

"Coffee," Colin snaps.

"Make that two," I add as the waitress gathers up our plates.

"Are you serious? You actually think I could be the man who raped you?" Colin looks around the crowded deli, as if half-expecting a cop to jump up from behind the next booth, wrestle him to the tabletop, and cuff his hands behind his back.

"Are you?"

"No. Of course not."

"Okay."

"*Okay?*" he repeats. "That's it? *Okay?*"

The waitress brings our coffee, depositing a bowlful of cream and sugar packets on the table.

"I don't understand. What are we even doing here, if you think I could have . . . ?" Colin asks as soon as she is gone.

"I don't think that. I really don't."

"Then why . . . ?"

"Can we just forget I mentioned it?"

"Forget you mentioned it? No, I don't think I can do that. What's going on here, Bailey? Were you trying to trick me into saying something incriminating?"

"No. I honestly wasn't."

"What then?"

"I don't know. Clearly, I have issues. . . ."

"Clearly."

Neither of us speaks for a good minute or two. Instead we sip at our coffee and stare at the rain.

"I take it the police haven't caught the guy," Colin ventures just as the silence is becoming unbearable.

"No, they haven't."

"I also assume you never saw the guy's face?"

"No, I didn't." Is he fishing?

"It wasn't me," he says. "I swear to you, Bailey. It wasn't me."

"I believe you."

"Okay," he says.

"Okay," I repeat.

He raises his cup of coffee to his lips, doesn't put it down until he has finished every last drop. "I really should be getting back," he says finally. "I have a patient in fifteen minutes." He stands up and reaches into his pocket, lays a twenty-dollar bill on the table. "I really have to run. . . ."

"I know. I understand. I really do."

"Are you going to be all right?"

"I'll be fine."

"I hope they catch the guy."

"Me too."

He pauses for another second, as if debating with himself whether to say anything else. When he finally speaks, the message is simple and crystal clear: "Goodbye, Bailey."

— T W E N T Y - S E V E N —

An hour later I'm sitting in a taxi in front of the building where Paul Giller lives.

"This the right address?" the driver is asking, regarding me suspiciously through his rearview mirror.

I know what he is really saying is that if this is the right address, why don't I get out of his cab? I've paid what I owe, and we are experiencing another temporary break in the rain. This would be the perfect time to make a run for it.

I hadn't intended to come here. My original plan was to go straight home. Yet when the seventy-something, gray-haired cabbie pulled to a stop in front of me, the address I gave him wasn't mine, but Paul Giller's.

I'm operating on pure adrenaline, and I know it.

Except . . .

I feel more in control than I have in weeks.

I am not crazy.

Yeah, right.

Tell that to Colin Lesser.

And David Trotter.

And Jason Harkness.

Tell it to Detective Castillo and Officer Dube.

Tell it to the judge, I think, and almost laugh.

A flash of light is followed, seconds later, by an ominous roll of thunder. Another major downpour is imminent. The prudent thing would be to abandon whatever hare-brained scheme my mind is cooking up and head for home. But, of course, since *I'm not crazy,* I do just the opposite, exiting the cab and running toward the entrance of the tall glass building. I push open the lobby door and head straight for the residents' directory.

The manager of the building is listed at the bottom, and I press the buzzer and wait.

"Yes?" comes the booming male voice seconds later. "Can I help you?"

I take an involuntary step back. "I want to inquire about an apartment."

"Be right with you."

I look around the sparsely furnished lobby, wondering if its minimalist content is one of design or necessity. There are hints the economy might be starting to improve, at least according to several pundits I've heard posturing on TV. Then maybe the real estate market will pick up, and people will start buying again. Condos won't have to resort to renting out their units by the month in order to stay afloat. Lobbies will once again overflow with furniture.

I watch a man in neatly pressed jeans and a bright blue golf shirt approaching from the other side of the glass door. He is short and middle-aged, good-looking. A full head of salt-and-pepper hair, excellent posture, a trim physique. He opens the door and motions me inside, extends his hand in greeting. His handshake is strong, almost crippling, my knuckles squeezing against one another before he releases me from his iron grip. "Adam Roth," he says. "You are . . . ?"

"Elizabeth Gordon." I'm seized with the fear that Adam Roth might actually know Elizabeth Gordon, that he could be one of her clients.

"Nice to meet you, Miss Gordon," he says. "Pretty nasty day

to be out apartment hunting." He leads me around the corner to his office.

In contrast to the large, empty lobby, the manager's tiny office seems more like a storeroom. In the middle sits a large desk piled high with papers, folders, and floor plans; behind it, a comfortable-looking brown leather armchair; in front of it, two brown leather tub chairs. Several folding chairs are stacked in a corner. A large bookshelf full of colorful binders lines the wall to the right of the desk, while to the left stands an easel with an artist's rendering of a tall glass building, probably this one, although it's hard to tell since they all look pretty much the same.

"This is shaping up to be quite the storm," Adam Roth remarks, sitting down behind his desk, and motioning toward the chairs in front of it for me to do likewise. "How can I help you, Miss Gordon?"

"I'm looking for an apartment."

"To buy or rent?"

"Rent."

He looks disappointed. "Are you sure? This is an ideal time to buy. Prices are down, interest rates are low. . . ."

"I'm not sure how long I'll be staying in Miami."

"I see. So we're talking more short-term."

"Yes."

"A year's lease or month to month?"

"Probably month to month."

Adam Roth smiles, although he looks even further dejected. "How big an apartment are you interested in, Miss Gordon?"

"A one-bedroom, preferably on one of the upper floors, looking west."

"Really? Most clients prefer an eastern view. Well," he says, sifting through the papers on his desk until he finds the folder he's looking for, "let's see what we have available."

I inch forward in my seat.

"As it turns out, we have quite a few one-bedroom suites available that face west. How does the eighteenth floor suit you?"

"How many floors does the building have?"

"Twenty-nine."

"Then I'd prefer something higher. Maybe around twenty-seven?" According to the directory, Paul Giller lives in apartment 2706.

"Well, I should warn you that the prices go up with each floor and the view is pretty much the same." He waves in the general direction of my building. "Let me see. I have a one-bedroom available on the twentieth floor, two on the twenty-first, one on the twenty-fourth, and one on the twenty-eighth."

"What number is the suite on the twenty-eighth floor?"

"What number? Uh . . . it's number 2802. Any particular reason you'd ask that?"

"Just curious. I once lived on the twenty-eighth floor of a building, and I thought it would be interesting if it were the same number." I give him a shrug and my most winsome smile, a smile that says "charmingly kooky," not "crazy." "I'd like to have a look at that one, if you wouldn't mind."

"Of course. That's why I'm here." He reaches inside his desk drawer for a set of keys. "The unit rents for sixteen hundred dollars a month. But for a down payment of only twenty thousand dollars, you could pay much less monthly and start building some home equity as well."

"Would that I had twenty thousand dollars to put down," I improvise, pushing myself to my feet and following after him as he exits the office.

"We do insist on a security deposit and first and last months' rent in advance," he tells me as we wait by the bank of elevators. "What is it you do, Miss Gordon, if you don't mind my asking?"

"I'm a therapist."

"Really? Physical, occupational . . . ?"

"Psycho," I say, thinking this might be the best term to describe me.

"A psychotherapist? Really? You look so young."

We take the elevator up to the twenty-eighth floor.

"This way." He points to his right and we walk down the gray-carpeted hallway. I'm looking toward suite 2806 as Adam Roth inserts the key inside the lock of suite 2802 and gives it a twist. "Miss Gordon? Or should that be Dr. Gordon?" he asks when I fail to respond to the name.

"Miss Gordon is fine." The door falls open and we step inside a tiny gray-and-white marble foyer.

He shows me around the small apartment. "Floor-to-ceiling windows throughout. Marble flooring in the main area. Granite countertops in the kitchen. Modern appliances, including a dishwasher, microwave, and stacked washer-dryer," he rattles off. "And now the bedroom." We step inside the small square whose entire westerly wall is window. "Wall-to-wall plush carpeting as well as a walk-in closet and marble en suite bathroom. Quite a nice size, by today's standards. So, what do you think?"

"It's lovely. Do all the one-bedrooms facing west have the same layout?"

"Yes. There may be minor variations, if people purchased before construction began, but essentially what you're seeing is the identical unit throughout."

I walk to the window, stare out toward my building, trying to determine which apartment is mine. But the rain makes it almost impossible to see anything. I lay my head against the glass, straining to pinpoint my unit.

"Miss Gordon?" Adam Roth asks. "Are you feeling all right?"

"Just trying to get a feel for things. . . ."

I try counting the floors of my building from the ground up, but this proves too difficult, and I'm forced to settle for a general sense of where everything is located. But it's obvious, even with the rain, even one floor removed and two units down, that Paul Giller has as good a view of my apartment as I have of his.

"Any questions?" Adam Roth asks as we return to the main living area.

"How much of the building is currently occupied?"

"Slightly less than half. We had a lot of speculators, and unfortunately, when the markets collapsed . . ."

"And the ratio of owners to renters?" I interrupt, wondering into which category Paul Giller falls.

"Probably about equal."

"Is there a high turnover with the renters?"

"Not really, no. I assure you, Miss Gordon, that this is a very safe building, if that's what's concerning you."

"No, I'm not concerned. I actually think I might know someone who lives here."

Adam Roth looks at me expectantly.

"I met him at a party the other week. I think he said he was an actor. God, what was his name? Paul Something. Gilmore? Gifford?"

"Giller?" the building manager offers.

"Yes. That's it. Paul Giller. Good-looking guy. I thought he said he lived in this building."

"He does, yes."

"Has he been here long?"

Adam Roth says nothing.

I pretend to take a closer look at the granite countertop in the kitchen. "I can't remember if he said he owned or rented."

"I'm afraid we don't give out such information. You'd have to ask him those things yourself."

"Oh, I doubt I'll be seeing him again. I was just curious. Guys tell you all sorts of stories these days. You know how it is."

"Is that what you're really doing here, Miss Gordon? Checking up on a potential boyfriend?"

"What? No! Of course not. I was actually under the impression that Paul Giller already had a live-in girlfriend."

"Again, something you'd have to ask him. Now, if we're done here . . ." He walks toward the door.

"I guess we are."

"I assume you're not interested in seeing any of the other units."

"No, thank you. I think I have a pretty good idea of what's available."

"Should I tell Mr. Giller you were asking after him?" Adam Roth asks as we step inside the elevator.

"I wouldn't bother."

"I suspected as much. It was lovely meeting you, Miss Gordon." The elevator doors open into the lobby. "Oh, look. There's Mr. Giller now."

I take a step back, knowing there is nowhere for me to hide and trying to will myself into invisibility.

"Oh, sorry," Adam Roth says, not even trying to disguise the smirk on his face. "I'm mistaken. It isn't Mr. Giller after all."

I stuff my hands into the pockets of my pants, partly so that he won't see them shaking and partly to keep from wrapping them around his throat. I stare at the floor, afraid to even glance at the man who is not Paul Giller as he walks toward us.

"Good afternoon, Mr. Whiteside," Adam Roth says in greeting.

"Hardly," Mr. Whiteside replies, stepping inside the elevator. "Have you seen what it's doing out there?"

"Good afternoon to be inside," Adam Roth agrees. "Try not to get too wet, Miss Gordon," he calls as I step out into the storm.

—

Heath is waiting in the lobby when I get home. "You look like a drowned rat," he says.

"Where did you disappear to last night?" I ask in response, shaking the rain from my hair and watching him jump to avoid the spray.

He shrugs, all the answer I'm going to get.

"Good afternoon, Miss Carpenter," Wes calls out as we pass by the concierge desk. "Hope you didn't get too wet out there."

"She looks like a drowned rat," Heath calls back.

"Thank you for that." I press the call button. "I'm really tired, Heath." While part of me—the concerned sister part—is relieved to see that he is safe and sound, resplendent in a pair of skinny black jeans and a black silk shirt, another part of me—the exhausted human being part—just wants him to go away so that I can crawl into bed and pretend that today never happened. "Is there something you want?"

He looks hurt, and I feel a stab of guilt. "Why do you always assume I want something? I'm not Claire. . . ."

"Claire doesn't want—" I break off. Heath obviously feels jealous and more than a little threatened by my newfound relationship with Claire. There is no point in trying either to explain or defend it. "I'm sorry," I say again. It's easier that way.

"Apology accepted," he says as the elevators doors open and we step inside. "Look. Now that you mention it, there *is* something you can do for me."

"Why am I not surprised?"

"I need a favor," he says. "I meant to talk to you about it last night, but . . . you kind of passed out on me."

A middle-aged woman slips inside the elevator just as the doors are closing, smiles at Heath flirtatiously, and presses the button for the fifteenth floor.

"What kind of favor?" I ask as soon as she gets off.

"I need some money."

"What do you mean, you need some money?"

He says nothing further until we reach my floor.

"Heath?"

"It's just a loan. I wouldn't ask you. It's just that I don't know where else to turn. I'm in trouble, and I need money."

"What do you mean, you're in trouble?"

"Do you think we could talk about this inside your apartment and not out here in the hall?"

"Do you think you could tell me what this is about?" I ask in return, unlocking my apartment door.

"I need thirty thousand dollars."

"Thirty thousand dollars? Are you kidding?"

"It's just temporary. You can take it out of my share of the inheritance."

"There is no inheritance. Not until this lawsuit gets settled. Which, I remind you, could take years."

"Well, then this could get tricky because I'm pretty much out of cash. And it seems I owe a few people money. People who aren't nearly as understanding about this sort of thing as you are."

"What are you saying?"

"It's pretty simple, Bailey. I made a few bad bets here and there."

"When did you start gambling?"

"I don't know. Five, ten years ago? And I'm usually pretty good at it. Just not lately."

"Are we talking loan sharks?"

"A quaint term, but an essentially accurate one. I paid them back most of what I owed when I sold my condo. For half of what it's worth, I might add."

"You sold your condo?"

"Why do you think I was living at Dad's?"

"I don't believe this." I wonder if there could be a connection between Heath's gambling debts and my assault. Was my rape intended as some kind of warning? Could my brother be responsible, no matter how inadvertently?

"I just owe another twenty thousand," Heath is saying, "and then I'm in the clear."

"I thought you said thirty."

"Well, I could use a little something to live on. Come on, Bailey. Consider it an advance. I'll pay you back every cent. Please. Don't make me beg. We're family. Not like some people I could mention."

"Can we leave Claire out of this?" I sink to the sofa, burying my head in my hands, partly because I'm reeling, and partly because he's right. I didn't think twice about writing Claire that check for ten thousand dollars.

"Careful," Heath warns. "You're dripping all over everything."

"I'll call the bank," I tell him. "Have them transfer the money into your account."

"That's great." The relief in his voice is palpable. "You're the best. You really are. You're my hero."

"Your hero," I repeat and almost laugh. Some hero. "You can't keep fucking up," I tell him. "I can't keep rescuing you. I don't have the strength."

"Are you kidding me? You're stronger than anyone I know."

I stare at him in disbelief.

"It's true," he says.

The phone rings.

"This is Wes, from the concierge desk," Wes informs me when I pick up the phone in the kitchen. "Your niece is here."

Jade is here? Why? "Send her up."

"Don't tell me," Heath says from the doorway. "Saint Claire is on her way up with milk and cookies."

"It's Jade," I tell him, wondering what more could possibly happen today.

"I should leave before she gets here." Heath gives me a big hug. "I love you. Never doubt that."

"I never do."

He pulls out of our embrace. "You really should get out of those wet clothes," he calls back as I watch him walk down the hall. "Call you tonight," he says, as I'm closing the door.

Seconds later, Jade is knocking.

"Just ran into that gorgeous brother of yours," she says by way of hello. She is wearing jeans that appear to have been painted on, a tight blue sweater, and at least three layers of mascara, her blond hair hanging in loose curls around her shoulders. On one side of her four-inch-high espadrilles sits a small suitcase, on the other a large overnight bag.

"What's this?"

"My mother didn't tell you? We're moving in."

"What?"

"Just for a few days, until things settle down a bit. She'll explain." As if on cue, the phone rings. "That's probably her now. Do you know you're soaking wet?"

I walk back into the kitchen as Jade wheels her suitcase and overnight bag down the hall. Caller ID informs me that Claire is on the other end of the line. I pick up the phone. "Start talking," I say.

—TWENTY-EIGHT—

It is eight o'clock Sunday evening, and Jade and her mother have been living here since Thursday night, Jade sleeping on the pullout bed in my office and Claire occupying the empty space beside me in my queen-size bed. Claire informed me—after I told her to start talking—that she'd made the decision to move in after receiving a phone call at work from Detective Castillo, confiding that he was pretty much at his wits' end as far as I was concerned and that he was counting on her to keep me in check before I did irreparable damage to either myself or my case. Apparently, Adam Roth, Paul Giller's property manager, contacted the police the minute I left his office, Adam Roth having already been briefed by Paul Giller about my so-called harassment. Detective Castillo told Claire that I was jeopardizing not only the police investigation but my own safety, that my behavior was such that any good defense lawyer would have no trouble getting a jury to question my sanity, and that whoever eventually got charged with my rape could very well end up walking free, especially if I continued to recklessly accuse every man in sight. The end result of this discussion was that Claire called Jade at school and told her to go home, throw a few things into a suitcase, and get over to my apartment, that she'd join us as soon as her shift ended.

When she arrived, I tried to explain what I'd been doing in Adam Roth's office, but I think whatever rational motives I might have had got lost amid the revelations of my quitting my job and ambushing Colin Lesser. Claire tried not to look too concerned as I was expanding on my meeting with Sean and my lunch with Colin, but I knew what she was thinking: that Detective Castillo was right, that I was out of control, that my credibility, my very sanity, was at risk.

It's been raining almost constantly since they moved in, so we don't go out. Instead, our days are filled with computer games and reality TV. We eat ice cream and watch movies and gossip about the newest salacious revelations in the Poppy and Aurora Gomez divorce, and as soon as the sun goes down, we get out the binoculars and take turns spying on my neighbor.

Paul Giller has done little this weekend of either interest or concern. He goes out; he comes home. Sometimes Elena is with him, sometimes she isn't. There have been no erotic displays, no acts of violence, not so much as a glance in our direction. "He's become very dull," Jade remarked after he and Elena came home before midnight last night and climbed straight into bed.

I'm finding it comforting having Claire and Jade around. As much as I initially resisted sharing a bed with my sister, I've discovered that there's something very soothing about having her there. What's more, she seems blissfully unbothered by my restless sleeping patterns, not scolding me when I get up several times in the night to use the bathroom, not urging me to be still, not telling me to settle down when a nightmare wakes me up. Instead, barely conscious, she pats my back and mutters that it was just a dream, that she's here and won't let anything bad happen to me. This seems to do the trick.

Partly out of respect—I know her job requires that she get a good night's rest—and partly out of fear—I don't want her to think I'm crazier than I fear she already does—I've cut way back on the number of times I search my apartment and the number of showers I take. Amazingly, I feel much less paranoid as a result. I'll be sorry to see them leave tomorrow, when Claire has to return to work and Jade has to go back to school.

"Here they come," Jade announces.

Both Claire and I run to the window.

"What are they doing?" Claire asks, straining to see through the rain that hasn't let up since Thursday.

"Nothing, by the looks of it. Oh, wait. Elena just went into the bathroom. She's shutting the door. Now Paul's taking out his cell phone, and he's looking back over his shoulder, like he's checking to make sure she can't hear, and now he's talking into the phone and smiling and laughing. Very exciting stuff."

"Let me see." Claire lifts the binoculars from her daughter's hands.

"How can you tell he's smiling?" Claire asks. "I can hardly see anything through this rain."

"That's because you're old and your eyes don't work so good anymore," Jade tells her, rolling her own eyes toward the ceiling.

"My eyes don't work so *well* anymore," her mother corrects.

"Exactly," says Jade.

Claire hands me the binoculars. I peer through them just as Paul is returning his cell phone to his pocket. A few minutes later, the bathroom door opens and Elena comes out, wrapped in several towels, one around her torso, another around her head; clearly, she has just emerged from the shower. She sits down at the vanity table and plugs in her hairdryer as Paul disappears into the bathroom. "Looks like they're getting ready to go out."

"Where do they go all the time?" Claire wonders out loud.

"Hello?" Jade says. "It's Miami. World famous for its nightlife. Not everybody's in bed by ten o'clock, you know."

"Gives me a migraine just thinking about going out in this weather," Claire says as I hand the binoculars back to Jade.

"So, what's happening with your brother?" my niece asks, returning the binoculars to her eyes. "Haven't seen him since Thursday."

"Heath was here?" Claire asks.

"Just briefly." I haven't said anything to Claire about Heath's visit or his request for money. Again I wonder if his gambling debts had anything to do with my rape. But sharing this concern with Claire will only complicate things further.

"This is boring," Jade says. "Can't we at least put on the TV?"

"Not till they go out," Claire tells her. "I don't want any light on in this room. Nothing that might tip them to the fact we're watching."

"I don't think he cares." Jade hands me the binoculars, although strictly speaking it's not my turn.

"Anything?" Claire asks a few minutes later.

"No. Yes! He's coming out of the bathroom," I announce. "Towel around his waist. Walking to the window. Oh, my God."

"What?" Claire and Jade ask together.

"I think he waved."

"What?" they ask again.

"Let me see that." Claire grabs the binoculars from my hand, raises them to her eyes.

"Is he waving?" I ask, my heart pounding.

"Not that I can make out. I mean, it's raining so hard, I can hardly see anything. It looks like he's just fixing his hair."

Is that what he's doing? I replay the motion in my mind, watching Paul Giller lift his hand to his head.

"Let me see," Jade says, and Claire gives her daughter the binoculars.

"Well . . . what's he doing?"

"Just standing there. Wait—he's taking off the towel. Damn it. He turned around. Nice butt!"

"Jade . . ."

"Well, it is."

"What's happening now?"

"He's walking into the closet. She's still drying her hair. Doing a lousy job, by the looks of it." Jade watches Paul and Elena for the next half hour as they continue getting ready to go out. "Okay. I think we're finally set to go. Terrible dress she's wearing."

Again, Claire commandeers the binoculars. "I think it's nice."

"I rest my case."

"What do you think of her dress, Bailey?" Claire asks. "Take a look."

I glance through the binoculars at what Elena is wearing: a sleeveless minidress with a scooped neckline and layers of ruffles at the hips. I search her exposed flesh for any bruises, but even if it weren't raining, I know I wouldn't see any, that the beating I was so positive I saw Paul administer happened only in my mind. What other explanation can there be? "She looks nice," I say as Paul Giller, wearing a print shirt tucked into a tight pair of dark pants, comes up behind her, puts his arms around her waist, and nuzzles his chin into the crook of her neck, his hands reaching up to cup her breasts. Elena playfully bats his hands aside and they head out of the room, both of them laughing.

A few seconds later, Paul Giller walks back into the bedroom to retrieve the cell phone he left on the bed. He approaches the window, staring into the downpour.

Then he lifts his fingers to his lips and blows me a kiss.

I gasp.

"What?" Claire asks as Jade looks at me.

I shake my head. "Nothing."

—

"That's it for me, guys," Claire announces at the conclusion of the eleven o'clock news. She grabs the remote from Jade's lap and turns off the television over her daughter's loud protests. "I'm going to sleep. I suggest we all do the same."

"But it's so early," Jade says. She is propped up between us in bed, looking imploringly from her mother to me.

"It's late," Claire tells her. "I have to be at work by eight o'clock, and you have school tomorrow."

"But they haven't even come home yet." Jade motions toward Paul Giller's apartment.

"And who knows when that could be? Go on," Claire tells her daughter. "You can watch TV in your room."

Jade groans and crawls over her mother on her way out of bed. "Okay. Have it your way. See you guys in the morning."

"Good night, sweetie," Claire and I call after her.

"We don't have to leave tomorrow, you know," Claire tells me as soon as Jade has left the room. "We could stay another week. Until you're feeling . . ."

"Not so crazy?"

"A little more secure," Claire says.

"No. You have your own lives to get on with. I can't expect you to babysit me forever."

Claire reluctantly agrees. "Only on one condition."

"What's that?"

"I need you to stop watching Paul Giller's apartment."

I'd pretty much decided this on my own already. "Okay."

"It's one condition with two parts," Claire qualifies.

"What's the second part?"

"I need you to hand over your binoculars."

"What? No. Those were my mother's."

"I know, and I'm not talking about forever. Just for a little while. Until you're feeling better. I'll keep them safe, Bailey."

"That's not the point."

"The point is that as long as they're here, you'll be tempted to use them." She looks at me with the same imploring eyes Jade gave me earlier. "Please, Bailey. Enough is enough."

I nod.

"Good girl." She kisses my forehead, then hunkers down in the bed. "Try to get some sleep."

I slide down beside her and pull the covers up over my head.

Claire flips onto her side, facing away from me. Within minutes, I hear her breathing deepen, and I try to emulate its calm, steady rhythm, each one of my breaths an echo of hers. Within minutes, I'm fast asleep.

—

The ringing of the telephone wakes me up some three hours later.

"Claire," I say as I grope for the receiver. "Claire, wake up. Do you hear that?" I answer the phone in the middle of its second ring. But even before I can say hello, I know no one is on the other end, that all I will hear is a dial tone. Probably it didn't ring at all. Still clutching the receiver, I turn toward Claire.

Except she isn't there. There is no one in bed beside me.

"Claire?" I climb out of bed, returning the phone to its charger and about to reach for the scissors when I see her.

She is sitting in the chair in front of the window, her head drooped forward, binoculars in her lap.

"Claire?" I say again, advancing slowly toward her, seized by the sudden fear she might be dead. "Claire?" I touch her shoulder, and then shake it when she fails to respond.

She startles and wakes up. "What? What's happened?"

"Are you all right?" I ask. "What are you doing?"

It takes a few seconds for her eyes to focus. "What time is it?"

"After two. How long have you been sitting here?"

"About an hour," she tells me. "I had to go to the bathroom, and I was coming back to bed when I realized the blinds were still up. I went to close them and I saw the light in Paul Giller's apartment was on. So I thought I'd take a look. And I guess I must have fallen asleep. . . ."

"I take it you didn't see anything very exciting."

"No. Not a thing. God, I'm thirsty. You feel like some hot chocolate? I feel like some hot chocolate."

"Hot chocolate sounds nice."

She pushes herself to her feet. "I'll go make it. You want to help me?"

"Would you mind if I stayed here and kept an eye on things?" I pick up the binoculars from the chair where Claire has left them.

"Bailey . . ."

"Last time, I promise."

"Okay. I'll be back in two minutes. Then you hand those suckers over."

I nod, sitting down in the chair she has just vacated as she tiptoes past the closed door of the room where Jade is supposedly sleeping, although I can hear the television. I raise the binoculars to my eyes and stare through the rain.

As if on cue, Elena comes running into the bedroom, Paul Giller walking slowly after her. She is shaking her head and gesticulating wildly.

"Claire!" I call out. "Jade!" But nobody hears me.

Elena makes a move for the bathroom, but Paul blocks her way, backing her up against the window. Elena raises her hands in the air, as if trying to ward him off. Paul has temporarily disappeared from my line of vision, swallowed by the ongoing downpour.

And then I see him.

He is advancing steadily toward her, his right arm extended. I stand up, move closer to the window, adjusting and then readjusting the lens of my binoculars, trying to convince myself that I'm not seeing what I think I'm seeing, and that is the gun in Paul Giller's hand, a gun he is waving menacingly at Elena's head. Elena is crying and waving her arms in front of her, frantically trying to persuade him to put the gun down.

"Claire!" I call out again. "Jade! Get in here!" I hear sirens emanating from the TV in Jade's room and the kettle's whistle in the kitchen telling Claire the water for our hot chocolate is boiled and ready.

And then suddenly Elena's hands are flying into the air above her head, and her body is lifting up and spinning around, her face flattening against the glass of the window. Blood is pouring from the gaping wound in her forehead, as her dead eyes search through the rain and stop on mine. Her fingers scratch through the blood on the window as she slides to the floor and disappears from sight.

Paul Giller walks slowly toward the window. He points his gun at me.

Which is when I start screaming. And screaming. And screaming.

Claire comes racing into the room, followed the next second by Jade, both of them trailing screams of their own: "What's happened? Bailey, what's going on?"

They find me on the floor, as if I've been shot myself. I'm crying and incoherent, unable to pull myself together.

"What is it, Bailey?" Claire asks again, her hands on my shoulders.

"He shot her! The bastard shot her!"

"What? What are you talking about?"

Jade pries the binoculars from my fingers and trains them on Paul Giller's apartment. "It's dark," she says.

"What? No!" I'm already scrambling back to my feet. "What do you mean, it's dark?"

"I can't see anything."

"The light was just on. You saw it," I tell Claire, my eyes pleading for confirmation.

"Yes, I did," Claire says. "The light was definitely on when I left the room."

"Well, it isn't on now," Jade insists.

"What happened, Bailey?" Claire asks. "What is it you think you saw?"

The words pound against my brain. What is it you *think* you saw?

I recount the exact sequence of events, starting from the moment Claire left my bedroom and Elena came running into hers.

"Are you sure you weren't dreaming?" Claire asks, her voice soft and kind. "Maybe you fell asleep. . . ."

"I didn't fall asleep."

"And you're positive he had a gun? I mean, it's raining really hard. Before, you thought you saw him wave, and now . . . How can you be sure it was a gun?"

"Because I know what a gun looks like," I insist. "Because what else could it have been? It killed her! Blew a hole right through her forehead. There was blood all over the window. There's no way she could have survived. We have to call the police."

No one moves.

"Maybe we should hold off on that," Claire says.

"What do you mean?"

"Think about it, Bailey. There are only so many times you can cry wolf."

"You think I'm crying wolf?"

"No, of course *I* don't think you're crying wolf. But it's what the police will think," she says, tears filling her eyes. "I just don't want you setting yourself up to be . . ."

"What?"

"I believe you honestly *think* you saw Paul Giller shoot his girlfriend."

"You just don't think it actually happened," I state, hearing the disappointment in my voice. If Claire doesn't believe me, who will?

"The police are going to say they find it odd that none of this happened until *after* I left the room."

"What? No. Why is that odd? It could have been a coincidence. . . ."

"That's some coincidence, Bailey. The three of us have been watching Paul Giller's apartment for days. Absolutely nothing happened in all that time."

"Well, it happened a few minutes ago. I'm telling you I saw Paul Giller shoot his girlfriend."

"Okay. Tell me again. Convince me. Then maybe we can convince Detective Castillo."

I take a deep breath, tell my story a second time, and then a third. There are only two possibilities: (1) Paul Giller did indeed shoot his girlfriend, or (2) I imagined the whole thing. "I know what I saw," I insist, although the truth is that I'm no longer as convinced as I was even minutes ago. Claire is right. The police will find it highly suspicious that this happened only *after* Claire left the room, that once again, I'm the only witness. If this latest incident proves to be another false alarm, it will only cement their suspicion that my rape has left me totally unhinged. "There *is* one other possibility," I say.

Claire and Jade stare at me expectantly.

"And that's that Paul Giller staged tonight deliberately," I continue, the idea beginning to flesh out, gain weight.

"What do you mean?" Claire asks.

"What if it's a setup?"

"I don't understand. What do you mean, a setup?"

"Maybe he just pretended to shoot his girlfriend."

"Why would he do that?"

"To make Bailey think she's going crazy," Jade says, latching onto my reasoning.

"You're definitely watching too much television," Claire says.

"What if I'm right?" I ask.

"About what? You seriously think that Paul Giller staged the shooting of his girlfriend for your benefit?"

"Not just that," I say, thinking out loud. "What if he staged everything? From the beginning. The wild sex in front of the window, the beating and rape that apparently never happened, the shooting I just witnessed."

"But why would he want to make you think you're going crazy?"

Three reasons spring to mind. "The first is that he's just a sick son-of-a-bitch who thinks this is fun," I expound, amazed at how calm, how rational I've suddenly become.

"Could be," Claire agrees, "but he'd have to be a real whack job. . . ."

"And the second?" Jade asks, interrupting.

"The second is that by making me think I'm crazy, I don't report what I saw tonight to the police, and he gets away with murder."

"I don't know," Claire says. "He's taking an awfully big risk. . . ."

"And the third?" Jade asks.

I take a deep breath. "The third is that . . ." I take another breath. ". . . Paul Giller is the man who raped me." I exhale slowly. "And if he can undermine my credibility by convincing everyone I'm crazy, that I've been harassing him for weeks for no good rea-

son, accusing him of anything and everything, then the police are
never going to charge him, and he gets away with it."

Claire and Jade give this theory a moment's thought.

"It still doesn't add up," Claire says, her eyes moving rapidly
from side to side, as her mind tries to grapple with everything she's
hearing. "How would he time everything? How would he know
when you'd be watching or when you'd be alone? How did he
know I'd left the room? It doesn't make sense," she repeats. "Something's missing."

I have to agree. How would he know any of those things? It
doesn't make sense.

I replay tonight's events in my mind, watching Elena run into
the room, cowering in front of her furious boyfriend as he raises
the gun in his hand and pulls the trigger, her blood splattering
against the window, her lifeless eyes pleading with mine. Did Paul
Giller stage the whole thing? And can I take that chance? Can I let
a man get away with murder because I didn't report his crime? "I
know what I saw," I tell Claire.

"Then I don't think we have any choice," she says.

—

Of course everything happens exactly as Claire predicted it would.

Claire calls Detective Castillo on his private line and tells him
what happened. He is not happy at having been woken up in the
middle of the night, and he's dismissive of our story. He keeps
Claire on hold while he checks with the station to find out if there
have been any reports of gunshots in the area or a call from someone else who might have witnessed the shooting, then informs her
that there have been neither. It is only when Claire lies and tells
him that she herself was a witness to tonight's events that he agrees
to send a police cruiser over to check it out.

"You shouldn't have lied to him," I tell her.

"I shouldn't do a lot of things," she says.

The rest of the night goes pretty much according to script: The
police go to Paul Giller's apartment; they find him alone and angry

at being awakened in the middle of the night; he gives them permission to search the premises; they find no trace of Elena, no signs of blood anywhere, no hint of a disturbance of any kind; while there are security cameras on all the floors, they haven't been turned on due to the low volume of tenants; there is no photographic proof that Elena might have snuck out or that she was ever even there. Paul Giller threatens to sue, not only me, but the entire Miami-Dade Police Department and Detective Castillo personally, if this outrageous harassment doesn't stop; the police come to my condo to relay this information and voice their dismay; they refuse to buy into any of our conjectures, parroting virtually all of Claire's earlier questions, although Detective Castillo concedes that if my third theory is right and Paul Giller *is* the man who raped me, then at least I'm right about one thing: I've pretty much ensured his never being charged. He warns me to stop watching Paul Giller's apartment or he will have no choice but to arrest me for stalking. He reminds Claire that it's a crime to lie to the police. And then he leaves.

"Well, that was a roaring success," Jade says after they're gone.

"I'm so sorry."

"It's not your fault."

"Then whose fault is it?"

"It's nobody's fault. It just is what it is," Claire says, clearly exhausted. "Let's not talk about it anymore tonight. Let's just get some sleep."

"I was so sure," I mutter.

I'm not crazy.

"I know you were," Claire says. "And I believe you. I really do."

"I believe you, too," Jade seconds.

"Unfortunately, the police don't," Claire points out. "And now we have a bigger problem."

"What's that?"

"Now they don't believe me either."

—TWENTY-NINE—

At seven thirty the next morning, having slept maybe a total of two hours all night, Claire goes to work. She leaves me with a verbal list of instructions: Stay away from the bedroom window; don't leave the apartment; leave Paul Giller alone.

She entrusts my binoculars to Jade and instructs her to drop them off at their house on her way to school. "I'll call you on my break, see how you're doing," she tells me. I know what she is really saying is that she'll call on her break to check up on me.

"Don't be late for school," she warns Jade on her way out.

"So, you want some scrambled eggs?" Jade asks as soon as her mother is gone. "They're my specialty."

"I didn't know you could cook."

"I can't. The only thing I know how to make is scrambled eggs. That's why they're my specialty."

I laugh. "Shouldn't you be getting dressed?"

Jade walks into the kitchen, quickly commandeering a frying pan and a bowl from their respective cupboards. "I'm not going to school today," she says matter-of-factly, tugging on the yellow polka dot pajama bottoms that have slipped halfway down her slender hips as she reaches with her other hand into the fridge for some eggs. She cracks four of them into the bowl, quickly fishing out some errant eggshells with her long, elegant fingers, before adding water, salt, and pepper, and then stirring vigorously. "I'm staying here with you."

"You can't. Your mother will be furious."

"Not if you don't tell her. Come on, Bailey. You really think I'm gonna be able to concentrate on algebra after what went down last night?"

I decide not to argue, having watched enough exchanges between my sister and her daughter to know that nobody wins an argument with Jade. Besides, I'm glad for the company. I no longer trust myself to be alone. I don't trust what I might see.

Or not see.

Minutes later, the scrambled eggs are on a plate, along with several pieces of buttered toast, all neatly arranged on the dining room table. Claire made coffee before she left, and Jade pours me a cup and then gets herself a can of Coke. "How can you drink that stuff first thing in the morning?" I ask.

"Caffeine is caffeine," she says. "I'm gonna need something to stay awake."

"Sorry about last night," I tell her, wondering how many times I've apologized already.

"Are you kidding? I loved it. It was like being in an episode of *Cops*."

I smile, swallow a forkful of eggs. "These are delicious, by the way."

"Thank you. They're my specialty." She yawns.

"Were you able to get back to sleep after the police left?" I ask.

"I dozed off and on. You?"

"A bit. Between nightmares."

"About your rape?"

"I guess. Indirectly. They're always the same: masked men chasing me, faceless women watching, sharks circling underneath my feet. . . ."

"Sharks?"

"My therapist calls them anxiety dreams."

"She needed a degree to figure that one out? You think they're trying to tell you something?" she asks in the next breath. "I mean, other than that you're anxious?"

"Like what?"

"I don't know. Dr. Drew once said that the reason people have recurring dreams is that these dreams are trying to tell you something, and you'll keep having them until you figure it out."

"Who's Dr. Drew?"

"*Celebrity Rehab?*" Jade asks with a shake of her uncombed hair. "Honestly, Bailey. How can you be a detective when you don't know anything about the modern world? It's like you're this visitor from another planet. Although maybe it wasn't Dr. Drew. It could have been Dr. Phil, or maybe even Dr. Oz."

"You ever think your mother might be right about your watching too much television?"

It's Jade's turn to shrug, which I have to admit she does magnificently, her whole body seemingly engaged. We finish our scrambled eggs and toast. I go into the kitchen and pour myself another cup of coffee.

"So, who called last night?" she asks as I return to the dining room.

"What?"

"Was it Heath?"

"What are you talking about?"

"What do you mean—what am I talking about? I fell asleep around midnight—in the middle of a *Law and Order* episode I've seen, like, five hundred times—and the phone woke me up about, I don't know . . . two o'clock?"

I feel my adrenaline starting to pump. Every hair on my body seems to be standing on end. My hands are shaking. "You heard the phone ring?"

"There's a phone on the desk right beside my head. How am I *not* gonna hear it?"

I burst into a flood of grateful tears.

"Bailey, what's going on?"

I tell her about all the mysterious phone calls I've been getting, the dial tone that regularly greets me when I lift the receiver to my ear, my suspicions that these calls are all in my head.

"You *do* know you can punch in star 69, that you can check the phone's history." Jade regards me as some sort of alien being.

"I do that . . . usually. It keeps coming up 'Unknown caller.' At first I thought it might be Travis. . . ."

"Who's Travis?"

"Or Heath."

"You really think your brother would be crank-calling you? Why would he do that?"

"He wouldn't," I tell her with more certainty than I feel. I no longer know what Heath might or might not do, or why.

Jade's eyes suddenly open wide, any hint of sleepiness vanishing. She jumps to her feet.

"What?" I hold my breath, as if I know what she's about to say.

"Do you think it could be Paul Giller?"

This isn't the first time I've considered this possibility. "It could be," I concede, resuming my pacing, an action Jade mimics on her side of the table.

"It makes sense. It's how he'd make sure you'd be watching."

I stop, turn toward her. "What do you mean?"

"Last night, one of the questions my mother asked was how he'd know you'd be watching. Well, if he phoned you, deliberately woke you up. . . . Think, Bailey. Did anyone call just before you saw him beat and rape his girlfriend?"

I think back to that night, rewinding the reel in my head and playing back the night's events in reverse order, first the rape, then the beating, then the phone call that woke me up, that started everything. "Yes. Yes, it did."

"And the other times?"

"I don't know. I can't remember." They happened too long ago for me to be sure.

"He knows you've been watching him, so he decides to use it to his advantage," Jade continues, thinking out loud. "He phones you, wakes you up, figures you'll see his lights are on and, being both naturally curious *and* a detective, you'll probably start watching. . . ."

"But that doesn't answer your mother's other question, how he'd know when I was alone. . . ."

This stops Jade cold. "Okay, okay. So, I haven't figured it all out yet. But I will. *We* will."

I walk around the other side of the table and take her in my arms, hug her tight against me. "Thank you."

"For what?"

"For being here. For believing me. For making me scrambled eggs."

"They're my specialty."

—

Jade is standing in front of my bedroom window, dressed in jeans and a white hoodie, binoculars in hand, staring toward Paul Giller's apartment when I finish my shower. "You're not supposed to be doing that," I tell her, securing my terry cloth robe around me as I exit the bathroom.

"No, *you're* not supposed to be doing that," she corrects. "My mother didn't say anything about me."

"See anything?"

"I think I saw him getting ready to go out. It's hard to make anything out in this light, especially with all the rain. I'm thinking maybe we should start building an ark."

I check the clock on the nightstand beside my bed. It's almost nine o'clock. The phone rings.

"Don't answer it," Jade says, rushing to my side to check the caller ID. "Shit. It's my mother. You better pick up."

"What do I tell her?"

"That I left for school ten minutes ago." She returns to the window.

I pick up the receiver. "Yes, she left a few minutes ago," I tell her. "She made me the most wonderful scrambled eggs."

"Shouldn't have told her that," Jade says as I replace the receiver. "You're ruining my reputation. Oh, wait. He's leaving."

I'm right behind her, peering over her shoulder. "I can't see anything."

"Here," she says, handing me the binoculars and walking toward the bedroom door.

"Where are you going?"

"To check out his apartment."

"What? No! Wait! You can't do that."

"Of course I can. Bet you anything he has the same shit locks you used to have."

"That's not what I'm talking about."

She stops. "There's nothing to worry about, Bailey. I'll be in and out before anybody even knows I'm there."

"But what are you going to do?"

"Just have a quick look around. See if I can find anything the police might have missed during their supposedly thorough search of the premises."

"I can't let you do that."

"You gonna chase after me in your bathrobe?" She is already halfway down the hall.

"Jade!"

"Keep watching. I'll call you when I get there."

"Jade!"

But she's already gone.

—

Fifteen minutes later, my phone rings. "I'm in the building," my niece says, and I picture her inside the sparsely furnished lobby, her hoodie pulled up over her head as she whispers into her cell phone. "I'm absolutely drenched. I had to wait about ten minutes, till I could sneak in as someone was coming out. I'm waiting for an elevator right now, dripping all over the damn place."

"This is crazy, Jade. It's too dangerous. If you get caught, they'll send you back to Juvenile Hall."

"I won't get caught. Just keep watching the apartment. I'll turn a light on when I get inside, so you can see what's happening."

"No. Just come back. . . ."

"The elevator's here. The doors are opening. . . ."

"Make sure you keep your phone on," I instruct.

"Uh-oh. Someone's getting on with me," she says just before the line goes dead.

—

"Hi," Jade says approximately a minute later.

"What the hell happened?" I cry into the phone.

"Sorry about that. I forgot to charge the battery, so it's kind of low, and elevators are always dicey anyway. And then this old guy got on with me, and I didn't want to call you back until he got off, which wasn't till the twenty-fifth floor."

"You almost gave me a heart attack."

"There's really nothing to worry about. Just don't freak out if we get cut off again."

"I'm freaking out already."

"Well, don't. I know what I'm doing. I learned from the best, remember?"

"This isn't TruTV."

"No, it's a hundred times better."

"Jade . . ."

"I'm walking down the corridor," she informs me, ignoring my concerns. "This building isn't nearly as nice as yours."

"Just turn around and come home."

"I'm standing in front of his apartment."

"Don't do this."

"Hang on a sec."

"Jade . . . Jade. Please . . ." I hear a succession of vague noises, followed by a few choice expletives. "Jade, what's going on?"

"Stupid lock is giving me a harder time than I expected."

"Then leave it and come home. . . ."

"Just a few more tries. . . ."

"Jade . . ."

"Got it! I knew it. Piece of shit."

"What's happening?"

"I'm in," she says.

—

I'm holding my breath as I raise the binoculars to my eyes, training them on Paul Giller's apartment. My hands are shaking so badly that it's hard to keep the damn things focused. "Where are you?" I ask.

"I'm in the living room," Jade says, flipping on the overhead light. "Can you see me?"

"No. I see a light, but it's raining too hard to see anything else. You have to come right to the window."

She obliges, approaching the window and shaking free of her hoodie, waving at me with the fingers of her left hand while holding the phone to her ear with her right. "It's very weird in here," she says, looking around.

"What do you mean?"

"There's, like, hardly any furniture. Not even a sofa. Just a couple of plastic lounge chairs, like the kind you take to the beach."

"Maybe he's still waiting for his furniture to be delivered," I posit. "I mean, if he just moved in . . ."

"I don't know. It's like nobody really lives here." Jade disappears from my line of sight.

"Where are you? Where'd you go?"

"I'm in the kitchen. There's, like, no dishes or anything in any of the cupboards. Just a couple of plastic glasses. And the stove still has all the instruction books inside, like it's never been used."

"Half the stoves in Miami have never been used," I tell her. "Lots of people don't cook anymore. . . ."

"Yeah, but they eat. There's absolutely no food in the fridge. This is really weird."

"Anything else?"

"Not so far."

"Where are you now?"

"Heading into the bedroom."

"Jade?"

"Right here." The overhead light in the bedroom suddenly comes on. "Can you see me?" she asks, coming right up to the glass.

"Yes. What do *you* see?"

"Pretty much what we see when we stare through the binoculars, except it looks better from a distance. There's the bed and a couple of end tables, a full-length mirror, a dresser and a vanity table, some lamps. It's all pretty cheap stuff. You know, like from Goodwill. There are no drapes anywhere."

"Any signs of a struggle?"

"No. Just an unmade bed. Oh, wait." She reaches into the sheets. "Idiot forgot his cell phone." She holds it up for me to see.

"Which means he could come back any minute. As soon as he realizes . . ."

"I'll be long gone," Jade assures me, tossing the phone back on the bed and suddenly dropping from sight. I picture her down on all fours.

"What are you doing?"

"Looking for blood."

"Do you see any?"

"Not a drop. No bodies under the bed either."

"What about around the window? Any sign of blood there?"

Jade's head pops back into view. "Nothing. Except for the water I'm dripping all over everything. You know what we could use? One of those special flashlights they have on TV, the kind that lights up the blood that people try to wash away."

"Okay, Jade. That's enough. It's time for you to leave."

"Let me check the closet."

"No. . . . Don't. . . . What's happening?" I secure the phone against my ear with my shoulder while furiously twisting the lenses of the binoculars in an effort to locate her.

"This is getting more and more bizarre," Jade informs me seconds later. "I'm in the closet, and there's, like, hardly any clothes.

A few pairs of jeans, a pair of black pants, a couple of men's shirts. A dress. Some kind of uniform. A pair of sneakers."

I bite down on my tongue to keep from screaming. "What kind of sneakers?"

"Nikes."

"Black?"

"More like charcoal gray."

Close enough, I think, my heart moving into my throat, causing my head to spin.

"You want me to grab them?" Jade asks.

"No." If we remove the sneakers from Paul's apartment, any evidence obtained from them would be inadmissible in court. "Can you take pictures of them with your phone?"

"I can try."

"Front and back, both sides, top and bottom."

"Okay. As soon as I hang up. First, I'm gonna peek into the bathroom."

I can barely make out her vague form as it moves away from the closet. "Anything?"

"Not much. A razor, some shaving cream, a toothbrush, some toothpaste. I'm opening the medicine cabinet. Wow—not even an aspirin. Shit . . . what's that?" Her voice has become a whisper.

"What's what?"

"I thought I heard something." Jade appears in the bathroom doorway.

My eyes shoot toward the living room window. "I don't see anything. Wait. Oh, shit. Someone's coming inside!" I watch in horror as Paul Giller enters the apartment, his head tilting toward the overhead light. "It's him," I tell Jade. "He noticed the light's on. Damn it."

Jade's head snaps toward the light switch on the wall by the bedroom door, as if trying to decide if she has time to run over and turn it off.

"Forget it," I say as Paul Giller kicks off his shoes and walks toward the bedroom. "Get under the bed. *Now!*"

"What's happening?" Jade whispers seconds later, and I can hear the fear crowding her words.

"I don't know. I can't see him. Are you under the bed?"

"Yes."

"Don't say another word. Just keep the phone tight against your ear and I'll tell you as soon as I see him."

"I'm scared."

"Shh. Don't talk. I still can't see him. Wait. There he is. He's coming into the room . . . he sees the light is on . . . obviously confused . . . he's looking around, checking the closet . . . now he's looking in the bathroom . . . he's walking to the window. . . ." I back away from my own window as quickly as I can.

"What's happening? Bailey, what's happening?"

"Shh! He'll hear you. Be quiet." I edge slowly back toward the window, relieved to see that Paul isn't there.

Except, where is he? Where the hell is he?

And then I see him. He's reaching into the middle of the crumpled sheets to retrieve his cell phone. He's just about to put it in his pocket when he stops. He remains motionless in this position for several seconds, his gaze focused on the floor.

Does he know someone is hiding underneath the bed, only inches from his feet?

He pivots slowly around, then bends down, balancing on his knees.

"Shit," I exclaim, the word escaping on a shallow breath as I watch his hand reach down to pat the carpet by his feet. "He knows it's wet," I tell Jade, my voice a strangled whisper. I watch in growing horror as Paul's body vanishes from sight.

"What the hell?" I hear him say.

"Leave me alone," Jade cries.

"Come on out, little girl," he tells her. "Nice and slow. Don't make me have to drag you out."

"No! Don't touch me!"

"Then get out here. That's it. Slide all the way out. On your feet."

I can see them clearly now. Jade, trembling, in front of the bed, Paul looming over her. He has yet to notice the phone secreted inside the palm of her hand.

"Who the hell are you?" he asks.

"Nobody. I'm nobody."

"Not good enough."

"I'm just someone who's been breaking into apartments in the neighborhood for the last couple of weeks," she improvises. "Please let me go. I didn't take anything. You don't *have* anything. . . ."

"What's your name?" he barks.

"Jade. Jade Mitchum."

"Jade Mitchum," he repeats slowly. "How'd you get in here?"

"I jimmied the lock."

"You jimmied the lock?"

"Those locks aren't worth shit."

"Good to know." He grabs her arm and pulls her toward the window. "See anyone you know?" he asks, staring in my direction.

With one hand, I press the binoculars tighter to my eyes, my other hand securing the phone to my ear.

"I don't know what you're talking about."

"Really? You don't know anyone named Bailey Carpenter? Why do I find that so hard to believe?"

"Please just let me go. You know Bailey's onto you. You know she's probably calling the police right now. . . ."

"Would that be the same police she called last night?" he interrupts. "The ones I've threatened to sue if they so much as show their faces here again? I doubt she'd be that stupid. But go right ahead, Bailey," he shouts at the window. "Call the cops. See how fast they come running this time."

I know he's right. Whatever credibility I had with the police disappeared with last night's debacle. There's no point calling them. I'm the girl who cried wolf, at best a pathetic victim of post-traumatic stress, at worst a total nutcase.

"What's this?" I hear Paul ask, his voice inching closer. "Is that a phone? Is it on?" I watch him wrest the phone from Jade's clenched fist. "Hello? Hello, Bailey? Are you still there?" His voice insinuates its way into my eardrum like a tiny serpent. "I think you are. I can hear you breathing."

Tell me you love me.

Oh, God.

The line goes dead.

Seconds later, his apartment goes dark.

—THIRTY—

I'm crying as I pull a sweatshirt over my pajamas and run from the room. Pushing my bare feet into a pair of flip-flops, I race down the hall and out the door. The elevator arrives almost as soon as I press the call button, and mercifully, there is no one in it. I should have called Gene and told him his niece was in trouble, urged him to contact the police. The cops might not believe me, but they most assuredly wouldn't argue with an assistant state's attorney. Not that Gene has any more faith in my judgment than Miami's finest does.

The elevator stops on the second floor, and I wait, holding my breath, as a man approaches, then stops abruptly. He is about forty, with a damp helmet of white hair and a blue towel around his thick neck. He is wearing gym clothes, and perspiration drips from his forehead and down the side of his full face. "Can you hold the elevator just a sec?" he says, more an order than a request. He glances over his right shoulder. "Donna, where are you? Come on, the elevator's here. People are waiting." He holds up his index finger and takes a step back.

"I'm in a huge hurry."

He ignores me. "Donna, what the hell are you doing back there?"

I lunge forward, pushing the elevator button repeatedly until the doors start to close. "Sorry," I mutter, the man's outraged expression the last thing I see as the elevator resumes its descent. "Come on. Come on," I urge, desperate to get out of the elevator and over to Paul Giller's apartment.

I should have called Sean, begged him to place the call to the police in my stead. Of course, he probably would have found all sorts of excuses not to comply. Sean is good at excuses.

At the very least, I should have called Claire, I decide, as the elevator doors open into the lobby. And told her what? That because of me, her only child is now in grave, perhaps even mortal, danger? I can't do that. I'm not ready for her to hate me yet. At least not until after I've done everything in my power to try to rescue her daughter.

Except, how can I do that? What can I do?

The answer is simple: Whatever it takes. Anything Paul Giller asks.

I run past the concierge desk, almost tripping over my flip-flops.

"Miss Carpenter," Finn calls out, "is everything all right?"

"Call the police," I shout back, my panic increasing with the sound of his voice. I can barely see him, so blinded am I by my tears. "Tell them there's a break-in in progress at 600 Southeast 2nd Avenue. Apartment 2706." But my words are swallowed by the combination of rain and the noise of hammering from the nearby construction site, and I'm not sure he even heard me.

I reach Paul Giller's building and all but collapse outside the front door, bending over from the waist and gasping for breath. No one seems to have noticed me. The few pedestrians I see are too busy trying to escape the rain. Nor does anyone pay me any mind as I fall back against the exterior wall, waiting for someone to come out of the building so that I can sneak in, the same way Jade did earlier. I contemplate ringing Adam Roth's office but quickly think better of it. There's no way Adam Roth will allow me entry. And if he sees me and calls the police, they will forcefully escort me from the premises without even bothering to check out my story, a story they will undoubtedly dismiss as the hallucinations of a crazy woman.

Finally, two women approach the door from inside the lobby, matching floral umbrellas in hand. Mother and daughter, judging by the same sour expression on both their faces. "I know you don't like him, Mother," the younger of the two is saying between tightly clenched teeth, as they push their way outside, "but it's my life."

"Which you seem intent on screwing up royally," her mother shoots back as I slip past them, head down. Once inside the elevator, I press the button for the twenty-seventh floor, closing my eyes in gratitude when the doors close quickly and the elevator begins its climb.

Seconds later, I'm standing in front of apartment 2706, prepared to do whatever it takes—whatever Paul Giller asks—to get my niece safely out of there. If it isn't already too late. I reach for the doorknob, emitting a small cry when it falls open at my touch.

Which means what? That the apartment is empty? That Paul has already taken off, my niece in tow? Or worse. Does it mean that the only thing I'll find inside Paul's apartment is my niece's dead body?

"Come on in, Bailey," a voice says from somewhere inside. "We've been expecting you."

Suppressing the scream I feel building inside me, I push open the door and step over the threshold.

"Shut the door."

I kick the door closed with my foot, my heart beating so loudly, I'm sure the whole building can hear it. The room is empty except for the two plastic lounge chairs Jade described earlier.

"Now put your hands up in the air," the voice continues, and I realize Paul is standing directly behind me. I picture the gun in his hands, the same gun he used to shoot Elena. "You know I'm going to have to frisk you," he says as I feel a tentative hand patting me down.

"Don't. . . ."

"Please be quiet," he says with exaggerated politeness as the hand moves slowly down to my waist, and then down farther, traveling from hip to hip before disappearing between my thighs.

I fight the overwhelming urge to throw up. "Please . . ."

"Shh," he says, his hand continuing down the inside of my legs, then stopping when he reaches my bare toes. "Love the flip-flops," he says before standing back up.

Tell me you love me.

"Oh, God."

"Oh, God, what, Bailey?"

"It's not you," I whisper, scarcely believing the words coming from my mouth. Paul Giller is not the man who raped me. His voice—so different from my attacker's in both pitch and inflection—just confirmed it.

But if Paul Giller isn't the man who raped me, then who the hell is he?

I turn toward him.

"Slowly," he cautions, taking a step back.

A wave of calm washes over me. This is not some faceless stranger overwhelming me in the darkness of night, but a man who, despite the weapon he is brandishing, seems almost more afraid of me than I am of him. My eyes absorb every detail of Paul Giller's casually handsome face. Unlike the photographs on his Facebook page, in person he is rather bland, the stand-in rather than the star. There is something surprisingly insubstantial about him. "Where's Jade?"

"Your niece is in the bedroom."

"I want to see her."

He waves the gun in the direction of the other room. "After you."

Jade is sitting on the bed, crying softly. "Bailey," she cries as I move toward her.

"Are you all right?" I sit down beside her and take her in my arms.

"Yes."

"Did he hurt you?"

"No. He just told me not to move or he'd shoot you."

"Don't be afraid," I whisper into her hair. "I'll get you out of here." I turn back to Paul Giller. "Who are you? Why are you doing this?" I demand, grappling with the disparate pieces of the puzzle my life has recently become. The pieces float above my head, just out of reach, evading capture. "I know you aren't the man who raped me, so why . . . ?"

"Raped you?" Paul looks genuinely astonished. "What the hell are you talking about?"

"There has to be a reason you're doing this," I say, my brain snatching at a fistful of the invisible puzzle pieces and straining to fit them together. What motive could he have? I know that motives are generally either personal or financial, and I've never met this man before, so it can't be personal. Unless he knows Heath. Unless this has something to do with my brother's gambling debts. Could there be a connection between Paul and Heath?

"Don't know any Heath Carpenter," Paul says when I voice this thought out loud.

I mention Travis and get a similar response, the same bemused look in his eyes that tells me I'm way off track.

My mind is racing, one thought tumbling fast on another. If Paul's motive isn't personal, that means it can only be financial. And what could Paul possibly stand to gain by taking part in this bizarre charade? He's an actor, I remind myself, a hired hand at best. Which begs the question: Who hired him?

"Someone is paying you," I say.

The almost imperceptible flicker of Paul's eyebrows tells me I'm right.

"I don't understand," says Jade.

I explain the situation as much to myself as to my niece, the puzzle pieces beginning to slide more easily into place. "He's an actor. He just memorizes his lines, follows direction, shows up on time, hits his marks, and collects his paycheck. You needed money to pay your hospital bills after your recent bout of pneumonia, didn't you?" I ask Paul directly.

He remains silent.

"Someone's been paying you?" Jade asks him. "To do what exactly?"

Paul Giller smiles. "Ask Bailey. She seems to have it all worked out."

"To rent this apartment. To make love to a bunch of beautiful women in front of the window," I answer, as still more pieces of the puzzle drop into place. "To pretend to beat up his girlfriend, engage in a little rough sex, act all outraged and innocent when the police come calling. The same thing again later, after pretending to shoot her with the toy gun in his hand."

"His gun's fake?" Jade jumps to her feet in outrage.

"A souvenir from a TV show I once did," Paul admits with an apologetic shrug, tossing the toy pistol onto the bed.

"Shit," Jade mutters, picking it up and weighing the lightness of it in the palm of her hand. "This was all an act? What about the blood Bailey saw?"

"Trick of the trade. But a major bitch cleaning off the window, I gotta tell you. Especially in the dark."

"And your girlfriend, Elena, she's in on this, too," I say, the puzzle now almost complete.

Paul smiles indulgently. "Everybody can use a little extra cash."

"How much cash? Who's behind this?"

Who would go to the trouble and effort to concoct and carry out such a complicated scheme, to take advantage of my delicate psyche, throw me further off balance than the rape has already thrown me, make me question my very sanity?

Who wins by making me think I'm losing my mind?

Who stands to gain?

"He phoned someone," Jade says as our heads snap toward the sound of the apartment door opening. "Before you got here. . . ."

"Took you long enough," Paul calls toward the door as Jade burrows in against my side. "We're in the bedroom."

And then it becomes painfully clear how Paul was able to time his nightly performances, how he knew precisely when I'd be watching. I know who is paying him. And I know why.

"What the hell is going on here that was so goddamn important I had to leave work . . . ?" the final piece of the puzzle demands from the doorway.

Claire.

My heart sinks.

"*Mom?*" Jade whispers.

In an instant, everything crystallizes: Claire likely began hatching this scheme the moment she entered my apartment, taking advantage of my extreme vulnerability, faking concern for my welfare while carefully playing on my neuroses, feigning generosity and selflessness while undermining my sense of self. Within a week, she'd set everything in motion: writing the script, hiring her cast, and selecting her location.

Heath was right all along. My sister was never interested in my welfare. She was interested only in my money.

I remember that it was Claire who "accidentally" stumbled upon Paul Giller while casually peering through my binoculars; Claire who dropped the disturbing hints about his resemblance to the man who raped me; Claire who ensured I was awake for each of Paul's soul-destroying performances with those disorienting phone calls in the middle of the night; Claire who timed her exits and entrances just so, secretly signaling Paul when it was time to begin; Claire who pretended to be on my side while slyly working to discredit me with the police; Claire who masqueraded as my friend, my staunch supporter, my loving protector, when the truth was that she was none of those things.

I recall how upset she'd been when I told her I'd started investigating Paul Giller on my own, that I'd looked him up on the Internet, that I'd actually gone to his apartment, that I'd followed him and his girlfriend, that I'd talked to Elena. She'd pleaded with me, made me promise never to do anything so foolhardy, so dangerous, again. I remember how touched I was by her concern.

Except it wasn't me she was worried about.

Did Claire really think that by making me believe I was going crazy, by setting herself up as indispensible to my well-being, I would willingly concede control of my fortune to her? Was she hoping that, given my fragile emotional condition, the State would ultimately decide I was incapable of managing my own affairs, and that it would be in my best interest to grant my loving sister power-of-attorney?

I don't know, and to borrow a famous line from one of my mother's favorite old movies, I don't give a damn.

Although the truth is there's a part of me that wishes Claire had succeeded in her scheme. Part of me would rather be crazy than to have been so totally, utterly, betrayed. I stare at my half-sister through a shroud of tears.

The color drains from Claire's cheeks when she sees us sitting on the bed. Clearly, whatever she was expecting when Paul phoned her, it wasn't this. "Oh, God."

"Mom?" Jade says again. "What's going on?"

"What are they doing here?" Claire asks Paul. She's so pale, she looks as if she's about to pass out.

"Your kid broke in," Paul explains. "Picked the goddamn lock. Just like on TV."

"What the hell are you doing here?" Claire cries, turning on her daughter.

"What am *I* doing here? What are *you* doing here?" Jade counters. "Would you please tell me what in fuck's name is going on?"

I wait for Claire to say, "Jade, language." But she doesn't. In fact, nobody says anything for several excruciatingly long seconds.

"I can't believe this is happening," Claire sputters. "Oh, God. I'm so sorry."

"What are you sorry about?" Jade asks her.

"Please understand, sweetheart. I did this for you, so you'd have all of the things I missed out on."

"What exactly did you do, Mom? Tell me."

"What can I say?" She's crying now, her breathing coming in a series of shallow bursts. "You want a confession, like the kind you see on one of your stupid TV shows?"

"A confession of what?" Jade is crying now, too.

"Bailey?" Claire asks, as if there's anything I can say to mitigate what she has done, anything I can do to make this better.

"So this was all about the money," I say. Even knowing this to be true, there is still something inside me that needs to hear the words out loud. "You knew that Heath would never agree to settle the lawsuit, and that the damn thing could take years to crawl through the courts, that there's a good chance you wouldn't win. . . ."

"Please try to understand, Bailey. You've always had everything. The looks, the money, the mansion, the father who adored you. And me? What did I ever get? A goddamn Elvis impersonator! That's what I got."

"Are you asking me to feel sorry for you?"

She shakes her head, vigorously. "I'm just trying to explain. . . ."

"Gene and the others, are they . . . ?"

"Involved? No way. No, this is all on me." Claire rubs her forehead. "Please understand. This was never personal, Bailey. You have to believe that. You're a really sweet girl. Sweeter than I ever imagined."

"Where did you find *him*?" Jade throws a disgusted glance toward Paul Giller.

"He was her patient," I say before Claire can answer.

"A sweet girl *and* a good detective," Claire says, a surprising note of pride in her voice. "I just never realized *how* good."

"But where'd you get the money to set all this in motion? You had to rent the apartment, pay first and last month's rent in advance. . . ."

"I called Gene, told him I was drowning in debt and that if I didn't pay off my credit cards, I'd have to file for bankruptcy. I knew his pride would never allow that."

"I'm sure that check I gave you helped with the carrying costs. Even if I did take some of it back," I say. "Although that kind of worked in your favor, didn't it? You knew I'd never suspect you were after my money when you kept refusing to take it."

Claire struggles to maintain eye contact, but her eyes are so full of tears, I doubt she can see anything at all.

"And getting me to a therapist was a stroke of genius. It would only bolster your attempts to have me declared incompetent, should that become necessary."

"I would never have done that to you, Bailey. Never."

"It must have been quite the balancing act," I continue, "trying to put yourself inside my head, figure out what my next move was going to be, which couldn't have been easy. I was all over the place."

Claire looks helplessly around, first at Jade, who glares back at her mother with a combination of shock and contempt, then back at me.

"You just never figured on *this* happening," I tell her.

"What I never figured on was how much I'd come to care for you. It's just so ironic when you think about it. You're more than my sister, Bailey. You're the best friend I've ever had. Maybe the *only* real friend I've ever had."

"Wow," Paul Giller exclaims. "I'd hate to be your enemy."

"I can't tell you how many times I wanted to pull the plug, how often I was on the verge of calling the whole thing off. . . ."

"But you didn't."

"No." Claire swipes at her tears. "I didn't. I couldn't. I'd gone too far."

"So, where do we go now?" Paul asks.

"Yes, Mother," Jade says, her cheeks red with anger. "What happens now?"

"Now?" Claire lifts her hands into the air in the universal gesture of surrender. "I guess we pack up our things and go home. I spend the rest of my life trying to make amends. . . ."

"Amends?" Paul repeats. "What the hell are you talking about?"

"I'm talking about the fact that it's over, finished, done. We cut our losses and call it a day. We haven't really broken any laws. Except maybe for Jade here, breaking into your apartment."

"What about lying to the police?" Paul demands. "What about interfering with a police investigation?"

Claire wipes away the last of her tears. "What investigation?

You were never a suspect in Bailey's rape. The police were only here at Bailey's instigation. What are they going to arrest you for? Public mischief? Believe me, it isn't worth their time."

"How about forcible confinement and threatening bodily harm?" Paul glances toward the gun on the bed.

"With a water pistol?" Claire shakes her head. "What were you going to do with it—squirt them to death?" She sighs. When she speaks again, her voice is flat, depleted of energy, devoid of emotion. "Do I have to spell it out for you? There's been no real crime committed, no murder, no fraud. Just an elaborate practical joke that got out of hand. Bailey won't press charges. For one thing, no one would believe anything she says, and for another, no matter how she feels about me, she doesn't want to get Jade in trouble. And for all her bravado, Jade doesn't want to go back to Juvenile Hall. Nor does she want her mother to end up in jail. Am I right?" she asks, not waiting for an answer as she turns back to Paul. "So, all you have to do is go home and forget this ever happened. It's over."

"What about the rest of the money you promised me?" Paul asks.

"In case you haven't figured it out yet, there won't be any more money."

"You're shitting me, right?"

"No, I'm most definitely not shitting you."

"God, Mom," Jade says, as the enormity of everything she has just heard begins to sink in. "What have you done?"

"I did it for us, for *you*," Claire says, as she said earlier.

"The hell you did!" Jade shoots back. "You did this for *you*! Don't you dare try to fool yourself that it was ever about anybody else."

"You don't understand. . . ."

"Oh, I understand all right. I understand that you're a liar and a fraud and that I never want to speak to you again."

"Jade . . ." Claire's gaze shifts from her daughter to me, her shoulders slumping, a fresh gathering of tears in her eyes. "Bailey, please . . ."

I stare long and hard at my father's eldest child, recalling all the things she's done for me these past weeks: the countless meals she prepared, the many hours we spent together, the myriad acts of kindness, the heartfelt confidences we shared.

"You have no idea how sorry I am," she says. "I know I've done a terrible thing. I can only hope that some day you'll be able to forgive me."

I think about taking her in my arms and telling her yes, I do understand, and that in spite of everything, all is forgiven. The way I always do with Heath.

But Heath is merely weak, not greedy. And for all his faults, he has never betrayed me.

So I don't take her in my arms and tell her I understand.

Instead I slap her, hard, across the face.

Because all is definitely not forgiven. It never will be.

—

The police, responding to Finn's phone call, arrive soon after. Thinking they are interrupting a robbery in progress, they haul us all down to the police station but mercifully hold off on making any arrests until the situation can be thoroughly assessed.

Detective Castillo and Officer Dube show up almost immediately, as does Detective Marx, newly back from her honeymoon. Suspecting we might need a lawyer, I call Sean. I'm told he's in the middle of an important meeting and can't be disturbed. His assistant promises to send one of the firm's junior associates right over.

Jade and I take turns explaining the morning's events to the police. Our stories sound incredible, even to our ears. "Are you crazy?" Detective Castillo asks when we are through, throwing his hands into the air.

This sentiment is echoed by my brother, Gene, who arrives at the station a short time later. "Are you out of your fucking minds?" he demands repeatedly, after listening to everyone's story.

I am many things: impulsive, reckless, even foolhardy. But I am not crazy.

"You're sure Paul Giller isn't the man who raped you?" Detective Marx asks me when we have a few minutes alone.

"I'm sure."

"Too bad. It would have been nice to wrap it all up."

"How was your honeymoon?" I ask her.

She gives me a shy grin. "Great. I really lucked out."

There are still some good men out there, I remind myself. Not all men are bad.

Not all women are good.

At almost two o'clock in the afternoon, no final decision having been made as to what, if any, charges will be pressed, we are finally granted permission to go home.

"I'm not going anywhere with her," Jade says, glaring at her mother, who turns away, refusing to meet her daughter's eyes.

"Jade, for God's sake," Gene says with an exasperated sigh.

"I'm sixteen, and I'm not going home with her, and you can't make me."

"You want to spend the night in Juvenile Hall?" Gene asks. "You're certainly not coming home with me."

"You're fucking right I'm not."

"Watch your mouth, young lady. I can still have you charged with breaking and entering. . . ."

"She can stay with me," I say quietly. And then louder, warming to the idea, "She's staying with me."

Gene shrugs and shakes his head. "Suit yourself." He walks over to Claire and grabs her elbow. "What the hell's the matter with you? What were you thinking?" He leads her roughly from the room. "You know what this could do to our lawsuit?"

I almost smile. Maybe I would if I weren't so utterly exhausted.

"Thank you," Jade says, appearing at my side. "I was kind of counting on you offering."

This time I *do* smile.

Jade slips her arm through mine and together we walk from the room, down the hall, and out the station's front door.

THIRTY-ONE

"Looks like somebody is here to stay," Heath is saying as we peek into my former office, now a second bedroom once again. It's half past nine on a Saturday night, and three months have passed since Jade came to live with me. Or maybe *I'm* the one who's living with *her*. Evidence of her takeover is everywhere: school books and fashion magazines lie scattered on every available surface throughout the apartment; skinny jeans hang from every doorknob; wellworn, high-heeled boots litter the hallway. My desk and computer have been moved to my bedroom, where they sit in front of my window, mercifully blocking much of my view of the apartment where Paul Giller once pretended to live.

"Her new bed arrives next week," I tell my brother, marveling at how happy he appears.

And why not? Good things are finally starting to happen for him. He landed a series of commercials for a popular chain of Miami gyms, the first one of which was shot last week. While the commercials are local and not more lucrative national spots, they do mean a little bit of money and a lot of exposure, at least here in South Florida. Heath is sure the ads—which take full advantage of his glorious face and trim, muscular physique—will lead to more and better things, and I hope he's right. At least he's no longer sleeping on the floor of Travis's apartment and has rented a furnished place of his own. He's also sworn off weed. "I need to look not only gorgeous," he told me without a hint of false modesty, "but healthy. Besides," he added, "if you can get your act together after everything that's happened to you, then the least I can do is try."

So far, so good.

"Bet she'll be happy not to be sleeping on this thing anymore," Heath says now, plopping down on the sofa bed and causing the laptop Jade left lying there to jump into the air. "It's a real backbreaker."

"Don't tell Wes that," I warn.

"Who's Wes?"

"One of the valets. Jade told him it's for sale and he's coming up later to have a look."

Heath leans his head against one of the purple velvet pillows and closes his eyes. "So, what else is new?"

I give the question a moment's thought. "Not much. My friend, Sally, brought her new baby over the other day."

Heath's eyes pop open. "You have a friend?"

I laugh, although the question isn't that far-fetched. "Amazingly, yes. Don't think you've ever met. She works at Holden, Cunningham, and Kravitz."

"Are you considering going back there?"

"Not a chance. I've actually been thinking of starting up on my own."

"What?"

"I know. It's a stupid idea."

"It's an awesome idea. 'Bailey Carpenter, Private Investigator.' Sounds great."

"Jade thinks 'Bailey Carpenter and Associates' sounds even better. She's already started looking into courses online."

"What a woman," Heath says, and I laugh. "God, it's good to hear you laugh again. It's been a while."

"Getting a little stronger every day."

"No more panic attacks?"

"Some," I admit. "But less frequent, less severe. And I'm sleeping better." I don't tell him of the deadly sharks that continue to swim through my nightmares, their fins slicing through the surface of deceptively placid seas.

Heath pushes himself to his feet. "Well, little sister, it looks like my work here is done."

"You're leaving?"

"You're not going to believe this, but I actually have a date. A real date, not just a hook-up."

"Wow."

"Nothing serious. Just, you know, this girl I met on set."

I follow my brother into the hall.

"What about you?" he broaches tentatively when we reach the door. "Given any thought to maybe dating again?"

"I think about it. I'm just not ready." I picture Owen Weaver and wonder if his invitation to dinner will still be open if and when I *am* ready.

"You will be," Heath says, taking me in his arms. "I love you, Bailey. Remember—you're my hero."

Tears fill my eyes. "I love you, too."

I watch him through the peephole as he disappears down the hall. Then I double-lock the door.

After all, my rapist is still out there.

My rapist, I repeat silently as I head toward my bedroom. As if he is someone I possess and not someone who once possessed me, possesses me still. *My* rapist, as if he is mine alone.

I doubt this is true. Experience tells me that, even in the unlikely event I was his first victim, it's even more unlikely I'll be his last. He won't stop until something—or someone—stops him.

I've thought a lot about him these past months. I've researched the kind of man who rapes, what motivates and drives him. Of course, there are as many motives as there are rapists, but I've learned that these men share a number of traits: Many are the product of meek mothers and brutal fathers, or weak fathers and overbearing mothers. Take your pick. Many were abused. Most feel inadequate in one way or another, often sexually, although rape has little to do with sex. It is a crime of power, of control and humiliation. In its quest to inflict pain, it cuts through class, economic boundaries and racial divides. One thing unites these men: Men who rape are men who hate.

Tell me you love me.

I've tried to reconcile these words with the act itself, to determine what kind of man would demand such an admission from a woman he'd just violated. I've discussed it with Elizabeth Gordon. We've postulated that the man who raped me might have been subjected to frequent beatings by his mother for even the most inconsequential of childhood transgressions, then made to apologize for his punishment and, in a final act of debasement, forced to declare his undying love. Another theory is that as a young boy, the man who raped me might have witnessed his father repeatedly abusing his mother in just such a manner. Both scenarios are possible, even plausible. Of course, it's equally possible that neither of these suppositions bears any relation to reality, that the man who raped me is the product of a warm and loving home and that his parents remain blissfully ignorant to this day of the monster their love created.

And ultimately, do reasons matter? The "why" is of consequence only if it leads to the "who." It's the "who" that counts.

I sink down on my bed, scoop up my remote, and turn on the TV, absently flipping through the channels. Stopping on *1000 Ways to Die.*

The reality is that I will likely never know who raped me, that he will forever remain faceless, nameless, that the biggest question in my life is the one I might never be able to answer.

But sometimes you have to be okay with ambiguity. Sometimes it's all you've got.

As an investigator, someone who solves mysteries for a living, this is hard to wrap my head around. Even more ironic is the fact that the mystery I *did* solve had nothing to do with the mystery I thought I was solving.

My rape masked a lot of things. For weeks, I was operating

under a huge distraction, a distraction engineered by my half-sister, a distraction that cut two ways. The rape distracted me from dealing with longstanding family issues, while my family distracted me from dealing with my rape.

Elizabeth Gordon—the one positive to come out of Claire's betrayal—will help me come to terms with both of these enormities. But first I have to figure out what is solvable and what is not. Now that I am no longer being overwhelmed by all the red herrings Claire threw my way, my focus is starting to clear.

Tell me what you see, I hear my mother say now, her voice mixing with the voices emanating from the TV.

The darkness of that awful October night instantly surrounds me. I'm transported from my comfortable bedroom into the middle of a circle of prickly bushes. I breathe in the deceptively warm air, the gentle breeze blowing the subtle scent of the surrounding blossoms toward my nose. What details have I overlooked? I ask myself, as I slide off my bed to crouch beside it, mimicking my actions of that night.

Reflexively, I retrieve my binoculars from the bottom drawer of my nightstand, conjuring up the scene and watching it play out again. I see the large rectangular window of the third floor corner apartment across from my hiding place. Occasionally, a woman walks into view. Once, she stops and lingers in front of the window, craning her neck, as if she might have spotted me. I'm growing tired, thinking of calling it a night. Which is when I hear the noise, feel the modest shifting of the air.

Tell me what you see, my mother prompts again.

I see a sudden blur of average height and weight, a flash of skin, brown hair, blue jeans, and black sneakers with their trademark Nike swoosh. I relive the onslaught of punches to my stomach and head, and strain against the roughness of the pillowcase that drags my hair over my face and burrows into my eyes, nose, and mouth.

The phone rings.

I jump at the sound, a familiar reflex. Taking a series of long, deep breaths to calm my newly jangled nerves, I grab the remote and turn down the volume of the TV. It's closing in on ten o'clock, and Jade is at a party. She's probably calling to see if I'll extend her midnight curfew.

But the number that comes up on my caller ID doesn't belong to Jade.

My heart is reaching into my throat as I push myself to my feet, my hand hovering over the receiver, as I try to decide whether or not to pick it up. On the television screen, a woman is choking on a plastic Easter egg she mistook for chocolate. "Number 912 . . . ," the announcer begins as I press the mute button and pick up the phone, sitting down on my bed and leaning back against the pillows. "Hi," I say.

"How are you?" Sean asks softly in return.

"Okay." Why is it that, in spite of everything—the revelations, the lies, the fact it's been months since he's tried to contact me at all—a part of me still thrills to hear his voice, a part of me wants nothing more than for him to come over and spend the night holding me in his arms, assuring me that his feelings remain unchanged and that he will always be there, to love and protect me, to keep me safe and out of harm's way?

Except, of course, he was never there for me at all. He never loved or protected me. His arms never kept me safe. How could they, when his grip was so deliberately tenuous?

"It's been a while," he says.

"It has," I agree.

"I still can't believe that Claire, of all people . . ."

"Yes."

"She seemed so nice."

People are rarely what they seem. "She had us all fooled." Why is he calling?

"Look. I hate the way things ended between us," he says, answering my silent question. I picture him hovered over his phone, keeping his concern for my welfare well away from his pregnant wife's ears. "I think about you all the time."

"I think about you, too."

"I miss you, Bailey."

"I miss you, too." A wave of shame washes over me. Have I learned absolutely nothing?

"I was thinking maybe I could stop by sometime soon. . . ."

It would be so easy to give in, to overlook, to surrender.

Except I've already surrendered too much of myself. And I'm tired of feeling ashamed. "Aren't you expecting a baby any day now?"

"That has nothing to do with us."

"Well, maybe it should," I say forcefully, surprised by how easily the words fall off my tongue.

"Bailey . . ."

"I don't want you to come by. In fact, I don't want you to call me ever again."

"You don't mean that. It's late. You're tired. . . ."

"And you're a liar and a fraud," I tell him, borrowing the words Jade threw at her mother. "Call me again, and I swear I'll call your wife." I drop the receiver back into its charger, my adrenaline pulsing through my veins, my veins threatening to burst. I want to scream. If I don't do something, I will explode. I jump off my bed and march into the bathroom, coming face to face with my reflection in the mirror over the sink.

While I've put back a few of the pounds I lost in the immediate aftermath of my rape and I've cut down on the number of showers I take, I'm still way too thin, and my hair continues to hang like a crumpled dishrag around my too-narrow face. Sean always loved my hair.

Reason enough to get rid of it.

I head back to the bedroom and retrieve the scissors from the top drawer of my nightstand, then return to the bathroom and impulsively begin hacking at what was once my crowning glory, slicing it off in clumps and tossing fistfuls of it to the tile floor. I continue recklessly, not stopping until all that remains of my once luxurious locks has been reduced to barely more than stubble, a five o'clock shadow run amok.

When I'm done, I drop the scissors to the counter and stare at my handiwork, my energy spent. "Holy shit," I whisper.

In the movies, when the anguished heroine chops off all her hair, she somehow manages to look as if she just emerged from a high-end salon, her hair short but expertly and stylishly layered, her new do even more fetching than her previous one. Not so in real life, I realize, staring at the mess I have made. "Holy shit," I say again. What else is there to say?

Overwhelmed by exhaustion, I collapse on top of my bed, turning back on the volume of my TV and watching as a woman wearing a billowing white bridal gown wades into a river, laughing happily, a photographer running along beside her on the shore. I hold my breath, knowing what is about to transpire. I remember reading about the growing trend of brides to do something outrageous in the way of wedding pictures, how this trashing of tradition has become all the rage. I watch the unsuspecting bride's gown become waterlogged, the weight of her dress ultimately dragging the now-struggling woman beneath the water's surface. I'm asleep before the announcer can tell me where her tragic drowning stands in the pantheon of *1000 Ways to Die.*

I turn on my side and tumble into a dream. I'm running down a sun-drenched street, pursued by half a dozen faceless men. They chase me to the edge of the ocean and I wade in, quickly becoming weighed down by both my billowy white skirt and the heavy blue waves. There is a raft in the distance, and I swim toward it, sharks gathering beneath my feet. I pick up the pace of my strokes, not noticing until I am mere feet from the raft that there is a man lying on top of it. He sits up, his silhouette familiar although his face is blocked by the glare of the sun. He extends his gloved hand toward me. "No!" I scream, flailing about helplessly in the water, my clothes wrapping around me like duct tape as a giant fin breaks through the ocean's surface, and hundreds of scissorslike teeth rip into my flesh.

Which is when I jolt awake.

"Damn it." I glance over at the clock, realizing that barely ten minutes have passed. A whole night of bad dreams to look forward to. I run my hand through what remains of my hair, deciding to go to the hairdresser's on Monday. Maybe they'll be able to do something. Maybe it's not as bad as I think. I walk into the bathroom and once again confront my reflection in the mirror. It's exactly as bad as I think.

I splash water on my face, debate taking a shower, then decide against it. I've regressed enough for one night.

What was it Jade once said—that we have recurrent nightmares for a reason?

So what exactly are these dreams trying to tell me?

"Probably that I'm watching too much damn TV," I say as the phone rings.

This time I'm so sure it's Jade that I don't even bother to check the caller ID. "No, you cannot stay out past midnight," I say instead of hello.

"Miss Carpenter," the familiar voice says. "It's Finn from the concierge desk. Wes just arrived for his shift, and he asked me to tell you that as soon as he changes into his uniform, he'll be up to check out that sofa bed."

A feeling of dread immediately worms its way into the pit of my stomach, and I swallow a growing panic. Don't be silly, I tell myself. There's nothing to be afraid of. Wes's visit is not unexpected. Jade made these arrangements with him days ago.

Except Jade isn't home, and I'm alone.

And a young man is on his way up to my apartment, a young man who's always made me feel vaguely uncomfortable, a young man of average height and weight, a young man with brown hair and a familiar voice, a young man whose breath occasionally smells of mouthwash. . . . "Oh, God."

"Miss Carpenter, is everything all right?"

I forgot I was still on the phone. "Could you come up with him?" I ask suddenly.

"What?"

"Please. Could you come up with him?"

"I'm just about to go off shift," Finn says, lowering his voice. "I'm meeting this girl. . . ."

"*Please.*"

"Sure thing," he agrees quickly. "What am I supposed to say to Wes?"

"Just tell him you're interested in the sofa, too."

"He's not gonna be very happy. . . ."

"*Finn . . .*"

"Yeah, sure. Whatever."

"Thank you." I hang up the phone, knowing I'm being ridiculous, that Wes is almost certainly not the man who raped me.

Except.

What if he is?

There's nothing to worry about, I assure myself as I proceed down the hall. I'm being paranoid, bouncing from one extreme to the other, from not being able to focus to focusing too much. Instead of letting go of what happened to me, I'm hanging on tighter than ever. But this is just a temporary setback. Elizabeth Gordon warned me to expect this, that my journey back to normalcy would not be a smooth one.

So I stand in front of my apartment door, bracing myself for Wes's arrival, praying that Finn won't let me down. Staring through the peephole, I watch as, minutes later, the elevator arrives and the two young men step out, Wes in his uniform, Finn in street clothes. My breath tightens as they draw near. I open the door.

"Sweet Jesus!" Finn exclaims.

"What the hell happened to your hair?" Wes asks in the same moment.

Their words combine and overlap, floating toward me on a breath of spearmint, threatening to topple me to the marble floor. I will myself to stand firm. "I . . . I felt like a change," I mumble as I usher them inside.

"You did that on purpose?" Wes sputters.

"It looks nice," Finn offers weakly. "Different. It'll just take a bit of getting used to."

Wes shoots him a look that says, *You're as crazy as she is.* "Is Jade here?" He glances uneasily down the hallway. My appearance has clearly unnerved him.

"She went out about eight o'clock," Finn tells him. "Said she was going to a party."

"She should be back soon," I add.

A moment of uncomfortable silence.

"Think we could have a look at that sofa now?" Wes asks.

Tell me what you see, my mother whispers in my ear.

I see a man who looks decidedly ill at ease in his neatly pressed khaki pants and short-sleeved, forest-green shirt, skinny arms hanging awkwardly at his sides, his hands too small and delicate to have fit so easily around my throat.

But I know all too well that appearances can be deceiving, that in order to really "see," sometimes you have to look beneath the surface, to spot the sharks lurking just below.

"Of course. It's right this way." I lead the two men down the hall toward Jade's bedroom.

"How much do you want for it?" Wes asks, examining the sofa carefully.

"I was thinking maybe three hundred dollars."

"Pretty good deal," Finn says, running his hands across the top of its corduroy surface. "Color doesn't really work for my place." He offers me a slight, conspiratorial smile.

"Would you take two hundred?" Wes asks.

"Sure," I agree quickly. It's worth at least ten times that, but I'd almost give it to him for nothing to get him out of my apartment as fast as possible.

"Great. It's a deal." Wes is about to extend his hand for me to shake, then obviously thinks better of it. "Well, I should probably get to work. Just let me know when I can pick it up." He walks back down the hall to the front door.

"Thank you," I whisper to Finn as we follow after him.

"No problem," he whispers back, leaning his head toward me as Wes opens the door.

Which is when I catch the whiff of mouthwash on Finn's breath.

It's nothing, I tell myself. They probably keep a bottle of the stuff in the concierge office, and Finn already told me he's meeting

someone, so it's only natural he'd use it to freshen up after his
shift. He was just going off duty when I all but insisted he accom-
pany Wes up here, which is why he's dressed in street clothes and
not the uniform I'm used to seeing him in.

My eyes absorb his casual attire, from his navy cotton sweater
to his dark blue jeans. How different he looks out of his uniform.
My heartbeat quickens. There's nothing sinister, or even unusual,
about the fact he's wearing jeans. What young man *doesn't* wear
jeans? He's just exchanged one uniform for another. My eyes continue down his legs toward the black sneakers on his feet. The familiar Nike swoosh winks up at me obscenely.

I gasp and stagger back.

"Miss Carpenter?" he asks. "Is something wrong? Are you all
right?"

"Is there a problem?" Wes asks from the exterior hallway.

"You better get to work," Finn tells him. "I can take care of
everything here." He pushes the door closed with his hand.

For the first time, I'm aware of what big hands he has.

"Miss Carpenter? What's wrong?"

She went out about eight o'clock, he said earlier, referring to
my niece. *Said she was going to a party.* Who has better knowledge
of my comings and goings? Who better to keep track of my every
move?

He's staring at me with genuine concern in his eyes. I realize he
has no idea what's going on in my head. And why should he?
More than three months have passed since that night. He feels safe
and invulnerable. He has no idea what I saw then, no idea what
I'm seeing now.

Tell me what you see.

I see a not-quite-handsome man of average height and weight,
with brown hair, a man between the ages of twenty and forty,
wearing blue jeans and black sneakers bearing the iconic Nike
swoosh.

But I speak to Finn almost every day. How is it possible I
wouldn't have recognized his voice, even one he buried inside a
low and angry growl?

Except maybe I *did* recognize it, I determine, as one thought falls quickly on top of the next, each thought occupying less than a fraction of a second. I recall the many times we've spoken since the night I was raped, my panic each time he announced himself on the phone, the anxiety I experienced each time I saw him. I attributed those feelings to whatever else was going on around me at the time, but maybe my anxiety was *because* of him. Maybe my subconscious knew all along that he is the man who raped me.

Tell me what you see, my mother says again.

I look deeper.

I see the sharks of my nightmares circling my feet, their fins gliding ever closer. Finally I realize what they've been trying to tell me.

His name: Finn.

"Miss Carpenter, are you all right?" he asks again.

"I'm fine," I tell him quietly.

"You're sure? You don't look so good."

"I just felt a bit faint there for a minute." I force a smile onto my lips as I lift my eyes to his. "I'm okay now."

"You're kind of pale."

"I'm fine. Really. You should go. You have plans."

"They can wait."

"No. Please. I feel guilty enough about making you come up here. You should go."

He shrugs. "Okay . . . if you're sure."

"I'm sure."

He turns toward the door, hesitates, then turns back. Our eyes lock.

He knows that I know.

We move at the same moment, almost as if everything has been choreographed in advance. He lunges at me as I vault out of his reach and race down the hall toward my bedroom. He's right behind me, his hands stretching toward my shirt. He grabs hold of it just as we cross the threshold, and he spins me around, effortlessly lifting me into the air and sending the scream emanating from my mouth flying uselessly off in all directions. Somehow I manage to struggle out of his grasp, flailing at him with my feet, trying desperately to evade his fists, his fury. We fall to the floor.

"You know you can't get away with this," I manage to spit out. "Wes knows you're here. . . ."

"He knows you're crazy!" Finn shoots back. "The whole building knows that." He pushes himself to his feet, looming menacingly over me. "And crazy people do crazy things. They make unfounded accusations, they attack people who are only trying to help them, people who have no choice but to defend themselves. . . ."

Is this what he's planning to do? To kill me and somehow make it look as if it were an accident?

"I had no choice," he whines plaintively, as if already rehearsing what he's going to tell the police. "She came at me. I pushed her away. She fell back . . . hit her head . . ." He reaches down and grabs hold of my arms, pulls me back up.

I will my body not to resist, allowing it to go slack, as my self-defense classes have trained me to do. Only when I'm on my feet, do I suddenly lash out, my knee slamming into his groin. He doubles over, gasping for air and letting go of my arms. I run around the bed, searching for the binoculars I left on the floor earlier. I'm reaching for them as he comes at me again. My fingers surround them as he throws me down and flips me over. I haul back and bring the binoculars crashing down hard against the side of his head.

It stuns him, but still isn't enough to stop him. As I struggle to my feet, he grabs hold of my legs, trying to drag me down as I stumble into the bathroom.

I'm reaching out to break my fall, to steady myself against the countertop, when I feel the scissors that are lying on top of a pile of my discarded hair. I grab them as Finn lunges at me again, his hands reaching for my throat. I plunge the scissors deep into his gut.

"You crazy bitch," he mutters in disbelief. Then he crumples to the floor at my feet.

I stand there for several seconds before walking back into the bedroom and calling downstairs, asking Wes to phone 9-1-1. Then

I sit down on the bed and wait calmly for the police and para-medics to arrive.

—

My niece arrives home at just before midnight. The ambulance has already taken Finn to the hospital for emergency surgery, and the forensic team is wrapping up. Heath came running back as soon as I called to tell him what happened, and he's been here ever since. "Holy shit," Jade says as he fills her in. "I can't leave you alone for a minute."

It's almost two A.M. before the police are satisfied and I'm able to convince Heath he can go home. They'll probably want to question me again in the morning, Detective Marx informs me, and I tell her that's fine with me. We can go over everything as often as she likes. She asks me again if I'd like to go to the hospital, and again I decline. Nothing is broken. At least nothing that X-rays will be able to reveal.

Even though the man who raped me is now in police custody, I'm not so naïve as to believe that everything has been miracu-lously resolved. I know I'll still suffer episodes of post-traumatic shock, some familiar, some new, as a result of tonight's events. I almost killed a man. And contrary to my earlier fantasies, I derived neither pleasure nor satisfaction from the act. I can still feel the awful reverberation of those scissors in my hand as they plunged deep into Finn's flesh.

I know I'll still endure moments of panic and paralysis. I'll still have nightmares, although at least now the man chasing me will have a face. And a name. The sharks will no longer find it neces-sary to swim beneath my feet.

And I know something else: that I am not powerless, that I can fight back, that I can win.

I have no idea how long it will be before I feel truly normal again, if ever, before I'll be able to experience pleasure at a man's touch, to trust others. I know I have a long way to go. Elizabeth Gordon and I will keep working on it.

"What are you doing?" I ask, watching as Jade climbs into my bed.

"I'm sleeping with you until my new bed gets here."

"You don't have to do that."

"I'm not doing it for you," she says. "Your bed is way more comfortable than that thing I've been sleeping on."

Claire was right about one thing: For all Jade's bravado, she's really not half as tough as she pretends to be.

"Holy shit," she says, as she said earlier.

I crawl into bed beside her. "I know. It's all pretty incredible."

She cuddles up beside me, lays a protective hand across my hip. "I was talking about your hair."

ACKNOWLEDGMENTS

It's been a tough road getting this book to print. As most of my readers know, I've been putting out a book a year for the past fourteen years. But last year marked the end of my long association with my American publishers, which upset my normal schedule. I'm thrilled to announce my new association with Ballantine Books (an imprint of Random House) and hope our partnership is both long and fruitful. With that in mind, I have a number of people to thank, starting with supporters of long standing: Brad Martin, Nita Pronovost, Kristin Cochrane, Adria Iwasutiak, Val Gow, Martha Leonard, and the rest of the truly wonderful crew at Doubleday, Canada (a division of Random House), all of whom have been exceptional in their advice, guidance, and encouragement. Nita, in particular, is an author's dream editor—caring, diligent, and sharp as a tack. She doesn't let me get away with a thing, and for that I'm very grateful; my agent, Tracy Fisher, and her assistant, James Munro, at William Morris Endeavor, who work tirelessly on my behalf and have seen me through a sometimes difficult year with grace and tact; and to my various publishers around the world, all of whom continue to be tremendously supportive and enthusiastic. While I can't name you all personally, I thank each and every one of you for the wonderful work you continue to do, including translating and publicity. I've established strong connections with many of you individually and love the fact that we communicate throughout the year via email on matters both professional and personal. I hope to see all of you in person soon so I can thank you again face to face.

As for my new American publishers, you know the expression "Everything old is new again"? Well, it seems I've come full circle. In 2000, I published a novel entitled *The First Time*. My editor at the time was Linda Marrow, a woman who had a knack for seeing the larger picture and zeroing in on what was wrong with my manuscript and what needed fixing. Unfortunately, we only worked together on that one book before she moved on. But now, serendipitously, we've found each other again—my mother always said that things have a way of working out—and it's like *The First Time* all over again. She remains a wonderful editor, and her comments regarding this novel were both insightful and spot-on. So, thank you, Linda. I'm so glad we're together again. Thanks also to her assistant, Anne Speyer, and the amazing crew at Ballantine. I know you'll do a terrific job.

I want to thank a special friend, Carol Kripke, a brilliant psychotherapist whose advice I sought when dealing with the therapy sessions in this novel. If these sessions ring true, it is because of Carol's expert advice. We play-acted these sessions, and she guided me through them line by line. If I occasionally put words in her mouth she might not use, I apologize and plead temporary insanity.

Thank you to Lawrence Mirkin and Beverley Slopen, names my regular readers will surely recognize, as they've been a part of my process so long they really feel like family. Your insights, patience, and advice have been—and hopefully will continue to be— invaluable. Larry reads my books as I'm writing them, a little at a time, careful to keep me on track, and tells me if I'm going the wrong way before I go too far. Bev reads the finished product, her fresh (and eagle) eyes there when I need them most. Both take the time from their already busy and crowded schedules to help me produce the best book I possibly can. Thank you, thank you, thank you. I love you both.

Thank you to Corinne Assayag, who designed and oversees my website. You are a constant source of dedication and great ideas, a terrific person who's terrific at what she does. Thank you for always being there, and stay well. And to Shannon Micol, who manages my Facebook and Twitter presences and also functions as one of my first readers. When the eBook versions of *Life Penalty, The Deep End, Good Intentions,* and *Kiss Mommy Goodbye* are finally released to the American market and arrive with fewer mistakes than readers might normally find in this format, it is the direct result of Shannon's tireless efforts.

And finally, to my wonderful family: Warren, my incredibly generous husband of forty years (!!!), whose advice I might occasionally resent but who is usually right (about most things); my daughters, Shannon and Annie, two of the world's most beautiful and capable young women; my son-in-law, Courtney, as loving as he is handsome; my two sweet, sweet grandchildren, Hayden and Skylar, for bringing such joy to my life and making me feel so loved and appreciated; my sister Renee, who is also one of my closest friends; and Aurora, my housekeeper of more than twenty years, who takes such good care of me and always goes above and beyond.

And of course, thank you to you, my readers. I can always count on you to bring out the best in me.

ABOUT THE AUTHOR

JOY FIELDING is the *New York Times* bestselling author of *Charley's Web, Heartstopper, Mad River Road, See Jane Run,* and other acclaimed novels. She divides her time between Toronto and Palm Beach, Florida.

www.JoyFielding.com
@JoyFielding

ABOUT THE TYPE

This book was set in Sabon, a typeface designed by the well-known German typographer Jan Tschichold (1902–74). Sabon's design is based upon the original letter forms of sixteenth-century French type designer Claude Garamond and was created specifically to be used for three sources: foundry type for hand composition, Linotype, and Monotype. Tschichold named his typeface for the famous Frankfurt typefounder Jacques Sabon (c. 1520–80).